The Virtuous Viscount

Susan M. Baganz

The Virtuous Viscount
COPYRIGHT 2017 by Susan M. Baganz

Contact Information: titleadmin@pelicanbookgroup.com

Scripture quotations, unless otherwise indicated are taken from the King James translation, public domain.

Cover Art by *Nicola Martinez*

Prism is a division of Pelican Ventures, LLC
www.pelicanbookgroup.com PO Box 1738 *Aztec, NM * 87410

White Rose Publishing Circle and Rosebud logo is a trademark of Pelican Ventures, LLC

Publishing History
Prism Edition, 2017
Electronic Edition ISBN 978-1-5223-9764-9
Paperback Edition ISBN 978-1-5223-9766-3
Published in the United States of America

BOOKS BY SUSAN M. BAGANZ

Black Diamond Regency Romantic Suspense
The Baron's Blunder (Prequel) novella
The Virtuous Viscount (Book 1)
Lord Phillip's Folly (Book 2)
Sir Michael's Mayhem (coming soon)
Lord Harrow's Heart (coming soon)
The Captain's Conquest (coming soon)

Orchard Hill Contemporary Romances
Pesto & Potholes
Salsa & Speed Bumps
Feta & Freeways
Root Beer & Roadblocks
Bratwurst & Bridges...
and others coming soon!

Historical Christmas Novella
Fragile Blessings
Gabriel's Gift

Short Story Compilation
Little Bits O' Love

Dedication

To Carol Hisel—
Your name is written in the Lamb's Book of Life and
this novel, which reunited us, is now in print. I'm
beyond grateful to you and honored to be part of your
journey. And no—this is not a 'bodice-ripper.'

Author's Note

During the tempestuous years between 1800-1820 or
the more specific "Regency" years of 1811 to 1820, it
was common for the upper classes, especially the men,
to drink various forms of alcohol as part of their daily
life. A glass of port wine was often savored by the men
after the evening meal. French brandy was considered
superior and highly coveted even though England was
at war with France. In these stories, my characters do
at times drink, and sometimes even to excess with
serious consequences for their overindulgence. This is
not in any way a recommendation on the part of the
author or Pelican Book Group to advocate the drinking
of alcohol or to abuse any substance. Laudanum is
actually an opiate that was often prescribed
medicinally (although many did become addicted to
the drug). The use of these in the story are merely an
attempt to use this period in history and its notorious
excesses as a backdrop where appropriate.

Lord, bring me a man
who is strong, faithful, and true.
~Miss Josephine Storm

Virtue:
Greek ἀρέτη aretē̄ ar-et′-ay properly manliness (valor),
that is, excellence (intrinsic or attributed): praise,
virtue. ~Strong's Exhaustive Concordance

And beside this, giving all diligence,
add to your faith virtue; and to virtue knowledge;
~Peter 1

PROLOGUE

Derbyshire

The Black Diamond stared at the pitiful Sir Archibald Bastian. He doubted the fool could deliver to him the virgin he demanded. The potential disappointment was worth the current pleasure of watching him squirm. If he failed, Diamond would own Bastian's estate, located conveniently on an inlet with access to the ocean. Perfect for his purposes.

"I made an offer of marriage. Her father insists on giving her time," Bastian whimpered. The man perspired and mangled the hat in his hand as he stood there, fidgeting.

"She is a virgin?" Diamond pounded his fist on the mahogany desk in front of him.

"Yes. Most certainly, my lord."

"Then let this be done before the season is over. You will wed her and return her to me untouched."

"Un-untouched?"

"Do you have a hearing problem, Bastian? That is my demand, and if you expect to have your gambling debts paid, you will deliver."

The bumbling knight swallowed hard. "Yes, my lord. It shall be as you say."

"Leave me." The Black Diamond snapped his fingers. The door on the opposite end of the room swung open.

Bastian nodded his head and backed away, bowing as he did so. The Black Diamond grinned. Sometimes his minions were far too easy to intimidate. Foolish Englishmen. They were all doomed anyway. Once he had his sacrifice, the war would turn. Soon, quite soon, the Black Diamond would equal Napoleon Bonaparte for power and wealth.

Ah, but the virgin. She was the key. He would crush his English rose and enjoy every minute. After all, it was what his own dark lord required of him. He was only following orders.

1

Spring
Oxfordshire

The gray gelding reared as a flash of lightning struck the tree by the road. Lord Marcus Remington held on tight and brought his mount under control.

Weariness seeped into the marrow of his bones, much as the rain did his exposed trousers. Fatigue weighed on him. He was weary of the hunt—the balls and soirees and the pressure to dress 'top of the trees.' He longed for the one place he was most at ease. Rose Hill. Home. His three friends, following behind, were equally miserable in the spring storm. Should they have waited out the deluge at the pub in Didcot? It hadn't seemed worth it when his estate was so close. They had agreed to ride on.

As he turned the bend, the Viscount's heart sank at the vision illuminated by another flash of light. Through sheets of rain, Marcus spied a carriage teetering on its side. The top half of it hung over a ditch filled with running water from the storm. The horses were free of the carriage. They struggled against their traces as a young man tried to calm them. Their frantic neighs added to the cacophony of wind, thunder, and rain. Two figures huddled under a nearby tree. He sighed as he slowed his horse.

"What ho!" Marcus shouted. He pulled up to await an older man, most likely the groom, who limped forward. Marcus dismounted. "Is everyone out of the carriage?"

The man pointed off the road toward the trees. "I got me mistress and her daughter out before the second wheel broke. One more lady is inside."

"Is she well?" Marcus implored as three other horses drew up close by and their riders descended. Blood pounded in his ears as he kept his eye on the carriage in its precarious position.

The man grimaced, and his hands rose in the air as he took in the four gentlemen in their many caped greatcoats. He backed away. "Ye not be here to rob us?"

Marcus shook his head, and raindrops danced off the brim of his hat. "Most certainly not. Lord Remington at your service. Excuse me." He turned aside. "Phillip? Will you ride to Rose Hill and bring back a carriage? We have one passenger to rescue. She may be injured, so have Fenton send for the doctor, and inform Mrs. Hughes to expect more guests."

"Right away." The tall, blond aristocrat spun on his heel, remounted, and rode off into the stormy darkness.

Marcus headed toward the carriage as he called out to his friends. "Theo. Attend to the ladies, please." Lord Theodore Harrow would charm the women and ease their anxieties. Marcus turned aside to a man of slighter build and lowered his voice. "Michael, a woman is trapped inside."

"Then a rescue is in order." The shorter, coffee-haired gentleman gave a cheeky grin to his friend even as rain dripped off his hat.

Marcus shook his head and struggled to master the corner of his lips that wanted to curl in response. Leave it to Sir Michael Tidley to see an adventure in what promised to be a challenging effort. He sobered. "Let's not waste any time. I do not like the way the carriage is balanced."

The two gentlemen drew closer to the equipage.

Marcus noticed the groom had gone back to removing the luggage from the boot. The horses had calmed. "I'll go in." Marcus pulled himself up to the side of the carriage. Once on top, he struggled to jerk the door open. It stuck. The carriage rocked over the culvert as Marcus balanced on the sky-borne side.

Michael grabbed hold of the underside of the carriage to add stability.

Marcus pulled at the door several times before it gave way and almost threw him off his elevated perch. He waited for the carriage to cease rocking. He knelt and peered into the darkness, barely able to see inside. The rain pelted him harder. *Could this night get any worse, Lord?*

A bolt of lightning illuminated the interior long enough to detect where the figure of the passenger rested. He ascertained an area he might stand without landing on her. After lowering himself in, he shut the door to keep out the deluge. His gloved hands moved around in the dark, searching. Oil had spilled from the lantern attached to its hook by the uppermost door. He waited for his eyes to adjust to the darkness.

Outside, Michael called to tie the horses to the carriage to keep it from tipping into the ditch.

"There you are." Sprawled out next to his feet, which were against the far wall of the carriage, lay a young woman. He knelt down beside her in the cramped quarters. Shadows from the skittering of lightning came in the windows. He removed his gloves and shoved them in the pocket of his greatcoat.

"Miss?" He moved lower to spy a crushed chip bonnet that at one time was probably quite pretty. "Miss? Can you hear me?" He untied the ribbons under the woman's chin, removed the hat, and tossed it aside. Dark waves of hair tumbled down, and he brushed them away to get a look at her face as his eyes adjusted to the dark. She did not respond to his touch or voice. He imagined she was pretty and sweet, like his younger sister, and his heart ached for this woman's suffering. He shook his head. This was neither the time nor the place for flights of fancy. His fingers touched something warm and sticky in her hair. Blood.

Please, don't let her be dead. He found her pulse weak but steady and released a breath he hadn't known he held. He glanced around and noticed the rear window of the carriage was the only space large enough to fit her through. Lifting her up to the door at the top would be nigh on impossible in her current state.

Marcus stood up and opened the door to find rain pelting him in the face. This was not how he anticipated spending his birthday. "Michael!" he growled.

"Here. How is she?" The shorter man's face popped into view.

"Unconscious, but alive. She received a blow to the head. I am going to try to break out the back window. We can pass her out that way."

"I'll be there."

Marcus sank down and closed the door. He reached into his inner coat pocket and pulled out a handkerchief to wipe the moisture off his face. *Lord, help me.* Marcus felt around for a carriage blanket and placed it over the young woman. A metal box that had probably caused her injury was near her head. The locked box most likely contained valuables, but there was nothing else to hand. He smashed it against the glass. A slight crack emerged in the thick pane. There wasn't enough space to get momentum. He tried again without success. He set it back where he found it.

Replacing his gloves, he grabbed the handle by the uppermost door and swung his feet toward the fractured glass. A resounding crack was his reward. He dismissed the sharp pain as he pulled himself out of the broken window. *Come on, Marcus, push!* He made another attempt.

This time, both legs pierced through, and glass sliced his trousers at the knees as he drew them back. He picked at the shards in his trousers. The third time, he shattered most of the glass. He dropped down to the unconscious woman and grabbed the metal box to finish off the sharp edges around the window frame.

Michael peered in. "Your valet will not be happy with you, Remy."

Marcus rolled his eyes. "Max will recover. I can always get a new pair of boots." Marcus removed the glass-covered blanket and set it aside before he squatted down to lift the woman. Time crawled as he gathered her in his arms. Her head rolled back as he moved her to the window. He glanced down as a flash of lightning illuminated her face. Marcus's breathing labored, and he swallowed hard. *Steady on.*

"I'm ready," Michael called, breaking the moment.

Marcus glanced up to see his friend there, waiting with one eyebrow raised.

Marcus struggled to wrap her in her cloak. The woman in his arms gasped. "Miss? Miss?" Marcus resisted the urge to shake her, fearing he would cause her pain. Her eyes fluttered open, and she gazed up at him. He couldn't ascertain their color. She gave a weak smile before her eyelids closed. He passed her through the window to the waiting knight. Once she was safe in Sir Tidley's arms, Marcus placed the safe-box outside the carriage. Due to his larger size, he could not exit the same way she had. He opened the door and pulled himself up into the stormy night.

Michael had brought the injured woman over toward the people standing under the tree to keep dry.

Lord Theodore Harrow stripped his greatcoat and spread the garment so they wouldn't place the young lady on the wet ground.

The rain abated for a moment, and Marcus strode over and handed the box to the older woman under the tree. "This is yours, I believe."

The matron with graying hair and imperial bearing, wearing a wet fur hat and fur-trimmed cloak, grabbed the box from his hands. She resembled a drowned dog. In spite of that, she managed to give Marcus a glare reminding him of a short-lived governess he once had. He shoved the unkind thoughts aside as the woman spoke, her voice strident.

"I am Lady Widmore, and this is my daughter, Lady Heticia Widmore."

"Lady Widmore, Lady Heticia, Lord Remington at your service. This is Lord Harrow and Sir Tidley. Our friend has ridden to my estate nearby to get help."

Lady Widmore nodded her head. "That was well done of you. This has been a most vexing evening. My carriage is ruined. It's bad enough that I have to replace two wheels, but now the glass too?" Her nose rose a fraction as her eyes snapped as much as a ruler to the knuckles.

The three men glanced at her nonplussed.

Lady Heticia simpered and batted her eyes at Marcus. "I'm cold and wet. How much longer before the carriage arrives?"

Marcus gave her a quick glance before he turned away. "Lord Westcombe will be here soon enough." He moved to kneel next to the unconscious form on the forest floor. "What is her name?"

"Miss Storm," Lady Widmore replied with a snort.

Marcus commenced checking the young woman's arms and legs to assess any broken bones. He watched her face as the clouds began to move past and the moon started to shine bright. Blood oozed from a gash on the side of her head. He loosened his cravat. "Michael, can you help me hold up her head while I bind her wound?"

Michael was next to their patient before the question was complete and lifted her head.

Marcus smoothed away the dark tendrils of hair stuck to the blood. He proceeded to wrap the linen around and tie it off. He brought the hood of the cloak up to cover Miss Storm's bandaged head.

"Max will have another charge against you, Remy." Michael gave a cheeky grin.

"There's a reason I left my valet in London, Michael. So I would not have to be hounded about boots, cravats, and my lack of dash." The flat tone delivered a warning to his friend. Marcus looked down again at the young woman.

Dark hair outlined her heart-shaped face, half covered with the white bandage across her forehead surrounded by the rich burgundy of her traveling cloak. Long, dark eyelashes splayed against pale cheeks. "Sleeping Beauty."

"I don't think a kiss will do the trick, though," Michael whispered.

Lord Remington startled. Had he spoken aloud? His cheeks grew warm. He was grateful to hear the rumble of a carriage coming from the west. "Phillip has arrived."

Marcus rose and strode to the road only to gape at the old, small gig his fastidious friend drove. Lord Phillip Westcombe pulled past and managed to turn the horse and buggy around before he came to a stop next to them.

"Sorry, ol' chap. Stickney is getting another carriage ready, but this one we were able to hook up in record time. I figured with an injured party, speed might be of the essence."

Marcus nodded before he turned and strode over to the group under the trees. He knelt to gather up Miss Storm in his arms. "I apologize, ladies. Another carriage will arrive posthaste."

Lady Widmore blocked his path to the carriage. "You cannot mean to leave us here? She will be fine waiting." Lady Widmore's spite-filled eyes glanced at the woman in his arms.

"Unless you would like the indignity of riding in the wagon of the gig, you will have to wait. The inconvenience cannot be avoided. You will have the company and protection of Lord Harrow and Sir Tidley. It's the best I can do." Marcus moved around her and strode to the carriage.

Michael followed.

"Let me help you, Remy." Michael took the woman from his arms while Marcus leapt up into the front seat of the open gig next to Phillip. Once settled, he lifted her up to him.

Marcus leaned the woman against his chest, with her head resting on his shoulder, before he gave Phillip the nod to drive off. Miss Storm's hair tickled his cheek, and he detected the sweet scent of roses emanating from her in spite of the damp. Something unexplainable stirred deep inside him. *Lord, how can I be attracted to an unconscious woman?* He shivered. He pulled her limp body closer to his own. Every protective instinct was aroused.

Through the uncomfortable ride, Marcus fought to keep his charge secure against the strength of the jolts as the carriage wheels hit dips in the road. Marcus's back ached from the strain.

"Sorry your respite from town life has eluded you once again," Phillip began. "You don't think—"

"—this was intentional?"

Phillip nodded. "I tend to be suspicious."

"Two wheels? Why, when one would suffice? Her traveling companions show little concern for her."

Phillip shrugged.

"Don't worry, Westcombe. With the four of us working together, I suspect we can manage to avoid being compromised."

Lord Phillip Westcombe glanced at the girl. "Are you sure she's really unconscious?"

"Yes, Phillip." Marcus glanced down at the pale face. "She cannot attend to our conversation."

Phillip drew the gig up to the front door and tossed the reins to a waiting groom. He jumped down from the equipage and hurried around to help Remington descend with the woman in his arms.

Marcus strode up the steps, and the doors opened to allow him entrance.

"Marcus?" Phillip called.

"Yes?" Marcus turned.

"I'll head back to help the others."

"Thank you." Marcus nodded and proceeded into the house and up the stairs as a frantic Mrs. Hughes urged him on. His dog, Charlie, yipped at his heels. At the top, they took a right turn, headed down the south wing of the mansion, and slipped into the room his housekeeper indicated.

Mrs. Hughes frowned at the damp state of her master and the woman in his arms. "Here, let me help you get her wet cloak off, and we will set her in the bed."

Together they managed to remove the garment, and Marcus placed her on the mattress by the pulled back counterpane. He stepped away as water dripped from his hat.

Mrs. Hughes moved to remove the girl's shoes and noted Marcus's continued presence. She chided him. "Young man, you need a hot bath, some salve for your legs, and something to eat. At least drip yourself dry in the hallway and not on the carpet." She turned her back on him in dismissal.

Marcus drooped. "I will leave her to your care." He strode to the door and paused. "Her name is Miss Storm."

"How appropriate," she muttered as the door closed behind him.

He stood in the hallway. Water dripped on the wooden floor in a sad rhythm. His terrier sat by his side looking at the door, waiting for her master's next step.

Drip. Drop. Drip. Drip. Drop.

For a moment, he did not know what to do. *Happy*

birthday, Marcus Allendale, Viscount Remington. Happy birthday, indeed. He shook his head and grimaced. He didn't want to leave but became more aware of how cold and damp he was. He strode down to another hallway, followed by the dog, toward his own suite of rooms to dry off and tend to his wounds before he returned downstairs to welcome his unexpected guests.

A short time later, Marcus paced in his study as Charlie watched. Fresh clothes and a sip of brandy warmed him, but he was restless. That was nothing new. For weeks, he held a conviction deep inside that it was time for him to seek a bride. *What would it have been like to come home tonight to someone other than paid servants? To have a wife minister to my wounds?*

He snorted. If only he might find a woman he liked, who had a perfect combination of purity as well as the ability to preside over his home and be a political hostess. If she were attractive, that would be a bonus. He longed for the kind of marriage his parents had. They had been in love. He understood such unions were rare amongst the *beau monde.* Hollowness ate at him from within.

But the girl upstairs. Something unsettled him when he looked at her. In a brief moment when her eyes had opened and she had gazed into his eyes, he was undone. Intrigue and hope vied for a place in his heart. Perhaps her unexpected visit here would give him opportunity to explore that further.

2

Marcus awaited his friends.

Dr. Miller had refused to stay for dinner. Miss Storm remained unconscious, which concerned the doctor as well as Marcus. This would not be a short visit for his guests.

Sir Michael Tidley entered the room. He glanced around. Spying only Marcus, he took a seat to consider his friend. Marcus's dog jumped up to receive some absent-minded petting from the knight.

"Charlie, dear dog, you should be aware that your master is already half in love with Miss Storm," Michael teased.

The terrier barked.

"I beg your pardon?" Marcus scowled as he sat down and proceeded to pick at his fingernails.

"I don't know when I've ever seen you look at any woman the way you did that young lady tonight."

Marcus steepled his fingers, tapped them against his nose, and avoided eye contact. "You imagine things."

"Hmmmm."

"What's *that* supposed to mean?" Marcus narrowed his eyes as he placed his hands on the arms of the chair, poised to move.

"You get grumpy when life doesn't quite go your way, and tonight definitely did not fit in your plans." Michael leaned back in his chair and extended his legs out before him, crossing them at the ankles. His slimmer figure shown to advantage in a well-fitted pair of buff colored pants and custom made boots. He tied his cravat simply, and his dark hair, cut shorter than Marcus's, had a little curl at the back where it met his shirt. Topped off with a brown jacket and turquoise vest, he was the image of a dashing Corinthian.

Marcus sighed. "I had hoped to come home and relax."

"Women are *not* relaxing."

"The one who is unconscious will not be a problem. I have serious doubts about the other two."

"Did they give you more grief when they arrived?" Michael's mouth twitched in an effort not to smile.

"Most certainly, but I doubt we will see any more of them this evening. Their servants showed up a half an hour ago in a separate carriage. Stickney awaited them at the turn-off."

"This was not an anticipated stop?"

Marcus shook his head. "You and Phillip are too suspicious. No. They were quite put out to be here, until they entered the foyer."

"Rose Hill is an impressive property."

"It's home."

"It would be an even nicer home if you had a lovely wife to share it with." Michael's voice was all seriousness.

"The thought has crossed my mind. I am eight and twenty. My brother Jared is off to war, and my sister, Henrietta, is happily married to Lord Percy. This house is empty without either of them here."

"Has anyone in London sparked your interest?"

Marcus gave a harsh laugh. "I am tired of the

masquerade of the *beau monde*. Maybe my standards are too high, but I cannot imagine living with a woman who doesn't share my faith."

"Somewhat difficult to weed out during a contra-dance. You don't really want a whey-faced Methodist do you?"

"Their faith doesn't make them unattractive, Michael, but some seem to think when one accepts Christ, they forgo any joy in living. Definitely not the kind of woman I want to spend the rest of my life with."

"But Miss Storm? You've not shared one word with her. What draws you?" Michael leaned forward.

Marcus rose to walk over to the drink table, picked up a glass, and motioned to the decanter. "Brandy?" Noting his friend's nod, Marcus poured two glasses. His friend delighted in baiting him. He was too tired to deal with this nonsense tonight.

"Thank you." Michael rose and strode over to accept the glass. The dog curled up on the other end of the chair to watch. "You are avoiding the question."

"I am not." Marcus brought the glass to his lips and sipped, closed his eyes, and swallowed. "I don't know the answer."

"You don't know the answer to what?" An elegantly attired Lord Phillip Westcombe strode in. He had meticulously combed blond hair and his cravat intricately tied. He wore black inexpressibles and polished boots. His coat fit him like a glove.

Marcus suspected a footman had probably been conscripted to help him get it on and would be needed later to remove it. "Good evening, Phillip." Marcus responded. "It is of no importance." He glanced at Michael with a silent plea to let the conversation drop.

"Well, I'm famished. Has your wonderful cook arranged for something hot to eat?"

"But, of course. We only await Theo to go in to dinner, but it will be simple fare."

"Anything your cook prepares is far from simple." Phillip patted his flat stomach. "In the past, I have left your home, even after short stays, struggling to get my clothes to fit properly."

Lord Harrow entered the room sporting country attire over his substantial form. While not as tall as Marcus or Phillip, he bore himself with understated dignity. He was barrel-chested but didn't hesitate to fence or box with his friends although he preferred more sedate entertainments. His short, sandy brown hair was styled simply. "Did someone mention food?"

Marcus's stomach growled in response. "Yes. Shall we remove to the dining room?"

~*~

They had already begun the first course when Lady Widmore and her daughter arrived to join them. The matron was dressed in a puce gown with low décolletage. She wore her greying blonde hair piled high with a few curls free on the side. Jewels sparkled on her neck, wrist, ears, and fingers. Lady Widmore stood ramrod straight at the table with her chin elevated as she acknowledged the men.

Lady Hetitia was dressed in a white gown that washed out her complexion. Green ribbon trimmed the dress. Matching adornment wove through her saffron locks. She was a younger version of her mother from the set of her chin, to her eyes and crooked teeth.

Marcus and his friends stood as a footman helped

the women to their seats.

"My apologies, Lady Widmore. I had been assured you and your daughter were weary from this evening's trials and planned to dine in your rooms." Marcus resumed his seat and picked up his spoon to eat his soup as a footman arranged place settings and assisted the women with their chairs.

"We decided it would be rude of us to hide away in our rooms and leave you bereft of female company." Lady Widmore tittered.

An uncomfortable silence fell on the room.

"We were on our way to London for the season." Lady Heticia volunteered.

"Was this to be your first season, Lady Heticia?" Theo asked, with an indulgent nod.

"Yes, my lord. I'm looking forward to the balls and recitals and seeing the sights of London." Miss Widmore's speech was rapid.

Lady Widmore placed a hand on her daughter's arm to stop her chatter. "We were unable to bring her out when she came of age but hope to make it up to her now."

"It's tragic that your trip has been interrupted by this unfortunate accident and Miss Storm's injury." Lord Westcombe spoke.

"Surely that needn't cause delay?" Lady Heticia glanced from the gentlemen to her mother, eyes wide and mouth agape.

"Hetty, dear, it may not delay us for long, but we cannot travel until our coach is repaired and Miss Storm is restored to health." Lady Widmore's nose rose even as she glared at her daughter.

Marcus exchanged glances with his friends. "I gladly offer you one of my own carriages to convey you to town, Lady Widmore."

"How generous of you, but Miss Storm would be without a chaperone in a houseful of bachelors. We cannot allow any scandal, which could taint my dear Hetty's chances to make a match in London."

"You are correct. We must protect Lady Heticia's reputation. You are welcome to stay here." Marcus leaned back in his seat and sipped his wine while the footman cleared his bowl to bring in the next course.

"That would be wonderful. Wouldn't it, Mother?" Hetty bounced in her seat.

"Calm yourself, my dear. Our first responsibility is to your dear cousin." There was a lack of sincerity in her tone. She turned her gaze to Marcus. "Has the doctor tended to her yet?"

Marcus's eyes narrowed as he nodded. "She remains unconscious. He was unable to ascertain the full extent of her injuries but is certain she has a concussion. I have a servant sitting with her."

"You have been most gracious in attending to our needs, Lord Remington." Lady Widmore applied herself to the roast rabbit and seasoned vegetables placed before her.

The rest of the meal passed as Sir Tidley entertained the women with tales of mishaps that occurred at previous seasons' balls. After the servants removed the final course, the ladies excused themselves to go to their rooms while the men remained to enjoy their port.

Marcus leaned back, let his head fall against the tall chair, and closed his eyes. "I thought that would never end," he groaned.

The other men chuckled.

"Happy birthday, Remy!" Theo cried out and

raised his glass. "May you make it through another year escaping the parson's mousetrap."

Marcus frowned, tilted his head, and glanced at Michael.

"What? Did I say something wrong?" Theo set his glass down. A furrow appeared between his brows.

Phillip sipped his wine and tapped at the side of the glass as he placed it back on the table. "I suspect perhaps our esteemed friend here is thinking of wrapping the noose around his own neck this year."

Marcus sighed. "I dislike coming back to Rose Hill alone."

"Alone? What are we, tripe?" Michael asked.

Theo laughed. "I don't think having any one of us greeting him at the door with a kiss would be quite his idea of a homecoming. Am I right?"

Marcus lowered his eyes as his thumb caressed the stem of his goblet.

"You've never been in the petticoat line, Remy. I have never even known you to be sweet on a girl, not even at university when the rest of us ran wild. Not even when we hit the town, thinking we were the answer to the world's problems. You always held yourself aloof from our mischief. You danced with the ladies and gave honor to the wallflowers, but never once did you single out any woman for your attentions." Phillip sipped his port.

"You've become adept at avoiding the snares set for you because you are careful and perfected your reputation. You are a paragon in everything you do. Certainly finding a bride will not be difficult." Michael wiggled his eyebrows.

"If I miss my guess, Lady Heticia would be more than happy to save you the trouble of another season."

Theo teased.

"Thank you, but no. Lady Heticia is not to my liking." Marcus sipped his wine.

"You will need to be doubly on your guard. I suspect hunting season has opened on the Rose Hill estate, and gentlemen, we are the prey." Phillip frowned.

Theo sighed. "I despise being hunted."

Marcus parted with his friends for the evening and started down the hallway to his suite of rooms. As he reached the door, his hand rested on the knob and his head leaned against the wood. He shook his head and turned to walk to the south wing. Marcus knocked on the bedroom door. The maid he had met earlier opened the door a crack. "Molly, is it?"

"Yes, m'lord." She dipped a curtsey.

"How fares your mistress?"

"She continues to rest." Worry etched her young face.

"May I enter?" He pleaded.

Molly's eyes grew large. "T'would not be proper, m'lord."

He sighed. "I only want to visit her. I'm not about to ravish an unconscious woman in my home. You may act as a chaperone."

Molly crinkled her nose as she considered him. She nodded and allowed him entrance. Molly closed the door and escorted him into the adjoining bedroom.

Marcus entered the room decorated with yellow rose bedecked wallpaper and a bedspread of similar flowers and white lace. As he drew near the bed, his eyes were riveted to the young woman under the blankets. Her brown hair spread out on the pillow, and his cravat had been replaced with a smaller bandage.

Bruising was visible on her pale face. He swallowed hard. She was so still. So pretty, even with the new bandage on her head. Marcus located a nearby chair.

He pulled it to the bed, sat, and bent his upper body forward. With his elbows on his knees and with folded hands, he silently prayed.

Lord, I'm not sure why You brought this woman to my home. It grieves me to see her so injured and unresponsive. Please place Your healing hand on her.

He glanced again at Miss Storm, the bed, and the window. It grew late. He grimaced and rose, releasing a long sigh. Fatigue overwhelmed him. He thought he had been tired before the adventure of this evening. He was even more so now.

Molly accompanied him from the room.

Marcus nodded his head. "Thank you, Molly."

The door shut firmly behind him.

Later as he stretched out in bed, Marcus could not shake the image of the girl from his thoughts. What did she look like when she really smiled? He remembered the weak one she gave him when her eyes had opened while in his arms. He wondered how her laughter sounded. Would he ever get the opportunity to find out? He fell asleep with these petitions on his heart.

He tossed and turned through the night and rose as the sun began its ascent. The storm had passed, and the day promised drier weather. In spite of this being a holiday for him, he had tasks around the estate to accomplish. First was to make sure the carriage on the road was moved for repair. Marcus holed up in his study after a solitary breakfast, when a knock disturbed his work on the papers before him.

"Come in," he called out.

The door opened, and in stepped his head groom,

Stickney. The older man had thinning hair.

"Beggin' yer pardon, my lord, but I wanted to report to you regardin' the broken carriage."

"Did you manage to get it into Didcot to the wheelwright?"

Stickney nodded.

"Good." Marcus returned his gaze to his paper. The groom cleared his throat, drawing Marcus's attention once again to his servant. "What is it, Stickney?"

"Beggin' yer pardon. 'Tis about the carriage." Stickney twisted his hat in his hands but fearlessly returned his master's gaze.

"Yes?"

"The broken axles. They didn't break on their own. They 'ad been sawed partially through."

"Are you saying...?"

"That twern't no accident, Lord Remington. Someone 'ntended for them wheels to break."

Marcus placed his pen back in its stand. "The carriage was sabotaged? At possible risk to the lives of those aboard, not to mention the possibility of injury to the horses?"

Stickney nodded. "The geldings 'ill recover."

"Good. Thank you for informing me. I shall look into this." With a nod to his servant, Marcus picked up his pen and dipped it again in the inkwell.

Stickney put his cap on and turned to leave, quietly shutting the door behind him.

Marcus started to write but returned the pen to its stand and leaned back in his chair. Why would someone deliberately seek to injure the occupants of that carriage? And who? Marcus massaged his right temple and shook his head before closing his eyes. This was not turning out to be a relaxing visit home.

He picked up his pen and wrote three letters. Two left within the hour, and the other only awaited an address. With a deep sigh, he rose to seek out Lady Widmore. He tracked her down in the sunny South parlor. "Lady Widmore, I was searching for you."

"Yes, my lord? I am penning a missive to my husband about our accident."

"As you undoubtedly should. I wrote a letter to post to Mr. Storm but do not have his address."

"I will take care of it for you." She took the envelope from his hand, inscribed an address, and handed it back to him.

Marcus glanced at the address. Strange. Miss Storm's address was Northampton, when the Widmore carriage traveled from the west. "I'll take this to Fenton to send out immediately. You can give him your correspondence when you are done, and he will post it for you."

"You are most kind, my lord." Lady Widmore bent her head to her letter, cutting off any further communication.

Marcus frowned. Every interaction with this woman challenged even his most basic training in manners. A shiver traversed his spine as he sought out his butler.

~*~

Widmore Estate

The corpulent lord grinned as he stroked his substantial stomach. When he became a widower, he could go to London and find another wealthy wife. If his peons failed, at least he could stop his whiny bride from spending money and bringing the attention of the debtors to focus on him. The Black Diamond had offered him a mint for his daughter. He'd balked at that. But if things became desperate...

He grinned. Maybe a well-written letter to his father-in-law would loosen purse strings without him having to sacrifice his only child? Even so, in the end, it still came down to a need for an heir, and his wife had not cooperated with his efforts. He'd be glad to eliminate either one or both of them.

3

Josie moaned. Her head ached as though she were a horseshoe being shaped and pounded on the anvil at the local blacksmith. She remembered once watching him pump air into the hot coals, which now took up residence in her skull, and the *clink, clink, clink* of the hammer on reddened metal thundered within. The doctor cautioned against the medication unless the pain became intolerable. Suffering was a subjective thing, though, was it not? Molly awoke her every few hours. The pain was inescapable.

She blinked her eyes against the darkness. The room smelled like sunshine, flowers, and furniture polish. She heard movement. She suspected it was Molly. Her faithful servant had cried earlier when the doctor gave her the sad diagnosis. She could tell from the sound of his voice that the prognosis was not hopeful. His voice carried regret and pity. She didn't want either. She refused to think about tomorrow. This day promised to be long and painful. All her energy would be required just to survive.

Tired. So tired.

~*~

Dr. Miller descended the stairs as Marcus returned from his discussion with Fenton.

"Bruce, come in and tell me how our patient

fares." Marcus escorted the doctor to the study and closed the door behind them. "Make yourself comfortable. Would you like me to ring for tea?"

"Thank you, no. Other patients await me." Bruce sat in a chair, and Marcus found one across from him and took a seat.

Bruce sighed. "Miss Storm awoke this morning during the exam."

"And?" Marcus leaned forward, rested his elbows on his knees, and clasped his hands together.

Bruce shook his head, stood, and started to pace. "I'm not sure. She is in pain but cannot move her legs." He squeezed his eyes closed tightly and released them, reaching up to grasp the bridge of his nose between his thumb and forefinger.

"What?" Marcus's voice was low and serious.

"She can't see."

"What can't she see?"

"Miss Storm is blind. She is also paralyzed from the waist down, as best as I can determine." Dr. Miller sighed.

Marcus leaned back in his chair and exhaled. "This is far worse than anything I imagined. Is it permanent?"

Bruce shook his head and turned, making eye contact. "I do not know. There's no reason I can discover for the paralysis although she reported pain in her spine. If the head injury were closer to her eyes or the back of the head, the blindness would make more sense. I'm flummoxed, and I have to admit I'm not comfortable with any of it."

"What is to be done for her?" Marcus asked softly.

"She cannot be moved. I apologize Marcus—she may need to remain under your roof for some time.

I've left laudanum, but I'm loathe to use it with a head injury."

"Miss Storm is welcome at Rose Hill as long as necessary. I've already written to my aunt to ask her to join us for an extended stay to protect the young lady's reputation."

"I wish I understood more. If you require anything, do not hesitate to send for me. I'll write to some of my colleagues and find out what else might help her."

Marcus came to stand by the doctor. "I trust you, Bruce. We have been friends for too long. We can pray for Miss Storm. God has His hand in this somehow."

Bruce sighed and shook his head. "I confess His ways confuse me. She's not had a chance to really live her life yet. It seems wrong to watch her resting there."

"May she have visitors?"

"Short visits and plenty of rest. I've already sent orders to your cook."

"She is under the best possible care with you as her physician. Thank you." Marcus placed his hand on the doctor's shoulder. "You will return soon?"

"Yes. I am grateful for your faith in me." Bruce turned and walked to the door, and Marcus followed. The doctor accepted his hat and coat from Fenton, picked up his medical bag, and headed out to his carriage.

Marcus returned to his study and sat down. Blind. Paralyzed. His heart grieved for the guest in the yellow suite. The loss of her dreams and her future. Who would marry a woman with those kinds of deficiencies? A heaviness cloaked his soul. He longed to see if she was still awake. He rose and departed the room.

Lady Widmore and her daughter descended the staircase as he approached. They wore dresses in a similar shade of blue, but Lady Widmore's was darker and exposed more flesh. The daughter resembled the mother in the manner in which she walked and moved. It was eerie.

"Ah, Lord Remington, just the person we hoped to see." Lady Widmore exclaimed. Her gaze assessed him.

"Your hopes are fulfilled, for here I am." Marcus forced a smile. Something about this woman set him on edge.

"We hoped you would do us the honor of a tour of your beautiful home." Lady Hetitia inquired.

A small bundle of fur flew across the marble floor and slid to a stop at Marcus's feet, where it barked and jumped. Marcus bent down. "Charlene. Stop this at once." His voice was stern, but he smiled at the small dog, who barked back as she sat down at his feet. The dog panted and her tail wagged as she gazed up at him expectantly. Marcus shook his head, petted the dog, and scooped her up in his arms. He received a lick on the cheek as a reward.

Lady Widmore scowled. "I can hardly believe you would allow this beast loose in your home."

"I apologize if Charlene's manners are not to your liking, but she had been kept in the stables in my absence and is happy to see her master return. Be glad that I don't have a whole passel of hunting dogs running lose around here. As a bachelor, I have no one to please but myself in these matters." His gaze dared her to gainsay him.

Lady Widmore sputtered, drew herself up a little taller, and raised her nose a fraction higher. "The tour?"

"Ah, yes." Marcus turned toward the front of the foyer. "Fenton?"

"Yes, my lord?" The older man, dressed primly in black, stepped forward.

"Would you locate Mrs. Hughes and find out if she would be able to give the ladies here a tour of the house?"

"Certainly." Fenton turned to leave.

"If you wait in the front parlour, first door on the right, I'm sure Mrs. Hughes will arrive soon."

Lady Widmore's eyes narrowed, and her lips pursed together in an unattractive way. Her daughter's shoulders visibly slumped. "Thank you," she said through clenched teeth.

"I have business I must attend to. Pardon me." Marcus set Charlene back on the ground and proceeded to climb the stairs. The dog followed at his heels.

~*~

Josie detected Molly off in the distance and the sound of a deeper voice. *The doctor, perhaps? No, his voice had been higher.* She lacked the energy for curiosity. She wanted to cry in private, if not for the diagnosis, but due to the pain alone. From the way things sounded, she had little privacy. She found that thought simultaneously stifling and comforting.

The soft padding of feet drew closer, and Josie sensed Molly's presence.

"Miss Storm?"

"Yes, Molly?" Josie turned her head toward her abigail's voice. *Clink. Clink. Clink.* The hammer continued as her head throbbed.

"Lord Remington desires to visit with you for a few moments. Would that be acceptable?" The words bounced around in Josie's head and competed against the pounding for comprehension.

Josie nodded and instantly regretted the activity, as her brain had become a bowl full of pudding and nails. "For a few moments. Stay close."

"Yes, Miss."

Josie imagined Molly bobbing a curtsy. The footsteps moved away. The pitter-patter of little feet scratched on the hardwood floors and muffled on the carpet. Heavier tread approached, and she sensed the mysterious presence of the owner of this place of her confinement.

"Miss Storm?" A deep, resonate voice called to her. It wrapped her in warmth and comfort like her favorite blanket when she was a child. She delighted in the sound.

"Yes? Lord Remington?" She turned her face toward that side of the bed and inhaled the soothing scent of sandalwood.

He cleared his throat. "Yes. How do you fare?"

Her weight shifted. "I've had better days." *Why pretend I am fine when I am not and may never be again?*

A slight weight bounced on the bed by her side, and little feet walked across her torso. Soon a wet nose sniffed her face. Josie reached up to touch the soft fur. "And who might you be?" The dog tickled her neck with its tongue. For a moment, she forgot her pain.

"May I introduce Charlene? Charlie, for short. I can remove her if she is a bother to you."

"Please don't. I love dogs." As Josie petted the dog, the hammering slowed its tempo.

"She may remain with you."

"Thank you." Turning her head from the dog, she once again faced her host. "I am grateful as well for your rescue last night and for the shelter of your home." She wished she could see him.

"I'm glad we happened upon you when we did. Not many people travel this road after dark. As for shelter, I could do no less since I lived close."

Silence hung between them, broken by Marcus. "I'm sorry to learn of the extent of your injuries. Are you in much pain?"

Clink. Clink. Clink. Josie took a deep breath and released it slowly. She nodded and suffered the amplification of the sounds in her head. She feared that if she were not blind already, the pain itself would accomplish the task for her.

"Is there anything I can do to help make your stay more comfortable?" Marcus's velvet voice soothed her.

"Visit me again when you are able. I would like that." Josie couldn't believe she had made that request, but something about his voice, the tone, called to her deep inside, and like a metal drawn to a magnet, she couldn't resist.

"I shall try. Would you like your aunt and cousin to visit?"

Josie closed her eyes. The pounding increased in intensity and speed. "No. Please. I do not wish them here." She squeezed her eyes as if doing so would stop the pain, but it was futile.

"I can tell you suffer. I will depart and return another time. Should you require anything, please make the maids aware and they will get word to me."

A large hand grasped hers and squeezed. The warmth of his touch muffled the *clink, clink, clink*. Tears welled up in her eyes, and she tried to blink them back. *I will not cry in front of him.* "Thank you, my lord." She turned her head away from him and into the soft fur of the dog curled up on the pillow next to her head.

"You're welcome," came the soft, deep response.

The careful tread of his feet as he moved away was the only sound. The pounding amplified, and the tears flowed. She shivered as if all the warmth of the room had left with him.

Later, Molly chattered freely as she helped Josie to eat. Josie warred internally against the sound of her maid's voice as it intensified the noise in her head and the pain in her back. She bit back the retort on the tip of her tongue. She had never been one to be short with servants, and she refused to allow these circumstances to attempt her to abuse such a trusted maid. Plus, she was curious about the master of Rose Hill.

"Miss Josephine, I nearly fainted when Lord Remington showed up at the door last evening." The maid spoke softly, almost conspiratorially.

"Last night? Wasn't I unconscious?"

"Yes, miss, but he only wanted to visit you, and he did something quite odd."

How strange. "What did he do?"

"He was charming and handsome. I didn't know how to say no to him, but he allowed me to stay, and he came to sit by you, and well…"

"And?" Josie closed her eyes to try to forestall the rapid tempo in her head.

"Lord Remington sat by your bed and prayed for you." Josie heard the astonishment in Molly's voice as she shared this secret.

"He prayed? Are you sure?" What kind of man did that?

"Oh, yes. Most definitely. Although he didn't speak aloud, he prayed."

Josie relaxed. "What's he like, Molly?"

"Tall, broad-shouldered, with wavy brown hair he pulls back in a queue. His eyes are kind. Deep brown like the coffee your Da likes." Molly sighed.

Great. My maid is half in love with the master of the house.

"The staff has spoken highly of Lord Remington. They are devoted to him and tell me he is generous and fair."

"There's no Lady Remington?" Josie had to know.

"No. Mrs. Hughes hopes this season he might select a bride."

"Has cousin Hetty set her sights on him yet?"

"I'm unsure. I suspect all four of the gentlemen present will be fair game for her."

"Four men?"

"Oh, yes, miss. There is Lord Harrow, who is kind but not quite as handsome as Lord Remington. Lord Westcombe is exactly how I would imagine an aristocrat to be—blond and untouchable. He doesn't view us like Lord Remington does."

"That accounts for three. I thought you said there were four men?"

"Sir Tidley. He seems a pleasant man with a ready smile and a twinkle in his eye. Mrs. Hughes said the men befriended each other at school and spent most of their holidays here at Rose Hill."

"I would like to be alone now." Weariness settled into the marrow of her bones.

Molly put the tray to the side and pulled the covers up to Josie's chin. "You rest, Miss Josephine. I will wake you in a little while as the doctor instructed."

"Thank you, Molly." Josie forced her muscles to relax in an attempt to shut out the hammering in her head. A metallic *clink, clink, clink* distracted her as she sought to imagine what the man with dark hair and coffee-colored eyes looked like. She groaned at the futility of it as darkness suffocated her soul.

4

Morning brought no relief from the constant pain. Josie longed to be left alone. Molly tried to be solicitous in taking care of her basic needs, but her efforts grated on Josie's nerves. Is this what the rest of her life was to be like? Her future looked as dark as her vision. *Lord, why did this happen? I don't understand. I had hoped for a husband and children and a home of my own someday.* She sighed. Her introspection cut off as a new physical presence had entered the room. She inhaled. "Lord Remington."

"How did you know?"

His deep voice wrapped around her in the most delightful way. She wondered if he smiled. Were his teeth as perfect as his soothing voice?

"I cannot see, but I can still use my other senses."

"May I sit?"

"Go ahead. I cannot stop you." Her voice sounded petty, even to her own ears.

"Do you want me to stay?" Uncertainty laced his words.

Josie sighed. Thoughts of *let me be miserable in peace* warred against the comfort she experienced in having him there. "Yes. I'd like you to stay. Please."

"Does conversation make the pain worse?"

Josie heard the concern. "No, I only tire easily."

"My visit will be brief."

"Regardless, I'm grateful you came."

"I would be a poor host if I did not tend to the comfort of my guests."

"And what kind of comfort do you extend to my aunt and cousin?" Jealousy seeped into her heart with these words. *Please, let him not like Hetty.*

"I'm not as good a host in that regard. I came home from London to relax and attend to estate matters, not to entertain. I've relied on my friends to help me with your family."

"They are extended and estranged family. I didn't meet either of them before Monday, when we departed my home."

"That would explain some things."

"Like what?"

"They show no great concern for you."

"I recognized from the first moment I met them I was a means to an end."

"How so?"

"My father funded a majority of the expenses for our season in London. My mother had saved money for my season when she was alive."

"The Widmores are not able to do this?"

"I don't know. Why would they take me up with them, when I am a country nobody lacking the illustrious connections necessary to make a match in London? They were just…"

"Rude?"

Josie nodded. "You've noticed? Of course. They may be nice enough people, but I've not been privy to their favor."

"If they left to continue the journey to London without you, how would you feel?"

"Relieved."

"Why?"

"I regret my injuries have kept them from their entertainments in town. If they go, I won't experience guilt. I also would not be obligated to visit with them, which eventually they may want for the sake of appearances."

"How terrible is your pain today?"

Josie brought both her hands up, placed them over her eyes, and began to rub her temple under the bandage as much as she could gain access.

"That bad?"

"And worse. The laudanum tempts me." Tears come to her eyes, and she could no longer hold them back. "I promised myself I would not cry, and I will rejoice in my sufferings, and yet I cannot. Oh, Lord, please help me." She dropped her hands, and the tears flowed.

He placed a soft piece of fabric in her palm. A handkerchief. She brought it up, wiped her tears, and blew her nose. *Handsome bachelor falls in love with injured woman after carriage accident. Ha! In your dreams, Josie.* She wiped her nose again. She must look awful.

"I cannot understand how difficult this must be for you. If I were able to take it away, I would. I've done everything I can to help, and it's not enough. Tell me what you need for me to do, and I will do it."

Anger at herself and her circumstances spewed forth. "I long to watch the sunrise again, to attempt to paint it. Can you make that happen? I want to walk again in the gardens and across the verdant fields and hills of England and paint every shade of green God has created. Can you make that happen?" She paused and took a shaky breath. Her voice grew softer. Sadder. "I would love to ride a horse again. Swim in a lake. I dream of dancing with a tall, handsome man who adores me. To meet his gaze later across a room and share a private joke. To someday marry him and raise children in our own home with laughter and love..." Her voice drifted away to silence for what seemed a long time. She turned her head away from him. Tears coursed unabated down her cheeks. "No one can do that," she whispered, "no one—not even you, Lord Remington."

A hand clasped hers, but he didn't speak.

"I am ashamed"—she sniffled—"I am inexcusably rude to speak like this to you. You are not at fault and are beyond gracious to me."

He squeezed her hand but again said nothing.

They sat in silence for several moments.

"You are correct. I am unable to bring you back to a reality in which I never knew you. I will do whatever I can to make your time here as bearable as possible. I offer you my friendship. I do not understand His actions, but I believe God is still good. I will continue to pray for healing."

The door opened, and the scratching of claws on the floor preceded a small bundle landing on top of her. Charlie leapt forward to give Josie several sloppy, wet kisses on her face, licking away any remnants of her salty tears. Josie embraced him, finding solace in the soft fur.

Lord Remington gave her hand one last squeeze. "I had better leave you to rest. I can tell you are well comforted by Charlie."

"Thank you. Your visits help more than you realize."

~*~

Marcus rode his horse across the estate to unwind and escape some of the company residing indoors. As hard as he tried, he could not stop thinking about Miss Storm, helpless and alone in the yellow suite. Her unseeing eyes had flashed at him, and her cheeks had turned a delightful pink during her short tirade. Marcus allowed himself a wry grin at the memory. She would not give in to her injuries. She was a fighter. He prayed her desire for recovery would not be in vain.

Returning to the stable, he dismissed the groom and brushed down his horse. He had missed this simple task while living in London and found the rhythm to be soothing. After he finished in the stables, he decided to return to the house through the gardens. Many of the plants were in full bloom and responded vibrantly to the rain followed by sunshine. They reminded him of his mother, who had spent hours in the dirt with her prized roses. The air was brisk and exactly what he needed to clear his head, even after his invigorating ride. He stopped in his tracks when he spied Lady Heticia up ahead.

Confound it.

She had spotted him.

He couldn't skirt around or go back to the stables. The sights of her weaponry focused on him—target number one. Marcus bit his lower lip. Maybe this was the best time to depress any plans she might have toward him. A man who smelled of horse and barn was not conducive to a romantic rendezvous, and he hoped to use that to his advantage. He was not in the mood for flirtation. Work awaited him in his study.

"La, Lord Remington, how wonderful it is to come upon you in this beautiful garden." Lady Heticia sashayed up to him in what he suspected she intended to be a seductive manner. She appeared silly.

"Good day, Lady Heticia." He spoke in his most formal tone and gave her a brief bow.

Her arm swept to one side. "I adore the gardens at Rose Hill."

Lord Remington made sure they were in full view of the windows of the house. "Thank you. My mother labored in love to establish the blooms here, and our gardeners work hard to maintain the grounds."

"I adore roses, especially these coral ones. They seem to be the most romantic flower with the sweetest scent. I hope in London I receive many bouquets of them." Hetty gazed at Marcus with wide eyes and what he suspected might be a flirtatious smile. Her lips alternated between a pout or turned up at the edges to a pucker as if she suggested a kiss.

He fought the urge to laugh and struggled to maintain a dour expression on his face. "Roses are well enough, but for a young woman of tender years making her debut, coral hued roses may be overblown. I would be suspect of any man who sent you such an outrageous offering. Lilies, daisies, or carnations would be far more appropriate."

A flash of anger crossed Heticia's countenance before her smile returned. "Lord Remington, I'm glad to learn about these things before I would show how green I am and unaccustomed to society. Do you enjoy the season when in town?"

Marcus strode toward the garden gate leading to the path to the house and stayed in view of the windows. "Recently, it has been a bore. Too many faces of milk-and-water misses dressed in identical pastel gowns presented for marriage to the highest bidder." He kept his tone flat. He was not lying about his perspective on London, but he rarely gave voice to his opinion.

Heticia's face clouded over, and her eyes narrowed. "Oh."

"Exactly so." Remy's clipped response cut off further conversation. He offered his arm to escort her to the side entrance. "I believe I spied your mother searching for you. Let me walk you to the house."

Once Marcus had arrived at the door, he opened it. "If you will pardon me, Lady Heticia, I have estate matters to tend to." He gave a nod of his head to her and strode off in the direction of the stairs.

Grasping matrons and desperate debutantes. That was the reason he left London. Of course, he desired a woman to share life with, raise a family, and fill Rose Hill with laughter and children. He didn't want to choose a woman for her appearance, or wealth, or title alone.

He gained access to his room, pushed the door shut, and leaned his back against it. The brief episode with Heticia was a narrow escape. While the Widmores had not intended to drop on his doorstep with a staged accident, they would not let the prime opportunity to snag a titled, wealthy husband slip by. He was equally determined they would fail.

After all, he wanted a wife, but on his own terms. Guilt stabbed at him, reminding him that his sister, Henrietta, didn't get that. From what he could tell, she was as in love with Lord Percy as he was besotted with her. He'd never regret his actions on her behalf. And he would do anything possible to avoid a compromising situation that could result in a misalliance for himself.

~*~

An hour later, a freshly attired Viscount descended the stairs and managed to gather his friends. They made their way to Lord Remington's study and locked the door.

"What are you about, Remy? You played least in sight and left the women to us to entertain." Lord Westbrooke continued, "My boots and top coat will never be the same after that rescue, but I shall recover. However, these women are beyond encroaching. They pop up everywhere. I was minding my own business, reading a book in the library when before I realized it, Hetty sat across from me, her mother nowhere around. I beat a hasty retreat. I don't think I can bear them for much longer."

"You know, Remy, there is some truth to what Phillip says. That woman is a shark, and I don't want her sinking her teeth into my hide. The questions she asks border on offensive. Is there a way to get rid of them?" Theo shook his head. "When can we be comfortable again?"

"We need a battle plan for dealing with the Widmores," Marcus started. "I stared down the barrel of a loaded gun this afternoon in the garden. None of us can ever be caught alone with Lady Heticia."

"Easier said than done," grumbled Phillip. "We entertained ourselves and tried to stay out of their way. This morning terrified me. I'll read in my locked bedroom from now on. I think, Remy, the greater danger lies with you as you travel around to manage your estate." Lord Westcombe leaned back in his chair.

"Michael and Theo, are either of you the object of her attentions?" Marcus asked.

"Lady Widmore has dropped broad hints and has tried to wheedle information out of each of us about the other. The standard drill. How much money a year we take in, properties we manage, investments, etc. It's possible Lady Heticia is merely seizing every opportunity she has to gain the interest of one of us." Michael went to the sideboard and poured a glass of brandy. "Since I carry the lowliest title and income along with being born on the wrong side of the blanket, I'm safe."

"Lady Heticia is a lovely young woman. But doesn't the daughter grow up to be like the mother?" Theo shivered and grimaced.

The others chuckled.

"They are guests here, however unexpected, and should be treated with respect. I do not think we need to go out our way to entertain. This is not a house party. My aunt will arrive within a few days, and hopefully we can dispatch the Widmores to London."

"Has the carriage been repaired, Remy?" Theo asked as he rose from his seat to get a glass of brandy as well.

"It should be done by tomorrow."

"Odd that both axles would break," Michael queried.

"Stickney discovered they had been tampered with." Marcus helped himself to a glass and poured one for Phillip.

Phillip reached for the glass. "Thank you. Tampered, you say? A dastardly business. Who would want to harm the occupants of a carriage?"

"That is what I would like to know. One passenger may never recover. Something should be done to bring justice to whoever would perpetrate such a crime."

Michael sat back down and sipped his drink.

"I've summoned Bow Street to investigate the matter. I expect a Runner any day."

"Good idea." Theo sat down.

"How is Miss Storm?" Michael asked.

Marcus expelled a sigh. "She is conscious and in a significant amount of discomfort."

"Poor thing. She appeared quite pretty from the brief moment I saw her," Theo commented. "What else have you learned about her, Marcus?"

"She requested no visits from her aunt and cousin. The Widmores do not even request to see her. I do not know much else. I sent a note to her father to inform him of her accident. According to the doctor, she cannot be moved safely for some time."

"Another reason for your aunt to come?" Phillip asked.

"Yes. I wish to preserve Miss Storm's reputation."

"Whyever for? She'll never see or walk. A season in London is out of the question. Her reputation is insignificant." Theo crossed his arms and leaned back in the chair.

Phillip chimed in. "You are talking to Remy here, remember? Maybe he's more interested in protecting his own reputation."

Marcus bristled, and his eyes narrowed. "The thought never crossed my mind." *If it had, I would not be visiting her as she lay on her sickbed.* Marcus shook his head. Sometimes a good reputation was a burden.

"Well, it should. Regardless of her injuries, if her reputation is ruined under your roof, you would be expected to marry her." Michael smirked.

Marcus closed his eyes as his friends continued talking. For some reason, being forced to marry Miss

Storm didn't horrify him as much as it would if it were any other woman of his acquaintance. She was easy on the eyes and had fit in his arms when he had held and carried her. His heart skipped a beat at the memory and fought the urge to go to her even now. Her scent reminded him of his mother, who was all purity, light, and joy. He didn't know yet if Miss Storm had those same qualities. He must be losing his mind to be meandering around in thoughts about possible marriage to the guest in the yellow room. He shook his head to attend to what his friends said.

"I think we need to be more concerned about how to avoid the parson's mousetrap with Lady Heticia Widmore. Miss Storm is the least of our worries." Theo rose and paced.

"Until the women leave, how shall we protect ourselves?" Phillip tipped his glass for a sip.

"That's what we need to figure out," Theo responded.

The men discussed possible ways to deflate the pretentions of the Widmores and keep themselves from any risk of compromise. Before they went to meet their dinner guests, Marcus cheered them with this thought. "It won't be long, fellows, before we can enjoy peace at Rose Hill."

"Peace? There hasn't been a moment's peace since we left London yesterday morning. Certainly not an auspicious beginning to your holiday, Remy." Michael frowned as he rose to pat his friend on the back before unlocking the door. He swung it open, and the two women stumbled into the room. Michael shook his head. "I rest my case." He glanced at the ladies posing with their elevated noses, and pushed past them without another word.

5

Dinner was a subdued affair. Lady Widmore made few attempts at conversation, and her daughter avoided eye contact with the men.

Marcus wondered what they might be scheming.

After servants removed the cover, the ladies left the men to their port.

Theo spoke up. "I sympathize with Lady Heticia."

Michael groaned. "Why?"

"I think she's being coached and forced to act in ways she's not comfortable with. I suspect her mother does not treat her well. Are any of you acquainted with Lord Widmore?"

Phillip shrugged and commented, "He rarely comes to town from what I recall, and he doesn't take his seat in Parliament. I could point him out in a crowd, but I have never spoken with him."

"Doesn't that seem suspicious to you?" Michael asked. "Why would a peer put his only daughter on the marriage mart and not participate in the process of vetting prospective suitors?" Michael gazed into his glass and shook his head.

"A lot of men avoid the season. We cannot fault Lord Widmore for choosing to stay home and tend to his estate." Marcus swallowed. "I pray I can find a woman who won't annoy me, though."

Theo chuckled as he spoke. "Are you suggesting Lord Widmore stayed home to avoid being with his wife?"

Marcus shrugged and emptied his glass. "Gentleman, I believe we need to provide entertainment of our ladies this evening, even if only for a short time." He pushed his chair back and rose.

Sharing tortured glances, the other three men stood as well.

Entering the drawing room, Marcus approached the women seated by the fire. "How have you enjoyed your stay at Rose Hill thus far?"

"This is a beautiful home, Lord Remington, but I am certain there was a draft in my room. How do you manage to keep up this grand house with such a limited and, ahem, inefficient staff?"

"Really?" Theo joined in, "a draft? I have never experienced any kind of drafts at Rose Hill." He turned to Marcus. "What did you do, ol' man, put them in the attic to sleep?"

Sir Tidley stood near the fire. "Perhaps they are sleeping in the cellars. That is certainly the only place I have ever experienced a chill."

Lord Westcombe coughed and cleared his throat in an exaggerated manner before exclaiming, "As for drafts, I've not noticed any in this mansion, and Lord Remington's staff is of the most excellent quality. Of what could you have found fault in their performance?"

Lady Heticia chimed in. "I rang my bell this morning desiring hot chocolate brought to my room, and it took more than a quarter of an hour before it arrived!" She nodded her head and crossed her arms with a "*hmpf!*"

Phillip placed a hand on his chest, and his eyes grew big. "You had to wait that long for hot chocolate?

Dear Remington, I didn't know you even liked hot chocolate. How would your staff happen to have that on hand when you start your day off with a bracing cup of coffee? How could it be possible your chef managed to come up with hot chocolate in such a short time?" He turned to Heticia. "My lady, you must understand this is a bachelor establishment, and as such, the servants are accustomed to meeting the needs of men. That you should get hot chocolate so fast is beyond belief." Phillip faced Marcus. "I hope you plan to give your chef a special bonus, or these ladies might attempt to offer him a position for such superior service."

Heticia stuttered, "You do not understand. I awaken to a steaming cup of hot chocolate at home. Whyever should I need to wait at all?"

Lady Widmore patted her daughter's knee. "Hetty, he already said they do not make hot chocolate, as the chef is used to preparing only coffee in the morning."

Heticia's eyes narrowed in confusion.

"I know what the problem is," Michael offered. "The root of your complaint is because this is a far larger home than you are used to being in and do not realize the time it takes for a servant to retrieve your desire from the kitchen and return to your room still hot and without spilling it."

Marcus nodded his head before speaking. "It truly astounds me how they do that. You are correct, Phillip. An increase in wages is in order." His mouth twitched at the corners. In truth, his staff were handsomely compensated.

"This conversation is nonsense. You cannot believe you employ superior help in this monstrosity of a house?" Lady Widmore bristled.

Lord Remington stood and narrowed his eyes as he glared at the woman. "Dear Lady Widmore, I extended my hospitality and yet you would pay me back with insults? I have no previous complaints from visitors to this home about the rooms, chimneys, windows, food, or the service. As this is my principle seat and has been in my family for generations, it is with great pride that my staff and I would offer hospitality to anyone. If you find us lacking, I will arrange for my carriage to transport you to The Crown in Didcot until your carriage is fit for travel. Your servant." With a curt bow, Marcus exited the room, giving his friends a wink on the way out.

The men would not find as easy an escape, at least until after the tea tray had arrived. It was an underhanded trick. He had not taken as much umbrage at the ladies' comments as he had pretended. With relief, he escaped the Widmores' presence. He hoped his friends would forgive him.

Marcus took the stairs two at a time and veered off to the south wing. He entered the sitting room doorway and walked across the carpet to the door to the bedroom. Miss Storm was speaking to the dog. Charlie wagged her tail and soaked up the attention. Marcus nodded to Molly, who sat over by the fireplace mending.

"Be careful, Miss Storm. If you spoil my dog, I may be forced to give her to you and let you suffer the consequences."

Josie grinned, and Charlie rose, stretched forward her front paws, leapt off the bed, and ran to the slightly open door. The dog made a quick glance at Miss Storm.

"Be gone, fickle wench!" Marcus laughed as Charlie barked a retort.

Josie bit back a giggle.

Marcus admired the dimple, which appeared for a brief moment.

Charlie scampered out the door.

"Do you mind if I pull up a chair?" Marcus asked.

"Please do." Josie smiled.

Marcus moved closer to the bed and sat. "How do you fare?"

"I am improved this evening, thank you. I am ashamed of how I reacted the last time you visited. I expect had I been able to see your face, I might have shown more restraint in your presence. In that regard, this blindness is a curse."

"No apology necessary. How is your pain?"

"Not as intense. The doctor has advised me to lay flat, but I doubt I will be able to do so for much longer. My head aches, and I'm irritated at not having anything to do. I am also unaccustomed to having my maid and others wait on me to this degree. It is humbling."

"I am unable to imagine how difficult this is for you."

"Thank you, Lord Remington."

"For what?"

"For listening and not judging me. I sense grace from you, which is more than I can give myself. I appreciate that you care."

"Molly and Charlie care too."

Josie gave a soft smile. "Molly does care, and I do not know where I would be without her. Charlie is a lovely dog, and I'm grateful to you for letting her stay with me. You, however, have no reason to care. You are not of my acquaintance, and yet you take time out to visit. You do not act as if my presence here in your home is an imposition. I am quite sure we upset the plans you had for your stay."

"Plans rarely cooperate. While mine changed, I do not begrudge your presence."

There was a sound at the door. Charlie pushed it open a little further and scrambled across the room, jumped onto Marcus's lap, and licked his face. "Scamp!" He laughed as he petted the dog.

Mrs. Hughes had also arrived.

"Miss Storm, I'm afraid I need to depart now." He set the dog on the bed near Miss Storm, and Charlie proceeded to curl up in a ball.

"Thank you for coming."

"My pleasure." Marcus walked to the sitting room door and carefully checked the hallway before leaving to make sure the Widmores did not discover him. He made his way to his suite of rooms.

He pulled off his boots and loosened his cravat as he sat in front of the fireplace. He picked up a tattered piece of paper, which had been delivered late. He was long overdue to hear from his brother, Captain Jared Allendale, but the January date and the state of this letter disturbed him before he even opened it.

Dear Marcus,

I pray Henri and Charles have returned safely to England from their honeymoon. I'm pleased with our sister's choice of a husband, and I'm certain you're relieved of the responsibility of finding her one. Well done, brother.

The war has been brutal, and in spite of my previous letters to detail the beauties surrounding an officer's encampment, life is hard here. I don't want to worry you, but you are a praying man and rumor has reached me of an invisible evil force gathering on England's shores to defeat our nation from within. How Napoleon has managed to woo members of the peerage to do his bidding is a terrifying thought. I pray you and your friends and others can withstand the attacks when they come. What form they would take, I do not yet know. Just beware evil lurks on the shores of bonny England, and I fear for our country.

Pray for me, dear brother. I am a hunted man. Every mission I undertake I fear will be my last. I have not forgotten the God of our parents, the one you so nobly follow. My fear, however, is He has forgotten me.

I long to see your face again. To fish the lake at Rose Hill. Give my regards to our friends. Tell them to stand firm when the devil comes knocking, for surely he will.

Captain Jared Allendale

Marcus paced and prayed late into the night as a deep weight of concern for Jared rested in his heart.

~*~

Josie was bereft at Lord Remington's departure. He hadn't even touched her hand, as he had during past visits. She stroked Charlie's silky fur. She realized proprieties kept the master of the house at a distance, and yet that seemed somewhat silly since a good reputation would not be of much value to her now. She would never make it to London, much less be a byword amongst the *ton*. Who would consider a blind cripple for a wife? Even if she came with a fortune, which she didn't, no amount of money could entice a worthy man to wed her. Why would anyone want her when she would not be able to participate in life alongside him as a helpmate? Josie imagined her future stretched out before her—dark, colorless, and loveless. She wept out of a depth of self-pity.

Charlie lifted her head to lick Josie's tears.

Against doctor's orders, Josie fought to roll to her side. She struggled to get her lower body to move and somehow managed to find a position where the sharpness of her pain lessened. Her legs tingled. She drifted off to sleep and dreamt of impossibilities.

The next morning, she awoke and listened carefully. Charlie softly snored in her arms, and pain radiated down her right leg. Someone else was in the room. She listened for sounds of movement. It wasn't Molly. This presence was different. She inhaled. *Sandalwood.* "Lord Remington?" she whispered. She was afraid there would be no response to her question and Molly would think she was losing her mind. Maybe she was.

"Good morning, Miss Storm," came the soft, deep reply. His voice sounded farther away than usual.

"I realize you cannot watch the sunrise, or paint the colors, but I thought I might describe it to you and somehow you would find some joy."

"It is time for the sunrise? You rose early." Josie held Charlie a little tighter, closed her eyes, and smiled. "I would like that."

"Very well," he replied. "The sky has been pitch black but is slowly starting to turn to a deep, dark sapphire blue. The stars are still twinkling above."

"I can imagine. I have witnessed this so many times." Josie surprised herself at the wonder in her voice.

There was a pause before Marcus continued.

She understood the colors changed subtly and

slowly.

"There are hills to the east which are part of the Rose Hill estate, and above those hills a few stretched out, thin, white, lacy clouds are beginning to be tinged with the faintest color of peach." Another space of silence. "The sky is now a much lighter blue, with streaks of vivid pink above the horizon."

Josie delighted at what he was doing for her. She had challenged him, and he wasn't able to make her physically view the sunrise, but he gave her one nonetheless. What a priceless gift.

He continued. "More yellow is emerging, and the sky is almost white with light. The bright pink is gone completely now, and a brilliance of white gold hovers along the horizon."

More silence ensued.

Josie spoke softly. "The heavens declare the glory of God; and the firmament sheweth his handiwork. Day unto day uttereth speech, and night unto night sheweth knowledge. There is no speech nor language, where their voice is not heard. Their line is gone out through all the earth, and their words to the end of the world. In them hath he set a tabernacle for the sun, which is as a bridegroom coming out of his chamber, and rejoiceth as a strong man to run a race. His going forth is from the end of the heaven, and his circuit unto the ends of it: and there is nothing hid from the heat thereof."

Silence.

"Lord Remington?"

"Hmm, the sun is about to make an appearance. The sky is getting brighter, and I can hardly bare to look with that bright orb popping up from beyond the horizon."

"Thank you, Lord Remington."

"Call me Marcus, or Remy."

"Please call me Josie."

"I'm glad to be of service, Josie."

"Will you sit beside me and visit?"

"I'm afraid I cannot this morning. Dr. Miller will be here soon enough. I will try to visit you later."

She bit back her disappointment. "I'm grateful for your gift of the sunrise. I'll look forward to your return when you are able." She tried to keep from sounding desperate.

"When I can manage to steal away, I will do so. I must go now, but I am continuing to pray for you."

"Thank you, Marcus."

His footsteps grew further away. She wondered at a man who would awaken early to do what he did. She snuggled Charlie as close as the little dog permitted and drifted back to sleep.

~*~

Widmore Estate

"You fools!" The man groaned and threw his glass across the room. The breaking glass and stain of wine on the wallpaper gave him perverse pleasure. "A simple task was all I asked of you." He slumped further in the chair. "Where are they now?"

"Lord Marcus Remington's Rose Hill estate just west of Didcot."

"Keep watch. If they leave and head for London, follow them and keep an eye out for other opportunities."

"The carriage is being repaired at Lord Remington's expense."

The lord smiled. "Good. Just remember, whatever happens needs to appear an accident."

"We won't fail you, m'lord."

"If you fail, heads will roll."

"This is not France, m'lord."

"Not yet. But you just wait." He growled at the servant. "Leave me." He took out a piece of paper to write. Perhaps a note to the Black Diamond could give him a reprieve from the debtors soon to be calling. If he played his cards right, he could get in on a bigger game than at any gambling den. He scratched out the note, sanded, and sealed it with red melted wax so very much like...blood. Yes. Blood would work. But it could not be his.

6

Marcus left Josie's room deeply unsettled. He had stood at the window for what seemed like the longest time. He tried to avoid staring at her as she slept but failed. Her dark hair shone against the white pillowcase. How could he not look? At least she wouldn't catch him observing her. He noticed furrows between her eyes, indicating pain.

He made noises in an effort to gain her attention while at the same time not awaken Molly, who rested on a pallet in the corner. Was it wrong that he had been unable to avert his eyes from his injured guest? In spite of her bruises and bandage, she radiated beauty. He didn't understand what drew him to her. They could never be more than acquaintances. Men and women in their world could never be friends outside of marriage.

For a wife, he needed someone who would be a political hostess. A woman who would ride across the estate and seek after the welfare of his tenants. A mother who cared for their children with the help of nannies but not abdicate to them. He wanted a lady who would love him like his mother loved his father. How presumptuous was he to present such a list to God?

But what would life be like for Josie? His heart grieved at the thought of her living out her days lonely and alone, perhaps in her father's home. Who would make her laugh, and how would she bear that kind of life? Would he willingly marry and be content with a wife who was so limited and unable to share his life? If he married and something like this happened, would he love his wife less? Where did love and duty meld? Marcus shook his head. He had no answers to so many questions.

Marcus grabbed his greatcoat, headed out the back door to the stables, and mounted Cloud. He often did his best thinking on horseback. Once he entered the courtyard, he urged his horse to a gallop. The brisk air was refreshing, and he gave himself over to the wind in his face, the rhythm of the horse's hooves pounding the ground, and the aroma of spring. His mind cleared, and the tension ebbed away, if only for a brief time.

After a few miles and taking several fences with ease, he finally stopped by a brook, tied his mare, and sat down on a rock by the bank. The ground was still damp from the rain. His breath hung in the brisk air. He leaned against a tree and savored the silence, alone with his thoughts and prayers. All centered on a certain young woman. Josie. His imagination ran riot with visions of her walking and dancing and smiling up at him as he held her in his arms. Since when had he become fanciful in his thoughts? Never before had a woman been the focus of his thoughts and aroused such emotion. But in the back of his mind was always this "what if...?" Did he dare hope and pray for her healing? Would God grant a miracle?

It never hurt to ask. He bowed his head to pray. When he finished, he remounted and headed back home at a more sedate pace.

~*~

Remington opened the door to his study and took

a step into the room.

His three friends stared back at him. Silence pervaded with the exception of a log falling in the fireplace.

He shut the door and turned the key. "Is this an interrogation?" Marcus asked as he made his way across the room to his desk. He sensed their gaze on him. This did not bode well. He sat at the desk, leaned back in his chair with his eyes narrowed and lower jaw stiffened as he considered his friends.

Phillip broke the silence. "We met last night and agreed there was safety in numbers, and you play least-in-sight. You left us to play host again to the Widmores. What's going on, Remy? Is there something you're not telling us?"

Michael walked over and placed a hand on Marcus's shoulder. "We wish you would confide in us. We are your friends, lest you've forgotten."

Marcus gave a chuckle. "As if you would ever let me?" He rose and walked over to a chair closer to where his friends sat.

Michael followed.

Marcus ran his hand through his hair and took a deep breath. "Someone planned the carriage accident. But who? I've not had a reply from Bow Street about providing an agent to investigate."

"We already knew some of this. What's bothering you?" Theo countered.

"Lady Widmore only once inquired of her niece and how Miss Storm fared. She has never asked to visit her. Those ladies seem at ease here and willing to take advantage of my hospitality to the degree my servants are being run ragged by their demands. I shall need to hire more if they are staying. I hope Mr. Storm or my aunt, Lady Grey, arrive posthaste. I find any moment spent in the Widmores' company to be vexing, and I wish them to the devil, or at least London, as soon as may be."

"What is driving you from your bed early in the morning and careening across the countryside?" Phillip met Marcus's eyes and held the gaze before Marcus broke away to focus on the fireplace.

"Miss Storm. I've visited with her a few times, and she is coping as well as she can with her injuries."

"You are attracted to her," Michael whispered.

Marcus leaned forward, hands clasped and elbows resting on his knees. "She has to be the most remarkable lady of my acquaintance."

Silence followed.

"What do you really know of her, Remy?" Phillip asked, his voice kind.

Marcus shrugged. "Not much more than many men do before they take a bride amongst the *ton*. She's lovely, considerate, and refreshingly honest."

"And she is blind and paralyzed," Theo added. "Those are definitely not 'selling' points for a potential wife, are they?"

"I didn't say I wanted to marry her. How could I? But the very fact her disability would stop me makes me question my own depth of character."

"How so?" Phillip now stood and came around behind a chair across from Marcus. "You are responsible, fulfill your duties, and help your friends. Your estate flourishes, and you are respected amongst political allies and detractors. What kind of defect of character might you possibly possess, Remy? You are perfect. Is it wrong to seek a wife who would complement that?"

Marcus frowned. "Isn't it selfish and vain to want a wife as an ornament and someone who would enhance my life? What about her needs?"

"She would gain security, faithfulness, and a title. A man others respect and admire. You are not bad to gaze upon, from what the ladies say. Almost any woman would gladly trade her unmarried status for any or all of those things." Michael grinned.

The heat crept up Marcus's face, and he shook his head. "Marriage should be more than a business arrangement."

Phillip chuckled as he spoke. "Very few marriages can stand up to the standards your parents set. Is that what you seek? Love? Affection? Devotion? If so, you were born into the wrong social class. Give it up and pursue a sweet young thing who will not shame you and give you the heirs you need."

Marcus shook his head. "I will not marry solely to get an heir. I do have Jared."

"Unless your brother doesn't make it back from the war." Theo tapped his cheek with his forefinger. "Remy, I don't understand much about this God of yours, but what if He brought Miss Storm here? Why would He tempt you with a woman who cannot possibly fulfill the duties of Viscountess?"

Marcus shrugged. "I don't know the answer to any of those questions. God has permitted this to happen. Why? I don't know. Maybe I was complacent and too self-absorbed to realize I've been more concerned about perfecting my reputation than honoring Him in my heart."

"I think you are too hard on yourself, Remy," Michael chided.

"Most certainly not." Marcus was not hard

The Virtuous Viscount

enough. They did not know how these things tortured him. He loved his friends in spite of their lack of appreciation for their faith. They tolerated his devotion to God even though they failed to understand it.

Michael stretched his legs and gazed at his polished boots. "Perhaps Miss Storm is exactly the wife you need and you just don't realize it."

"Her circumstances present a difficult starting point for any kind of courtship." Marcus frowned.

"If you had married her before the accident and this had happened, would you have abandoned her?" Michael's voice was soft.

"Most certainly not." Marcus growled, and Michael's eyes grew wide.

Phillip walked around and put a hand on his friend's shoulder. "What can we do to help?"

"Pray."

"I think you may have lost us with that request, Remy. I sincerely doubt God's interested in anything I might say." Phillip removed his hand.

"I disagree, Philip. I believe God is very interested in anything you would wish to share with Him." Marcus bowed his head.

"Remy?" Michael asked. "You run a risk by visiting Miss Storm. You don't want to be forced into matrimony because you were caught in her room."

Phillip's eyebrows shot up. "Remy? Do you think visiting Miss Storm is appropriate?"

Marcus leaned back and sighed. "Her maid is always present. I wish Aunt Dorothea would arrive."

"Amen." Theo smiled. "Not to mention she is a delightful lady. If she comes, the Widmores can depart, right?"

Marcus laughed. "Couldn't happen soon enough

for me."

"Maybe one of us should fetch her?" Michael asked.

"She'll come," Marcus countered. "Never fear. With the way I worded my letter, she wouldn't be able to stay away."

The men chuckled.

"Will we get the pleasure of meeting Miss Storm soon?" Theo asked. "It's not fair you get to spend time with her and we don't."

Phillip piped in. "She will likely be under your roof for quite some time. Maybe we can take turns visiting her and cheering her up?"

"I'm not sure if that's wise." Marcus frowned as his eyes shifted and avoided contact. He did not want to share Josie—as if she was...his.

"Will she be able to be brought downstairs at any point?" Theo asked.

Marcus shrugged and shook his head. "I expect she will be permitted to be down here soon. She has to be bored sitting in her room alone. I hope you don't intend to make a May game out of her, gentlemen. She is a lady of gentle birth, and I would not have her trifled with."

"Whoa, ho, ho, dear boy." Theo's eyes grew wide. "I think we've been insulted, men. Do you dare think we would trifle with the affection of a young woman suffering injury and under the protection of your roof? If I didn't know you were such a good shot, I would challenge you to a duel over that."

Marcus laughed. "I wouldn't dare meet you for a duel, Theodore. Who would second either of us?" He shook his head. "I apologize if I offended you. I've not been myself, and I regret having been such a poor host.

I appreciate you entertaining my guests. Hopefully it won't be too many more days before we observe the backside of the Widmore women."

There was a knock on the door to the study, and Michael rose to answer it. Noting that it was Dr. Miller, he motioned him into the room and locked the door again.

"Any news, Bruce?"

The doctor had a seat amongst the circle of friends. They had all been at university together. The doctor glanced around the room and settled on Marcus before he began to speak. "I'm not sure whether to be encouraged or cautious about Miss Storm. She is experiencing pain lower in her back, a feeling that didn't exist a few days ago. She is beginning to experience some sensation and reflexes in her legs."

"Are you suggesting she may regain her ability to walk?" Marcus sat up straighter now.

"It's too soon to tell. As swelling decreases, there is a possibility she may regain use of her legs."

"Would that hold true as well for her sight?" Phillip asked.

Bruce shrugged his shoulders as he looked at Lord Westcombe. "It's too early to know. She suffered a bump on the head, but as swelling decreases, it might relieve pressure and give her back her sight. I would hate to raise false hopes. While pleased with these new developments, her spirits are still low."

"Will it be possible for her sit up for short periods? Perhaps join us for meals or relax in the drawing room so she would not be so isolated?" This time Michael inquired.

Marcus turned his head away. Why was he afraid of his friends being acquainted with this woman?

Bruce spoke. "I will assess that day by day based on how she's progressing. I don't want to do anything to jeopardize her recovery." Bruce rose to leave. "My other patients await. I'll return tomorrow."

Marcus walked Dr. Miller to the door. "Thank you." He unlocked the door, let his friend out, and turned to his friends. "Are we finished?"

Phillip looked to the other two before answering. "Yes, for now."

Marcus motioned to the door. "Will you all let me return to my estate business? It was why I initially entered this room."

"Gentlemen, we are dismissed." Michael rose and gave Marcus a pat on the back as he exited.

Theo and Phillip followed him.

"Remy?" Phillip spoke softly.

"Yes?" His one eyebrow rose. He'd thought the interrogation was over.

"Lock the door behind us. Lady Hetty is not to be trusted." Phillip winked and departed after his friends.

Marcus smiled as he shut the door and turned the key. He walked to his desk. He was glad his friends were gone, but being alone with his thoughts was not comfortable. Settling in his chair behind the large mahogany desk, he began sorting through the day's mail. All the while, the image of gray eyes and dark wavy hair taunted him. He groaned, threw the letters down, and leaned back in his chair.

A log fell in the fireplace, jarring him from his stupor.

He picked up the top letter, opened it, and began to read. Anything to get his thoughts off the young miss upstairs.

7

Josie longed to stare out the window, if only to experience the warmth of the sun upon her face. Molly had helped her move her legs in prescribed exercises, and Josie's lower back and legs hurt more than ever. In spite of that, she was encouraged by the sensations in her legs and feet. The doctor had permitted her to take the laudanum to ease her discomfort if necessary, but she wasn't ready to cave in. She longed for a visit from Marcus. She thought about him often. She wondered what occupied his day.

Charlie had abandoned her for the nonce, but she figured the little mutt needed her own exercise outside. She was grateful for the warmth and affection she received from the small dog. Homesickness beset Josie, and she wondered what kept her father. Shouldn't he have come for her by now? She longed to see him, yet another part of her hoped he was delayed. She didn't want any excuse to leave Rose Hill. At least, not yet. There was someone here she hoped to become better acquainted with.

Josie also wondered about her Aunt Janet and Cousin Hetty. Their behavior on the day of the accident had been unexpectedly rude, and she still smarted from the pain of rejection she had sensed from them before the accident. Maybe having the trip interrupted like this was a blessing in some way. Could a season with them have been worse for her than the pain she now experienced?

Sir Bastian's pursuit would certainly end, surely a blessing. Being a distant neighbor at home, he had pursued her, and his attentions made her uncomfortable. He was older, and his breath often smelled of rotten fish. Josie shivered at the memory of his proposal of marriage. He had not taken her rejection well. At least her father supported her. Certainly, he would not want a blind or crippled wife. Maybe this accident had saved her from more than one disaster.

Too often, her thoughts turned to her pain and the uncertainty of her future. She would never paint again, ride a horse, or dance at a ball. She wouldn't enjoy the colors of a floral arrangement or witness the look of adoration in a man's eyes. Sir Bastian's gaze had not been one of admiration, but more of calculated lust. She had cringed in the face of his pursuit.

Then there was Lord Remington. A man who prayed. He had listened to her and not caviled at her rant. He had visited her, given her a handkerchief, squeezed her hand, and shared a sunrise. What kind of man was this, whose servants spoke highly of him and yet he flouted convention by coming to her room? Even with her abigail present, it was simply not done. Oh, but she was glad he had not stayed away.

Foolish heart! Don't you go reading more into this than friendship. A man of his status and vitality would never condescend to love a woman like you. Maybe the dream, though, would be enough to sustain her in the years to come. That there had been a man who cared about her and was not put off by her bruises and disability. Even though he could never marry her, she could dream. Was this a comfort, though? Or would the Viscount be one more memory to eventually tease and torture her in the lonely, long days and nights extending into her future?

Josie wished her eyes worked. She longed to see the face of this lord of the manor who had invaded her thoughts and livened her lonely days. *Selfish girl.* He was probably busy managing his estate and playing host to her relatives.

Molly had mentioned three other friends who were also visiting and had assisted in her rescue.

They made her curious. What kind of men did Lord Remington call "friend?"

She despised this isolation. She could not read or draw to pass the time and found herself at the mercy of her thoughts. They led her down dangerous paths of despair. There would be no season in London. No marriage, home, or family of her own someday. It was frustrating. She had always been the one to care for everyone else. Was her value and contribution to this world over? Darkness surrounded more than her vision.

The door opened, and her heart leapt.

"'Tis only me, Miss Josephine," Molly said.

The scamper of little feet preceded Charlie as the fluff ball availed herself of the open door and came back to jump on the bed. Josie gave the dog a squeeze and settled down to snuggle as best she could in spite of her pain. She could only rest and wait for a certain visitor to arrive.

~*~

Marcus had tried hard to focus on the numbers before him. He had sorted through his mail, disappointed at no correspondence from Mr. Storm or his aunt. He fought the urge to go check on Josie. The image of her gray eyes and wavy brown hair constantly seemed to blot out the figures on the ledger he tried to balance. In frustration, he rose, changed his clothes, and headed out for another ride on Cloud.

He had no real plan for where he would travel. He galloped for miles. Only upon entering the shade of the woods did he slow. Cloud was foaming and showed signs of fatigue from the hard ride. He brought her to a canter and headed toward the river weaving through the woods.

That was his last thought before an unseen branch caused him to take a hasty dismount from his horse and an unplanned nap.

~*~

Pain as well as boredom became more intense for Josie. The pounding of horse's hooves had broken the stifling silence of the late afternoon. She grew despondent when Molly insisted on closing the windows as the temperature cooled.

Molly mentioned a fog rolling in.

Josie wondered about the horse and rider out in the fog and encroaching darkness. While she was accustomed to the dark now, she recognized how deadly it could be on horseback. She had nothing else to think about and even fretted at the lack of returning hoof beats. Josie struggled through her meal. She had no appetite, and her pain increased. "I'm sorry, Molly, I cannot eat."

"I will remove the tray, Miss Josephine." Molly took the tray and left the room.

Josie struggled to settle under the covers. She felt abandoned when Marcus had not returned to visit her. Her heart ached as well as her body as she struggled to find a comfortable position.

Molly soon returned.

"I think I would like to try the medicine tonight."

"You would? You must be in terrible pain. Let me get it for you." Molly dosed out the medication.

Josie shivered at the bitter taste. Soon, drowsiness overtook Josie as the opiate began to work. Perhaps she'd find refuge in sleep.

~*~

Marcus pried open his eyes and, at first, wondered where he was. His head throbbed. He sat up, and the world spun. Cloud stood nearby, munching on grass. Shadows overtook the dense forest. Marcus whistled for his horse, who came near enough to nuzzle her master. Marcus rose and tested out his limbs. He came through his mishap with nothing more than a knot on his head and a few scratches and bruises.

Standing, he held on to the saddle until the world stopped swirling. Finally, he mounted his horse, swallowed, and closed his eyes as the world wobbled once again. "Well, Cloud, shall we return home before we are missed?"

They retraced his path out of the woods.

Marcus kept his head low to avoid any other branches that might have dastardly designs on him.

As they emerged from the tree line, fog enveloped them. He sighed. To save his horse injury and to minimize the throbbing in his head, he could not travel as fast as he had previously. Clucking to Cloud, he struggled to sit up straight, and with a slight squeeze of his knees, they moved into the misty evening air.

His thoughts once again were of Josie. Hadn't he come on this ride to escape this obsession with her? Marcus experienced a tinge of guilt for avoiding her all day. The sight of her in bed snuggling Charlie this morning had stirred something deep inside him. He had wished he were his dog. He shook his head and regretted the action as the world tilted and slowly righted itself.

Why did she fascinate him? True, he had longed for a woman to call his own, to share his name and his home. Might Josie be the answer to his prayers? He laughed aloud as he looked to the heavens where the moon eerily shown through the fog. "You definitely possess a sense of humor, God. Please help me understand what to do. I can't seem to stop thinking about her."

He spent the next half hour covering the ground slowly and gingerly with Cloud. He shivered and fought back nausea caused by the pounding in his skull. Off in the distance, he squinted and hoped he was not imagining things. Maybe he had more of a head injury than he thought.

Slowly, the ghostly images became clearer. His friends shouted his name.

When they were close enough, he returned the call.

"Well met, gentlemen. Are you out for an evening ride, or are you searching for someone?" He hoped the hint of humor in his voice served to let his friends know he fared well.

"We couldn't think of better weather in which to escape the house," Michael retorted. "We had hoped for a good thunderstorm as well but have been sorely disappointed."

"What happened to 'safety in numbers,' Remy? We were worried about you. Any one of us would have joined you for a gallop." Phillip's face was stern. He really had been worried.

Marcus was humbled. "I didn't even think about that. I needed to escape my study. I am not used to having to find a partner for everything. As it was, my forehead met an invisible branch, which resulted in me taking a nap on the forest floor with a rock for a pillow. I'm a little dizzy but otherwise fine."

"Might not be a bad idea to have Bruce come and take a gander at you." Lord Hughes rode to his right.

"If you insist, I will submit myself to inspection, but can it wait until morning? I would hate to bring him out on a foggy night for nothing more than a mild concussion."

Phillip grinned. "I think this was a ruse to keep you out of the way of our encroaching houseguests."

Marcus chuckled. "The lengths I will go to avoid entrapment." He sobered, and a tremor shook his body. "Something sinister is at work."

Theo pulled up alongside. "Are you reacting to the fog or the nefarious nature of the branches in your woods?"

"Neither. The carriage. The strange behavior of the Widmores. The fact Mr. Storm has not written or come. Nothing is right about any of this."

"And a young lady suffers as a result," Phillip added. "When you put the pieces together, huge gaps exist in our understanding. Why Miss Storm? Why here? Why you?"

"I don't know." Marcus frowned, but without a

doubt, the struggles he faced in his own head were nothing compared to the events unfolding around them. He recalled Jared's haunting letter, along with the Scriptures about battles not being of flesh and blood. In the mist of this late spring evening, it was believable that evil was afoot, even in his peaceful corner of England.

A shiver traversed his body, and Cloud shook her head and skittered sideways in response.

"Easy girl." Marcus patted her neck.

Phillip glanced over but said nothing.

They rode back in companionable silence, handed their horses off to the stable hands, and strode in the back door of Rose Hill.

Marcus gave a message for food to be set out in the dining room. They all went their separate ways to change, meeting again on the stairs and traveling to the dining room.

Lady Widmore came out of the drawing room and stood with her arms folded as the men descended. "Wherever have you been? It is the height of insolence to abandon your guests."

Lord Remington stepped forward, extracted one of her hands, and lifted it to his lips as he bowed. He refrained from the customary kiss. His eyes met her glare as he released her hand, which she promptly snatched back. "I am sorry for the inconvenience. I rode out earlier to inspect some of my estate and met with an accident."

Lady Widmore gasped as she took in the scratches and bruising on his forehead.

"My friends, concerned for my welfare, came in search of me. I beg your forgiveness for my lack of consideration."

"While I am sorry you were injured, did you really need three men to rescue you?"

Lord Westcombe, checking his cravat in the hallway mirror, coolly responded, "We are as close as brothers, and our fear for the welfare of our friend overcame any sense of other responsibilities. We are famished now and will again abandon you to satisfy our hunger." Phillip headed off toward the dining room with a slight bow that the other gentlemen mimicked as they took leave of the befuddled woman.

After dinner, the men chose to avoid the ladies and seek their rest.

Marcus decided to pay a visit to Josie's room to observe how she fared. Cautiously entering the room, he found everything in shadow.

"Shhhhh." Molly came forward and did not allow him entrance to the bedroom. "Miss Storm is sleeping with the help of the laudanum."

"She was in considerable pain?" Marcus's concern and guilt taunted him because he had not come earlier.

Molly frowned as she nodded.

"I'll come back tomorrow. Good night, Molly."

"Good night, Lord Remington." The door closed behind him as he entered the hallway, and a hollowness enveloped him. He hoped Josie had not been disappointed when he had not stopped by earlier. He also hoped in some way she had missed him.

8

Josie awoke in a foul mood, groggy from the opiate. She was angry Marcus hadn't visited her. She chastised herself for thinking she should be important to a man she had only met a few days ago. She apologized for her crossness with Molly but couldn't seem to break through the darkness in her heart. She resumed her trial of lying in her bed, bored.

After hours of unrelenting silence, Molly stepped out of the room.

Josie decided she would try sitting up by herself since her legs itched to move.

Charlie whimpered at her displacement from her favorite spot. The dog sat on the floor, watching and growling as Josie struggled to bring her legs around to the edge of the bed and pushed herself into an upright sitting position.

The bed was higher than she expected, and her dangling feet did not touch the floor. She had thought to try to make it to the chair near the bed if it was where she expected it to be, but she experienced too much pain to try to stand. She sat, feet exposed and shivering in the cold air. Tears of frustration flowed down her cheeks.

Charlie barked at her and pawed at her legs, trying to get her attention.

Josie reached out one hand to stroke her soft fur. "Charlie, I'm such a fool to attempt this."

The door opened from the sitting room and quickly closed.

"Josie! What are you doing?" Marcus asked.

Josie's face flushed with heat at the realization that her lower limbs were exposed where her nightgown hiked up from the effort to move to this position.

He approached and grabbed her hands in his.

She wished she could watch his face. Was there concern written there? Or anger?

"What are you doing? Are you in pain?" His voice was tender.

Josie nodded her head. She took a deep breath, exhaled, and lowered her eyes even though she could not see him anyway. "I could not stand lying here anymore. I thought... Oh, it hurts." She leaned toward him as he held her hands steady.

Marcus bent over and wrapped her in his arms. They were strong and warm.

She buried her head in his shoulder. She inhaled the scent of sandalwood she associated with him.

He maneuvered her back into a lying position in the bed.

Shame inflamed at his observing her this way. When he released her arms from around his neck, she sank into the mattress. A brief expanse of cool air preceded the blanket as it was pulled up, but it did not replace the warmth and comfort she had found from his embrace.

Charlie jumped back on the bed and snuggled next to her head on the pillow.

"I'm surprised you tried something like this with no one here. Has the doctor given you permission to be out of bed yet? Don't you realize you might have further injured yourself? You are starting to make progress, and you would jeopardize that because you lacked entertainment?" Frustration and fear marked Marcus's words. He *did* care.

"You didn't come to visit. In addition, yes, I was bored and thought I could do this. I was wrong. Thank you for coming to my assistance. If you would send Molly in to me, I would appreciate it."

"What do you mean I didn't come? I did, although it was late and you were already asleep. You will fob me off now because I offended you by not coming earlier. I am well aware of the impropriety of even coming to visit you at all." There was an edge to the tone of his voice.

She had offended him, and he had been nothing but gracious to her. "I appreciate the risk you take. Heaven forbid you end up married to a blind cripple only because you attempted to be a good host." She couldn't keep the frustration from seeping into her voice. What was wrong with her today? Was this really all a result of taking laudanum last night? Or her pain? "I'm sorry. I am poor company today. I am not normally this irritable." She closed her eyes and hoped that he would go away and leave her to her shame.

"Pain is not a comfortable friend by any means." Marcus paused.

Josie held her breath, wondering what he might say next. Had she pushed him too far?

"I hope you are better and can rest. I don't know what I can do to alleviate your boredom. I cannot stay and am not certain when I can return. I should have never come at all."

Here it comes. He's going to say he cannot return.

"I want to be able to stay and help you." He whispered those words as he reached out to clasp her hand. "I think about you often and pray for you." He gave her hand a squeeze before he released it. His footsteps moved across the room.

Josie wanted nothing more than to beg him to stay, but all that came out was a soft, "Thank you, Marcus." She heard him pause, the door open and close. His departure sucked all the warmth out of the room. Shivering, she pulled the blankets up higher and maneuvered herself to her side. As her hand came up by her face to rest on the pillow, she thought maybe, just maybe, she detected the scent of sandalwood.

~*~

Marcus slowly descended the grand staircase into the foyer as the front doors opened. He again found himself preoccupied with thoughts of Miss Storm. Her delicate feet and ankles dangling off the bed. The tears had left a trail on her cheeks. Her glorious hair, unbound and teasing him around her shoulders. He didn't know whether to admire her for trying to sit up or be afraid for her, that she would suffer further injury. He shook his head. This preoccupation with her disturbed his peace of mind.

He reached the last few steps to the foyer when Fenton opened the front door.

Dearest Aunt Dorothea, Lady Grey, younger sister to his deceased mother, sailed inside. She was dressed outrageously in various shades of orange from head to toe and a smile that appeared when she spied her nephew.

Marcus always viewed her as pleasingly plump and merry, and he was grateful she had arrived.

"My darling, Marcus! How delightful of you to

invite me to visit." Lady Grey's gloved hands came forward.

He grabbed them both and leaned in to plant a loud kiss on her cheek.

Lady Grey laughed. "You naughty boy. How precious it is to be one of the few women on whom you bestow such favors."

Her blue eyes twinkled up at Marcus, and he gave her a hug.

"I am relieved and grateful you have come. I desperately need you."

"Well, my dear boy, we will sit down for a chat in a little while. First, I need to go to my room and change out of my traveling clothes. Come to my sitting room in three quarters of an hour and we shall have a coze." She reached up, patted his cheek, and followed Mrs. Hughes up the staircase to her usual suite of rooms.

Marcus stood aside as commotion ensued with the unloading of luggage. He sought the sanctuary of his study. As he closed the door and turned, he pulled up short at the realization that another visitor awaited him and been forgotten in the chaos of Lady Grey's arrival. He stepped further into the room. "I apologize if you've been kept waiting. I'm Lord Remington, and you are?"

"Nigel Neville, Bow Street at your service." The man gave a bow.

Marcus pointed to some seats, and the men sat across from each other. "I have a puzzle for you to solve." Marcus shared the events that had occurred with the carriage accident.

The runner left in time for Marcus to find his way to Lady Dorothea's sitting room located in the family portion of the West Wing.

Marcus anticipated his tête-à-tête with Lady Dorothea. She was the youngest child in her family and the most notorious. Of medium height, with wavy brown hair distinguished by silver highlights, she often had a warm smile on her face and a twinkle in her brown eyes. Some had remarked at his similarity to her in that regard. She held her beauty even after losing all three of her children shortly after birth. She had lost her husband to a hunting accident three years past.

Maybe because of her losses and the closeness she had with her sister, she doted on Marcus. While no one could take the place of his mother, Marcus found comfort in her company. She stepped in to offer comfort and counsel when his mother had died suddenly of unknown causes. He had been one and twenty. She came again when his father passed away, some thought of a broken heart, a year later.

Marcus valued her approval as he took over the reins of the estate and made it prosper. She appreciated his faith, which she also shared. He knew she prayed he would find a young woman of quality, faith, and breeding as an acceptable bride.

Only recently had Marcus sensed a calling deep within to settle down. His sister recently married. His brother, Jared, served in France as an aid to Sir Arthur Wellesley, a respectable position but fraught with potential danger since England seemed continually at war with France.

When Marcus entered her sitting room, he could not contain his relief. "Aunt Doro, you are a godsend. Thank you for coming." He gave her a bracing hug, lifted her off the ground, and spun her around while she squealed in delight. He laughed as he set her down and stepped back.

"Now, Marcus, I would do almost anything for you. Would you explain what is happening? From what Mrs. Hughes revealed, you host some interesting guests." She motioned him to a chair and sat in the adjoining one.

"Interesting and frustrating. My prayer is that you will help me get rid of the two in the latter category."

"This sounds intriguing. Why don't you start at the beginning?"

~*~

Lady Dorothea Grey entered the drawing room to find Marcus, Lord Harrow, and Lord Westcombe already present. They greeted her with affection.

"Well, my dear boys. Marcus told me you were guests, and I could not be more delighted to have the company of such charming and handsome young gentlemen."

"We eagerly anticipated your arrival, my lady," Lord Phillip said, "and you look to be in prime twig."

Lady Dorothea twirled around in her gown of various shades of green. "You always were full of flattery, Phillip," she teased.

Phillip winked at her. "You have always been ripe for a little harmless flirtation."

Lady Grey chuckled.

"Ahem."

Two female guests stood in the doorway.

The Lady Widmore sailed in as if she owned the place. "I am afraid we have not had the pleasure of being introduced. Gentlemen, would one of you please do the honors?"

Lady Dorothea Grey looked to Lord Harrow with

one eyebrow raised.

Theodore stepped forward and in his most formal voice, fulfilled the request. "Lady Dorothea, Dowager Countess Grey, this is the estimable Lady Widmore and her daughter, Lady Heticia. They are here as the result of a carriage accident."

Lady Widmore had inhaled quickly, and her eyes widened at the mention of Dorothea's exalted title.

"What a pleasure," purred Lady Grey. "My nephew had informed me of his unexpected guests. I'm sure you are eager to depart Rose Hill as soon as possible, to prepare this lovely young lady's wardrobe for the whirl of the season."

Lady Widmore stammered. "My lady, we would love to depart as soon as may be accomplished, but there is a member of our party who was injured. Surely I could not abandon her to a bachelor establishment or be easy while we enjoyed the gaiety of London as she recuperates."

"Marcus did mention an injured young woman. As I am now in residence, I can provide chaperonage for your niece while she recovers. Her reputation would not suffer under my protection. I can also assure you these young men would never step beyond the pale with the young lady. How soon will your carriage be available?"

Sir Michael Tidley entered the room at this question.

All eyes turned toward Marcus as he stood by the fireplace watching events unfold. "My groom has informed me the carriage will be available for use as early as tomorrow morning if need be."

Michael came up to give Dorothea an exaggerated bow and a kiss on her hand, which sent her into a whoop of laughter as she playfully slapped his arm. "You delightful rogue!"

Lady Widmore and her daughter stared wide-eyed at this display.

"How singularly strange," Lady Widmore murmured.

Dinner was enjoyable. They petitioned Lady Widmore and Lady Heticia to join in the conversational gambits thrown out by the other diners, but they refrained.

Lady Dorothea invited the ladies to withdraw with her while the gentlemen enjoyed their port.

Lady Widmore smiled and nodded as she rose to leave the room.

~*~

The men entered the drawing room a short time later and joined the women in a game of charades. The men fared far better than the women did, and Lady Widmore's color grew higher as the game progressed.

"Lord Remington, thank you for your kind hospitality. Would it be possible for my carriage to be ready by ten in the morning for our departure to London?" Lady Widmore had set down her teacup and saucer and rose to her feet.

The gentlemen did likewise.

"I will make sure everything is in order, Lady Widmore and Lady Heticia. May you have a safe journey." Marcus gave a brief bow, and the Widmore women left the room.

Lady Heticia's eyes had been darting from Marcus to Lady Grey to her mother.

Lady Widmore clasped her daughter's elbow and

led her out of the room.

The door closed behind them, and Marcus hugged his aunt. "I knew I could count on you."

"But of course. And tomorrow you can count on me taking over the care of the other guest you have." Dorothea's eyes tried to search Marcus's, but he looked away.

Wine was called for, and the merry party drank a toast to the redoubtable Lady Dorothea, Dowager Countess of Grey.

~*~

Sir Archibald Bastian arrived in London to keep an eye on his fiancée. Of course, she wasn't his, *yet*, but he longed for the delights of town, and while he awaited invitations to events where he might dance with his intended, the rest of the time he spent gambling and visiting Madame DuBois's establishment. He daily sought to visit the house the Widmores and Miss Storm had rented for the season and grew more concerned at their failure to appear. *Josie had better not be crossing me in this matter. I will have her, and my money too, regardless of what the Black Diamond says.*

He earned some relief from his financial straits with the use of his property for smuggling from France. Being a traitor didn't bother him at all. What had England done for him anyway? *Soon, Miss Storm. Soon you will be mine.* He grinned as he tapped his cane and ascended the steps to Madame's establishment. It was only a matter of time.

9

The next morning, Josie was out of sorts and picked at her breakfast.

Molly came to announce Lord Remington was there, with his aunt.

In frustration, she slammed her fork down. *I don't want to meet anyone right now. I'm in no mood for company. Unless it's Marcus alone...* She took a deep breath. *Lord, help me through this.* She exhaled slowly. "Thank you, Molly. Would you take my tray and send them in?"

Josie pushed back fickle strands of hair as she turned her head toward the sounds of footsteps. "Good morning," Josie said calmly, hiding her inner turmoil. The scent of gardenias wafted in the air.

A woman's voice responded, filled with warmth and acceptance. "Thank you for receiving us, Miss Storm. It is a delight to finally meet the woman who has put my nephew at sixes and sevens." A chair moved across the carpet, and someone sat and rustled clothing. "I am Lady Dorothea Grey, Lord Remington's aunt. I have assured Lady Widmore I will be in residence to protect your reputation while you recover. They removed themselves to London this morning." With a *de soto* voice she added, "We will be far more comfortable here without them underfoot."

Josie's emotions tumbled together. Anger. Relief. Fear. Grief. "My aunt has gone on to London? With

Hetty?"

"Yes, dear. Did I not say so?" Lady Dorothea's voice sounded concerned.

"I'm stunned they would abandon me so easily."

"Miss Storm, consider instead they abandoned the hunting grounds here, and be glad for the sake of me and my friends, who can now relax."

Josie heard the smile in Marcus's voice. "Was Hetty pursuing you all?"

"As much as we would permit."

Molly returned. "Dr. Miller is here."

Dr. Miller entered. "Good morning, Lord Remington, Lady Grey. I'm here to tend to our patient. If you would excuse us?"

"Certainly," Marcus replied. "I hope to visit you another time, Miss Storm."

Marcus and Dorothea rose to leave.

"I'll return later when we can get better acquainted, Miss Storm." Lady Grey said as the sound of feet moved away, and a door opened and closed.

~*~

Marcus grinned through dinner as his aunt employed her talents as hostess. Before she left them to enjoy their after dinner socialization, she told them she would retire for the evening.

"Well, your aunt has done what we couldn't. She vanquished the dragon." Theodore smiled as he raised his glass. "Cheers!"

"Cheers!" the rest of the men joined in.

"Miss Storm's father has not responded to the letter I had posted. I expected him on my doorstep by now." Marcus's brow furrowed. "It's been six days."

"Who addressed the letter?" asked Michael.

"Lady Widmore. Miss Storm was not conscious at the time."

Phillip gazed into the purple liquid in his glass. "I wonder if she misdirected the correspondence?"

"Why would she do that?" Theo asked.

"Why would she possess no desire to connect with Miss Storm but be accompanying her to London for the season?" Marcus set his glass down. "In spite of her injuries, Miss Storm may have had a fortunate escape from Lady Widmore."

"I've heard Lord Widmore is under the hatches," Michael offered.

Marcus shook his head. "Why would that matter? I despise gossip, Michael. It still wouldn't explain any disregard for Miss Storm's well-being."

"Sorry, Marcus, but it might be worth bearing in mind. In this day and age of war and untold evils, even men of the peerage do underhanded things to maintain a lifestyle they cannot afford." Sir Tidley sipped his glass of wine. "I eagerly anticipate meeting the fair lady upstairs. You cannot hide her away forever. You need to share." He winked.

Avoiding looking at Michael, Marcus set his glass down and sighed. "Miss Storm's social life is not mine to determine. That will be up to her, my aunt, and the doctor."

Lord Phillip took a sip of his drink and with a twinkle in his blue eyes and a smirk, proclaimed, "I suggest we make our first attempt on the morrow, gentlemen."

Marcus fidgeted and longed to escape to visit the very woman the men were eager to see.

The men sat with their thoughts for a moment.

Lord Harrow broke the silence. "Have you had any letters from your brother recently?"

Marcus startled at the change of subject. "Jared is a poor correspondent, which makes it ironic that he serves as an *aide de camp* for Wellington. I had a letter a while ago, which contained some ominous warnings about traitors on our shores. He had previously been more light-hearted and would talk about local beauties he encountered. I anticipated he would find himself leg-shackled before the war was over. This letter contained a darker tone, and he seemed afraid. He asked me to pray..."

"You must miss him," Phillip stated, his voice low.

Marcus nodded. "In some ways, I envy him. He experiences adventure, travel, and does something to help change the world, while I go to Almack's, balls, soirées, picnics, and return here to rusticate in comfort. By comparison, my activities seem of little value."

"Has the wine made you buffle-headed?" exclaimed Theodore. "You saved Miss Storm's life, and you have been on hand to help out every one of us at some time or another. Your staff and tenants thrive under you stewardship, and your estates prosper. You use your voice in Parliament to good effect. To think your life is more protected because of the faithful services of people like your brother does not mean it is any less valuable."

"You kept me from financial ruin, the shame of which would have harmed my entire family," Phillip said thoughtfully. "You never used that to make me feel guilty or obliged to you in any way."

"I wasn't searching for praise. I'm sorry, friends, I've been overly reflective since arriving home and a poor host." Marcus rose. "If you don't mind, I'm going to turn in for the evening." Marcus experienced guilt at leaving his friends. He needed escape from being the center of their speculations. He strode up the stairs and, without realizing it, found himself outside the yellow suite. He dropped his head and took a deep breath. Did he dare? He knocked.

"Who is it?"

"Lord Remington."

"Please, come in."

Marcus entered to find Josie propped up in bed absent-mindedly petting Charlie. She smiled as she turned her head toward him.

Molly sewed in the corner.

"How are you this evening, Josie?"

"I am able to move my legs more, and the doctor is optimistic about my recovery."

"Wonderful." He pulled the chair up near the bed and sat down. "Are you still in pain?"

"It lingers, but my headaches are improving. I hope to sleep tonight without the medication. I dislike being muddled the next day."

"That is good news, Josie."

Her facial features were not as pinched as they had been. Her cheeks held a rosy glow, and her gray eyes twinkled.

It saddened him they didn't twinkle because she could see him. She likely never would. His heart grew heavy.

"Would you do me a favor, Marcus?"

"If I can."

"Would you read something from my Bible? I asked Molly to leave it on the bedside table."

"I would be glad to." Marcus reached for the book and came back to sit down. "Any preference? Surely not the story of Job."

Josie gave a wry grin, but it faded quickly. "I suppose Job wouldn't be bad. It would make my momentary troubles pale in comparison to what he suffered. But I think I would prefer something from the book of Psalms. You choose."

Marcus paged through the Bible. Psalms was one of his favorite books to read. "Here's one, Psalm. A Song of degrees. 'I will lift up mine eyes unto the hills, from whence cometh my help.'" Marcus stopped and cringed. "I'm sorry, Josie. Perhaps a different one?"

"No, please keep reading."

"My help cometh from the LORD, which made heaven and earth. He will not suffer thy foot to be moved; he that keepeth thee will not slumber. Behold, he that keepth Israel shall neither slumber nor sleep. The LORD is thy keeper: the LORD is thy shade on thy right hand. The sun shall not smite thee by day, nor the moon by night. The LORD shall preserve thee from all evil: he shall preserve thy soul. The LORD shall preserve thy going out and thy coming in from this time forth and even for evermore."

Marcus started at the words. Would Josie ever gaze upon hills again? Would her feet truly ever move? All evil? Had God protected her, or did he read too much into these words meant for Israel? Was it wrong to want them to be true for the young woman in front of him?

"Thank you, Marcus. That was beautiful."

Marcus searched for words and failed. He swallowed and blinked back the moisture in his eyes as he closed the book and placed it on the table.

"Will you visit again tomorrow?" Her voice held uncertainty.

"I will try to come to visit you. I must warn you my friends are eager to make your acquaintance as well."

Josie gave him a small smile. "I would enjoy meeting them."

But will you like them better than me? And why should that matter? "I will let you rest." Marcus rose and pushed the chair back. "Pleasant dreams, Josie," he said as he headed for the door.

"Pleasant dreams to you as well, Marcus."

~*~

The next morning, the sun seemed to shine brighter. Marcus smiled and felt lightness in his step as he moved about his morning ablutions. His commitments for the day were relatively minor, and he hoped he would get to spend more time with Josie.

As he headed out the door to his suite, he paused to gaze out the window again at the sun as it emerged over the horizon. What was it Josie said? *Like a bridegroom emerging from his chambers.* Why did he remember those words? Would he ever emerge from this chamber to go meet the bride of his dreams? And what would she look like? Who might she be? He could only imagine her as Josie. He shook his head as if to clear out the questions rattling around inside, closed the door behind him, and entered the shadowed hallway to proceed to the breakfast parlour.

At breakfast, Marcus's friends surrounded him, all dressed with a bit more care than normal for a country retreat.

Phillip, always dressed to the nines, surprised Marcus the most with his purple waistcoat under his gray jacket and his cravat tied in an intricate and unusual way. "What do you think, Remy? Will Miss Storm like this? I created it in her honor and call it *The Storm*."

Marcus swallowed a surge of jealousy that his friend would try to woo Josie. "I think it is wasted on a woman who is blind." Marcus's reply was dry as he sipped his coffee.

"Remy scowls like a dog afraid someone is taking away his prized bone," Michael commented with a smirk on his face.

Marcus glared at his friend but remained silent.

"Come on, Remy, Miss Storm has to be something special to tie you up in knots. At some point, we will meet her. Regardless of what you think, you cannot keep her locked in that room forever." Lord Harrow also dressed as if he were in London about to make the rounds and do the pretty to all the misses of the *ton*. He even wore a daisy in his lapel.

Michael set down his cup of coffee and leaned forward with his elbows on the table. Even he had a superbly tied neck cloth. "Regardless of your sensibilities, my dear friend, Lady Dorothea informed us this morning that we may visit the mysterious Miss Storm at half past ten, and we accepted."

Marcus shook his head and rose without speaking to visit his study, shutting the door loudly, yet firmly, behind him. Once inside, he strode to his desk and started sorting through his mail to distract his mind with something other than the breakfast room conversation. The letter he sought was not there.

Why had Mr. Storm failed to reply to his correspondence about his daughter's injuries? What kind of parent would not rush posthaste to his daughter's bedside?

He opened a drawer, extracted a piece of stationery, picked up his pen, and inscribed another missive. He looked back at his scribbled pages of the address Lady Widmore had put on the previous correspondence, for he had copied it down before the letter had gone out in the post. He shook his head. With his scrambled brain that evening, he'd scribbled it down in so sloppy a manner the ink had smudged. He couldn't make out all the information. Later, he would seek Josie for directions to her family home. This letter would have more positive news to share.

~*~

Josie awoke anticipating the new day. There was movement in the room. "Molly?"

The maid's quick movement came toward her bed. "Lady Grey has decided you shall have a bath and your hair washed. The bed linens will be cleaned today, and you will sit in a comfortable chair by the fireplace so the gentlemen can come to visit with you." The excitement in Molly's voice was infectious.

Josie chuckled but grew cynical about these plans. "How does she propose to move me around to accomplish all of this?"

Another body moving toward her and the scent of gardenias told her it was Marcus's aunt. Lady Dorothea spoke. "The servants here are hardy and strong, and between us women, we will manage to make sure you are comfortable without causing you any discomfort."

Josie sighed. Obviously, her days of lazing around bored were ending. She had some misgivings about the upcoming agenda. Would Marcus's friends like her? Would she like them? What more would she learn about the master of the house, who seemed to occupy a more than inordinate share of her heart? Setting those thoughts aside, she gave into the agenda with grace.

"I leave myself in your capable hands."

Soon she soaked in the soapy water of a rose scented bath. Contentment wrapped around her, along with a little bit of hope that her days of loneliness and isolation would be over for good.

~*~

The hot water had done wonders for Josie's back, and her pain level had decreased. Her hair was damp and left long to dry instead of putting it up as would be normal for a miss receiving gentlemen callers. Josie occupied a comfortable chair, and her legs perched on a footstool. Her favorite slippers peeked out from under the blanket. She had donned a simple walking dress made of lightweight cotton. She felt more human, being dressed for the day.

A knock echoed from the sitting room door.

"Half past ten. Right on time," Lady Grey said.

Molly's distinctive footsteps walked to the door.

"Come in, gentlemen," the older woman called. She proceeded to introduce Lord Phillip Westcombe, Lord Theodore Harrow, and Sir Michael Tidley.

Josie grew suddenly shy. Three gentlemen of the *beau monde* sat across or near her, and she could not see them. These were men more exalted in station than her family. With her humble origins, they might never have asked her for a dance in a London ballroom. Had the bruising on her forehead gone away? What would they think of her? Insecurity gnawed at her insides. She wished she had not eaten so much for breakfast.

"What a pleasure it is to finally meet you. I hear you were present and a part of my rescue. Thank you."

Lord Phillip was to the right of her. He had a confident tone to his speech. "It was an awful night, but it is not often we get to play knight errant to a damsel in distress. While not enjoyable at the time, I am pleased to observe how far you have come since then."

"Well spoken, Lord Westcombe. Lord Remington told me you managed to ride through the storm for help and navigate back with a skittish horse and carriage to transport me safely here. I'm guessing you were drenched in the process." Josie offered a smile.

"We all were. I think you, my lady, were the only one who remained dry, as Theo sacrificed his coat to the cause."

"It's remarkable you survived. Lord Remington was inventive in affecting your rescue. We followed orders and only did whatever he asked of us. He did the hard work."

Josie thought this was Sir Tidley speaking, sitting across from her.

"True, Michael, it was a cold and miserable evening. But there was nothing more that men of honor could choose to do but lend a hand. It is a pleasure to finally meet you." Lord Harrow's voice came from the left.

More conversation and laughter followed, but soon Lady Dorothea shooed the men out of the room, amidst dramatic protests from them, which made Josie smile. Why had she been afraid? Marcus had chosen well when he had selected these men as his friends, and she found herself wondering more about the one gentleman who was conspicuously absent. When would the man she longed to be with most come to her? Time weighed heavy in the waiting. Josie picked at her lunch. She lacked an appetite, and her back began to throb.

Dr. Miller came and carried her back to bed. "I'm pleased you were able to sit up and enjoy company. I can tell the gentlemen helped the color return to your cheeks."

Josie bit her lip.

"Your legs are starting to gain more movement. Tomorrow I want to see if we can have you take a few steps with some support so you can regain some strength."

"I would love to try." Hope surged within. She tamped it down as doubts assailed her. Would she walk again?

"I cannot guarantee you will be able to walk, but we won't know unless we make the attempt."

Josie nodded. "Thank you."

"Rest well, Miss Storm. You still have much healing to do."

Charlie jumped up on the bed to snuggle with Josie, and both were soon asleep.

10

Marcus joined his friends for lunch, but his attitude had not changed much as the men gushed about how delightful, charming, and beautiful Miss Storm was. Maybe they were right. He acted like a dog salivating over a bone he refused to share. Except Miss Storm was not a bone, but rather, a woman with choices. He had no right to be jealous because she had enchanted his friends. He just hoped she liked him better.

Theo broke Marcus's reverie. "Have you heard from Bow Street?"

"A letter arrived in the post a few minutes ago. I've yet to read it."

Michael rose, his chair almost tipping over in the process. "We should look at it now."

The rest of the gentlemen followed suit.

Marcus shook his head, sighed, and pushed back his chair. "As you will."

Marcus strode to his desk, grabbed the letter, and opened it. He read aloud to his friends.

Lord Remington,

I am still in the process of investigating the carriage accident that injured Miss Storm. I regret we have no suspects as of yet. The inns I investigated reported Lady Widmore was rude and tight-fisted. She failed to make a good impression anywhere along her journey to or from Rose Hill. With incentive, the Widmore servants revealed they have not been paid for several months and do not leave due to threats of bad references being given.

Please be assured I will keep you abreast of any new developments. Regards,

Mr. Nigel Neville

Marcus threw the letter on his desk. "It is not unusual for someone to be under the hatches, and being rude isn't a crime, either."

The four sat staring at each other. They threw around some possible ideas for why those axles would be cut, but none were credible. They grew frustrated.

"We cannot give up. Certainly Mr. Neville will find something if given enough time," said Theo, hoping to lighten the heavy mood in the room.

"Time is the one thing we have," said Michael.

~*~

Dr. Miller informed Marcus that Josie was resting. Bruce was hopeful about her recovery, and they talked about the prospects for her healing.

Marcus had received word of flooding issues at the home farm. He rode out in the afternoon to meet with the tenant and arranged for necessary repairs. After he arrived home and changed out of his muddy boots and work clothes, he strode down the corridor to inquire if he could visit Josie.

Aunt Dorothea met him at the door. "Marcus, Miss Storm had a delightful morning but is now in great discomfort. Your visit must be short."

Marcus nodded to his aunt, went into the bedroom as she followed, and sat by the fireplace. His heart skipped a beat as he gazed at Josie lying in the bed.

From her furrowed brows she was suffering, but

she still looked lovely. Her head turned toward him as he crossed the carpet. She smiled, and his heart did a jig.

"Marcus, I missed you this morning."

Marcus was silent. He could hardly confess his fear of competition from his friends for her affections. Since when did he ever compete for a woman? He shook his head at his errant thoughts. "I had work to tend to. My friends informed me I could no longer keep you to myself."

Josie's eyes squinted. "What kind of work?"

"Estate business, letters, and some flooding issues on part of the property. Aunt Doro says I cannot stay long. I am sorry you are in pain. However, I am in need of some assistance from you." He pulled the chair up and sat down.

"How might I be of help?"

"After the accident, I had your aunt address a letter to your father. He has not responded, and I desire to send another one. However, I was careless in copying down what she had written, and I cannot make out the direction. Would you give it to me? I will send out another missive. He must be worried for you."

"Thank you for caring about me and my family." Josie proceeded to give him the address.

Marcus wrote it down slowly with graphite and repeated it back to her. "I shall send this out in the morning." He put the piece of paper and pencil in the pocket of his coat. "How did you enjoy my friends?" Did he really want to know? He closed his eyes, took a deep breath, and let it out slowly. When they opened, he saw her lips curve softly.

"I liked them exceedingly well and appreciated

their visit. They treated me as a younger sister, which put me at ease. They seem like proper gentlemen. Men worthy of your regard. None of them would take credit for their part in my rescue when I expressed my gratitude. They gave all credit to you for your sacrifice and leadership."

Marcus blinked. "Sacrifice? What did I lose by rescuing you? They obviously lie. Don't believe a word they say."

Josie's dimple showed as she spoke. "Their voices spoke of deep devotion and affection for you, my lord."

"We are not back to 'my lord' now, are we?"

"Sorry, Marcus."

"That is better. Sometimes I think the title and all that comes with it to be far more of a burden than I would prefer. However, I was born to do this. I must fulfill my destiny to the best of my ability. There are benefits that come with wealth and position."

"Like what?"

"I can give to charities and other endeavors that I believe in. I can use my influence in the government to effect positive changes in our country."

"I would love to hear more about that." Josie yawned. "I'm terribly sorry, Marcus."

"I have reached my time limit anyway." Marcus spied Aunt Doro rising to insist he leave.

"I think this conversation needs to be saved for another day, when Miss Storm has more stamina to endure the lengthy lecture that might ensue." Lady Grey laid a hand on Marcus's arm as he rose from his chair.

Marcus scowled playfully at his Aunt and turned again to Josie. "She is right to keep me from boring you with my pet charities and causes. It would be better if you were stronger and had other, more pleasant conversations between us, lest on the basis of this one you would choose never to allow me to visit again." Marcus noted his Aunt had moved to the doorway. He picked up Josie's hand, stroked it lightly with his thumb, and gave it a squeeze.

Josie sighed as he released her hand. "I don't think much of what you could say to me would ever be boring, Marcus. I am a captive audience for the time being."

"Marcus, you scamp. Please leave before I forcibly remove you. You will be late for dinner if you don't hurry." Lady Grey's eyes danced with laughter even though her voice was stern.

"Yes, ma'am. Good night, Josie." Marcus gave his aunt a slight bow and a peck on the cheek and exited the room with a spring in his step.

He hurried down to his study, pulled out the scrap of paper, and compared it to his scribbled note. The addresses were not in any way similar. For some reason, Lady Widmore had misdirected his first letter to Mr. Storm. This was information to pass along to the runner. He copied down the address and took the letter out to the salver, where his butler would tend to it in the morning. The thought continued to plague him—why would Lady Widmore give him a wrong address? He entered the drawing room as the first dinner bell rang. He sensed Phillip's gaze on him, and it shook him out of his reflections.

"You look preoccupied, Remy."

Marcus frowned. Had they read him so easily? "I am, and I apologize. How has your afternoon gone?"

"It was quiet and relaxing, unlike yours, I

understand. Trouble at the home farm?"

Marcus nodded. "Too much rain, too fast. I think we've come up with some solutions so we are not vulnerable in the future. Messy work."

"Somehow, I'm guessing what is on your mind has nothing to do flooding issues." Michael helped himself to a glass of brandy and took a sip, never taking his eyes off Marcus.

Marcus gave a half-smile. "You always were perceptive, Michael."

"Would it perhaps have to do with the lovely lady upstairs?" Michael teased.

Marcus nodded. "Correct, as always."

"Always? I'll remember that." Michael came over with a glass of brandy for Marcus. "Here, maybe this will help."

"Thank you."

"So, you now have our attention. What is bothering you, and how can we help? We will be more than happy to render any assistance needed." Phillip held Marcus's eyes. "You are not in this alone."

Marcus nodded again.

At that moment, the gentlemen were disturbed by Lord Harrow, who led in Lady Grey. Soon the men playfully argued over who would have the honors of escorting in the lone lady to dinner, and Aunt Dorothea tittered like a schoolgirl over their antics.

Theodore asserted, as he was the oldest of them all, it was his right to lend his arm to take her into the dining room. Light-hearted humor filled the dinner that followed.

As the servants brought out the third course, Marcus decided to inquire as to the men's visit with Josie.

"You never told us she was able to sit in a chair," Michael said, in-between bites of salmon.

"Really?" Marcus raised an eyebrow toward his aunt.

"Doctor Miller and I spoke yesterday, and he agreed she might be allowed to sit up for a short period of time to receive visitors," Lady Grey defended.

"I found Miss Storm to be a delightful and charming young miss," Theo gushed.

Soon the others chimed in about their impressions of their guest, and Marcus fought against the unspoken threat their admiration aroused in him. He stabbed at his food, and the footman refilled his wine glass. The men appeared oblivious to Marcus's changed mood, but his aunt watched him closely.

She cleared her throat loudly and gave the other three gentlemen speaking glances.

One by one, they turned to look at Marcus, who refused to make eye contact. He was very much aware of their perusal.

Phillip leaned back in his chair, away from his empty plate to allow the footman to clear it. He sipped his wine and spoke. "You mentioned earlier you had news pertaining to our patient?"

Marcus's gaze shot to Phillip's, and he laid down his fork. "Today I wrote another letter to Miss Storm's father, but the direction Miss Storm gave me differed from the one Lady Widmore inscribed."

"Are you sure it wasn't a mistake?" Lady Grey asked.

"They had been traveling from the west to head to London and had only left Miss Storm's residence that morning. If my memory of geography classes holds true, the address Lady Widmore gave me is from far north of London. I was a fool to have not paid attention to that detail earlier."

"Why ever would someone do such a thing?" Theo asked.

"That is what I wondered," Marcus said.

"Will you be letting Bow Street know?" Michael asked.

"Of course, yet I cannot figure out how this fits in with the carriage accident."

"Puzzling indeed," said Phillip. "Did you mention the discrepancy to Miss Storm?"

"No reason to alarm her. She is unaware the carriage was tampered with. None of this makes sense." Marcus's frustration rose.

"Is Miss Storm in any danger?" asked Lady Grey.

"I do not think so, Aunt, but I cannot be certain. I do not want to be seeking trouble around every corner, and yet these things don't add up. I suggest we stay on our guard."

The men were quiet as they finished their dessert. The evening ended with the men playing cards with Aunt Dorothea.

Marcus pleaded exhaustion and headed up to his suite. At the top of the stairs, he paused. He wanted to visit Josie one last time. He headed down to her rooms.

Molly answered his soft knock. "My lord, Miss Storm is sleeping," Molly whispered.

Marcus bent his head. "Thank you for keeping watch over her, Molly. Good night."

Deflated, he headed to his own room.

~*~

Marcus tossed and turned for the better part of the night as a thunderstorm flashed and boomed outside his window. Finally, he gave up his attempt and threw on breeches and his robe. He made his way through the darkened hallways to Josie's room. *Has it come to this? Skulking about in my own home in the dead of night?* He slipped into the room quietly, not even disturbing Charlie. *Not much of a watchdog, are you, girl?* Marcus grinned to himself as he grudgingly admitted he missed having his dog follow him around all day.

Molly was a sound sleeper on her pallet in the corner.

Marcus sat next to the bed in the chair left from earlier. He bent his head to pray as the storm raged.

Josie's scream startled him.

Charlie's head came up.

Molly snored.

Marcus tried to calm Josie with whispers. "There is nothing to fear. Just a storm. You are safe. Josie, you are safe, and you will be fine."

Josie sobbed and started to calm but never awakened or seemed to be aware of his presence. He sat and watched, helpless, as she tossed and turned before finally relaxing into sleep. Marcus prayed, and when he noted her breathing became slow and even, he rose to seek his own bed.

The storm continued through the night.

Before Marcus drifted back to sleep, he wondered if the roads would even be passable on the morrow for the mail or for other travelers, and hoped there would be no more accidents. He would need to pursue further repairs on the main road. Another task for a drier day. Soon his eyes closed, and his thoughts grew mute.

11

The day dawned shrouded in fog. Marcus's eyes scratched like wool as he stood, stretching by the window overlooking his estate. Weariness settled over him as he glanced back at his bed. His shoulders slumped, and he bent his head, shaking it as if to clear the cobwebs that had sprung up during the few hours of sleep he had managed. He leaned forward and let his forehead lean against the cool glass for a few moments. *Lord, help me get through this day.* He finally stood up straight, went to the washstand, and splashed his face with water. Revived, he attended to shaving and dressing for his day. Reluctantly, he left his room.

It appeared everyone either slept in or had breakfast in their rooms.

Marcus sat alone with his coffee and some toast and eggs. He wondered how Josie fared and what had caused her terror in the night. Was it a flashback to the accident? Maybe part of her remembered. He ached for her fear and wished he could take it all away—the fear, pain, blindness. *Lord, would I have been drawn to her if we'd met in London?*

Fenton disturbed his thoughts with the information that a visitor awaited him. Directing Fenton to show the unknown person to his study, he finished his coffee and withdrew to learn who had been brave enough to venture forth on such a damp and dreary day. Marcus hoped the servants had lit the fireplace. He shivered as he entered the open door to find Mr. Neville. "Good day to you, Neville. You have news?" Marcus motioned to chairs near the cheerfully blazing fire. "I'm surprised you traveled on such a day as this."

"I knew you were anxious for Miss Storm, and since I was investigating in the area, it seemed timely to meet with you."

"I'm glad you came. There is some information that may or may not be related to this I had intended to forward to you."

Nigel nodded, but he pursed his lips and he paused for a few moments before beginning. "Someone has been poking around at the posting houses inquiring about the carriage accident, and it is not one of my men. This personage wore green and gold livery, the same colors boldly painted on the Widmore carriage."

"So a Widmore servant is checking up for Lord Widmore? I do not recall Lady Widmore ever posting any correspondence to her husband, although she indicated she had planned to do so."

"That is as much as I suspected. Reports reached my ears that the Widmore marriage is not a happy one. Lord Widmore has more often than not been a ramshackle excuse for nobility, if you ask me."

"I didn't."

"I beg your pardon, my lord. My gut instinct tells me he may be the instigator of the accident. If he has staff asking around, he will already be aware Lady Widmore has moved on to London. I suspect injuring Miss Storm was not part of his original plan. Regardless, it shows a wanton lack of regard for human life. Attempted murder is serious business."

"So if his marriage is unhappy, does that necessarily make him guilty of tampering with his own carriage? Can you really be sure Miss Storm was not the intended victim and is safe from further danger?"

"I believe she is safe, but I only have my suspicions at this point. No proof to back up anything, much less take to a magistrate. If you want me to investigate, I will do so. It is possible Lady Widmore and her daughter may still be in danger if one or the other were the intended victim."

Marcus pressed his left thumb and index finger together at the bridge of his nose and closed his eyes. Why couldn't this be easier? Should he continue to pay for this investigation if Josie was safe and recovering? Why would he care about the Widmores other than they were human beings? After all, they were not his responsibility. *Lord, what to do?* He pulled his hand down and released a breath. "I'll continue to fund the investigation. We do not know for sure that Miss Storm is not still in danger until we identify who instigated the accident and why. It seems caution would be prudent."

Nigel nodded. "You said you had some information that might be pertinent to the case?"

Marcus relayed the misinformation he had received from Lady Widmore regarding Mr. Storm's real address. "The address she had given is in a different part of the country than from where Miss Storm hails."

"Are you suggesting Lady Widmore deliberately delayed Miss Storm's father from coming here?"

"It would appear so."

"This could not be a simple error on her part?"

Marcus shook his head. He rose, and grabbing a

piece of paper off his desk, he returned and handed it to the Runner. "Here, compare the two addresses."

Nigel met Marcus's eyes, took the page, and scanned it. He frowned, and his dark eyes shot back to Marcus. "I'll check out both these addresses to make sure. I would suggest we post one of my men here, just in case."

"In case of what? You said she should not be in danger. There are four men on the premises, and I can guarantee you we are all capable of defending Miss Storm should the need arise."

"I'm sure you are, but an extra person in hiding on the outside would possibly alert you to danger before it comes knocking on your door."

"Fine. Make sure I meet the man, though. I don't want to accidently shoot him for a trespasser."

"Done. He will present himself to you. We shall get to the bottom of this."

Marcus smiled. "Good, I'm paying you to succeed." He stood, as did the runner.

Soon Nigel Neville was on his way from Rose Hill, disappearing into the fog quickly as Marcus watched from the front window.

Josie might be in danger. The unknown of it grated at him. He was used to his life ordered and tidy. Nothing was certain when it came to the young woman upstairs. Marcus noticed his half-smile reflected in the glass. Life had definitely become far more chaotic since that particular storm blew her into his life.

He gazed at the hazy view from his window. His lovely estate, normally shining bright and beautiful in the sun, reminded him of a scene from one of Radcliffe's gothic novels. *A mysterious attempted murder* and a damsel in distress upstairs trapped against her will by fates beyond her control or knowledge. Marcus let out a bark of laughter. What had happened to him? Since when did he engage in such melancholy and macabre reflections? Josie was far from a tragic heroine of a story. She was a fighter.

Yet something sinister out there threatened, and as long as she was under his protection, he would do all in his power to keep her safe. He glanced at the mantel clock. His aunt had requested his assistance this morning. Marcus smiled broadly, and his spirit lifted as he turned to leave the room and climbed the stairs two at a time. It was never good to keep a lady waiting.

~*~

Josie woke with a start and stretched. Had it stormed last night? A damp chill in the air left goose bumps on her arms in spite of the fire lapping and crackling at the wood in the fireplace. She smiled to herself. She had dreamt Marcus had been with her during the night, reassuring her that she would be fine. She hugged the thought to herself because for a moment she felt loved, and the warmth it brought to her heart was something she wanted to savor before reality crashed in around her. Dreams of being loved and cherished by a man may be the closest she would ever get to realizing her hopes. For who would want a blind woman for a wife?

She had given up the fear she would never walk. She was determined to succeed, and Lady Grey had promised her today they could try based on the doctor's instructions. Maybe later she would be able to visit with Marcus and his friends again. As dark as her vision was, the future held some bright spots.

Molly bustled in with Mrs. Hughes to help her dress. Once that was accomplished and her hair finished, a footman came to carry her to a chair by the fireplace and a blanket was placed over her lap to keep her warm.

She relaxed against the back of the chair. There was a time to sit up straight like a lady, but not now, when she was recovering her strength. She relished the freedom to relax. Still, sitting up was not much fun with nothing to do. She couldn't read a book, and there was no one to talk to. It was difficult to keep positive with so much time spent alone in the darkness of one's own soul. She shook her head at how dramatic, at times, her thoughts became.

She should recall Scripture instead. Or sing. But she didn't want to do either of those things. For right now, loneliness was more comfortable to wrap around her like a woolen cloak. She shivered. Time crawled for her in the dark, and she grew weary and exhausted. Had she not slept well? After all, she'd had wonderful dreams, did she not?

Oh, if she could only keep the dark thoughts at bay. The fears of her future. The desire for more time with the men in this house, especially the master. She hugged Charlie close.

Molly had described Lord Remington to her, but she still could not envision his face. Dark wavy hair that brushed past his collar in the back. Dark, brooding eyes that also twinkled when he grinned. A strong chin. Tall and broad shouldered, but debonair in his posture. Molly had talked about him after every visit, even when she had not allowed him entry. The maid had gushed about the lord of the manor and how the other servants revered him.

Josie had sensed a tenseness in him at times and wondered at it. Was he uncomfortable around her? Is that why he hadn't been here? Or was it because he had defied convention to visit her while she lay abed? A man like him could never have any lasting interest in a woman such as her. She lacked a title and wealth, the two hallmarks of any bride a titled man like him would select. She wasn't even especially beautiful and, at present, certainly lacked a graceful walk. How would one even flirt with a fan when one cannot even make eye contact with the object of one's desire? Josie groaned aloud at the direction of her thoughts. *Foolish girl, have you fallen in love with a man you could never aspire to?*

"Miss Storm, are you all right?"

Josie startled.

Lady Grey had entered the room so quietly Josie never heard her.

"I am well enough, Lady Dorothea. Why?" Josie was happy to have a real person to converse with.

"You groaned, and I hoped you were not in pain. You looked like you were somewhere else. Molly stepped out to take care of your clothes."

Heat rose in her cheeks as she smiled. "No pain except for perhaps the fruitless direction of my thoughts." She struggled to sit up a bit straighter. "Have you come to visit for a while? I would be glad for the company."

"I have come to oversee your program of rehabilitation." Lady Dorothea sat across from her now.

"That sounds dangerous. Should I be afraid?" Josie grinned.

"Never dangerous, for I have brought with me someone who will be helping you learn to walk, and he will tend to your safety."

Josie leaned back in her chair again. "I'm at your disposal, Lady Dorothea. How do you propose we do this? I cannot see to hold on to anything or avoid tripping over my own two feet." Josie paused. "Wait, did you say 'he' will help me? Who? Is someone else here? I didn't hear any footsteps." She closed her eyes and inhaled. Sandalwood. *Oh, yes. Marcus.*

"I stand more than ready to assist you."

She heard a smile in his deep voice. Her heart sped up. Hadn't she been thinking of him? "I'm not sure I'm ready for this."

"We shall see, won't we? It cannot hurt to make the attempt." Marcus lifted the blanket, picked up Josie's hands, and bent down to place one arm under hers and around her back to help her rise to her feet.

He held her as they stood. The warmth of the length of his body against her side caused a strange skip in her pulse as she leaned against him. She turned her head up toward the sound of his voice. "It doesn't hurt. I was afraid it would." Her voice softened.

Strong arms supported her.

Being close to him made her dizzy. She turned her face forward and swallowed. One deep breath in and out. "I'm ready."

"Can you move a foot forward to walk?"

Marcus's gentle and encouraging words made Josie suspect she could fly if he asked it of her. She loved being close to him. Why did that seem familiar? Her dreams had certainly seemed as real as this moment. She lifted her right foot, moved it forward, and transferred her weight so she could move her left.

Marcus's grip was firm even though her steps were awkward. After a few steps forward, Marcus gently turned her around. Soon they were back to the chair, where he helped her down and returned her blanket as she shivered.

"Are you cold?" he asked.

Josie smiled. "No, thank you." She could never admit aloud that she had shivered at the loss of his body heat and closeness, and that slipping back into her own space, separate and alone, scared her. Awe overwhelmed her at the realization of what she had done. "I did it," she whispered, almost as if saying it aloud would bring a denial that it happened.

"You walked," Dorothea spoke. "How do you feel?"

Heat rose in her cheeks. "Wonderful. When can we do this again?" She couldn't keep the eagerness out of her voice. But to walk again would at least release her from the prison of this room.

Both Marcus and Dorothea chuckled.

Josie found the sound refreshing to her soul.

"We cannot move too quickly but will make another attempt this afternoon if you are able." Lady Grey spoke with tenderness.

"We don't want you to overdo things and hurt yourself." Marcus added firmly, but she heard the approval in his voice.

"I will try to be patient. What a wonderful gift you and God have given me this day." Josie hugged herself. Her shoulders raised up almost to her ears before she lowered them and relaxed into the chair, suddenly exhausted from her limited efforts. How frustrating.

Lady Dorothea rose, and Josie heard the rustling

of her skirts as she walked away. "I will leave you to visit. Molly has returned and can be your chaperone. I have some work to do with Mrs. Hughes. Josie, I am expecting you to join us downstairs for luncheon today."

With that pronouncement, Josie heard the door open and close.Josie's head snapped to where she heard Marcus take a seat. "Downstairs?"

"That is what my Aunt indicated, and she is one to be believed. There are three other men who will be delighted to have you joining us at the table."

"How will I be getting to the first floor?" Did she dare hope?

"I will be your transportation," Marcus stated.

Josie smiled. "Thank you for making this possible."

"It is my pleasure, Josie. How did you fare through the storm last night?"

Did he know something? Had her dreaming of him become transparent? Josie's heart beat faster. "I had a nightmare but do not remember what it was about." She couldn't tell him she had dreamed of him.

"I had wondered if storms would bring back any memories of the accident." Marcus's voice was soft as velvet.

"I had an impression of being in the carriage." She wouldn't tell him about the gentleman she recalled in her dream. It had only flashed through her thoughts, but she wondered if it was Marcus. Had she somehow seen him before her sight vanished? Or had her mind made up that face out of desperation? Josie yawned. "I'm sorry. This is the second time I've done that to you as we conversed."

"You must be tired. Let me get you back to your

bed to rest." She heard Marcus rise but stay by her side and Molly moving around in the background. He leaned down, and she inhaled his scent again and bit back a smile. It would not do to have him thinking she was possibly falling in love over him, even though that was exactly what was happening. Strong arms lifted her, and she heard his heart beating as she rested her head against his chest. Crossing the room went by too quickly, and before she was ready to let go, he was laying her down on the bed as Molly removed her slippers.

He removed her hands from his neck, and holding one hand in his, he left a soft kiss there. As he set her hand down, she was dizzy, happy, and disconsolate all at once.

Charlie jumped up on the bed, licked her cheek, and snuggled up next to her.

"I will come for you later, Josie. Rest well."

She heard him walk to the door and could have sworn she heard him say, "lucky dog" under his breath.

12

Marcus was pleased that Josie would be joining them for a meal. He was anxious for her because he suspected that eating without sight might make her self-conscious. They would all work to make her comfortable, but would she really be able to relax and enjoy the meal? He hoped so. It was a hurdle she would have to overcome if blindness was a permanent reality in her life. Marcus arrived at Josie's room with a spring in his step.

From the first time he had held her in his arms, something about the experience tugged at something deep inside him. He couldn't describe or explain it. All he knew was every time he held her next to him, whether helping her to walk or carrying her, he was needed, strong, and at least, perhaps in that brief moment, more alive.

He grinned as he strode into Josie's suite even though he knew she would not witness it. "Your chariot has come to give you a ride to the dining room." He observed a rosy color suffuse her cheeks.

She sat on the bed awaiting him. Molly had braided her hair and pulled it away from her face. Her dark eyes appeared wider and her lashes longer. Her cheeks were pink, and her dimple was evident.

For a moment, he wanted to keep her here away from the others. To touch her hair and taste her lips. *Whoa, stop it right there. Since when have I ever been tempted like this before?* He struggled to corral his thoughts.

"I'm ready, Marcus." Her eyes dipped as the lashes came down before she gazed, unseeing, back up at him.

She couldn't have heard his thoughts, could she? "Good, because I am hungry." He came over and displaced Charlie, who whined at that Turkish treatment. Marcus scooped up Josie with ease. "What have we been feeding you? I declare you must have gained at least a stone since you first arrived."

Josie playfully batted his shoulder before returning to clasp his neck. "You are horrid." She smirked but added, "I'm not too heavy for you, am I?"

"Doubting my strength, Miss Storm?" He relaxed his arms as if he were going to drop her, and she let out a little squeal and hugged his neck all the tighter. Marcus found he did not mind that at all.

Aunt Dorothea had witnessed this byplay. "No time for games, Marcus. Let us get this young woman to the table with as much grace as you can muster."

"Yes, ma'am," said Marcus with feigned humility, which earned him a *tsk tsk tsk* from Lady Dorothea. Marcus headed out the door with a grin on his face and inhaled the scent of roses. He was unaccountably lighthearted.

Entering the dining room, Marcus set Josie down in a chair seated to his right.

Michael offered her a dish with cold meat, bread, and fruit and informed her of where they were on her plate. Marcus was sad to realize she did not need any more help from him. All those days of eating alone, she'd obviously developed a system to make it a manageable task.

Lord Harrow congratulated Josie on being able to join the group. "You cannot imagine how boring Remy has been lately. We are delighted to have someone new to converse with."

Josie simpered. Marcus scowled at his friend.

"Like you don't have your dull days either, Theodore? There are definitely tales I could tell," Marcus quipped.

"Boys..." Lady Grey warned.

"Remy?" Josie asked.

"We saddled him with that moniker when he became Viscount." Theo stated.

Michael took up the gauntlet to share tales of adventures they had in school. Phillip and Theo joined in the telling of these tales while Marcus remained silent, listening and watching Josie's animated face as she asked questions and her smile showed her amusement at their tales.

When the meal was finished, Josie asked for help to stand and requested that she be allowed to walk to the drawing room. Marcus lent her his aid, and Josie made the journey, a bit uncertainly, but triumphantly nonetheless. With great fanfare, she settled into a seat near the fireplace.

The men fought to sit near her while Marcus stepped back to watch.

"Miss Storm, would you please tell us about your family?" Sir Tidley made the request with a needling voice.

"We are nothing out of the ordinary. My father owns a modest estate, Westwood, near the village of Stone in Gloucestershire. He fell in love with my mother, who was the daughter of an Earl. He disinherited her when they married against his wishes.

I have two younger brothers, one at Oxford and another still in the schoolroom, and one younger sister. My mother passed away two years ago when influenza swept through the village. That was why I did not have a season earlier. After that, it was unclear who would take me until my aunt volunteered to sponsor me along with my cousin Hetty."

"Which Earl is your grandfather?" Lord Westcombe asked.

"Lord Chester, but we have no relationship with him."

"Chester? I've heard him speak in Parliament. He is a powerful man." Marcus started to pace around the periphery. He couldn't keep still. This girl was more than landed gentry. She had noble blood running in her veins. He glanced at his aunt and raised an eyebrow.

"Does your grandfather know that your mother has passed on?" Lady Dorothea asked.

"I'm not sure. We have no contact with him. I didn't even know my aunt existed until a few months ago, when she wrote to my father suggesting I join them for a season."

"News can have its way of getting around in the *ton*," Michael added.

"But we don't socialize amongst the *beau monde*. We are not worthy enough for that. I did not expect a grand entrance in London, not even tickets to Almacks. I am a mere 'miss' with no grand connections." Josie's fingers fiddled with a ribbon from her dress. "I have no desire or expectation to meet my grandfather. God calls me to forgive, but it is hard to do that when someone you have never even met has been cruel to someone you've loved. My mother was such a kind and beautiful woman. She never complained about our humble circumstances. She was a joy to be around." Tears began to well up in Josie's eyes, and she blinked them back.

Theo pressed a handkerchief into the palm of her hand. "Please don't weep, Miss Storm. You must know that it unmans us. We never know what to do with a woman's tears."

Josie gave a tremulous smile as she sopped up her errant tears. "I'm sorry. Since the accident, I've missed my mother more than ever."

"I would expect that is only natural, dear." Lady Dorothea reached to clasp Josie's free hand to give it a squeeze.

"What occupied you at home? What kind of activities did you enjoy?" Marcus hoped to steer the conversation to safer ground. This wasn't the first time he'd been unsettled by her tears.

"I loved to draw, paint watercolors, read, play pianoforte and violin. I enjoyed managing the household for my father and helping with the tenants on our estate. I loved long walks and riding my horse. I was content with my life there."

Marcus looked away. Most of those activities she would no longer be able to enjoy. His heart was heavy for her loss. But she still had some things, didn't she? "Miss Storm, we have an excellent pianoforte—you are welcome to use it any time you want. I have had little time to play it myself. It was my mother's instrument."

Theo jumped up. "How about right now?" He grinned and came to stand by Miss Storm's chair. "Would you honor us with a song?"

"Now? I don't know…"

"You don't have to, but if you would like to, we

would be a most grateful audience," said Lord Westcombe.

"Perhaps she is fatigued." Lady Dorothea offered her an escape.

Josie sighed and conceded defeat. "If you wish, I could try."

"That's the spirit!" cheered Michael.

Theo helped Josie rise since he was by her side but handed her off to Marcus as she crossed the room. He assisted her to the pianoforte and helped her find middle C, although he realized a moment later that she had not needed assistance. He whispered in her ear, "I would help you turn your pages, but I guess that would be an obviously useless excuse for the opportunity to sit next to you."

Josie blushed. She ran her fingers up and down, playing scales to warm up. When she was finished, she launched into a hauntingly beautiful Bach selection.

The group sat spellbound, watching her play and listening to the emotions that flowed through the notes and filled the room. When she finished, the room erupted in applause and the request for another selection.

This time, Josie played an unfamiliar tune. She managed to use the knee levers with ease. As the music rose and fell, her face reflected joy and contentment.

No one clapped or spoke when the last vibration of the final note ended.

"Did everyone leave?" Josie asked as she gripped the bench with both hands.

"No," Marcus whispered from close by. "We were transported by the beauty of what you played. We were still lost in it when you had finished, and it seemed almost too holy a moment to mar with applause."

"I agree," said Lady Grey. "You play beautifully. However, now I think it is time you got some rest if you hope to meet with us again for dinner. Marcus, would you give Miss Storm a lift to her room? I suspect she's fatigued."

Marcus nodded to his aunt and bit back a smile of self-satisfaction.

His friends protested.

"Just one of my duties as host." He settled Josie in his arms, and she sighed as she wrapped her arms around his neck. She laid her head close to his, and he inhaled the sweet scent of her hair.

She smiled as he climbed the stairs.

"Spending the afternoon with you and your friends was delightful," she whispered.

"I agree."

"Marcus, can I beg a favor of you?" Her voice sounded uncertain.

"You may. What is it?" What could she possibly want that he had not already provided? He found his curiosity piqued.

"When we reach my room, before you leave" —she paused and exhaled deeply before she continued— "may I touch your face?"

What an extraordinary request. Marcus stopped at the top of the stairs and searched her face for clues. "Why?"

Josie looked away but leaned her head against him. "I cannot see you. I can hear you, smell the soap and cologne you use, but I want to see through my fingers what you really look like."

Marcus grinned. "Then yes, by all means." He proceeded to her room and set her on the bed. He drew up the chair until he was right in front of her. He brought her hands up to his face.

She closed her eyes and give a gentle smile as her soft fingers touched his hair, all the way to the back of his head. She traced the shape of his ears and on to his chin before she moved up his jaw to his forehead and traced his eyebrows.

He had to close his eyes as she traced them but opened them again as she did the same for his nose, cheekbones, and lips. Her own lips part slightly as she ran a finger across his. If this were any other woman, he would have suspected he was being seduced. Her touch was feather light, and he struggled against the desire for more and to be able to touch her. The entire experience was so—intimate. His pulse accelerated. Finally, he put his hands up to pull hers away. "Satisfied?"

She opened her eyes, smiled, and tipped her head to one side. "Yes. Thank you, Marcus."

Molly came forward to pull off her slippers and help her to bed.

Marcus rose to leave.

~*~

Marcus headed to his own sitting room. His face tingled where she had touched him, and he missed her light touch on his skin and in his hair. He was drawn to her, yet how little did he know of her? He sighed and was about to go to his dressing room to change when a knock came to his door. He opened it to find his aunt there.

"May I enter, Marcus?"

Marcus stood back, allowed the door to open

further, and motioned for his aunt to enter. He raised one eyebrow as he shut the door and followed his aunt to the furniture on the other side of the room. They both sat on the sofa and turned to each other.

"You cannot hibernate in here all the time."

Marcus shook his head. "I came to change clothes to ride out to the home farm."

His aunt nodded her head, and as if she believed him.

"And this is the only place where I have any privacy." He glared at his aunt. "I was mistaken."

Aunt Dorothea narrowed her eyes. "What do you make of this business with the Earl of Chester?"

"What am I to make of it? He has a right to do what he wants, even though it seems hard-hearted and does not reconcile with the man I've met. I do not know him well, though."

"I think you should write to him."

Marcus frowned. "And tell him what? You have a closer connection with him, if I recall. Why don't you write if you think it will be beneficial? I suspect you might stir up a hornet's nest, and Josie has had enough challenges to face."

"Perhaps you are right. I'll pray on this. I'm inclined to send a letter but would need to be careful how I go about it."

"Sounds reasonable, you wise old woman," Marcus teased.

Dorothea rose and leaned over to plant a kiss on the top of his head. "You love her." She stepped back and gazed down at him. Her eyes radiated compassion and approval.

Marcus looked back at her but said nothing. He wasn't ready to confide in anyone the depth of his attraction for Miss Storm when he didn't understand it himself. She had him tied up in knots.

Lady Grey smiled and nodded her head as if he had spoken aloud. "I thought so." With that, she departed.

Did he love Miss Josephine Storm? Marcus didn't know. He rose and went to change. Duty called.

~*~

Josie had taken a good nap and awakened happy. Molly worked to get her dressed in one of her nicer evening gowns, but Josie was too preoccupied to care. She kept thinking of the smell and the texture of Marcus's skin and the rich timbre of his voice. She wondered if he sang, because she thought it would be a beautiful sound if he did. Dare she ask?

Dinnertime arrived before she realized it, and Marcus had come again to carry her. It was odd to be floating in his arms as they moved across the hallway and down the stairs. She was safe and secure and somehow knew that this man was more than capable of protecting her from any harm.

She heard the voices of the other men as they entered the dining room, and Lady Grey greeted her as well. She was grateful that Marcus sat to her left. He told her where on the plate the food was. She could more easily find it and not feel conspicuous. She was among friends and comfortable. The men went out of their way to make her forget her disability.

Josie found that peas were her one downfall, and it soon became obvious. She shook her head at the absurdity of it all. She didn't even like peas all that much. Finally, she placed her spoon down in frustration.

"Peas giving you some trouble?" Michael asked, but she could tell there was a hint of humor in his tone.

"If anyone of you laughs at me, I will fling a spoonful of these peas at you. I may not be able to see, but I can hear where you are."

"Tempting thought. It would be a fun thing to witness, but I am not sure how Marcus's servants would like cleaning that off the carpet or walls." Lord Harrow's humor was a bit drier, but she appreciated his comforting words. They would not make sport of her.

"I will pass, because given the company at this table, it might result in an all-out food fight. I suggest we all keep our peas on our plates if they are not making their way to our mouths." Lady Dorothea sounded in good spirits. "If we were outside having a picnic, however, I might encourage you."

Laughter followed as the men shared stories of food mishaps that took place at school, including a food fight or two.

Josie managed to eat the rest of her meal, having opted to skip the peas.

The men bypassed their customary glass of port and instead followed the women to the drawing room.

Lord Harrow begged to "escort" Josie across the hall.

Josie had already grown stronger and more confident in her ability to walk. Was it only this morning that she had started the attempt?

Once they were seated, Marcus announced a surprise. He came to stand by Josie. "Miss Storm, you tantalized us with your musical talent this afternoon on the pianoforte. I hope I am not being too bold, but would you also play this for us?"

Josie sighed as her hands touched the cool wood. Her violin! She gently caressed the sides and tested the strings, adjusting them as needed. She held out her hand for the bow, and Marcus placed it where she could grasp it. Placing the instrument under her chin, she ran the bow across, played some scales to warm up, and tuned as she did so. Then she played. As the last of the chord hung in the air, Josie lifted the bow and laid it across her lap.

"Breathtaking."

"Lovely."

"Incomparable."

"Bewitching."

Marcus spoke, and her heart skipped at his words. "Miss Storm, you have definitely shown forth the glory of God with the beauty you have coaxed from that piece of wood. You have a musical gift."

"You are kind. Thank you." Josie raised her bow. "Would you like me to play something else?"

They all expressed agreement.

Josie grinned, closed her eyes, and proceeded to fiddle an energetic little tune that soon had the group clapping and laughing as the violin led their hearts in a merry dance. When she was finished, she handed off the instrument to Marcus to put away.

"Miss Storm, every time we meet you, you become more enchanting in my eyes." Lord Harrow's voice was sweet to her ears.

Heat rose to her face. "I assure you I am not without faults. I also, at times, struggle with my faith. Especially Scriptures like, 'We know all things work together for good to them that love God.'"

"That verse is incomplete my dear," said

Dorothea. "It continues by saying 'to them who are called according to His purpose.' I would suspect the difficulty in your circumstance is not only trusting God for His goodness but wondering what your purpose is when you suffer."

"Interesting, Lady Dorothea," Phillip interjected as he rose, and Josie heard him move around. "I've never been interested in church beyond the duty of attending. Probably because I've never experienced anything there that bears any relation to the things you speak of, where people believe those words. It's like you have something personal with God, but how can you trust Someone you can't see?"

"Lord Westcombe, I have not seen Lord Remington with my eyes. Because I have heard his voice and spoken with him and know he has heard me and has my best interests at heart, I can trust he will do all that is in his power to help and protect me. I have no fear of him dropping me, either. Yet, I have never seen him. God speaks through His word and in prayer, and sometimes He even speaks to me through others. It takes time to learn to hear His voice. It is a relationship not based on sight. If it were, I would have to question *your* existence."

Laughter followed this, and Phillip joined in. "Flush hit, Miss Storm. I bow to the truth you have presented and consider your words carefully. I do not hear God as you do."

"Miss Storm," Michael interjected, "what might God's purpose be in your infirmity?"

Sincere curiosity tinged his question.

Josie shrugged. "I wish I understood. All I am certain of is that if I stay faithful to God, I can trust Him. When I remember that, I am not as discouraged. I wish I might see all of you, but maybe God has something to teach me in the dark."

After tea, Marcus walked her to the stairs. She stopped to turn to him, placing one hand on his arm. She bit her lower lip. "I would like to attempt the stairs."

"I do not think that would be wise, Josie." Concern colored his voice.

"Why, Marcus, I believe you might be afraid that I will fall and maybe you won't be quick enough to catch me."

"Maybe"—he sounded serious—"but you only started walking today. You don't know how many steps there are." He sighed. "And I worry you would do injury to yourself."

"Balderdash. The worst that could happen would be that I might find myself a bit sore on the morrow, forcing me to walk less and you will need carry me around more. Please, Marcus, let me try?"

"I'm at your disposal." His resignation was clear.

Josie nodded, smiled, and grabbed the banister. With Marcus's hand on her back, she took a step and pulled herself up. Using her other foot, she took the next and pulled herself up. One step after another, she sensed her muscles cramp and weaken, but pride would not allow her to quit. Marcus's hand was firm and steady. She reached the top and bit back a moan at the twinge of pain that traveled down her legs. "You can carry me now."

He picked her up in his strong arms.

She laid her head against his shoulder and silently chastised herself for her willfulness.

Susan M. Baganz

13

Marcus arose the next morning to bright sunshine which burned up the fog and cast everything in a rosy glow. Another visit to the home farm was on the agenda for him, but first he made his way to Josie's room. Disappointment weighed heavy on him when he found Michael there ahead of him, hoping to carry Josie downstairs. Miss Storm apparently had other plans, and for once, Marcus rejoiced in her feistiness as much as it had frustrated him last night.

"I would like to try to walk down. Would you be willing to assist me?" Josie asked.

Michael's face fell, although his friend recovered quickly.

"Gladly, Miss Storm." Michael extended his arm and placed her hand on his forearm as they navigated the room. Michael gave Marcus a look of triumph.

Marcus bit back a growl. Resigned to sharing her and figuring that she was in safe hands, Marcus took off down another set of stairs that led to the kitchen. He grabbed a scone and sipped some coffee before heading out to the stables. He saddled Cloud, and soon the two were off for a ride through the sunshine and mud.

Marcus spent the entire day at the home farm and helped dig irrigation ditches to funnel the overflow of water. The work was physically demanding. A layer of mud and sweat covered him. His thoughts were preoccupied with Josie. How did she fare in his absence? Did she even miss him? How long before she left his home to return to her own? Mr. Storm might arrive any day. Would he ever see her again? Did he want her enough to do whatever it took for her to remain at Rose Hill? That thought brought him up short. The only way that could happen would be to marry her. He had not known her long. Yet most marriages amongst the *beau monde* had far less knowledge of their spouses. Marcus knew more than most men about a woman they considered marrying. Still, was it the right thing to do? *Lord, help me to know for sure.*

He returned home in time to bathe and change for dinner and found himself once again usurped in escorting Josie to dinner.

This time, Lord Harrow had begged the honor.

Marcus's only consolation was that Josie sat by him through the meal. In spite of that, she did not give him her undivided attention but interacted with everyone equally. Marcus berated himself for his selfishness, and his physical exhaustion pulled him inward. He struggled to insert himself into the conversation.

As dinner finished, Lord Westcombe escorted Josie to the drawing room and, after some covert whispering between them, took her directly to the piano and helped her sit.

Marcus went to stand near the fireplace mantle. He was absurdly jealous of his friends as they surrounded Josie. In spite of his fatigue, he wished he could work off some of his negative energy with a bout with any one of them in the boxing ring at Gentleman Jackson's.

"Why so bleak, Marcus?" He startled when Lady Grey interrupted his wayward thoughts. She put her hand on his arm and searched his eyes. He had to look back or risk being rude. "I will have you escort Miss Storm upstairs tonight. She complained she had not seen you all day."

Marcus's heart surged with hope. She missed him. Weariness kept him from a show of enthusiasm, however. "Thank you. I was at the home farm all day."

"You look fatigued. You work too hard." She glanced over at Miss Storm. "I wonder when her father will arrive to take her home."

Marcus's spirits sank. Mr. Storm should have arrived by now. He could arrive at any time. He closed his eyes against the headache he knew was imminent. Miss Storm broke into his dark, brooding thoughts.

"Lord Remington? Where are you?" She sat at the piano, and the men backed away.

He had a clear view of her face and figure, accented by the soft blue empire waist dress with square neckline and a small locket around her neck. Marcus gulped. "I'm over here." Could he have sounded more lame?

"I want to dedicate this song to you, Marcus." Josie placed her hands above the keys and closed her eyes. The song played out simply but built in complexity. It soared, sank, and ended on light cheerful notes that resolved slowly in the silence.

Marcus walked over to the piano, picked up Josie's hand, lifted it to his lips, and gave the barest whisper of a kiss. "That was beautiful. Thank you." Reluctantly, he released her hand and stepped back as the other men vied for her attention.

Soon Josie laughed with the men as she played a

playful ditty that they all knew.

"I will play one more song tonight, gentleman, but under one condition."

"And that condition would be?" Phillip asked with a smirk on his face.

"That Lord Remington accompanies me with his voice." Josie looked down at her fingers in her lap as she awaited his response.

Marcus was nonplussed. He did not perform for audiences and reserved his singing for worship in church. It was not that he could not sing, but it was a private thing for him. If it had been anyone else asking, he would have refused. But this was Josie. Almost before he realized what he was doing, he was by her side and whispering in her ear, "Any particular song you would like to hear?" He thought he detected a shiver run through her.

"Remy? You sing?" Theo had gone to sit down close by, where he could observe what was happening.

"I guess you'll have to listen to find out, won't you?" Marcus grinned.

"How about *Amazing Grace*? I know it's a relatively newer song by Newton, but I love the words and can play it adequately." Josie tilted her head in waiting for his answer.

"If you can play it adequately, I believe I can sing it." Marcus gently touched her back. "Shall we?"

He watched her long fingers leave her lap to find their place on the black and white keys and begin playing. He strove to forget that others watched. Marcus closed his eyes and sought to focus on God as he sang. As the piano filled the room in a magical dance with his voice and the words of the hymn, it was as if God were there with them in a real and tangible way. When the chords resolved, he once again opened his eyes to gaze down at Josie.

She looked up at him with tears in her eyes and a small smile. "Thank you, Marcus."

After tea, Marcus walked beside Josie to the stairs and guided her ascent. When they arrived in her suite, Molly sat off to one side mending. Marcus sat down next to Josie on a loveseat and turned his body toward hers.

"I missed you today."

"I missed you too, but dash it all, Josie, every time I turn around, another man has you on his arm."

Josie tilted her head. "Are you jealous?" She smirked. "You needn't be. It would be unusual for me to have a man pining for my company."

"You are a desirable woman. Were the men in Stone blind?"

She shrugged. "I didn't lack for partners, but I never found a man worthy of knowing better. One, Sir Bastian, has pursued me, undaunted by my repeated rejections of his suit. But I held no affection for him. I am not desperate for a husband. If God wants me to have one, He will bring that about in His own way."

"Isn't that naïve? If you stay at home, how would that man ever find you?"

"Isn't God big enough to make it happen?" Josie's hand rose to stop Marcus from speaking. "I'm not naïve. I was on my way to London if you recall, to partake of a season where I might or might not find the man I would wish to marry." Her hand came down, and Marcus watched her smile fall away.

"Your father could show up any day."

"I've been spoiled here. It will be difficult to leave." Josie fidgeted with her hands. "Do you think a man might ever come to love a blind woman? Even a little?"

A knock on the door prevented his answer.

Lady Grey entered. "It's time to leave, Marcus. I will assist Miss Storm."

Marcus sighed, clasped Josie's hand in his much larger one and brought it to his lips and softly whispered so only she heard. "Yes." He rose and departed.

~*~

Josie tossed and turned during the night. Had she been too bold with Marcus? Had she practically asked him if he could love her? Was his whispered "yes" for her and him or for her and someone else? She growled and punched her pillow.

Morning came, and she was still frustrated. She hated having to wait on the men, even though they were most courteous of her. She could not stand being a patient any longer. At some point, she needed to get up and learn to live in spite of the darkness. She would not let this defeat her.

Once Molly had finished assisting her with her morning toilette and had left to find her an escort, Josie decided to make the journey downstairs on her own. With that determination, she found the door and slowly made her way down the hallway by running her hand along the top of the wainscoting that was there. When she came to a corner, she knew that she had to move across to the top of the banister, which she managed. Slowly, she worked her way down the steps, and remembering Marcus's turns as he carried her, she found her way into the breakfast parlour.

A footman procured food and she sipped her tea.

Footsteps heralded Marcus's entrance to the room. It had to be him because of his distinctive scent and purposeful stride. He halted in the doorway.

She smiled and set down her cup.

"Miss Storm. Who escorted you here? Molly came to fetch me to do the honors. We returned to find you gone. Yet here you are breaking your fast."

"I decided to manage without an escort."

He stepped closer to her. "Don't ever do that again. You have only been up walking for what, two days? You don't know the layout of the house and might have fallen and been seriously injured. Or worse." Anger emanated from him like a physical force invading her space.

"I appreciate your concern, Lord Remington. I am a grown woman. At some point, I have to learn to navigate a house, stairs and all. It cannot be avoided, and I refuse to be cooped up in that bedroom, as comfortable as it is, all day long to stay *safe*." Josie struggled to keep her voice calm. Was Marcus concerned, or was he irate with her? "Life will not always provide me with an escort."

"You are too independent."

Had he clenched his teeth? The words sounded strained and not meant as a compliment.

"Children," interrupted Lady Grey as she entered the room. "I think this should be set aside for now. Yes. I overheard. How could one not when your voices were audible in the hallway? Marcus, I understand your concern. I expect Josie would hope to be proficient at getting around here so she can adapt more quickly when she returns home, where she will not have four gallant men to escort her everywhere. Josie, you taking the stairs terrifies me as well, but this is not the place to have this discussion."

"Yes, Aunt." Marcus sounded contrite as he sat near her and a footman clattered a plate in front of him. "I don't want Miss Storm hurt."

"I appreciate your concern, Lord Remington. I will strive to be very careful as I move around the house."

"Fair enough," Lady Dorothea said. "Now, can we eat our breakfast in peace?"

After breakfast, Marcus excused himself to meet with his steward regarding road repairs.

Was he was still angry and trying to avoid her? Josie decided that she would become acquainted with the layout of the house. She wandered around 'seeing' the rooms with her hands as much as possible.

Lady Grey had returned to her room to tend to some correspondence.

Josie suspected someone was following her around and was grateful she wasn't totally alone as she explored. She wandered from room to room, and since the other men had gone fishing, she encountered no one. She entered a new room. The door had been partially open. She gently opened it further and made her way in. She stopped. This room had a different scent. Books. There had to be books. Sandalwood. Marcus. She smiled.

"Josie?" She jerked in surprise as Marcus strode toward her, his footsteps muffled on the carpet. He reached her and gently clasped her hand in his. "I'm sorry for my behavior at breakfast. My aunt was right to take me to task for my Turkish treatment of you."

"I was vexed that you had made such a big deal about this." Josie bit her lower lip.

"I take my responsibilities seriously. You are

under my roof and protection. I would keep you safe."

"Would you expect your wife to give you instant obedience as well?" Josie bristled.

"I would hope I would trust and respect my wife enough that I would express my concerns and be heard and followed. I would never demand obedience. I've never needed to, even with my servants."

"I'm sorry as well. I'm on edge after our conversation last night."

"How so?"

"I long to see my father and home but am not ready to leave Rose Hill." Josie reached out to touch his hand and experienced a bolt of lightning shoot up her arm. She grew lightheaded. Marcus's hand engulfed hers, and she was—safe. His thumb caressed her wrist, and she knew of a sudden why women wore gloves. The tingle was pleasurable. Some unknown part of her urged her to reach out and kiss him. But she could never be that forward. How fast would he think her? But if she were only to ever have one kiss from a man in her lifetime, she would want it to be his.

Marcus stepped back, and heat flooded her face. Could he read her thoughts? He cleared his throat. He still held her hand. "As much as I would hate to see you go, I hope your father comes soon. Even with my estimable aunt providing chaperonage, people might still gossip, and I would hate to have harmed your reputation in any way."

"Like being found alone in your study with me?" Josie was being sassy as she said that. *Kiss me!*

Marcus dropped her hand and took another step back. "I have no designs on your virtue."

"Maybe I have designs on yours." *Oh, my, did I really say that aloud?* She heard him walk toward the door. "I was only teasing you. I didn't think your virtue would be easily stolen." She walked toward the door herself, placed her hand on his arm, smiled at him, and gave the muscle a squeeze before letting it go.

"Saucy wench." Marcus had said the words so softly she wondered if she had heard him correctly. But his firm hand on her back propelled her out of the room, and before she realized what had happened, he had not only shut the door behind him but had locked it as well. Josie hugged herself and smiled. Maybe she affected him as much as he did her.

~*~

London

Sir Bastian walked up to the home where Josie was to have stayed. He knocked and waited. He knocked again. The slow shuffle of feet preceded the door opening and an elderly butler looking down his thin nose at him.

"I've come to see Miss Josephine Storm. I am her fiancé."

"There is no Miss Storm here." The elderly man intoned with clipped words.

"Is this not the Widmore residence? My understanding was that she was to be with them in London."

"I've not been privy to prior plans. There is no Miss Storm here."

The door closed in his face, and Bastian growled. Josie would pay for making him wait. There was no reason he should wait until the season...and what the Black Diamond didn't know wouldn't hurt him.

14

It was a merry bunch at dinner that evening.

Josie struggled inside with her growing attraction to Marcus. There was something about him that thrilled her when he was near. She had never experienced that with any other man of her acquaintance, not even his friends. They treated her well but were more like brothers. But Marcus. She would remember her fingers on his lips when he had allowed her to "see" him that way. The image she had in her mind was of someone quite handsome. Between how Molly had described him and her own sense of touch, she figured this man was too gorgeous to be true. If she regained her sight, would she be disappointed?

Josie blinked as bright lights sparked in her mind. Another headache? They had been coming more frequently and with greater intensity over the last few days. She was tired of being an invalid, though, and had not told anyone, even Dr. Miller, of her new complaint. She did not want him to restrict her to bed again. She prayed they would go away soon or that she would learn to live with them without becoming one of those cantankerous old women always seeking attention for every ache and twinge. She took a sip of water. She had not been able to eat much and hoped no one would notice.

Time was running out for her to be at Rose Hill,

and in spite of the pain of her injuries and her blindness, she was grateful that God had dropped her on this doorstep so she would meet this man. She grinned to herself because Marcus had doubted God could do it.

"What's so funny, Miss Storm?" His voice spoke from her left.

"Hmmmm?" She had been lost in her own dream and had dropped out of the conversation around her. "Oh, nothing really, just a silly thought that came through my head, which I found entertaining. But not"—she shook her head—"something I wish to share here."

Marcus leaned in so close his breath tickled her ear. "Later?" he asked.

"Perhaps." She tilted her head his direction and blinked. She chastised herself. When had she become a flirt? She wanted to savor every moment, but her desires were not all that a young woman was supposed to have. Were they? She did not know, and her mother had been gone for the past two years. She doubted she would go to Lady Grey with her longings and questions. She was Marcus's aunt, after all. Then who? *Lord, can you send me some help?*

After dinner, the women retired alone to the drawing room, having encouraged the men to enjoy their glass of port.

Marcus's absence from her side left a deep ache. What was she becoming when desire blossomed within her?

Lady Grey sat next to Josie on the couch. "I spoke with Dr. Miller today after he came to check on you. He is pleased with your progress. When he first had come to take care of you, he had little hope of you walking again. How are you? I hope you have not been overdoing it, especially with those stairs?"

"I am well, Lady Grey. As I told the doctor, I have some mild muscle spasms but not the pain I originally encountered. I am able to sleep without discomfort. It is good to be free of the sickroom."

"Have you and Marcus mended things since this morning? You seemed to be getting along better tonight."

Josie nodded. "Yes, we have spoken." Heat rose to her cheeks at the memory of her desire to kiss him. Maybe her blindness was a gift. If she really saw Marcus, would she be more prone to act on her attraction? "I'm grateful that Lord Remington asked you to come to Rose Hill to bear me company."

"Did I hear my name?" Marcus asked as the gentlemen entered the room.

"We were speaking of how wise you were to bring me here," Lady Dorothea said, a tint of laughter in her voice.

Marcus soon stood before them. "I can think of no one else I would rather have, Aunt Doro." He pulled up a chair nearby and sat.

Michael interrupted. "I have an idea for tonight's entertainment."

All talking stopped.

"Since Miss Storm has been gracious enough to share her musical gifts with us, I think we owe her a return favor."

Marcus gave a short laugh. "Really? Do you have any talents?"

Lord Harrow sounded affronted. "I resent that. You, dear Remy, will start with your own exhibition of your piano talents while Tidley, Westcombe, and I prepare for our part of the evening's entertainment."

Josie smiled and turned toward Marcus. "I would love to listen to you play."

Lady Dorothea defended him. "He is a competent player and would fare better with practice. His mother had a gift for music and played often for company. Marcus is not quite so prone to exhibit his skill."

Marcus rose and headed over to the instrument. "I hope my talent is not too inferior to yours. My aunt is correct. I am out of practice. Miss Storm, what kind of music are you in the mood for this evening—a ballad, concerto, or do you want me to select something?"

"Play whatever you wish, my lord." Josie leaned forward in anticipation.

Murmuring came from the far side of the room, but Marcus began to play and she soon found herself hearing only the music flowing from his fingers. She sighed deep inside as he played a romantic ballad that made her wish for things she would never have. A passionate concerto followed and filled her spirit as she closed her eyes and swayed to the music.

Marcus played a silly folk song that he also sang with his rich deep baritone.

Josie and Lady Grey were giddy and applauding by the time it ended.

Sir Michael came forward. "We will now give our expression of talent."

The three men positioned themselves not too far in front of her.

Marcus sat nearby.

Phillip grumbled, "I am participating under duress."

The three men proceeded to recite, in a comical way, a story. The various men took turns giving sound effects to the tale, and soon tears trickled down her cheek from repressed mirth, as Dorothea and Marcus chuckled.

"The court jesters. Excellent. Does Prinny know of your talent? You could be regulars at the Brighton Pavilion." Marcus crowed.

"Mention this to him and I will meet you in the ring, Remy." Phillip sounded truly aghast at his friend's suggestion.

The rest of the evening filled with lighthearted conversation over the tea tray, and too soon, Josie yawned.

Lady Grey escorted her up the stairs to her room. Once inside, she gave Josie a hug. "I am most glad that my nephew had the wisdom to invite me to be here. You are good for him."

Josie drew back. "Am I? How could that be? A man like him would never take a woman in my condition to be his wife."

"You are referring to a woman with beauty, talent, grace, and enough bottom to keep him on his toes."

Josie shook her head and frowned. "Thank you. I was referring to my blindness and my lack of a substantial dowry or family connections. I am aware of how marriages in the *ton* are partnerships designed to fill coffers and enhance alliances. I would never expect to aspire as high as a Viscount."

Lady Dorothea held both of Josie's hands in hers. "You have met my nephew and spent enough time in his presence to realize those are not the things that weigh heavily with him."

Josie pulled her hands away. "Maybe not, but my blindness definitely should." Josie took a few steps until she was able to grip the back of a chair. She turned toward Lady Dorothea. "Lord Remington is a good man, but he has responsibilities and needs a wife who can assist him with those here at Rose Hill, and in London. A blind wife would only hold him back from all that God has given him to do."

"Marcus has obligations, true. He also has a duty to his family, but I would never desire for him to choose a bride merely for convenience. Your lack of sight may be blinding you to other truths at play here."

"Maybe so. But my fanciful heart could not bear to be broken if my hopes soar higher than they ought."

"So you do care for him?"

Josie nodded. "More than is good for me."

Lady Dorothea sounded confused. "Why is that?"

Josie inhaled deeply, held her breath, and exhaled slowly. "Your nephew tempts me."

"Tempts you?" Dorothea sounded pleased at this.

Josie nodded. "I'm too attracted to him. T'would be better if my father came quickly before I act totally out of character and throw myself at him."

Dorothea laughed and came close and placed a hand gently on Josie's shoulder. "I'm glad he tempts you without you ever having seen him. He has had women sighing over him since he was a lad at university. I have never seen his eyes light up as they do when he looks at you, Josie. I suspect you may be more temptation to my virtuous nephew than you realize."

Josie shook her head. "'Tis hopeless. Nothing could come of our attraction."

"Do not be too sure about that, my dear."

Josie turned to find herself embraced by this older woman. When she pulled back, she swiped a stray tear. "I cannot dare hope."

"Yes, you can. And pray, as well. It was no accident that God brought you to Rose Hill, Miss Storm." With that, Dorothea stepped back and called for Molly to tend to her mistress. "Pleasant dreams."

~*~

"I am concerned that we have still not heard from Mr. Storm. If Josie remains here too long, her reputation might suffer." Marcus relaxed in his chair and sipped from a glass of brandy.

"Your aunt is here. There is nothing improper about that. Miss Storm's reputation is safe."

Lord Westcombe leaned his back against the side of the mantel and watched his friend.

"If it would help, I could ride to Stone to talk to Mr. Storm." Sir Michael Tidley sat, leaned back in a chair with his legs stretched out and his boots crossed at the ankle. "Besides, as much as I enjoy your hospitality, I am itching for adventure. I would gladly take on that errand for you."

"If you wouldn't mind the company, I'll join you," Phillip said as he pushed away from the fireplace area and came to stand near Michael.

"I had not considered sending someone to her home. Perhaps that would answer. What do you think, Theo?"

"It's a brilliant idea. I will stay here and bear you and the ladies company."

"When will you depart?" Lord Remington asked the other two men.

"Tomorrow morning. If we have decent weather, we could easily make the trip in a day, overnight at an inn, and approach Mr. Storm the next morning."

Phillip smiled.

"Excellent." Marcus grinned.

The men finished their drinks and headed off to bed.

Marcus sighed in relief. He did not want Miss Storm gone, but he feared what he might do if she stayed much longer. He had never had a woman who presented such a temptation to him before. Flirtation and provocative clothing amongst the women of the *beau monde* had never created a desire in him for any woman he had met. Yet under his own roof, a young woman of passion, beauty, and spirit was leading him to thoughts he really should not be having for anyone other than his wife. Was Miss Storm the one God had designated to fill that role? How could he really know?

~*~

Josie awoke to a loud pounding in her head and rolled over with a groan. She took some deep breaths and slowly opened her eyes. Bright lights stabbed behind her eyes and made her close them again. They wouldn't cease. She pushed up, and when the room no longer spun, she sat up, and rang for Molly.

She rose, stumbled across the room, and finally grabbed the back of a chair to steady herself. If only she were able to move around to sit. The pain seemed to increase with every breath, and the floor rolled like the deck of a ship in a stormy sea. She took a few steps before she floated into darkness.

~*~

Hoofbeats heralded the men's departure.

Marcus exited his bedchamber and headed for the stairs. Molly's scream brought him up short. He turned and ran to the East wing. He entered Josie's sitting room to find it empty and dashed to the bedroom door.

Molly knelt by the crumpled body of Miss Storm, who rested on the floor with her head against the base of the fireplace. The crimson pool of blood looked bright against the white and gray of the marbled stone.

Fenton and Mrs. Hughes rushed into the room as Molly continued to wail.

"Quiet!" Marcus bellowed. "Fenton, send someone to get Dr. Miller."

The butler left.

Molly continued to hiccup and whimper over her mistress.

"What happened?" Marcus knelt down on the other side of Josie and placed a hand by her neck. Her pulse was steady.

"She pulled the bell, and when I arrived she was...here." Molly looked at Marcus with fear in her eyes.

"Molly, you did nothing wrong." Marcus checked for other injuries. Josie still wore her night rail, and her bare feet were exposed, but he found nothing that seemed injured other than her head. Marcus stripped off his cravat, gently lifted her head, and wrapped it around to help staunch the flow of blood.

The linen was soon saturated, and Mrs. Hughes left to get more bandages.

Marcus carefully lifted Josie up off the floor, carried her back to the bed to deposit her on the mattress. Molly arranged the pillows as he reclined his burden. Marcus stepped back and looked away as the abigail covered up her mistress.

"Why art thou cast down, O my soul? and why art thou disquieted within me? Hope thou in God: for I shall yet praise him, who is the health of my countenance and my God." The words sprang to his lips as a whisper before he was even aware of them. Marcus sank to his knees beside the bed, grasped Josie's limp hand, and prayed like never before as fear gripped his heart.

When Dr. Miller arrived, he shooed Marcus from the room.

Lady Dorothea came to sit with Josie.

Lord Harrow met Marcus, grabbed his arm, and led him downstairs to the breakfast parlour. "This may be a long day, my friend, but you will do Miss Storm no favors if you make yourself ill."

"I doubt skipping a meal will put me on my sickbed, Theo." Marcus grabbed a cup of coffee and wandered to stare out the window. "Thank you for your concern." Bright sunshine poured through the window with a warmth that did not reach the ice that choked his heart. He returned to the table, sat, and picked at the plate of food a footman placed in front of him.

Dr. Miller eventually joined them and accepted the offer of breakfast. He sat down and frowned as he glanced at Marcus. "I'm sorry, Remy. I realize how much you have come to care for and admire Miss Storm."

Theodore piped in. "We all do. She is an exceptional young woman."

Marcus nodded and, with little hope in him, regarded Bruce. "What is the prognosis?"

"She struck her head when she fell. Marble is an unforgiving surface. Another head injury this soon after the first one is a concern. The sooner she regains consciousness the better."

"Which tells me nothing new, Bruce." Marcus pursed his lips together.

"I wish I could give you more. We do not know why she fell. Did she trip or faint? Without that information, I have nothing to go on. All we can do is keep watch over her and try to get fluids into her. I am sorry, Marcus. I am a doctor, not God. If you want more, you shall have to ask Him."

"Hmph." Marcus shook his head. "I already have."

"Wait and pray. Right now, that is all this doctor can advise." Bruce finished his coffee and rose from the table. "I shall return later today, but if you have need, do not hesitate to send for me."

Marcus nodded but did not rise. "Thank you, Bruce."

Dr. Miller tipped his head to Theo, who had sat silently through the exchange. Bruce passed Marcus, gave his shoulder a squeeze, and without another word, departed.

Marcus rose and paced the room twice before stopping to look at Lord Harrow. "Would you excuse me? I need to be with her."

Theo nodded. "Do not worry about me, ol' chap. I can take care of my own entertainment."

Marcus frowned and strode from the room. He took the steps two at a time and brought himself to Josie's room.

Molly sat sewing in the corner.

Lady Grey took one glance at him when he came in and stood to allow him the chair next to the bed. As he moved past, his aunt enfolded him in a hug. When she released him, she held him with one hand on each bicep. She said nothing, but her eyes told him of her care and that she understood his need to be there. He blinked back a tear as she released him and left. He sank into the chair by the bedside to keep vigil.

15

Marcus claimed the night shift with Josie. Lady Grey argued in vain against him being in the sickroom, but Marcus prevailed.

"You cannot control her recovery by being there, Marcus." His aunt admonished with a solemn look.

Marcus gave her a hug. "I know, but I can pray."

"You can pray from your own room."

"I need to be here."

"Molly will be asleep on a pallet in the corner, and I know you would never do anything to compromise Miss Storm, but realize her father will arrive in probably two days. Are you ready for that?"

Marcus shook his head. "How am I to tell him about this when I sent a positive report?"

"This was not your fault. We will leave the future in God's hands." Lady Grey gave her nephew a peck on the cheek and took off for her own bed so she would be ready to take over in the morning.

Marcus prayed, read Scripture, and even sang hymns. Josie slept. Her pulse was steady and she breathed, but that was it. Periodically, he sat on the bed and tried to raise her head up to dribble some water down her throat. He gently caressed her hair as he laid her back on the pillow. "Come on, Josie. Wake up. Please?"

Charlie fell asleep in Marcus's lap since Josie did not respond to her kisses or pet her.

Morning came, and after a small breakfast, he collapsed into his bed for a few hours of rest before he attended to estate business.

The next two nights were a repeat of the first.

Marcus functioned on less sleep than usual and occasionally lapsed into slumber next to Josie's bed. The next morning, Marcus went to bed exhausted. Today was the day Mr. Storm might arrive with Michael and Phillip. The heavy weight of despair settled over him until he slept.

When Marcus awoke, he found most of the day had passed. He had wanted to rise earlier, but his aunt must have countermanded his request so he might rest. He finished sticking a pin in his cravat as he heard hoof beats coming down the lane. He glanced out his window and observed two horses ride in followed by a carriage.

Mr. Storm had arrived.

Marcus descended the main staircase into the entryway of his home to witness a portly, older man with a receding hairline remove his hat and hand it to Fenton.

"Lord Remington?" The man came forward. "Herbert Storm. I hear I have you to thank for the rescue and care of my daughter."

Phillip and Michael entered the house.

"Marcus, we brought him," Michael proclaimed.

"Would you join me in my study?" Marcus turned to walk down the corridor. He spied Theo, took him aside, and whispered, "Explain to Michael and Phillip what has happened."

Theo nodded and intercepted their friends.

Shutting the door behind him, Marcus moved past Mr. Storm and motioned for him to have a seat.

"Brandy?" he offered.

"Much obliged. The roads were dusty, even encased in a carriage." Mr. Storm accepted the glass and watched Marcus with an eagle eye. "Is there a problem?"

Marcus nodded and sipped his own glass. "When I sent Westcombe and Tidley to you, the news was promising. After they left, however, Jo—Miss Storm suffered an accident. We do not know how it happened. She was found on the floor with a gash in her head."

"I wish I had paid more attention to your correspondence. I did not recognize your name or realize that it would report tragedy. If only I had…"

"Regrets will not do either of us any good now, Mr. Storm. May I escort you to her room? We have someone sitting with her all day and night in case she awakens. The doctor is concerned that she has not yet opened her eyes."

Mr. Storm's gaze lowered to take in the pattern of the Persian carpet. He took another sip of his brandy and set the glass down on the table. He rose. "I'm indebted to you for all you've done, Lord Remington. I would like to see my daughter now."

Marcus led the somber procession to the East wing. He knocked lightly before entering. As they entered, he pointed to the spot where Josie fell. The marble no longer showed signs of the disaster. Marcus stood aside as Mr. Storm sat by his daughter's bed.

Mr. Storm spoke gently to his daughter, laid a hand on her arm, and bent over her in prayer. When he finished, his shoulders sagged and he turned to approach Marcus. He placed a hand on Marcus's shoulder. "Thank you for all you have done for my daughter."

Together, the men returned to the drawing room, where Marcus introduced Mr. Storm to his aunt and Lord Harrow.

He would have remained, except that Fenton had come to inform him that he had another visitor. Marcus's brows knit together. *Who could it be now?* He left the room and followed the regal butler to the front door, where a distinguished older gentleman with snowy white hair stood waiting. Marcus stepped forward. "Lord Chester, welcome to Rose Hill. I'm Lord Remington." He gave a bow to the esteemed Earl.

"I've come to meet my granddaughter, Miss Storm. I apologize for arriving without notice, but it was urgent that I come as quickly as I could."

"Am I to assume Lady Grey corresponded with you?"

"Correct."

"And your intentions towards Miss Storm are honorable?"

The Earl gave a broad smile. "Is that the way the land lies? Good for her. I come with the intention to mend a breech that should never have occurred, except for an old fool's pride and stubbornness."

Marcus smiled. "Will you join me in my study? I have news to share with you." Turning to his butler, he said, "Fenton, please prepare a room for the Earl."

Marcus entered the study with the Earl, closed the door behind him, and offered a drink. *Déjà vu. Hadn't he just done this?* He explained Josie's original accident, the recent one, and that Mr. Storm had arrived.

"Am I too late, then?" The Earl's face fell, and the light dimmed in his eyes.

"We do not know for certain. You are welcome to

stay here, but I suggest you make peace with Mr. Storm."

"I had intended upon that course of action. Would you send him to me?"

Marcus nodded and left. He brought Mr. Storm to his study and abandoned the two men to sort through the past, present, and move on to a better future. If only Josie were awake to witness this. His heart heavy, he went to join the others in the drawing room. The dinner bell rang.

~*~

The meal was pleasant.

Lady Grey was a consummate hostess and made both of the newcomers welcome and comfortable. Conversation flowed freely, but Marcus could not help but yawn.

"Marcus, maybe you should go to bed early tonight," Michael stated. "You look a little rough around the edges."

"Thanks. As it was, I slept all day and only rose shortly before your arrival."

"You slept all day?" Phillip coughed in shock.

Lady Grey smiled at her nephew. "Marcus has been keeping watch over Miss Storm during the evening hours."

All heads swiveled as one to face Marcus. He shrugged. "Someone needs to do it."

"Couldn't a servant take that role?" Mr. Storm asked.

"Are you worried she might still be in danger, Marcus?" Michael's gaze was intense as he focused on him.

"Perhaps. We don't know why she fell."

"You suspect foul play with this recent accident?" Lord Chester asked.

Marcus shook his head. "No. Well, we do not know. It is unclear if she was the intended victim in the carriage accident. Could she be in more danger? And why?"

"Josie has no enemies," Herbert stated firmly.

"I can well believe that," Marcus defended. "But someone planned the accident which injured her. Why would she fall on a level floor?"

"We do not know for certain if she would be in danger, but Bow Street has recommended caution," Lady Grey stated.

"If you will excuse me." Marcus rose, left the room, and headed upstairs to assume his vigil over Josie. Marcus fought against boredom and worry as the sun set.

As usual, Molly sewed in the corner.

Night after night, Marcus prayed through the hours over Josie. His aunt and guests would spend the evening playing cards and talking. Marcus struggled to manage estate business due to his fatigue.

When he was not able to be by her side, other members of the household visited Josie. They developed a rhythm around the care of Miss Storm.

It had been over a week, and Marcus found his nerves frayed. He looked haggard, or so his aunt informed him.

"You know we can find one of the household staff to do this."

Marcus shook his head. "I can't explain why, but I need to be there."

During his evening watches, Marcus talked to

Josie. He told her about how he felt when his parents died. How the responsibility weighed on him. He spoke of his questions about God and his determination to live a life that would honor Him. He shared his dreams for the future, of a wife and family, and he even confessed he hoped that she would figure into those dreams if only she would awaken. He longed to see her gray eyes. He thought she still looked beautiful, but she took on a frail appearance as the days went by.

Charlie continued to provide solace and snuggled in Marcus's lap.

Occasionally, Marcus would drift to sleep as the long nights took their toll on him. He did not sleep well or long during the day.

Midway through another long night, Marcus put booted legs up on the edge of the bed, crossed one over the other at the ankle. He sank down in the chair to relax. He had not intended to sleep but could fight it no longer.

~*~

Light penetrated.

Josie fluttered her eyelids open, and the brightness hurt. Where was she? The bright morning sun streamed in the windows, illuminating the yellow roses on the wallpaper and almost blinding her. Blind. *Wait. Wasn't I blind? How am I seeing?* She stretched her arms and legs and tried to push herself up but collapsed in weakness. Something must have happened. She gazed to the left, and noticed scuffed boots. Her eyes traveled up the muscular legs to a man slumped in the chair, his head tilted to one side, a small brown dog snuggled on his chest. Both slept.

The man had dark hair, a little long in the back and a lock that fell on the forehead. A handsome face with a day's growth of whiskers looked innocent in repose. Peaceful. This man filled out his jacket nicely, and his cravat was untied, his shirt open at the neck. One hand cradled the dog as if he had been petting it when he had drifted to sleep. Josie smiled. Marcus. This had to be Marcus. But why was he sleeping in a chair by her bed?

She drank in the sight of him. How was this man not married? He was divine. She already knew he had a beautiful heart. She had believed Molly's description, but even touching his face had not led her to this image in her mind.

She could see! She had been blind. Now she saw. She grinned. She was no longer condemned to darkness. She relaxed back into her pillow and gazed at the man sleeping before her. She would never forget this moment. Waking up to this sight was a wonderful gift.

His eyelids fluttered, and soon her gray eyes met his brown.

Marcus sat up. His boots came off the bed and landed on the floor with a thud.

Charlie was displaced and whined about it. The dog jumped onto the bed and curled up to resume her nap.

"Josie?"

"Marcus, what are you doing in here? It is improper."

Molly snored away in the corner.

"You are awake." His eyes blinked rapidly as he attempted to wake up.

She nodded. "I'm thirsty."

Marcus jumped up to get a glass, filled it with water, and held it for her to drink, supporting her upper back with his arm. When she had indicated that she'd had her fill, he gently settled her back down and put the glass on the table. He sat. "We were worried about you."

Josie frowned. "What happened?"

Marcus shook his head. "We found you on the ground by the base of the fireplace with a head wound."

Her eyes narrowed. "How long have I slept?"

"Over a week. I am not sure. I lost track of the days. How are you?" He leaned forward with concern etched in the lines on his forehead and between his eyes.

"Weak. However, my arms and legs all seem functional. And I can see."

"You can—see?" Marcus held up a hand with some fingers raised. "How many?"

"Three."

"What color is my vest?"

"Green and white."

"You *can* see. I have to call for Dr. Miller to come. And your father. I'll go get him. And your grandfather, Lord Chester, will be pleased." Marcus jumped up and grabbed Josie's hand. He flipped it over, kissed her palm, and closed her fingers over it. "Molly! Come tend your mistress. She's awake, and she can see!" He dashed out the door as Molly came to her side.

Josie held her hand close to her heart to treasure the warmth his kiss had ignited inside her.

Chaos erupted.

The doctor came, and she visited with her father

and was introduced to her grandfather.

Lord Westcombe, Lord Harrow, and Sir Tidley made brief appearances, and of course, Lady Grey shepherded her through it all. She saw Marcus no more that day. She grieved the loss of his presence keenly.

16

Marcus was both elated and exhausted. After listening to Dr. Miller's report on Josie, he plodded to his room and collapsed into a deep sleep. He dreamt of Josie—rescuing her, holding her in his arms, her anger at her circumstances, her face as he described a sunset, her music. He also relived the terror of finding her and all that blood. He remembered the first time he was mesmerized by those gray eyes that opened briefly and met his when he'd rescued her.

Was it then that he fell in love with her?

His dreams twisted with images of her walking away from him with her father, entering a carriage, and leaving his life forever. He dreamed that life had turned to black and white without her there to smile at him.

When Marcus opened his eyes, it was to discover he had slept through to the next morning. His aunt had posted a footman to stand guard at his door so no one would disturb him. He grinned and whistled as he walked down the hall. He loved his aunt and was grateful for her care, but he longed to see Josie.

In spite of the early hour, Marcus found Mr. Storm in the breakfast parlour.

Josie's father was pleased that his daughter was recovering.

Dr. Miller had cautioned against her traveling for at least a week, however, to let her gain strength and make sure that her injuries were not serious.

Marcus asked to meet with him in his study after they'd eaten.

"Thank you for your care of my daughter, Lord Remington. I will depart tomorrow to go home but will return in a week to bring her home to Westwood."

"Both you and your daughter are welcome here for as long as you need." Marcus had been seated but stood to pace. "I will waste no more time. I have come to love your daughter, and I would like permission to request her hand in marriage."

Mr. Storm smiled. "I suspected you had a tendre for her, and from what I have seen and heard of you, I have no objection to such a match for my daughter should she wish it. I will give you permission to court my daughter. You have known each other under adverse circumstances, and you have been her hero. Josie has not been amongst the *beau monde* in which you live and move. She has not had the experience of being sought after by various men or living with the challenges of London society. She needs to be comfortable with these things.

"I cannot have her marry without those experiences to weigh her decision as to whether the life you live is one that she could adapt to. She is a country girl. Would she be comfortable being the kind of hostess you would expect? How would she deal with other men paying attention to her? How would you cope with that as well? She cannot know those things until she has had the opportunity to experience them firsthand." He put up a hand to keep Marcus from interrupting. "I do not doubt that you care for her and her for you. I want Josie to have time to learn more about the *ton* before she commits her heart. Lady Grey has volunteered to escort Josie through the next season. You may court her during that time, and if you both still feel the same way at the end of the season, I will be more than happy to grant you permission to wed."

"Do you doubt that my love will be steadfast?"

"No. But my daughter's heart is untried. She needs the opportunity to meet other men, but she also needs to watch you interact with other women and be confident that she can trust your love. This should not be an onerous task for you, given your reputation. I would not have either of you marry with regrets or doubts."

Marcus nodded. "What you say is fair. I will abide by your wishes."

"If a marriage between the two of you is meant to be, your love will be more mature for the wait." With that, Mr. Storm rose, shook Marcus's hand, and went to find a partner for billiards.

~*~

Josie soaked in every visual detail of her suite. She had spent a little time gazing out the window at the beautiful vista below with the rolling hills and green trees in the distance. She itched to explore the estate, or at least the gardens. She sketched as she sat before a fire that chased the spring chill from the room. She longed to go downstairs, but Lady Grey and the doctor had suggested one more day of rest before she ventured out of her rooms. Josie sighed with frustration but was determined that she would be grateful for the gift God had seen fit to give her with her sight and not bemoan her temporary captivity. It would not be for much longer. She itched to explore the rest of Marcus's home.

Molly allowed a visitor to the room.

Josie's heart rate sped up as her mouth grew dry. Words escaped her as she gazed upon the Viscount's handsome features and figure. Heat rushed to her cheeks as she absorbed his image. She wanted it branded into her memory for the future.

He strode across the room, and his brown eyes twinkled as he lifted her hand to place a light kiss on the back.

A strange tingle traveled up her arm at his touch. Emptiness enveloped her heart when he moved away. How could she be comfortable and yet nervous now that she could see him?

"Good morning, Josie. How do you fare?" He was tall and strong. And he sat down with elegance and grace.

Her heart skipped a beat. "I am well. I can see. My day is brighter for your visit." She frowned. "I missed you yesterday."

"I am sorry I disappointed you." He motioned to her sketchbook and pencils. "You've been drawing?"

She nodded. "I'm attempting to. Later, I hope to do some watercolors. But for now, I'm trying to capture some images on paper."

"I would love to see them sometime." His lips twitched, and a dimple appeared on his cheek.

Fascinating. She forced herself to look away. She did not want to be caught staring. Hadn't she done enough of that while he'd slept yesterday morning? A shiver of delight coursed through her body at the memory—or was it because of the vibrant man in front of her? "I've been informed that I have a week left of recovery at Rose Hill before I return home. It seems that my father and your aunt have plotted for a season in London in the fall."

"I also heard that." He grinned. "I hope I will get a chance to dance with you there."

Her heart lightened. "Does that mean you will be calling on us when we are in London?"

"As you will be staying with my aunt, I expect you may find me darkening your doorway on occasion. In the meantime, I look forward to showing you around Rose Hill for what is left of your stay here."

Josie blinked. A beautiful home, a handsome man, and a bright future. Those many nights of despair already seemed a distant memory. "I would enjoy that."

"There might be some competition for your favors. You have charmed my friends."

"They are admirable gentlemen. I am grateful for their friendship."

Lady Grey entered the room and informed Marcus that his visit was at an end. "If Josie is up to it, you may visit her again later."

Marcus rose, lifted Josie's hand, and kissed it as he raised one eyebrow.

She got lost in the warm chocolate of his eyes.

He turned and approached his aunt, picked her up in a bear hug, twirled her around, and gave her a buss on the cheek.

Lady Dorothea laughed. "You rascal! What was that for?" She sat near Josie and sounded out of breath.

"For being you." With a wink to Josie, he left the room.

~*~

The next morning, Josie was able to leave her room and have breakfast with her father before he departed. She was sad to watch him go but grateful for another week at Rose Hill before she resumed her duties managing her father's home. After she broke her fast, she was able to have a *tete-a-tete* with her grandfather.

Lord Chester pace in the drawing room.

The room was exquisite, decorated in creams and golds with accents of deep green and burgundy. It was lit up by tall windows with the draperies pulled back. Pastoral scenes done by master painters hung on the walls.

"Miss Storm." The Earl of Chester cleared his throat.

"Josie, or Josephine, if you desire." She wanted him to be at ease.

"Josie." He stopped and looked at her, sorrow etched in the lines of his face. "Did you know you were named for your grandmother?"

"I had not known. Mama grew sad whenever she spoke of her home and family. We tried not to remind her by asking questions."

"I was a fool. Blind to anything but money and position. I hope you would understand. I loved my daughters and had the highest expectations that they would marry well amongst the *ton*. Your mother had my strong will and flouted me at every opportunity."

"My mother?" Josie gasped. "I would never have guessed." Josie thought for a moment. "I recant. She was a stickler about our behavior, and we did not dare go against her rules or we'd suffer the consequences. My father was the more gentle about discipline of the two. She ran a tight ship."

"That would have been her. She met and fell in

love with your father, and I refused his offer of marriage. I knew not his character, and I refused to learn. All I knew was that he was not good enough for my Martha. She was inconsolable and eloped. She knew that I would write her out of the will and deny her the dowry I had been prepared to bestow. She said she would marry for love and called her dowry a 'bribe.'"

"Did you marry for love, Grandfather?"

"No, but love found me eventually, and my wife became my dearest companion and friend. I have been lost without her. She never quite forgave me for what I did to your mother." He pulled out a handkerchief and blew his nose. "When I got Lady Grey's letter, I had already lamented the errors of previous years. Her letter compelled me to come and meet you. I hoped we might mend the past. I have discovered your father is an estimable man.

"I learned the hard way over the years that neither a title nor wealth equates with true value and influence. As you may already know, my other daughter, who married as I desired, has not been the happier for it." He came to sit across from her, his posture rigid. "I've made things right with your father as much as I can. Will you forgive me for the hurt I have caused you and your family?"

"Yes. Of course. My mother would have wished it."

"I'm sorry to have learned of her passing. I depart tomorrow for Westwood to meet the rest of your family. I wanted a few moments today to get to know you better."

"I would like that very much." Josie smiled at her grandfather. She was amazed at what God had done because of a random carriage accident.

"I had several conversations with your father. I have agreed to cover the expenses my daughter, your aunt, had charged to his account. I also will finance your season in the fall. You can go and enjoy all the delights without worrying about having to count guineas. I have also rewritten my will. I have more money than I could spend in three lifetimes. I know it will never make up for all the years and the pain I've caused. I stopped in London before coming to Rose Hill. You will now have the dowry that I had intended to give your mother. However, you will not want that bandied about the *ton* or you will be the object of fortune-hunters."

"I don't know if I will be particularly interested in most of the men there." Josie was reluctant to share more. How could she tell him about her affection for Marcus?

"Lord Remington is a worthy man, Josie. Enjoy your season. Meet other men before you decide. You have that luxury now."

He rose, and taking both her hands in his, he held them between them. "You are much like your mother, Josie. You look a lot like your grandmother as well. I have no doubt you will create quite a stir in town. It will be a joy to watch."

"You will be there?"

"For a few weeks. I was too busy with my own career when my daughters came out. I missed those last months of Martha's life with us. Had I been around more, maybe I would have understood Herbert's worth. Thank you for giving an old fool another chance."

Josie smiled at him as he lifted her hands and

kissed them both before leaving her alone. She sat and stared at nothing. Ironic that now she could see and yet wanted to tune it all out to take in what she had learned. She was an heiress, and her grandfather, an earl, would claim her in London, elevating her status. She hoped she would not disappoint him. She rose to find Lady Grey. There were many things she needed to understand. In spite of it being her destination several weeks back, she now realized how ill-prepared she was for mingling with the upper ten-thousand.

~*~

The next morning was a mass exodus.

Lord Chester departed for Stone to visit with the Storm family at Westwood.

Michael claimed he had business to tend to in London and had been gone longer than he intended.

Phillip and Theodore left for Phillip's new estate.

All the men made it clear that they planned to meet Josie again in London when she made her debut.

An emptiness marked Rose Hill and taunted Marcus. For a moment, standing at the front door to wave everyone off, he again experienced the loneliness that had brought him home to pray about his search for a wife this season. Someone who would bring color and life to the estate. And children. As he had traveled west, he had no image to accompany that dream. Now he did. He envisioned Josie as the mistress of Rose Hill.

A dispirited Lady Grey was still in residence. The bounce had gone out of her step, and her smile appeared forced.

Marcus caught her out in the garden and ambled alongside her.

"Mr. Brown has done a marvelous job in maintaining the garden as it was when your mother lived." Dorothea spun a daisy in her fingers.

"I remember him working with Mother designing, planting, and pruning these roses and the other flowers. Mr. Brown has refused to change anything out of honor to her." Marcus broke off a pink rose and handed it to his aunt.

She took the rose and inhaled its scent.

Together they walked in silence until they came to the gazebo, where they sat down. Birds chirped and flitted in the bushes and trees. The garden thrummed with activity of busy bees doing their work. Dragonflies, with vibrant colors shining on their wings, swooped by. A small lake nearby reflected the shadows of trees, and little circles on the surface of the water gave evidence to fish in residence.

"You seem melancholy, Aunt Dorothea," said Marcus.

"It has been an eventful few weeks." She brought the rose to her face again and sighed. "I came here to help you, and I'm glad that I did. I am tired and miss some of our guests."

"In a few months, you will have Miss Storm with you in London for the season. Are you looking forward to that?"

Lady Grey's lips turned up at one end. "I am. I expect her to take the *ton* by storm. You may find you have to fight for her attention when she arrives in town."

A heaviness settled over him. "I am aware. I requested permission to pay my addresses but was told to wait." He glanced at his aunt. "What if she finds some other young buck who sweeps her off her feet?"

"Have a little more faith in her, Marcus. If your affections for each other are true, they will survive a season. It might be refreshing for you two to interact in a different circumstance than the ones you've experienced here."

Marcus clenched his teeth. "I understand. I have waited a long time to meet a woman I admire. I hate that I am forced to wait longer with no guarantee."

"Life doesn't come with guarantees. You, of all people, understand that. It will be worth it, dear boy." Lady Dorothea winked at him and laughed. "You are much like your father was. When he gave his heart, he gave it completely. I doubt you have anything to fear, but do not let jealousy become your friend. It will not serve you well."

After more conversation about the garden and some of the challenges Marcus experienced on the estate, they rose to go back to the house. After they parted, Marcus realized how masterfully his aunt had moved the conversation away from herself. He wondered why.

He had not minded carrying Josie downstairs since she was still weak. Dinner that evening was intimate with only Miss Storm and Lady Grey as his guests. Marcus found himself trying to encourage Josie to eat more to regain her strength from her illness.

After dinner, Marcus relished sitting next to Josie on the piano bench as they tried to work out a duet of a piano sonata that had been one of his mother's favorites. There was laughter as they each made mistakes, but soon they found their rhythm and were playing the piece competently.

After tea, Marcus escorted both the women upstairs to their prospective rooms.

Josie insisted on walking this time.

~*~

Marcus struggled to fall asleep. Josie occupied his thoughts. His fear about a season. He imagined her dancing in the arms of other men, and rage burned within him. He was ashamed at his lack of trust in her and at his strong emotions. He was the one who was always in control of such things. For some reason, this young woman had unleashed intense feelings within him that left him frustrated, confused, and humbled. He had never physically been so attracted to a woman before. Not that there weren't pretty enough ones around. But he had never met a woman who had the physical and spiritual beauty he observed in Josie. If he saw it, certainly other men would. Would they be more worthy of her than he was? Watching her dance and enchant the *beau monde* this fall would be a difficult test.

Finally, after praying and seeking God with his fears, he fell asleep.

~*~

Widmore Estate
Lord Widmore,
I regret to inform you that the deadly snake we placed in the carriage was ousted and trampled before it could strike. A small fire on the property was quickly put out as well. A carriage hired to run down a pedestrian likewise failed.

It has also come to my attention through reliable sources that Lord Chester has rewritten his will, and Miss

Storm will now benefit, as will her siblings. He has cut off any further communication with us regarding the assistance you requested with your debts.

Please let me know how I may be of further service to you. Mr. Caper

Lord Widmore crumpled the letter up and was about to throw it in the fire. Wait. Chester had bequeathed money to the chit injured in that accident? How dare she take what should be his. Hmmmm…maybe there was a potential there for recouping his losses. He dropped the crumpled letter in the flames and watched them lick and dissolve the paper to ash. He nodded his head.

Miss Storm would suffer an equally painful fate for stealing money he desired to claim for himself.

17

Early the next morning, Josie spent hours by her window, alone, praying, and drawing in her sketchpad. She worked hard to preserve images of Marcus. Love and passion compelled her art. A knock at the door interrupted her.

"Miss Storm, Lord Remington wishes to escort you to breakfast."

"Thank you, Molly. Tell him I shall be right there." Josie folded up her sketchbook and set it aside with her charcoal pencils. She washed and dried her hands and joined Marcus at the door. "Good morning, my lord." One corner of her mouth twitched up.

He looked much better in reality than in her imagination.

They enjoyed a quiet breakfast together.

Josie didn't know quite what to say to the handsome man beside her now that she could *see* him. Why should looking in his eyes leave her nonplussed?

Marcus broke into her thoughts. "I was wondering if you were up to a stroll in the gardens this morning."

"That would be delightful."

Molly fetched a bonnet and shawl for Josie, and soon they were stepping out the back door on to the garden path.

Josie expressed her appreciation of the flowers and their vibrant colors in the late spring sunshine combined with the smells of roses and earth.

Marcus walked alongside her saying nothing. He grinned at her, and she noticed that the lines on his forehead were gone. Being here relaxed him. Had he also been uncertain when they were together?

They reached the gazebo.

Josie entered and did a pirouette in the center. Marcus sat down, and she joined him. How close was too close? They were alone out here, and she shivered in excitement at the thought. But what did she really want? *A kiss*. She wanted a kiss. But not on the back of her hand. This man was the charming prince of many girls' dreams, and he was with *her*. Marcus always acted with propriety. Would he ever unbend enough to do something like that?

They were close enough to touch. Shadow and light played on his dark hair and it curled unbound over his cravat at the back of his neck. His coat fit his form well. It showed off his broad shoulders and trim midsection. His inexpressibles...well...

She gulped and blushed as she realized where her gaze had gone. He wore those scuffed boots. She frowned. "Can I ask you something, Marcus?"

"Hmmm?"

"You dress well, yet your boots are scuffed. Do not men of your station have valets to care for things like that?"

Marcus glanced down at his boots as he stretched his long, muscular legs in front of him and crossed them at the ankles. His dimple played peek-a-boo. "I kept my valet in London as my sojourn here was intended to be of a short duration. I have other boots. However, these are my most comfortable and do not require the assistance of a valet to remove them. Those scratches remind me of my one opportunity to play the knight errant to a beautiful woman." He glanced at her with a twinkle in his eye.

"You scratched your boots when you rescued me?" She placed her hand on his arm as she leaned forward to gaze into his face.

Marcus nodded. He had a silly grin on his face as he looked back at her. "That makes them special."

Josie beamed.

Marcus looked away again, but his face became troubled.

"You are preoccupied in your thoughts. I should be put out that I cannot capture your full attention." Uneasiness assailed her. Josie removed her hand from his arm. She leaned toward him and inhaled his distinctive scent.

Marcus leaned back against the bench. "Your accident wasn't really an accident."

Josie startled. "That doesn't make sense."

"The axles did not 'break' on their own. They had been damaged."

Josie gasped. "Someone planned for the carriage to crash." She rose and walked the short length of the gazebo. "But why would anyone want to hurt me?" She rubbed her arms as goose bumps appeared.

Marcus stood, came up behind her, and wrapped his arms around her. He whispered in her ear. "We do not know that you were the intended victim."

Josie felt safe in Marcus's arms. She turned within the circle he had created and placed her hands on his chest. Her eyes squinted. "Was someone trying to hurt my aunt or cousin?"

Marcus planted a kiss on the top of her head. "We don't know. Bow Street is investigating."

Josie gave a sigh and leaned her forehead against

his chest as her arms came down to his sides. "That's good."

"You are taking this well."

She looked up into his face. "As tragic as it was, it brought you into my life. I am grateful for that."

"Maybe it was the other way around—God, after all, brought you to my doorstep." He grinned, but his smile slowly faded as he gazed into her eyes.

"You have been a detour on my way to London. I'm grateful God brought me to Rose Hill." Josie wondered if he would kiss her now. Instead, Marcus relaxed his arms from around her and stepped back. She hugged herself and rubbed her arms at a sudden chill left in the absence of his warmth.

Marcus wandered to the opposite side of the gazebo with his back to her. "I am sad that our meeting involved much suffering on your part."

Josie's heart drooped. "I cannot say that I've enjoyed that part of this journey. I'm thankful to be past that." She sat down and wrapped her shawl about her. She looked away from Marcus to the garden surrounding them.

"Josie?"

"Yes?" She stole glances at him.

He continued to look out the opposite side of the gazebo. Marcus turned to face her before he spoke again. "What if you had not been healed? What if you had been unable to walk, or see, for the rest of your life? Would you still praise God? Would you still call Him good?"

Josie looked to Marcus and saw tears in his eyes. "I think so. I hope so."

Marcus paced. "All those nights I prayed for you. I wrestled with those 'what ifs.' I begged God for your healing. I am thankful He answered those prayers. But I wonder..."

"Why does that matter, Marcus? I am able to stand and walk. I *can* see you."

"What if you hadn't been healed?" Marcus stopped and again looked away from her.

"Then we might be having a different conversation." Josie frowned. "I don't want to think about that. I spent enough time looking at a dark future. I want to enjoy what I have now." She walked over to him. "You can't beat yourself up over 'what ifs.' You were faithful in your care of me. You prayed. You kept watch." She clasped his left hand with her right and looked up into his eyes. "You even described a sunset to me."

Marcus held her gaze for the longest time. "Josie."

She swallowed and broke eye contact. "You are a good man, Marcus."

"Not as good as I would like. I have failed where it mattered most." He brought his right hand, closed in a fist, and placed it over his heart.

"I refuse to believe that."

"I am not a saint."

"None of us are."

Marcus looked down at Josie.

Her heart raced at the intensity of his gaze. For the longest time, he was silent.

As if he snapped out of some kind of dream, he looked away. "I should get you back to the house." He offered her his arm, she placed her hand on it, and together they walked through the garden back to the house.

There wouldn't be a kiss. She dropped her head in disappointment. She knew that his reticence was a testimony of the virtue she had heard his friends speak of.

Upon entering the house, Lady Grey hurried to meet them. "Marcus. Josie. Have either of you seen Charlie? She hasn't come to the kitchen this morning to eat."

They responded at the same time. "No."

Everybody split up to look for the dog, and the staff helped. Lunch came and went without discovering Charlie's whereabouts.

Lady Gray dispatched Josie to the yellow suite to rest.

Josie yawned, reclined on the bed, and closed her eyes.

A noise came from the adjoining wardrobe.

Molly had the afternoon off, so it couldn't be her. Josie padded across the room in her bare feet and walked into the closet. The noises continued to guide her. Soft sounds. Josie was almost afraid to push clothing aside. She had yet to observe any rodents in the house. *There is nothing to be afraid of.* She hoped.

With a deep breath, she pulled back the clothes to peer in. One of her older day dresses lay bunched up on the floor, and at the center of the pile lay Charlie, with three tiny, blind puppies.

Charlie looked up and her tail wagged.

Josie grinned. "You sweet thing. Look at your babies." Josie left to go find Marcus and Lady Grey.

The housekeeper made up a new bed in Marcus's study.

Charlie and her pups were relocated.

After the move, Josie finally got her nap.

~*~

Marcus had a hard time focusing on his company at dinner. After the meal, he sat alone with his port, not knowing how he would share his news with his aunt and Josie. His respite from London was over. He shook his head. Since when did he come to believe he orchestrated the universe? God had certainly blessed his hard work, but that didn't mean that his plans were God's. But Josie...how could he do this to her? To them? He walked into the drawing room, sat down, and rested his head on the back of the chair.

"Marcus, you were quiet through dinner. Is something amiss?" Lady Grey asked.

Josie leaned forward and showed that she was eager to know whatever troubled him.

He frowned. "I received a letter today from the Home Office in London."

Lady Grey gasped and placed a hand over her heart. "Jared. Is he...?"

"He's alive. He was a prisoner of war. He was rescued but was injured, and is in rough condition."

"How serious?" Josie asked.

"I'm not sure of the nature or extent, but the letter seemed to indicate that the injuries are severe. Potentially life-threatening." He paused and sighed. "Jared has asked for me."

"You will depart in the morning." Lady Dorothea stated this as a fact.

Marcus nodded. "I despise leaving you." He didn't name any names but looked at Josie and met her silvery gray eyes.

"He is your brother, Marcus. Of course you must go." She gave him a teary smile.

Marcus took comfort in that. *She will miss me.* "I

shall depart early."

Lady Dorothea rose and came to clasp Marcus's hand. "I am weary. I will see you off in the morning." She winked at him and closed the door behind her as she left.

Some chaperone.

Josie sat across from him. Lost in thought, she played with ribbons from her blue dress.

He took in her dark hair and the loose curls that had a life of their own. He longed to twirl a lock around his finger. Inwardly, he groaned.

Josie rose to her feet. "I should retire as well."

Marcus stood in front of her, and stayed her by gently holding her left arm. "Josie," he whispered.

She looked up at him as he brought his other arm around her waist and pulled her closer. She tilted her head back to gaze at him. A kiss wasn't proper, but he wanted to taste her. Something to savor, remember, and hold on to until summer was over and she was in London.

He fought the temptation. He backed up a step, picked up her left hand, bent down, placed the lightest of kisses on her palm, and closed her fingers over it. It would have to do. He released her hand and dropped his arms. "Good night, Josie."

She gave him a sad smile as he took a step back. "Good night, Marcus. Have a safe journey. You and your brother will be in my prayers." With that, she turned and slipped out the door.

18

Marcus's thoughts jumbled as he rode Cloud toward London. Prayers interspersed with anxiety over his brother and curiosity about what he would find. He loved his brother but wondered at Jared's faith. It had seemed that since joining up with the war effort, his brother's penchant for gambling and womanizing was the stuff of legend. It grieved Marcus to watch his brother walk away from the beliefs and teaching of their parents.

Although Jared had mentioned in his previous letter he had not entirely abandoned it. Their mother would have been heartbroken if she had known how her youngest son lived his life. Maybe that would change as he recovered from these injuries and all he'd endured as a prisoner.

What a spring. Marcus never anticipated spending the season taking care of wounded and injured people.

Both labors of love.

He arrived at his home that evening. He changed out of his dusty clothes and found his valet, Max, eager to serve him now that he had returned. Marcus took the carriage to the hospital.

The building was a shabby affair, poorly lit, and filled with patients in various states of pain and distress. The stench of disease, filth, and death overwhelmed his senses. This makeshift hospital had originally been an old church. Now, blood stained the floors. With too many wounded men crowded into the space, and too little help, many of the men here suffered and died without the comfort of another human being. Too many would never reunite with family. Some were unidentified and, if their recovery was slim, left to die. Amputated limbs often became infected and fatal. The staff, while proficient in their own way, for their own survival had become numb to the suffering around them.

Evening sun coming through the stained glass windows brought a million dust particles to life in the air and cast the macabre scene in twisted colors of yellow, orange, blue, red, and green.

Marcus reached for his handkerchief to cover his nose and mouth in an attempt to fend off the odor as his stomach revolted. He should have passed on dinner before coming. He doubted he would have been hungry after the visions he beheld here. After a lengthy search, he found his brother. He was shocked at how changed Jared looked from when he saw him last, cleanly shaven and handsome in his uniform.

There was little to resemble that dashing officer now, as his brother lay unkempt, battered, gaunt, and motionless on a rough-hewn pallet layered in rags.

"Jared, I'm here." He gently touched his brother's shoulder. He called again with more intensity. He waited. Impending doom overtook his heart until Jared's blue eyes flickered open. look took several moments to register the face of the person bent over him.

When he did, he gave a weak grin. In a barely discernible gasp, Jared rasped, "Take me home." The eyes closed. "Please?"

Marcus failed to cajole him to open his eyes again

or to speak. "I will do what I can to bring you home." He received no response. Fear gripped Marcus's heart. He might lose his younger brother. He rose and began a frantic search for a doctor. He was able to discover the extent of the life-threatening injuries. Soon he and his servants managed to convey him home.

Once Jared was settled in his old room, Marcus's days revolved around seeing to his brother's care. A family physician in London tended the patient, and Marcus hovered even more than he had with Josie. Eventually, Jared's infection subsided and the fever was gone.

Marcus urged him on, and his brother soon ate and slowly regained his strength.

~*~

Josie greeted her father and hugged him. Lady Grey invited him to spend the night before they departed for Rose Hill the next day. Josie teased her father that this time she would have to play chaperone for him and Lady Grey. She was surprised when he blushed at her words.

Once back home, *ennui* was Josie's nemesis. Nothing interested her, and the tasks she normally did seemed pointless. She wondered how Marcus and his brother fared. The weeks ahead loomed long and dismal.

A few short weeks after she returned to Stone, a visitor arrived for Josie.

The housekeeper had placed him in the drawing room.

Josie pulled up short in the doorway when she realized it was Sir Archibald Bastian, a distant neighbor, and persistent and most unwanted suitor. Josie fought down a disquiet within. She hoped her father would come post haste.

Sir Bastian stood in the middle of the room, dressed in black with the exception of his snowy white cravat. A black onyx stickpin was nestled in its pristine folds. The style of his dress, however, did nothing to minimize his portly figure, and his spectacles made his eyes look too large for his round, florid face.

"Sir Bastian." She gave a slight bow and stayed close to the open door. She would not invite him to sit. "My father should arrive soon." *Please, Lord, protect me.*

"It is you I came to visit today, not your father."

An unpleasant shiver traversed the back of her neck. "I cannot imagine why, Sir Bastian."

"Have not we known each other long enough that you could call me Archibald?" He stood now with his hands in his trouser pockets as he rocked back and forth on his heels. He toyed with her.

"I fear doing so would give rise to expectations that are not proper." Josie spoke confidently, although inwardly she cringed as his milky green eyes perused her body from head to slippered toes.

"I would like to rectify that. Several months ago, I approached your father for permission to ask for your hand in marriage." His mouth tried to form a smile, but it looked more like a sneer to her.

"I was aware you had spoken with my father. I am also aware he had insisted you were not to ask for my hand until after I had my season in London. I have not yet had that season, so you will have to wait. I'm not inclined to favor your suit."

"No season? But...? You dare to refuse me?" His cheeks puffed up, and his face grew a deeper crimson shade.

"Due to an accident, I never made it to London. I will depart in a few weeks for the season. Even should I return home unattached, that should not give you hope I would favor your suit any better." Josie folded and clenched her hands in front of her.

"What kind of response is this to a respectable proposal of marriage? I know what I want, and I will get it regardless of what you think. Beware of crossing me, Miss Storm."

Josie stepped back as the older man thundered past her out of the room. She collapsed in a nearby chair and waited for her pulse to return to normal. Sir Bastian's words and presence frightened her. But why? A palpable evil resonated around him. She would tell her father about the threat and leave it in his capable hands. After all, she had a different man in mind for the role of husband.

~*~

"I'm glad you are sitting up now to eat. I got tired of having to feed you myself." Marcus teased as they sat at a table in the sitting room after a simple meal together.

Jared smiled. "It's good to rejoin the land of the living. Hell was not a fun place to visit."

"Care to talk about it?"

"No."

Marcus nodded as his brother's eyes avoided his own. This was not the first time he had tried to find out what his brother had endured while in captivity. With as many scars as his brother had, the ones on his soul would take far longer to heal. Jared thrashed at night when in the throes of night terrors. That alone convinced Marcus that the experiences had been horrific. "How about a game of chess tonight?" Marcus offered.

"I'll pass. I want to be alone. You smother me worse than Mother ever would have. When did you start with that?" Jared's blue eyes sparked at Marcus, and his words came out harsh.

Marcus sat back, nonplussed, and looked at his brother. What kind of gratitude was this for someone whom Marcus had come close to planning a funeral for? Marcus was only a few years older than his brother, but now he felt ancient. When had the weight of responsibility ever seemed so heavy and uncontrollable? He sighed. Jared was alive, and that was what mattered most. "I apologize. I'll back off. You are well enough now to not need me." Marcus rose from his chair with a sigh. "I will see you on the morrow, but only when you send word. Sleep well, Jared."

"Marcus, I didn't mean..."

Viscount Remington gave a wave of dismissal and closed the door to cut off his brother's words. He strode to his study and sorted through the mail that had accumulated. The days grew longer, and he figured he would work until he was exhausted. Melancholia beset him. Josie had returned home, and he would see her again in another month. His brother was on the mend, and if Jared was a bit testy, that was understandable. The soldier was a man of action cooped up in a room, a prisoner of a body that had not fully recovered.

Marcus grabbed his letter opener, selected the first envelope, and ripped it open with a flourish. Fifty more of those and he might begin to feel better.

~*~

The day finally came when Josie undertook her journey to London in the company of her father. It was an unremarkably boring carriage ride, and she was weary by the time they reached Lady Grey's house. They pulled up in front of what looked like a grand estate. The door opened before they reached the top step, and as they crossed the threshold, Josie found herself embraced by Lady Grey.

"Miss Storm, I have been eager for your arrival. How do you fare?" Lady Grey placed her hands on each of Josie's arms and stood back to survey her. "You look wonderful, but I think we need to put a little meat on those bones if you are to keep up with all the activities we are to be engaged in." She turned to Josie's father. "Mr. Storm, what a pleasure to see you again. Will you be staying in town?"

"I'm putting up at my club and will remain for a week to see Josie settled. I will tend to some business while I'm here."

"Will you stay for dinner with us this evening?"

"I regret that I need to decline your gracious invitation, my lady." He smiled warmly at Lady Grey, lifted her hand to place a kiss on the back, and turned to embrace his daughter.

Before Josie knew it, he was gone.

The following days were a whirlwind of shopping. They selected dress designs, fabrics, and all the necessary accessories. Hours-long dress fittings. The amount of money spent on such fripperies dismayed Josie. She gave thanks to God for the benevolence of her grandfather, who made her delayed season possible.

In addition to the myriad of shops were the afternoon teas that Lady Grey took her to, where she made the acquaintance of matrons and other young ladies of the *ton*. These events she found interminably boring, and the gossip impossible to avoid. She refused to engage in gossip and tried to depress the nasty words and innuendo shared, but this often left her uncomfortable.

She soon discovered that if she asked questions about the women she spoke with, they were more inclined to avoid the more lurid details of the lives of those she did not know. She figured she would need to learn how to navigate these dangerous social waters if she were to marry Marcus someday, as she hoped. Being a political hostess would require finesse if she were to deal well with the powerful people in society.

One such social call was with Lady Harriet Astley.

"My dear, Dorothea. How lovely to have you come and visit. Who is this delightful young chit you have with you?"

Josie bristled at the scrutiny as the woman looked her up and down. She determined to stand confidently in the presence of this intimidating matron.

"Lady Harriet, I would love to introduce my charge, Miss Josephine Storm. I always longed for a daughter, and God has seen fit to indulge me with this girl for several weeks, to aid her widowed father. Miss Storm, may I present to you Lady Astley."

Josie curtsied to this *grande dame* of society elite, sat when and where she was bid, and observed her hostess.

Lady Astley was tall and thin and sat in her chair

with her back ramrod straight, which only emphasized her lack of bosom. Her silver hair was swept up and elaborately curled in a much younger style than her years would indicate appropriate. That, added to her pale complexion and light peach colored dress, gave her the look of a wraith.

The woman's drawing room boasted excessive decor in the Egyptian fashion, and gilt was everywhere.

Josie likened it to being a horse put through her paces as her hostess begged her to serve the tea and scrutinized her closely. The perusal was uncomfortable, and questions came rapidly.

"So how is it that you have come to be acquainted with Lady Grey?"

Josie swallowed discreetly—she didn't want the story of her accident and extended stay at Rose Hill to become common knowledge amongst the *beau monde*. "We met through her nephew, Lord Remington."

Lady Astley's bushy gray eyebrows rose at this. "You are acquainted with the Virtuous Viscount? How interesting. How did you come to know him?" The questioner's eyes penetrated as she directed that question to Josie.

Josie had the image of a dog who sniffed for prey as this woman awaited details. "We accidently met in the spring." The less said the better. She thought about the moniker that Lady Astley had used to refer to Marcus. He had a reputation for virtue. She didn't doubt his integrity but found it interesting that his behavior would be considered unusual enough to have earned that designation. Inwardly she smiled She wouldn't want a husband who had a reputation that was anything less than virtuous, would she?

"Quite true." Lady Grey responded. "Harriet, do you remember where you ever found that extraordinary plum hat I observed you wearing the other day in town? I admired the style and would like to discover what other creations the designer might have."

Lady Astley abandoned Josie in favor of talk about hats and other new designers on the town this season, until other guests arrived.

Lord Harrow strode in accompanied by Lord Remington.

Josie concealed her pleasure at seeing Marcus after such a length of time. Forgotten was her disappointment in him at not having come by to visit her before this. He looked devastatingly handsome.

When Marcus took her hand in greeting, his eyes met hers with a twinkle. His skin appeared more bronzed than she had remembered. He had tied his hair back with a black ribbon. A lone curl escaped on his forehead.

Lord Harrow expressed delight at seeing her. "My dear, Miss Storm. You have arrived on the town at last. The season can now officially begin for me now that you are here. Will you be attending the Amberly party this evening?"

Josie nodded and smiled at his congenial countenance.

"Excellent. I pray you will save me a dance."

"I would be delighted to, Lord Harrow," Josie said softly and averted her eyes. She experienced a stab of disappointment that Marcus had not tried to claim a dance.

Lady Audrey Walsh entered with her two daughters, Amber and Angela. The girls were dressed in flounces that showed off their plumper figures in an unflattering way.

Josie found conversation difficult, as the girls only had eyes for Marcus and were determined to catch his attention.

Lady Amber leaned over and whispered to Josie, "Are you acquainted with Lord Remington?" Without waiting for an answer, the young woman nattered on. "Isn't he the most handsome man? He looks delicious." The young woman licked her lips as she gazed at the object of her desire as if he were a pastry she longed to devour.

"I am acquainted with the Viscount," said Josie softly. She was determined not to be jealous of this woman's designs on Marcus.

He had not glanced a second time at the newcomers after the initial greetings were exchanged.

"What is he like?" whispered Angela.

Josie was relieved from the burden of an answer as at that moment, Lady Grey indicated it was time to depart. They said their farewells and walked out to their carriage.

Josie leaned against the squabs and sighed. "Why do we have to go through the torture of these visits? The tea was tepid, the cakes were stale, and the gossip...I wanted to scream."

"I'm glad you did not give into that temptation" — Lady Grey frowned — "although that would have given them something new to talk about. These are a necessary part of a season. To see and be seen, to make all the right connections will help you gain *entre* to the best parties to help you become the toast of the *beau monde*." She gave her charge a conspiratorial wink.

"I wished I might have spoken with Marcus. It is

difficult knowing he is in town but has not come to call. Why is that? Have I offended him?" She blinked back the moisture that obscured her vision.

Lady Grey ordered the driver to take them home. "No more visits today. We both need to rest before tonight's ball. I'm sure your dance card will fill quickly."

Josie sat up and started at Lady Dorothea. "You changed the subject. Why has Marcus not come?"

The older lady sighed and closed her eyes for a moment before opening them again. All traces of the former laughter were gone. "He desires to give you space to meet other men and know your own heart. I believe he chafes at the separation. Perhaps you will see him tonight. I hear Jared is doing much better and may even accompany him. You will like Captain Allendale. In his uniform, he is deemed to be quite handsome, even though he is as fair as Marcus is dark."

Josie dropped her shoulders, releasing the tension she did not realize she had been holding onto. "I will just have to wait, but if this goes on much longer, I may have to consider my options."

"Josie, you have done a wonderful job of protecting your reputation. I'm proud of how you have handled these visits. By tomorrow, I expect you will be besieged with male visitors." The carriage pulled up to the curb, and a footman opened the door. "For now, let us seek our rest. We shall need it." Lady Dorothea allowed the servant to help her down the steps, and Josie followed.

~*~

Derbyshire

The Black Diamond encircled the sniveling Sir Bastian as he sat in the wood chair. "What do you mean you have not yet married her?"

"She did not have a season, because she was injured. She refused me out of hand. Her father won't consent—"

"I do not need a *willing* virgin. You promised me. If you fail to deliver her, soon you will find yourself in more trouble than you can grasp." The Black Diamond placed a foot behind a leg of the chair and shoved Bastian in the chest. The chair toppled backward and splintered apart under the weight of the knight.

Ah, that felt good.

All the air in Bastian's lungs had been forced out, and he gasped for breath as the Black Diamond towered over him with his walking stick strategically placed under his chin. "Do. Not. Disappoint. Me. Again." He raised his eyebrows as he glowered at the fool on the floor. The delay had not been fatal, but it slowed his progress. He thirsted for blood.

Bastian inhaled on a gasp and struggled to stand. He ran out the door, stumbling over his feet and running into the wall in his clumsy haste.

Bumbling idiots. No wonder England would fall. The aristocracy was filled with in-bred, useless fools. Soon he would rule them all with his superior intelligence and power. He had to bide his time, but only for so long.

And heaven help those who stood in his way.

19

Josie twirled in front of the full-length mirror in her room. The rose-colored empire waist gown was flattering to her figure and not cut as low as the seamstress had wanted. White gloves and pink slippers added to the effect. Ribbons and pearls wove through her hair. She stopped and smiled. *I hope Marcus is there tonight.* Her heart raced at the thought of seeing him again and perchance even dancing in his arms. She remembered how sad she had been when she could not walk and she had thought those dreams had been stolen from her. God had graciously allowed her this moment, and she was determined to enjoy it.

She descended the stairs into the ballroom a short time later and found herself separated from Lady Grey, who acquired her own court of admirers.

Lord Harrow was one of the first to make up the group of men that swarmed around Josie.

They all pleaded for a spot on her dance card.

"Josie, you look a picture," Lord Harrow gushed.

"You are all kindness, my lord," said Josie as they took their place for the quadrille.

"I believe I am the envy of every man here," he said as they came together again in the figure of the dance.

"I am not one for Spanish coin, Lord Harrow." Josie laughed as his eyes got big and a hand went to cover his heart.

"'Tis no flattery, Miss Storm. You have emerged as a beautiful swan this evening."

Their hands joined again.

Josie indulged in a spark of mischief as she smiled at her partner. "Does that mean I was an ugly duckling before?"

Theo's eyes narrowed as he studied her face. Once he ascertained she was teasing, he laughed, drawing the attention of the other dancers. "Most definitely not, but may I say instead that I have never seen you look better."

They turned again and moved in the pattern as the music played.

"Why, thank you, my lord." Josie curtsied at the end of the dance, and Lord Harrow bowed before escorting her to Lady Grey, where her next dance partner awaited her.

Throughout most of the evening, Josie danced with nary a pause. She was happy to see Sir Tidley and Lord Westcombe present, and each had signed her dance card. She had not yet seen Lord Remington. Her heart sank when she spied Sir Bastian roughly brush aside a young man to get to her side.

He proclaimed brusquely, "This dance is mine." He dragged her to the floor as she searched the room for any sign of rescue.

Josie's face heated as she stifled the urge to scream. A shiver of fear went up her spine as the cotillion began.

~*~

Lord Remington watched Josie smile and talk with several men, and his heart clenched. She hadn't seen him yet. He had not made his presence known but had hung toward the back of the crowd that surrounded the dance floor. Jealousy boiled over inside him as he witnessed the portly older man's rough possessiveness toward her.

Marcus had seen the flash of fear as she had scanned the ballroom. She had quickly schooled her features to give away nothing. The older man was huffing and puffing through the dance, and his face was florid. Josie appeared to be bearing it with strained grace, a forced smile on her face and her eyes seeking to avoid looking at her partner whenever possible as he muffed the steps of the dance.

Marcus itched to level the man. However, starting a fight in the ballroom would not be the action of a gentleman. He ground his teeth as he waited for them to exit the floor.

Josie recoiled when the older man tried to place her hand on his arm. She pulled it back and held both hands in front of her body, clenched together.

Marcus stepped forward and impeded their progress. "I believe the next dance is mine."

Josie glanced at her dance card and back at him when she realized his name was on it. Her brows furrowed together for a moment before her shoulders relaxed and her eyes spoke her gratitude. "Why, so it is, my lord." She gave the cut direct to Sir Bastian as she placed her hand on Marcus's arm and allowed him to escort her back to the dance floor.

Marcus didn't speak during the first measures of the dance. He drank in the vision before him.

Her cheeks flushed, and she avoided his gaze. When she finally did look at him, hurt and confusion were in her eyes.

He winked and squeezed her hand as they went through the movements of the dance. He couldn't keep back the question that haunted him. "Who was that bore?"

"Sir Bastian. He is attempting to coerce me into marriage."

Instantly, Marcus stood straighter. "How do you know him? I have not seen him around town."

Josie glanced around before answering. "He is a neighbor. His estate is on the banks of the River Severn. He has been most disagreeable over my repeated refusals of his proposal."

Marcus's eyes narrowed. Josie did not have a large dowry. Why would Sir Bastian pursue her?

"Let us forget about him and enjoy these few moments together." Josie pleaded.

He nodded, and as the dance ended, he escorted her to supper. After getting her a plate of delicacies, he sat beside her at the small table he had selected. "Will you join me for an early morning ride on the morrow? I have a lovely mare that I believe would suit you."

Her eyes lit up as she finished chewing her food. She swallowed. "I would be delighted. It has been some time since I have ridden. We mustn't go far or I will regret it."

Marcus grinned. "I'll come for you at eight, and we can talk more then."

She rewarded him with a smile.

As much as he regretted leaving her for the rest of the night, he knew that undue attentions on his part would prohibit her from experiencing all that a season had to offer. He needed to trust that if their love were true, she would still choose him over all the bucks of the *ton* who would pursue her. He had no desire to subject himself to the pursuit of debutantes eager for his title, so he departed after seeing Josie settled into a dance with her next partner.

~*~

Josie tossed and turned throughout the night with her memory of her dance with Marcus. That warred with anxiety over the threat from Sir Bastian. If only she were married. Sir Bastian would leave her alone then, wouldn't he?

She awoke early, ate a light meal in her room, and donned a burgundy colored riding habit with matching hat. She liked what she saw when she looked in the mirror with her brown hair twisted in a becoming fashion, topped with a hat placed at a saucy angle. She was downstairs before Marcus arrived. Marcus's eyes opened wide as he was welcomed into the parlour. Was it because of her appearance or because she was ready? She didn't know and didn't care. He led her outside to a sweet-tempered horse named Windy. Josie patted the nose on the chestnut mare. She offered Windy a lump of sugar tucked into her pocket and earned a soft nudge to the shoulder as the mare asked for more. "Maybe later, Windy. Let's put you through your paces and find out if we suit as well as your master thinks we shall."

Marcus assisted Josie up into the sidesaddle and adjusted her stirrup. Soon they were off for their ride in Hyde Park. Marcus kept Cloud to a gentle pace. The day promised to be beautiful.

A groom followed discreetly behind, far enough to allow for private conversation.

Josie smiled at the pure joy of riding the sweet

goer beneath her. The spritely mare was responsive to the lightest touch. The steady gait of the horse, the sunshine, and the handsome man beside her made her believe the morning could not possibly get better. She admired the way Marcus sat his gray mare. His muscles in those buckskin breeches showed to advantage on a horse. She had a hard time looking away, and her gaze travelled up to collide with brown eyes and a smile that told her he was aware of her wandering eyes. Heat crept up her neck. She recalled those times lying in bed blind, wondering about this man when she would hear the horse's hooves as he would ride off across the estate. She smiled again at how God answered prayers and not only could she see and admire the man beside her, but also ride alongside him.

The park was far larger than she had expected, and she tried to take in every aspect of the beauty around her, from the flowers to the lawns and the trees growing along the banks of the Serpentine River. The early morning dew was on the grass and sparkled in the sunshine like jewels. Flowers opened to the warmth of the day, and the world smelled fresh.

They set their horses to a nice trot and arrived at a large meadow. They allowed the horses to have their heads and enjoyed a brief gallop. As they pulled up under the shade of some trees, Josie coaxed her horse to prance in circles. "Thank you, Marcus! It has been so long since I've done that. If we weren't in the city, you would find me wishing to try this beautiful mare over a few hedges."

Marcus gave a broad grin. "Not quite the time or the place, Miss Storm." He then spoke conspiratorially. "But I would race you to those hedges if it were."

They slowly set off together, side by side. Their horses' hooves matched in perfect rhythm. Marcus spoke up again. "Are you enjoying the season?"

"Last night was my first ball. Most of my partners were charming, and I had supper with a most remarkable man. Other than that, I will defer comment." The sunshine disappeared behind a cloud, and the image of Sir Bastian came to her mind.

"What is it you dislike?"

She sighed. "Visiting all the starchy matrons, hearing gossip, and finding my personal business scrutinized."

Marcus nodded in agreement. "I find gossip abhorrent myself. Have you found it difficult to distract them?"

"If I can ask questions about themselves, they soon forget their own impertinent inquiries and abandon blackening someone else's reputation with innuendo and speculation."

"Not an easy task. No wonder you are exhausted. It takes a lot of fortitude to rise to that challenge amongst the *beau monde*."

Josie was silent.

"Josie?"

"Hmmm?"

"It has been my heart's desire to openly court you. Now that I have danced with you at a formal ball, we can meet, but I must stay in the background. I would not want to do anything to harm your reputation or your opportunity for choices amongst your suitors."

Josie looked at him but forbear to answer. She longed for Marcus and none other. Didn't he understand that? Why would she need space to choose suitors? How could she let him know she had already made her choice?

They covered some distance in silence before she spoke. "How does your brother fare?"

"Captain Allendale is recovering as well as can be expected. You will probably soon observe him by my side at social events, slaying all the ladies with his regimentals and golden good looks."

Josie winked at Marcus. "Are you afraid he will steal your thunder and that I may fall for him?"

Marcus shrugged. "It has been known to happen. I doubt Jared would cut me out with you, and he will be redeployed with Wellesley before too long."

"Have you enjoyed your time with him now that he is home?"

"I missed him when he left for war. The distance and the fear of losing him combined for a double sense of loss when he was abroad. Even more so since losing our parents."

"I delightfully anticipate making his acquaintance."

"He is the opposite of me in appearance. He takes after our father more in his coloring, where I take after our mother."

"That is an added benefit to you since I am partial to brown wavy hair and eyes the color of dark chocolate." Josie glanced at Marcus and noticed color in his cheeks. She doubted it was from the crisp morning air or their gallop.

"I am grateful that my appearance has found favor in your sight." Marcus smiled and nodded, showing a dimple on his right cheek. Just as quickly, a dark look come to his eyes. "What about Sir Bastian? How will you deal with him? He seems like a dirty dish."

"I do not know. I will ask Lady Grey to refuse him

admittance to the house. What else can I do in public to depress his attentions without calling undue attention to myself?"

"I suspect he will not be easily thwarted given his attitude last night. I am sure my aunt will give you sound advice." Marcus glanced around as they had circled around to come back to the meadow. He gave a discreet nod to the groom behind them. "What do you say to a final gallop before I escort you home?"

Josie grinned, and with a quick flick of her whip without it touching her mare, they flew across the meadow in response to his question.

Marcus pursued her.

Josie gasped for air as she slowed down with Marcus by her side. Her hair fell out of its coil, and her hat had tipped askew.

A look of appreciation filled his gaze.

Too soon, they were back at the Grey house and he helped her dismount.

Warmth traveled through her gloves as she placed them on his strong shoulders while he lowered her to the ground. She removed her hands, as if burned by the contact. She was conscious of the possible gazes of those from around the square who would watch for any misstep.

Marcus gently placed a hand under her elbow and guided her up the stairs.

"Thank you for the delightful morning, Marcus."

"The pleasure was mine." He tipped his hat, turned, and headed down the steps before she entered the house.

Josie went up to her suite of rooms and with Molly's help, changed into a demure yellow muslin morning gown. She was uneasy about wearing such muted shades with her coloring, but the dressmaker had been clever in the use of ribbons and trim to make sure the shades did not make her look unnaturally sallow. Josie went to Lady Grey's suite to see if she was awake and available for a coze. She found her hostess sitting up in bed sipping a cup of hot chocolate.

The older woman motioned for Josie to enter. "Come in, my dear." She set her cup down on the table next to the bed and patted a spot on the mattress close to her. "Did you ride out with Marcus this morning?"

Josie smiled and nodded. "Yes."

"I am glad you were able to spend a few unexceptionable moments with him."

Josie looked down and fiddled with the ribbons on her dress.

"What bothers you?"

"I need your advice. Last night, an unwanted suitor from back home showed up at the dance. Sir Bastian is serious in his pursuit, but I cannot be easy in his presence. He is determined I will marry him, regardless of my repeated refusals of his proposal. I don't know what else I can do to depress his attentions."

"We will refuse him admittance to the house. Beyond that, if you give him the cut direct in public it will give rise to undue speculation, but do so if you must. If you desire to refuse to dance with him, you may do so. That alone may not deter him. We can only hope he will not create a scene. You do not have enough credit yet amongst the *ton* to protect you from public censure should he do that. I shall have to pray for wisdom on this."

"I will spend some time alone in my room. I shall pray as well." Josie bent over to give the older woman a kiss on the cheek before she departed.

~*~

Flower tributes from young men intrigued with Miss Storm based on their dances with her the previous evening arrived at the house.

Josie expected callers later that afternoon, and she dreaded it. Sir Bastian's bouquet had unsettled her. Most of the arrangements that arrived contained beautifully arranged flowers, daisies, white carnations, and other symbols of purity, beauty, and love. Those tributes were sweet. Remington's bouquet of pink roses reminded her of her time at his estate and included gardenias, which indicated secret love.

She placed them in her room by her bed to cherish.

Sir Bastian, however, sent red roses with one black one at the center. A black rose?

Josie was not quite sure what that meant, but a shiver of fear and revulsion forced her to send the flowers to the kitchen with instructions to do what they wished with them.

Callers arrived, and Miss Storm and Lady Grey were besieged by young gentlemen, some who came with sisters or their mothers.

Lord Harrow, Sir Tidley, and Lord Westcombe showed up to add cache to a young woman in her first season.

They all heard a disturbance at one point.

Lord Westcombe left the room to see to the matter at the request of Lady Grey.

A short time later, Lord Westcombe re-entered the room with Lord Remington by his side.

He bent to whisper in Lady Gray's ear, but Josie

was uninformed of what had occurred.

Josie fought a blush as Marcus bent over her hand and whispered, "Did you receive my flowers?"

She nodded and felt the corner of her lip quirk. "Yes, thank you. I have them in my suite to enjoy privately."

Marcus nodded and gave her a smile that melted her heart. She reluctantly let her hand go as he moved around the room to interact with some of the other young dandies who were there to vie for her favor. She watched sadly as, after the appropriate length of time for his visit, he departed.

Overall, Josie was flattered at the attentions of the young men who surrounded her. Most reminded her of her younger brother up at university, a bit green, awkward, and not at all the kind of men she would desire for a husband. She sought not to encourage them but asked questions in the hopes that she would at least be friends and not arouse passion in their young hearts.

20

Lord Remington visited his mother's old friend, Lady Sally Jersey. This matriarch of the *ton* greeted him warmly as he entered her drawing room. It was Wednesday, and she made particular mention that both he and his brother were expected to be at Almack's that evening. A few discreet words dropped in the right ear gave Marcus an assurance that Josie's success amongst the *beau monde* was established.

That evening, Marcus and his brother made their appearance in those hallowed halls. They came upon an altercation with the majordomo and Sir Bastian. The older man was barred entrance due to his lack of appropriate attire.

Marcus straightened his shoulders and smiled inwardly. At least Josie would have one less concern tonight. Once inside, Marcus and Jared encountered Lady Jersey and her cronies. Various eligible young misses were pointed out and introduced. Marcus and Jared parted ways as Captain Allendale found friends to converse with along the periphery of the dance floor. He was not yet able to dance. The Captain would make the evening more enjoyable for the less pursued misses who decorated the walls.

Josie danced with Sir Tidley and Marcus experienced a twinge of envy. Would he ever relax and not worry that she would choose another? She was graceful, and her dress suited her to perfection, trimmed in peach lace that complimented the color in her cheeks. He didn't have to worry about Michael cutting him out with Josie. He paused. Or did he? Michael was handsome in his own right and financially well off enough to marry an untitled miss. He stood to gain a lot by marriage to Miss Storm now that her connection to the Earl of Chester had been uncovered. They did make a striking couple as they were about the same height and both had dark hair.

Marcus tried to school his features to hide his inner turmoil. He couldn't let anyone observe his attraction to Miss Storm lest he frighten off potential suitors. He wanted her to want him for himself, not his title, money, or looks. Women had pursued him for years for those reasons.

Josie had known him thus before she was aware of his other attractions. He shook his head in remembrance of all they had been through not that long ago. Thank God, she was able to see and dance now.

He smiled as the dance ended and approached the couple as they came off the dance floor. Marcus bowed before her. "Miss Storm, may I request the honor of your hand in the next dance?"

Josie blushed as she gave a small courtesy. "Lord Remington, I'd be delighted."

Josie placed her gloved hand on his arm as they moved to take the floor. Josie stopped and glanced at Michael. "Thank you for the dance, Sir Tidley."

"My pleasure, Miss Storm." Sir Michael grinned at Marcus and turned to find another partner.

Marcus placed Josie's hand on his arm as the music began. "Relax."

Josie looked at his cravat before glancing up with a

shy smile. "Everyone is watching."

"Pretend they are not and that it is only the two of us."

Josie averted her eyes as she glanced around while they turned to the music. She followed his lead beautifully. Her gaze held his gaze A soft, small smile graced her lips.

Marcus's heart skipped a beat. He inhaled the scent of roses in her hair, and having her the prescribed distance was torture when what he really wanted was to hold her tight and never let her go. The rules of society prohibited him from giving into his baser instincts, and it rattled him that this one girl was the one to give rise to temptations in him he had never before experienced. But here in his arms was a woman, alive and vibrant and thrumming with life. *It is better to marry than burn.* Unable to do that at present, he would have to struggle to master urges that had never before been a challenge. Possibly because no woman had ever captured his heart as this one did.

"You dance beautifully. You have emerged from tragedy as a butterfly from a cocoon."

"Very prettily said, my lord."

"I thought I was Marcus to you."

"Yes, my lord, except that we are in public and I would avoid arousing undue speculation."

"I have singled you out for a dance, my dear Josie. You have already given rise to speculation by looking at me the way you do."

Josie laughed softly at this, and they resumed the dance in silence. When it ended, Marcus guided Josie to the supper room and introduced her to his brother.

Lady Grey joined them.

Marcus decided he would not stand by watching

others dance with Josie. Jared looked weary. The two brothers departed shortly after the meal as another suitor came to claim Miss Storm's hand.

Marcus sensed his brother's gaze on him even in the darkened carriage. "Out with it, Jared. You have something to say. Say it."

"I approve, Marcus. I know you do not need that from me, but I like Miss Storm and believe she would be the perfect wife for you."

Marcus released a breath of air he had not realized he had been holding. "Thank you, Jared." Silence prevailed for a few blocks. Marcus tensed. "I'm consumed with dread, and I'm not sure what to do about that."

"I have learned to pay attention to those kinds of things. Pray. I shall do the same. If you need anything…"

"Jared, you pray? When did this happen?"

"I may have a wicked reputation to maintain, Marcus, however, there is a difference between the fantasy and illusion of what some would like to be true and what really exists. I have chosen to live a secret life of virtue since last year. Outwardly, it might cost me my life if I were to set aside what appeared to be a penchant for wine, gambling, and the sweet seduction of a beautiful woman. Stock in trade during a time of war, it has saved my neck many a time. When the war is over and my duty is done, I long for a woman who wants me for who I am, not for my looks and reputation between the sheets." His voice sounded weary.

Marcus nodded as he studied his brother in the dark shadows.

They were now closer than ever before.

~*~

Josie collapsed into bed that evening. Her feet ached from being stepped on by many a young man. Her only fond memory of the evening was her dance with Marcus. She felt safe, secure, and desired in his arms. Even dinner with him and his brother was a treasure.

When they'd left the ballroom that evening, the air had become stale and heavy in their wake.

She struggled to give her undivided attention to the parade of gentlemen who vied for her favors. Apparently, she had done well as more floral tributes arrived the next morning.

Josie had not seen Sir Bastian the previous evening, yet a bouquet arrived with two black roses amongst the red ones. A shiver went up her spine as she sent them off again to the kitchen. She found out later that the staff believed the black roses to be an evil omen and had taken to casting them in the fireplace.

Josie received a note two days later from Captain Allendale. He requested permission to take her for a ride in the park at the fashionable hour. She sent an affirmative reply and eagerly awaited the opportunity to get to know Marcus's brother better.

When Captain Allendale appeared at her door, she was impressed again with his appearance out of uniform. His build was slighter than his brother's, due to his recent injury, yet she sensed his strength as he helped her up to the carriage. The perfectly matched black horses gently pulled forward.

She complimented the Captain on the well-sprung carriage.

"It came with Marcus's title, and he allows me to share in the benefits." He paused, and she watched his blue eyes darken a shade. "May we dispense with the formalities, Miss Storm? I give leave for you to call me Jared."

"It seems unusual given our brief acquaintance, but in private I will use your given name, if you will return the favor and call me Josie."

"I'm glad my brother found you. You are different from the other women who make their debut here in London. Marcus has set a high standard for himself and avoided the pitfalls most men our age fall into. He needs a woman who can appreciate those values."

"You sound as if you approve of his way of life, but your reputation belies that."

Jared shook his head and gave a rueful grin. "My brother has excelled at a more pure way of life that I disdained, much to my shame. I rebelled in every way possible from the example he set. Marcus never failed to accept me in spite of that, and pray for my health, safety, and soul. He purchased my colors at my request. I worked my way up through Field Marshall Wellesley's ranks. I am not who I once was, and I'm glad I have never sought to offer that poor excuse of a man to any young woman as a prize. It amazes me at how many of these girls sell themselves short for a title and a fat bank roll, and overlook the character of the man they marry."

Josie's heart melted at his speech. She suspected it was more than he usually said. She wanted to reach out to touch his arm and offer encouragement to the young man who sat beside her. "I'm grateful God is not only a God of judgment but also offers mercy and forgiveness. From what I can discern, many of those young women do not have much choice. Parents or circumstances force them to settle for less than what their hearts may desire. I'm fortunate to have parents who loved each other. My father would not barter my future happiness to benefit himself."

"He would not wed you to Sir Bastian?"

Josie could not quell the tremor that involuntarily shook her body. "Did Marcus speak to you of him?"

Jared nodded, and the lines between his eyes and on his forehead showed the depth of his concern for her. "Has Bastian been bothering you? I heard how he tried to bully his way into my aunt's home a few days hence."

"I knew nothing of that, only that he daily sends me black roses." Another shiver followed that memory.

"Does my brother know of this?"

Josie shook her head. "I've not had opportunity to mention it to him."

"Is this man a threat to you?"

Josie nodded. "I fear he will cause a scene at some public event. I have refused his offer of marriage, but he doesn't believe me to be sincere. He is determined, but I cannot grasp why. I have neither fortune nor title to bring to him, and certainly there is no affection on my side."

Jared glanced away from her. "It makes one wonder why he would persist in his suit." He glanced back at her and made eye contact with a half-smile. "Not that you are not a valuable treasure to be won, Josie. You are most certainly worthy of any suitor's attention, but why would someone you have rebuffed continue? It does not make sense."

The question was rhetorical, and Josie forbore to

answer since she did not know what else to say. After a few moments of silence with the exception of the clip clop of the horses' hooves and the bustle of other carriages in the park, Josie spoke again. "How long will you be home?"

Jared shrugged with his good shoulder. "I am unsure. I'm not up to driving a carriage yet. I'm getting stronger and expect I'll be in the Peninsula in about a month or less."

"I'm glad you have recovered well. I'm sure Marcus and your aunt are relieved to have you home safe for now."

"Safe is definitely not a word I would equate with life in this uncertain world, Miss Storm."

"Josie."

"Josie. Surely you have learned that already, have you not?"

Josie glanced away, momentarily transported to a dark, lonely bed at Rose Hill. She fought against the sting of tears that memory brought forth. "I hope I am done with tragic accidents and can move on to a happier future." She grinned as she looked at the handsome man beside her. "Not very grounded in reality, am I? I pray for safety for loved ones, yet I know that God does not promise to grant that in the ways I would prefer."

Jared returned her smile. "Understandable. We long to protect those we love from physical or emotional harm. Most often, we are powerless to prevent tragedy, even with our prayers. Or so it would seem. When the enemy captured and tortured me, I knew there were no guarantees I would survive, and part of me wished I would not. I only knew that God was with me, even if I didn't make it home alive or whole. I was one of the fortunate ones. Before that, I lived as if I were immune from any real threat and sought pleasure any way I could." His face had taken on a hard look as he spoke. Lines appeared on his forehead, not quite hidden by the hair that fell across his brow. Jared's jaw was tense as deep emotion undergirded his words.

Josie placed her hand on his on the seat between them and gave a small squeeze before withdrawing it. "I'm sorry for what you have suffered, Jared. I was unaware you had been tortured. It must have been awful."

A flash of pain crossed his features. "It is a part of war, Josie, but one that most young men don't think about when they enlist. When I purchased my commission, I only had dreams of heroism and thought I would be exempt from danger. I was wrong."

"I am glad you survived."

Jared let out a laugh as he looked back at her. "Thank you. We are complex beings, are we not?"

"We are."

"Now, pretty lady, let me beguile you with some flattery so that my reputation as a rake does not suffer amongst the *ton*."

Josie put a hand to her chest and grinned. "Really? A rake is escorting me? How delightful."

With that began a lighthearted banter until it was time for him to return her home.

Jared helped Josie down from the carriage once they arrived. He escorted her to the door and placed a gallant kiss on the back of her hand as they parted.

Josie entered the house having enjoyed her afternoon with Jared but realized that, as with every other man she had met thus far, none compared to Lord Remington when it came to engaging her affections.

As was their regular practice on Sundays, Lady Grey and Miss Storm attended church in the morning. Josie was uncomfortable sitting in the Grey family pew. It was not that far from the Remington pew. This morning, she observed the two brothers side by side. She heard Lord Remington's distinctive baritone when they sang a hymn. Josie struggled to focus on the message with Marcus being near. She prayed for the ability to focus on God and not make a man her idol. After the service, she found it difficult to face the affable pastor, since she could not give any comment on a message she had not heard. She finally disengaged herself from him and stepped out into the sunshine to await Lady Grey.

Marcus stood at the foot of the church stairs talking with a beautiful woman with blonde hair and sparkling blue eyes.

The woman was close enough that Josie observed the way she beamed at him. Other commotion around obscured any opportunity to hear words spoken between them. Josie despised gossip. She had never been one to eavesdrop. That did not stop her from watching with interest.

The young woman had a hand possessively placed on Marcus's arm as they conversed. She flirtatiously used her fan and giggled in response to something Marcus said. She then leaned toward Marcus and reach up to kiss his cheek.

Josie perspired and grew lightheaded and nauseous. She was relieved when Lady Grey came and they moved to enter their carriage. What she had seen?

The woman had been lovely, and with the way she had gazed at Marcus, it was obvious there was great affection between them.

Josie fought back tears at the evidence of Marcus openly flirting with the beauty. He had not even spoken to Josie. She wondered who the woman was and what she meant to him. She was afraid to ask, terrified of what she suspected in her heart. Maybe Marcus did not care for her as much as she'd thought. By the time they arrived home, Josie was truly ill and escaped to her room without responding to Lady Grey's questioning glances.

21

"Marcus, I need your assistance."

"You know I would help you any way I could, Jared."

The brothers had opted out of the evening's entertainments to spend a quiet evening at home.

"I would not be so hasty with that offer without knowing what I am about to ask of you. It will involve risk and sacrifice. If you agree, you can tell no one of this conversation or what I am about to request of you."

"You have my full attention. It sounds serious."

"On a hunch, I launched an investigation that unearthed a political matter, but at issue is also the safety of your potential bride-to-be."

"This has to do with Josie?" That sense of foreboding returned, and Marcus's heart seized tight.

Jared nodded and gave his brother a grave look.

Marcus had rarely seen that expression on his devil-may-care sibling.

"I took Miss Storm for a ride a few days ago. I found her delightful, by the way, and would heartily approve if she should accept your proposal—especially after what I'm about to ask of you."

"Go on." Marcus swallowed the bitter bile of fear and leaned forward, intent on hearing every word his brother had to say.

"I was curious about this Sir Bastian, who seems to

be making a nuisance of himself with your potential fiancée. It piqued my interest, and I wanted to help. I investigated him."

"What did you find?"

"Whitehall has kept an eye on him. He has unexplained wealth and harsh appetites. Definitely not good *ton* by any means."

"And this involves me how?" Marcus wished he would get to the point.

"Patience, dear brother. We discovered that Sir Bastian has a favorite place to go, and we need someone to check out a contact there, to glean information that we might use to prosecute him."

"So you will be doing this?"

"No. We need you to do this."

"Who is this contact?"

"One of Madame DuBois's girls. Miss Maribel Smith."

Marcus leaned back in his chair and shook his head. "I'm confused. Are you saying you want—no *need*—me to go to a house of ill repute and interview a *barque of frailty*?"

"For Josie, if not for your country, you will. Reports indicate he is desperate to have Miss Storm as his bride and might act rashly in an attempt to claim her."

"Josie cannot stand the man. She would never permit it."

Jared leaned forward, looked intently in his brother's eyes, and spoke with a soft but firm voice. "Josie will have no say in the matter. It is probable that if he does what I suspect, your beloved will not be long for this world."

"If I help you, England, and save the woman I

love, I may well damage my reputation and jeopardize my relationship with Miss Storm."

Jared's mouth was taut, and his eyes had a militant glint to them Marcus had not seen since his brother was a rebellious adolescent sent down from school for his pranks on campus. "Those are the benefits and liabilities."

Marcus rose and paced the room. "Dash it all, Jared. How dare you do this to me? You won't let me explain my actions to Josie, either?"

"No one can know the real reason you go into that home. Whitehall is asking you to serve your country as a spy."

Marcus turned as fury welled up within him, and he pointed to his brother. "You! Why can you not do this? Isn't this your 'stock-in-trade'? It's not mine."

"I offered. I would have spared you this, but my orders are clear and I have been forbidden to go. In this circumstance, my reputation works against me." Jared's eyes looked weary. This entire situation pained him. "You must trust me on this. Remember that even Jesus met with prostitutes and tax collectors and faced unjust criticism for doing so. The fact is, we believe they will trust you and share the information with you because of your stellar reputation. They will not entrust the information we seek to anyone less worthy. We've tried and were unsuccessful." He paused and looked down at his hands clasped in front of him. "We only want you to go and talk to her. Talk. That's all."

Marcus spun around, away from his brother. He strode to the fireplace, leaned against it, and studied the flames. Anger, fear, grief, and skepticism all vied for prominence in his heart. After several deep breaths and with tight control on his emotions, he softly asked,

"Do I have time to pray about this? Does this need to be done immediately?"

"Every moment we wait puts Miss Storm's life at risk."

"You cannot detain him on what you already know?" Marcus glanced over to his brother.

Jared's shoulders sagged. He shook his head as he looked at his brother. "No. We need proof. If he is guilty of treason, we can move quickly. Only you can get the proof. I would rather do that than risk an attack on Miss Storm. I have your friends keeping an eye over her in case he acts."

Marcus sat across from his brother and buried his face in his hands before sliding those hands down enough to look at Jared through his fingers. The thought of that man accosting Josie made him physically ill. His dinner did not sit well in his stomach. He knew in his heart what he needed to do, but he grieved what he might lose in the process. He expelled a deep breath. "Is tonight soon enough?"

"Ideal. Let me brief you on what information we are searching for."

The two plotted together before Marcus rose and went to his room to change for his task. He prayed all the while. Prayed for Josie's safety. Prayed selfishly that his reputation would withstand this. What would happen if word got out amongst the *beau monde*? Would Josie love him enough to overlook this without an explanation? He feared she would not trust him as much as Whitehall seemed to. His heart was heavy, but duty trumped his own personal comfort. If he could protect Josie from harm, he would accept the consequences. He did not have to like it, though.

Marcus called for a hackney to take him to the less

desirable part of town. He came to the well-kept establishment, paid the driver, and walked up the stairs. A fission of fear traveled up his spine. He prayed quietly as he raised his hand to knock on the door and laughed to himself at the irony of a man asking God's blessing before walking into a brothel.

A burly doorman admitted him. Instead of Miss Maribel Smith, he found himself presented to Madame DuBois.

Her receiving room was plush in red and purple velvet. Garish and gilded with gold trim. The overpowering scent of perfume almost caused him to gag. He felt tainted. He noticed the curiosity in the woman's eyes and tried to think about how Jesus would have seen a woman like this.

She was heavy-set with an ample bosom that was barely covered, and her gown clung to every curve, of which there were many. Her hair was a riot of blonde curls that fell down her back. He wondered if they were real or a wig. Hazel eyes gazed at him above her heavily rouged cheeks, and a fortune in jewels dripped from her ears, neck, and fingers. He doubted they were paste. She raised one questioning eyebrow at his perusal. He wondered how and why she ever chose this type of employment and quickly realized that the injustices of society often forced women into positions like this. He fought in Parliament to find solutions. The issues were complex and not the reason for his visit. He schooled his expression and greeted her as warmly as he would a Countess.

"Very nicely done, my Lord Remington. I must say I am curious as to what would bring the 'Virtuous Viscount' to my doors specifically asking for one girl. The normal procedure would be for me to meet with you and ascertain your desires for your evening of entertainment so I may select the young woman who would best meet that need."

"I'm not here for 'an evening of entertainment.' I only wish to meet with Miss Smith."

"Miss Maribel is not available."

"I understand, but would she at least be willing to talk with me?"

"Talk? You came to a brothel to *talk*?" She looked at him carefully, her eyes taking in everything, and Marcus struggled to stand still and meet her gaze when they came back to his face. "You promise you will not take advantage of her?"

"I give you my word as a gentleman, although I fully recognize that my reputation as such may have suffered injury for having walked through your portal."

Madame smiled and laughed. "You plan to remain virtuous even if no one sees you. I like you, Lord Remington. I'm aware of the fine work you do in Parliament. Does that surprise you? I am first and foremost a woman of business and keep abreast of politics as best I am able." She chuckled. "I think I can trust you to hold the line. It must be important if you would risk your reputation to be here." Madame rose and indicated that he should follow her.

Marcus followed the abbess to a suite of rooms that was tastefully furnished.

She bade Marcus to sit and be comfortable while she went to fetch Miss Smith.

Marcus tapped his foot as he sat there, tense. The room looked like a normal sitting room, but his mind could not forget the purpose of this house. And he wondered...

The door opened.

Miss Smith entered, and Marcus was able to understand why she was not serving customers. The petite young woman was perhaps all of seventeen years of age. Her brown hair was up, and her small heart-shaped face was swollen and colored various shades of black, blue, purple, and yellow. Her arm hung in a makeshift sling. She walked slowly with a pronounced limp. Pain etched grooves in her forehead.

Marcus's eyes met Madame's in question.

"You may ask her. The client who did this is no longer welcome here." With that, Madame DuBois left the room and closed the door firmly behind her.

Miss Smith sat down across from Marcus with a suspicious look in her eyes. "Wat's a fine gent like yoos want wit the likes o' me?"

"I mean you no harm, Miss Smith. I seek information, and I heard you may be able to help me."

"It'll be costin' you."

Marcus laid some coin on the low table that was between them, and her eyes grew wide. "I will give you this now in good faith, and more of the same when I get what I came for."

She eagerly grabbed at the gold with her good hand. She looked up at him and smiled.

Marcus thought she might be quite pretty when she was not sporting bruises. "I need to know everything you can tell me about Sir Archibald Bastian."

She stiffened, and her eyes narrowed. "I swear if'n I's sees 'im again I'll kill 'im!"

"What did he do?"

"This!" She pointed to her arm, face, and leg. "He's the bloody cove that did this to me."

"Did he say why?"

"Hez angry at some gel named Josie and swore she'd be gettin' it soon. I feelz sorry fer her if'n this be her gent."

"What else can you tell me?" Marcus was sick to his stomach again.

"He sez he is rich 'n rivals Prinny wit 'is wealth. He sez he 'as some dealin's in free trad'ng and 'e's too smart for dem coves in the gov'ment to find 'im out."

"Interesting. Did he say anything else?"

"'e needs this Josie chit to make 'is vic'try. And 'e sympathizes with that frenchy."

"Napoleon?"

She nodded. "Him and some black diamond."

Marcus spoke with Miss Smith for a short time longer and paid her well with strict instructions not to say a word to anyone as to why he was there. "If you must say that I came for your favors, so be it. We know the truth."

"You's be a 'andsome gent, I w'ld be able to 'andle sumat your needs for you." She flirted now.

Marcus was shocked at how low a bodice could instantly go.

"If'n not, I tw'ld welcome ya back 'nother time."

"I, um, thank you for your generous offer, Miss Smith." Marcus gulped at the expanse of flesh exposed and her indecent proposal. His cravat choked him. "I hope you will not be too disappointed if I decline, in spite of the temptation."

She was definitely giving him an eyeful.

"I have promised God I would keep myself pure until I wed."

"Youz a strange gent. I'fn ya change yur mind…"

Marcus rose, leaned over the petite prostitute,

kissed her hand, and turned it over to place in it the extra coin. He left as quickly as he was able. He closed the door behind him, leaned against the wall, and let out a breath he had not realized he held. *Lord, this had better have been worth it.* He pushed off against the wall and skipped lightly down the steps, wanting only to get home and bathe the scent of this place off him.

Madame DuBois emerged from her sitting room door as he approached. "Would you join me for a cup of tea, my lord?"

He wanted to refuse but nodded instead. "Thank you." He followed her into the room.

A servant appeared with a tea tray, left, and closed the door behind her.

Madame motioned for Marcus to have a seat in a small sitting area where the tea and cakes awaited. She sat down and served the hot beverage. "You have not been here long enough. I would forbear having you leave too early and undermine your investigation."

Marcus raised an eyebrow as he accepted the refreshments.

"Yes. I eavesdropped, as I have at other times. Secret passages and peepholes can be convenient...and entertaining." She winked at him. "I have shocked you. Come, let us be honest with one another. You want information on Bastian. He is not allowed here anymore. If you know this Josie chit, you had best warn her of how dangerous he is. The man is a brute and should be stopped."

Marcus frowned, relief now replaced with anxiety for Josie's welfare. He nodded to his hostess.

"It may surprise you that I am a patriot of England. I do not admire the Little Emperor and refuse to have any dealings with those who do. What Miss

Smith does not know is that Sir Bastian has spent time in here bragging to me. Having French origins, he believed I would sympathize. I thought maybe my report to Whitehall had been overlooked. Who would think that a madame would take on the role of a spy? I am glad they have sent you, Lord Remington. I do not know that I would have trusted any other man entering this building to be true and worthy of these confidences. I suspect some of my patrons at Whitehall knew that."

Madame DuBois handed over an envelope with some handwritten pages on it. "These were left here by Sir Bastian in his haste to depart." She grinned. "He was unwillingly escorted off the premises before he was able to gather his belongings." She pointed to the envelope. "There should be enough evidence against him in there. You should know that there is someone higher in the peerage involved. He goes by the name 'Black Diamond.' I have been unable to ferret out his identity, but not for lack of trying."

Marcus nodded. "Miss Smith mentioned a black diamond. I had not realized it was a person." He tucked the envelope into an interior pocket of his coat. "I will ask that you do not convey to anyone the nature of my business here. I appreciate what you have done to aid our country, and Miss Storm. If you think my visit has been of sufficient duration, I beg that you would let me leave as I have much work to be accomplished post haste." He leaned forward to set down his cup and saucer and rose to leave.

Madame also stood. "You have stayed a sufficient amount of time. My Maribel was right, though. Any one of my ladies would be more than willing to initiate you into the pleasures of the flesh should you be interested." She sidled up to him and trailed a finger down his chest. She maintained her eye contact with him as she purred. "I include myself in their number."

Marcus reached for her hand and placed a kiss on the back of it. "Thank you for your offer. My hope is that I will soon be wed and my wife will assume that role."

"If you ever change your mind, you are always welcome here."

Marcus gave a brief nod of acknowledgment and departed. Upon exiting the building, he flagged a hackney and returned home to find Jared dozing in front of the fireplace in the study. Marcus shook him.

Jared yawned, stretched, looked at his brother and then at the clock. "You are home. Were you successful?"

Marcus nodded. "I am fearful for Josie's safety."

"I have her covered. Relax, pour yourself a brandy, and tell me what you learned."

22

That same evening, Josie engaged in the typical and exhausting whirlwind of *ton* parties. She was at her third ball and had finished her dance with Sir Tidley. Josie was about to accept the hand of another admirer when Sir Bastian shoved him aside and grabbed her arm.

"Come with me. Now." Sir Bastian's voice was low and guttural.

It sent shivers up Josie's spine. She struggled to get free of his grasp, but Sir Bastian was stronger than he appeared. "You are hurting me," she hissed as she stomped her foot on his only to find that satin dancing slippers didn't do much damage.

"If you want to avoid a scandal, you will come with me and smile as you do." Sir Bastian sneered through clenched teeth.

Josie looked around the room for any hope of escape as he dragged her toward an exit.

"Your Lord Remington is not here tonight to come to your rescue, nor is his meddling friend, Lord Westcombe. You are mine, and I will not be thwarted again." He jerked her arm, and pain exploded in her shoulder.

Fear and anger overtook her. She stomped down with her heel on his foot, harder this time, and his grip loosened. She tried to move away, but the crowd hemmed her in.

Did anyone witness what was happening? Would scandal truly be worse than what this man had planned?

Sir Bastian recovered and jerked her close to his sweaty body that reeked of cigar smoke and alcohol.

Josie cringed and yelped from the pain. "Let me go! You are hurting me!" She yelled as loudly as she could, repeatedly, until the music stopped and the dancers stared at them.

Lord Westcombe, Sir Tidley, and Lord Harrow appeared out of nowhere, and the crowd watched avidly at the tableau playing out before them.

Lord Westcombe bowed to Josie. "My darling, Miss Storm, is this man inconveniencing you?"

Josie nodded.

Sir Bastian blustered. "Stand aside and let us pass. Miss Storm is my affianced bride, and I am taking her with me. Now!" A growl emanated from her captor.

Josie had no doubt of the brutality that awaited her if he succeeded in leaving with her.

Suddenly, Sir Bastian's grip loosened, and she turned to see Sir Tidley, although somewhat shorter than Sir Bastian, twisting her attacker's free arm from behind. "I suggest you let the lady go," Michael growled.

Sir Bastian gasped in pain and released Josie, who ran to find Lady Grey as tears streamed down her face.

"I will call you out for this!" Her attacker yelled above the murmurs of the crowd as they parted like the Red Sea so she might pass through.

Josie heard no more of what happened.

Lady Grey clucked over her as they escaped the ball. In the carriage, Josie wept on Lady Grey's shoulder while the older woman remained silent. "I'm ruined." Sniff. Hiccup. "I want to go home." Body-shaking sobs overtook her. "I cannot stay in London."

Lady Grey's hand caressed and patted her back. The shudders subsided, and Josie was able to breathe and sit upright. By the time the carriage reached home, she was able to exit with dignity. Upon entering, she ran up the stairs to her room and fell onto her bed with a fresh paroxysm of tears. Josie shook inside.

She longed for Marcus to comfort her. Where had he been? How would he react to what happened? Would he even want her anymore? Her season in London was certainly over. There would be no way to overcome the scandal of what happened tonight. She dreaded tomorrow and having to face the harshness of the *beau monde* when on the prowl, salivating over fresh meat to chew up and spit out for the sake of their entertainment. Tomorrow she would be the main course.

Josie struggled to get ready for bed without Molly's help. She wanted to be alone with her heartbreak. She sipped a glass of brandy to relax. The liquor burned in her throat before it warmed her. Soon she was able to fall asleep and dreamt of Marcus coming to her rescue from the fate that awaited her.

The next morning, Lady Grey summoned Josie.

Josie knew her eyes were puffy from crying. Although Molly had done her best to make her presentable, she thought she looked pale and scared when she glanced in the mirror.

Lady Grey rose to greet her and walked her to the chairs on one side of the room. "I know you want nothing more than to go home, but we must brave the gossip this morning."

Josie recoiled inside. "Please. Do not make me go."

"This will prove your character and grace. If you can stare this down and weather this irritation, you will be able to handle anything that comes your way as Lady Remington."

Josie's gaze instantly rose to look at the older woman and noticed that her mentor looked tired and worn out. "Do you think so?"

"I am certain. It may be rough, but we can do this. I am not saying that this will blow over. It may last until some new tidbit tickles the ears of the elite. Until that time, we shall hold our heads up with dignity. Nothing that happened last night was your fault. Sir Bastian was arrested, and I received notice from Lord Westcombe that your tormentor has been placed in the tower and will be brought up on charges of treason."

"If he was wanted on charges of treason, why did they wait until he attacked me in public to arrest him?"

"They awaited proof, but someone thought you might be in danger and placed a guard around you until they had what they needed to arrest him. Someone watched out for you." Lady Grey raised her eyebrows.

"Lord Remington?" Josie couldn't help the rise of hope that perhaps he had been behind her rescue after all.

"I do not know. I have not heard from Marcus for several days."

"Oh." Josie frowned. "Where has he been? I thought he would be courting me here in London."

"You will have to ask him when next you see him. I do hope he will show up soon. His presence would give you prestige."

"If only he would bend enough to allow his attentions to be public."

"Trust him, my dear. He is worthy of that."

"I know. I should be more grateful for all he has done for me."

"I don't think you are ungrateful. You are a young woman longing for more from the man you love. You're chafing at the separation—try to be patient. Who can understand a young man's mind?" Lady Grey rose to her feet and grabbed her wrap. "Shall we prepare to enter the lion's den?"

Josie took a deep breath. "The sooner we get this over with the closer I will be to going home and being done with this entire pretense."

Lady Grey nodded and led the way to the carriage.

The first home they visited was that of Lady Wilhelmina Landsdowne. She was a widow who was stick thin, weak, and sickly in appearance. She rarely left her home, as the *ton* came to her. She was infamous for her ability to know everything and could help make or break a career in the marriage mart with the words she would utter.

"Do not fear, Josie. I have known Wilhelmina from our season in town. She can be our best ally as I am aware of certain secrets that she would not want spread."

"You would blackmail her into supporting me in this?" Josie whispered as the carriage drew up to the home.

"No. There is an unspoken understanding between us. I have never called in my favor with her, and now is the time. Do not fear, Josie." With that, Lady Grey patted Josie's gloved hands and prepared to exit the coach.

Josie inwardly trembled as they entered. The sitting room displayed dainty furniture and a gilded throne-like chair at the center of the room. The expensive surroundings had delicate figurines placed everywhere, which did nothing to ease Josie's nerves.

"My dear, Wilhelmina!" Lady Grey sailed in toward the hostess with no evidence of fear. "It has been far too long since I have seen you. Let me present to you my charge for the season, Miss Josephine Storm. I have been blessed to finally have a young lady, like a daughter to me, to enjoy a season with."

Lady Landsdowne put a looking glass up to her right eye and squinted. It made her eyes seem too huge on her horse-shaped face.

Josie fought the urge to giggle that this odd-looking dragon of society would scrutinize her. She managed to keep a sober look on her face but could not hide the twinkle in her eye as she curtseyed to this woman with a soft, "It is a pleasure, my lady."

"Very pretty gel, Dorothea. Nice manners too. Will you be seated? I had many visitors this morning, but it is quiet now and we can enjoy a bit of a coze." Looking at Lady Grey, she spoke in clipped tones. "What is this I hear about your nephew, Remington? I admired his prudishness as it was quite a diversion, but last night, he had to go and throw it all away on a young woman in a brothel? What is wrong with the dear boy? Has his heart been broken?"

Lady Grey jerked to attention, and her eyes blinked rapidly before she tilted her chin up. "I am not sure of what you speak, my lady. Viscount Remington entering a house of ill repute? I am sure there must be some mistake. Are you sure it was not Captain Allendale? It would suit his reputation to do so."

"Initially, that was my first thought as well, but they do have different coloring. It was most definitely the Virtuous Viscount, although I suppose that title does not apply now. Pity." She reached for a newssheet and handed it to Lady Grey.

Josie leaned over to glance at the drawing depicting none other than Marcus, a tilted halo on his head, in bed with a voluptuous woman barely clothed. Josie blinked several times herself. Marcus was depicted shirtless, the rest of his body hidden beneath a sheet.

Lady Landsdowne tittered. "Every girl loves a man to be a bit of a rascal. Maybe he finally succumbed to temptation. They all do eventually."

Lady Grey met the other woman's gaze. "If for some reason my nephew *was* there, I would guarantee it was not for what you and the rest of the *beau monde* would think. Remington holds his virtue and dedication to God higher than almost anything else. While he is human, I doubt he would fall this far and fast into sins of the flesh."

Lady Landsdowne nodded. "I wondered, as his reputation is unparalleled. But sometimes people appear virtuous to hide secrets. We do not ever know what is going on in someone's mind, do we? Men will be men and have their needs. I would expect that he would be faithful to his wife if he ever chose to wed."

"I will choose to believe he is faithful to his future wife even now," proclaimed Lady Grey, but her voice lacked confidence.

The rest of the short visit passed with the usual inanities of weather and war, and Josie's tussle with Sir Bastian was only mentioned briefly as, "You poor girl. That Sir Bastian was an evil man. I hear he is in the Tower. I'm glad you were rescued from his clutches."

Josie was grateful and horrified that Marcus's

scandal trumped hers.

The rest of the afternoon involved several similar conversations. Individuals delighted in the Viscount's apparent downfall, and Lady Grey defended his integrity.

Miss Storm spent most of these visits sitting quietly pouring tea under the watchful eye of matrons who evaluated and assessed her. Josie's stomach churned, and she only sipped her tea for fear she would not be able to keep even that little bit down with any modicum of grace. She struggled with the detailed drawing brought out at every visit to show proof of the Viscount's transgression. She wanted to run and hide from that gruesome reality. It was with great relief that they returned to the Grey house.

"You must not believe the gossip, Josie." Lady Grey's voice quivered. Even she struggled to trust the Viscount's integrity in the face of the gossip assaulting them today.

"How can I not? You observed the drawing. I also saw Marcus with a beautiful young woman on Sunday, and she flirted with him. She put her hand on his arm and leaned towards him as she laughed at something he'd said. He never sought me out. I have not seen him in over a week. No flowers. No note. No rides in the park. Now this? What am I supposed to conclude?" Josie could not stand in the foyer any longer and ran up the stairs to the sanctuary of her room and her pillow, grateful that they had decided earlier that they would not attend any events this evening.

~*~

In her room, Josie gazed out the window into the

back garden and let the tears flow unhindered down her cheeks. Marcus indicated an affection for her, but that was in the country with no other women present. Many misses in town surpassed her in beauty and accomplishments. Why would she attract someone like Sir Bastian and expect a glorious specimen of manhood like Lord Remington to glance her way? She was nothing compared to that blonde beauty he had talked to after church.

Josie was realistic. Her figure was proportionate. How could she, with modest endowments, compete with the image she saw in the newssheet this morning? She had hoped that would not matter to a man who loved her. She couldn't erase the image of Lord Remington in the arms of that other woman. Marcus *in flagrante delicto*. And the entire town knew. Weren't most men more discreet in their illicit liaisons?

Josie sighed. Most gentlemen of the *ton* frequented brothels or had mistresses before they were married. It was a rite of passage. She understood this. She was aware that Captain Allendale had a checkered past, and probably Sir Tidley, Lord Westcombe, and even Lord Harrow did, although she couldn't imagine it of him. Many other young men she'd danced with every evening most likely did too. However, they didn't have their likeness depicted in the London papers.

So what did that make her? Convenient breeding stock? Her grandfather was an Earl, so she had the blue blood to qualify to marry into the peerage. Didn't most men want a nice young woman from the country who would bear a houseful of heirs and dutifully raise children in the country while their husband spent time in town with willing widows or mistresses?

That was not what she wanted of marriage. She

couldn't bear to think that Marcus was like that. Was it as innocent as Lady Grey tried to paint it? How could it be otherwise? If something had happened and if he was not culpable of what the paper said, why had he not warned her? Why was he silent and absent? Why wasn't he with her when Sir Bastian attacked? If he really loved her, why was he not here now, wiping away her tears?

They were not married. Not even engaged. He had no official obligation to her. If he was not faithful, then why should she not flirt and consider other suitors? Maybe she had been wrong to settle on the first man to capture her heart.

Oh, but what a man! She smiled softly at the remembrance of him sitting by her bed when she had awakened from her fall and had regained her eyesight. It seemed so long ago now, yet it had only been four months. She had already spent more time in his company than any other man of her acquaintance. More than most of the women in the upper ten thousand get to spend with a man before they marry.

So why did she doubt him now? Why did she doubt herself? She could not think. Frustration, grief, anger, and confusion all warred within her soul. The comfort she sought was not to be found. She wanted to pray but realized with guilt that all she would do was complain to God. She already had more blessings than most. Why mourn the lost virtue of one man? He was free to do what he wanted.

Well, then. So was she.

~*~

Saint Giles, London

Lord Widmore paced the room he had rented out in a seedier part of town. His creditors were becoming more persistent, and since he could not escape the drain of his wife's expenses, he now needed to seek the windfall mistakenly bequeathed to Miss Josephine Storm.

Big Red had shown up with a scrawny partner.

"You have failed repeatedly to kill my wife. Do you think you could do even one job right?"

"Youz ain't paid us."

"I shall pay you if you can accomplish this task."

The men stood still, waiting.

"Miss Josephine Storm. I want her dead, and I want proof you've done it. Bring me a finger, at least. I don't care where or how it's done. Just do it, and quickly before she leaves town."

"I'z need money for 'xpenses," Red asserted.

Lord Widmore pulled out some pound notes and thrust them in the brute's hands. "Once she's dead, I'll get her inheritance and can pay you richly for your labors."

The men nodded and left, slithering into the darkness from whence they came.

Lord Widmore headed to the local brothel to satisfy his thirst for opium and the ladies.

It would be a fine thing to be wealthy again.

23

Marcus had not gone out amongst society that day but had spent most of it with his brother and the officials at Whitehall. He had been surprised at how quickly Sir Bastian had sought to kidnap Josie and was grateful his friends had been there to protect her and stop the assault. He wanted, more than anything, to go to her side and make sure she was unharmed but had been required to attend meeting after meeting with government officials. While Marcus had only been a small part of the puzzle, he had been vital to the case, and he was grateful that it netted safety for Josie. He chafed at the obligations it placed upon his time and prayed that Josie had recovered and been unharmed by Bastian.

Sir Tidley had ribbed him about his visit to the brothel and showed him the drawing from the newssheets.

Lord Westcombe teased him about his fall from grace.

Since he was not at liberty to tell them why he had been there, he had silently put up with their laughing at his visit to a bordello.

Michael had taken him aside. "Marcus, we may tease, but for whatever reason you were there, we all know it was not for what this rag claims."

Marcus fought tears. His faithful friends would rib him, but they stood firm in their belief in his integrity regardless of evidence to the contrary. Their solid friendship humbled him. If only Josie had that kind of faith in him as well, he would be content.

He finally returned to his townhome and found a letter from Lady Grey. He rushed over to her house in response to her summons. It was already late in the day.

Marcus sighed as the carriage pulled up. He longed for, and dreaded, facing the music of his actions. He hoped against hope that Josie would overlook such a public fall from grace. Somehow, his heart sank with the realization that his hopes might be in vain.

When Marcus arrived at Lady Grey's home, he was escorted to her private sitting room. He entered and crossed the room to give his aunt a kiss and a bear hug.

"How is Miss Storm? I heard about last night and wanted to come earlier but was unable to get away from obligations that demanded my attention."

"Obligations? Hmmmm. We will get to that in a minute. Josie is in shock and heartbroken."

Marcus's shoulders slumped. She had already decided he had really done what everyone said he did. She had not trusted him. He swallowed hard. "Has the gossip been that bad?"

"We expected that her incident with Sir Bastian would be the talk of the town and cause her to be hoisted up for ridicule. Instead, she found sympathy and the entire *ton* gloating over the fall of the *Virtuous Viscount*."

Marcus winced. He hated that moniker. He sat down across from his aunt.

"So. Is it true? You entered a house of prostitution?"

Marcus bit his lip and nodded, yet maintained his eye contact with his aunt. The inquisition he feared had begun.

"What do you have to say for yourself?"

"I would have a lot to say if I could. But I cannot."

"You will not defend your actions?"

Marcus shook his head and frowned. He looked down at his hands. "No."

"I apologize if you find me less than understanding, Marcus. You were raised better than that, were you not? What happened to your determination to live a life that was a witness and avoid the temptations and lures that society threw out?" She paused, pursed her lips, and exhaled loudly. "To say I am disappointed in you is an understatement."

"I understand and anticipated that. Do you think that you and Miss Storm will be able to forgive me?"

"Are you sorry you were there?"

"I cannot say that I am."

Lady Grey glared at her nephew with narrowed eyes. "If you were to do it over again, would you have made a different choice?"

"I made the best decision I could at the time. I know I did what I had to do to for the noblest of reasons."

"Noble? How dare you call your actions noble? Indefensible, and yet you want forgiveness. Unrepentant, and you want it overlooked? How am I to forgive you if you show no remorse?"

"I am sorry if my actions have caused you and Miss Storm any pain or embarrassment."

"It was humiliating for me to defend you when I knew nothing of what had transpired. Josie suffered a terrible shock last night and today discovered that the man she believed to be true had instead been unfaithful. How do you think that made her feel?"

"After all we have been through, I had hoped she would know better than to believe ill of me."

"It is hard for either of us to do that when you admit that what the gossips say is true." Lady Grey's posture sank a bit as she continued. "Josie reported that on Sunday, a beautiful young woman flirted with you after church. I didn't observe this. I am unaware of who might have sought your favors, but it disturbed Josie."

"Sunday?" Marcus leaned back and tried to remember. Whom had he seen on Sunday? "I remember trying to focus on the service when all I wanted to do was look at Miss Storm. I could not tell you what the sermon was about, to my shame. I do not recall any women flirting with me. Henrietta is back and delighted in telling me about hers' and Charles's trip to the continent. She enjoyed herself immensely, and marriage seems to suit her well. She is now setting up her household and redecorating the rooms. I daresay my sister will have Charles in the poorhouse before long." He shook his head and smiled at the memory.

"Henrietta is in town? And she has yet to come and visit me? I long to see her. Was she happy?"

"Blissfully. Do you think that might have been whom Josie saw me with? She has never met my sister, and Henrietta and I are close. Perhaps that was what she witnessed?"

Lady Grey frowned. "Quite possible." She looked at her nephew. "She has missed you, Marcus. You've stayed away far more than necessary."

"I have a reputation for not singling out any particular woman. If I were to have done so with Josie, it might have hindered her attempts to have a wider choice of suitors to experience. I want it to be her choice, not the man who was convenient."

"If you had paid more attention, maybe this recent behavior would be more easily overlooked by her."

"Or she would be even more hurt and singled out for pity amongst society. At this point, you are the only one tainted by any shame. I apologize for that."

"I still do not understand why you would jeopardize Josie's affections and your reputation by such foolish actions."

Marcus leaned forward on the chair with his hands clasped in front of him, elbows on knees. "Sometimes a man has to make difficult decisions and weigh the bad against the worst. I did what I had to for reasons I cannot explain. I will say this. If I would have had to die to accomplish what I did, I would have done so."

"Die?" Dorothea breathed out the word as she searched Marcus's eyes.

He maintained her gaze and hoped that his unspoken plea...

Lady Grey sighed. "I will not pretend to understand, Marcus. I love you, believe in you, and will stand by you."

"I appreciate that. It is the best I could hope for at this time. May I see Miss Storm?"

"Not at this moment. She is resting. If you want to try to visit tomorrow or send a note around to her, I would approve. Tread carefully."

Marcus nodded, relieved to have won his aunt to his side. But Josie? Would she understand without knowing the truth? "She's had a rough time of it. Pray that she forgives me even though it appears I don't deserve it."

"I will, dear boy."

With that, Marcus rose and left.

~*~

The next day dawned gray and damp. Josie's mood matched the weather as she sat at her window lost in thought. Carriages went by with grooms hunched over and hats pulled low. Horses plodded down the streets with their heads bent. She spied footmen running to deliver messages. No birds sang, and a gossamer layer of fog cloaked the houses. It was too early for the *ton* to be out, as most would have arrived home well after midnight.

Josie did not have any excuse to sleep anymore. With all her shed tears, she was weary and drained. She did not want to face this day.

She refocused her gaze on the raindrops splashing against the glass. Memories of her time at Rose Hill with Marcus rose before her. The weeks of her recovery were a haze compared to the vibrant memories she had of conversations, dinners, and walks in the garden. With Marcus. It was always Marcus. Even his friends faded into the background of her remembrances. How different life was there compared to London. What if she had married Lord Remington and found out about his wayward actions later? It was too late for her heart, but at least she wasn't trapped in a loveless marriage. Tears came. She wiped them away.

She tried to draw, but creativity had fled. The page showed dark colors, and as much as she tried to think of other images, the only ones that came to mind were the newssheet or the beautiful blonde who laughed up into his eyes after church. She would not paint that. She cleaned up and threw her brushes into their storage box.

She meandered to the music room and sat at the pianoforte. Her fingers caressed the keys, on the darker minor chords. They suited her mood, and the sounds that resulted were somber. They built in intensity as a melody emerged and her fingers floated over the keys. The rise and fall of volume, and the plaintive cries of higher notes against the backdrop of doom pounding in the lower register, gave voice to her heart. When the notes stopped and the vibrations hovered in the air, she closed her eyes, spent but relieved.

"That was devastatingly beautiful," whispered Marcus as he entered the room and closed the door behind him.

Josie startled but remained silent. She watched him move across the room, all strength, grace, and so handsome. Longing warred with anger in her heart. The reality of his deception was like a splash of cold water on her face. She sat up straighter and lifted her chin as she watched him warily.

"I've not heard that composition before."

"It was an original," she said flatly.

"May we talk, Josie? I think there is much to be said between us."

"I do not know that you could say anything to make this present reality any better."

Marcus was by her side and knelt down on one knee by the piano bench. "I love you, Josie, and would never do anything to intentionally hurt you." He saw her bruised arms. "Bastion hurt you?"

"Why would you care? You were not there. Apparently, you had more important things to do." Josie diverted her gaze to her hands lying in her lap. "I wonder if I really knew you."

He grasped her hand, and she tried to pull away, but he held firm.

"I am tired of being bullied, Lord Remington."

Marcus brought the hand up to his mouth, placed a kiss there, and handed it back to her. "I could never bully you into loving me. I would give my life for you if it was required."

"Spanish coin, my lord."

"I would hope you would never find me untruthful in anything I say. If you want me to leave and not return or be found in your company, as much as it would pain me, I would bow to your wishes."

Josie looked out to the windows at the rain that continued to run like a living curtain against the windowpane. What could she say? The warmth of his kiss lingered on the back of her hand.

A kiss of Judas perhaps? Part of her longed to kiss him, and the other part wanted to slap his handsome face. Without a word, she rose and walked over to the window to gaze outside. She observed him there reflected in the glass. She closed her eyes and leaned her forehead against the cool surface.

After what seemed like an eternity, Marcus spoke in the silence. "I'm disappointed but understand. Farewell, Miss Storm."

She heard the outside door close, and the tears descended.

~*~

That evening, Lady Grey insisted they attend some

balls and hold their heads up high in case there was any murmuring against Miss Storm.

Josie wore long gloves to cover up the bruises left by Sir Bastian, and she found that she had no such way to cover up her heartbreak. She lacked her usual vitality but found plenty of partners willing to lead her out on the dance floor.

Lord Harrow was amongst them. "My dear Miss Storm. What has given you a case of the blue-devils?"

"I know not of what you speak, Lord Harrow." She avoided meeting his penetrating gaze.

"You cannot pull the wool over my eyes, my dearest Miss Storm. If you are concerned about the incident with Sir Bastian, trust me when I say the collective *ton* has sighed in relief at his downfall."

Grateful for the distraction from the real cause of her heartache, Josie eagerly jumped into this line of conversation. "It was a distasteful incident."

"I suspect you still have bruises you are hiding under your gloves."

"You are too astute, my lord."

"I suspect you also have bought into the *beau monde's* recent gossip about Lord Remington."

Josie stiffened her spine, resolved to show that it was of no consequence to her what Remington had done. "I would prefer not to discuss the topic."

"I bow to your wishes."

Lord Harrow's face had fallen with her statement, and she sensed disapproval emanating from him. Did he blindly trust his friend's integrity against the reality of what everyone knew happened? Maybe Lord Harrow was not as sharp as she had first thought. That she should lose the friendships made at Rose Hill saddened her. These were men she had grown to like and trust. The dance ended in silence and a courteous bow as Lord Harrow handed her off to another partner seeking her hand.

It seemed as if her popularity had soared in the wake of Sir Bastian. She had never been sought out and fawned over as much as she had this evening. Her heart was not into engaging in even the mildest of flirtations. All the men seemed silly and immature. She wondered at their extracurricular activities in spite of their stellar appearances at a ball and courteous manners. Were they all engaged in liaisons with women other than their wives? The reality of it was that many of them probably were.

The last of the scales of naiveté fell from her eyes as she surveyed the mass of humanity around her. All immersed in some kind of sin but loathe to confess it. One small misstep away from scandal, they found fault in others so as to deflect it from being revealed in themselves.

Unfortunately, was she any different? She may not have engaged in any indiscretion, but she had been harsh and judgmental. God called her to forgive, but she found that hard to do when her heart ached. All the while, as she danced, she forced a smile on her face and gave these dubious men her attentions for the span of the measures of a dance. She would be gone from town soon enough.

~*~

Lord Remington arrived at the ball later in the evening and watched Josie go through the motions of the dances with a variety of dandies and Corinthians. Her smile was pasted on. He had promised he would leave her alone, and that meant he needed to ignore her when every fibre of his being called out to him to draw closer to her. He ached deep inside as he watched her on the arms of other men. He longed for her heart to belong to him alone. She glistened like a diamond amongst paste. He felt tawdry at the attentions lavished on him by many women in the *ton*. Married and unmarried alike viewed him far differently than before, and the innuendos were distasteful. It galled him to think that his standing amongst the *beau monde* had actually risen due to his alleged indiscretion.

But oh, at what a cost.

Later at home, he reflected on the new alliances he had gained that evening. He reflected on the irony of gaining the world and losing his own soul. Except for him, it was Josie who had his soul. Anguished prayers preceded a restless sleep.

Morning dawned bright and sunny. Marcus had an appointment for an early morning ride in the park with Jared.

"How you doing, ol' boy?" his brother asked with a smirk.

"Not well." Marcus gave him the evil eye. His eyelids scratched like sandpaper.

"Josie did not take it well?"

"That would be an understatement. No questions. No accusations. Presumed guilty."

"I feared that outcome but had prayed it would not come to pass. You did the right thing. She is alive today because of you."

"I knew the risks going in." Marcus sighed.

Jared looked at his brother with brows furrowed together. "Is there anything I can do?"

Marcus shrugged. "I doubt it. I have gained far more support for my bills against poverty and prostitution. Some believe I was there doing research." Marcus gave his brother half a grin. He slowed his horse to stop at the side of the pathway, and Jared pulled up alongside. "I would never have wanted harm to come to Miss Storm, but the idea of her marrying another man churns my insides. How do I live with this?"

"You could have never lived with yourself had you done nothing and she had perished. If you had not acted, Sir Bastian would have also been a part of the demise of more British soldiers and possibly tipped the war in Napoleon's favor. You have no idea the amount of smuggling that was going on through his estate. We have found the correspondence that implicated him, and while we have not identified who this Black Diamond is, Bastian is still undergoing interrogation and we may know soon. He is going through withdrawal from opium. He was a madman and certainly had plans to hand Josie over for torture and possibly death as a means to some larger end we haven't quite discovered."

Marcus nodded. "I needed to hear that. But is she really out of danger?"

"Why do you ask?" Jared started his horse forward, and Marcus followed alongside.

"We never did resolve that carriage accident. Bastian didn't own to that, did he?" Marcus inquired.

"He professes to know nothing of it, and on that score, I believe he tells the truth."

"Jo...Miss Storm might still be in danger."

The men exchanged glances.

"I am at your disposal as I'm sure the rest of your friends will be."

"I hope to leave for Rose Hill as soon as she is safe.

Will you join me?" Marcus asked.

"Changing the subject? I have a few more weeks before I am expected to return to the Peninsula and would be glad to join you at home for some fishing."

"I will be grateful of the company. This was not the way I had envisioned my autumn. I had hoped to end the season with a wedding."

"I know, and I am sorry."

Jared spurred his horse forward and with a "Whoop!" Marcus was soon on his heels as they tore across the meadow before they returned home.

~*~

"What now?" Marcus said as he strode into his house after his ride with his brother.

A guest awaited him. Mr. Neville bowed before him as he entered the library. "I apologize for inconveniencing you so early in the day, my lord. I have information that may be of interest to you."

"Let us have it." Marcus motioned for the man to have a seat and took the chair opposite.

"I have continued my investigation of Lord Widmore at Lord Chester's request due to the carriage accident that befell the Widmore women and injured Miss Storm. I trust Miss Storm has recovered?"

"Yes. She was in fine health when last I saw her."

"Lord Chester begged me to seek you for advice while he was out of town to save time traveling to and from his estate."

"I recall that conversation."

"Let me tell you what I've learned since then."

"Please do." Marcus leaned forward, full of curiosity.

24

Another night. Another ball. Josie found the enchantment of these events wore thin when she could no longer anticipate dancing with a certain someone. It was not that her partners lacked charm, grace, good looks, or even fortune, should those have been selling points for her in finding a husband. She could not like any of them. She missed Marcus.

Lord Westcombe danced with her twice and took her into dinner, for which she was grateful.

"Excuse me for saying this, Miss Storm, but you look decidedly down pin this evening. Are you weary of the season already?"

"I will be glad for it to end and to be home again. Finding enjoyment in all this frivolity is beyond my ability at present."

"Chin up. Smile. There, that is much better. You cannot let the old tabbies over there think you are anything less than enamored of my presence. My reputation must be upheld." He winked.

Josie forced a grin. "I am sorry I am such poor company this evening. I have the beginning of megrims. I will ask Lady Grey to take me home before the dancing resumes."

"I will help you locate her when you are done eating. I wanted to inquire how you and Lord Remington fared."

"We do not."

Phillip frowned. "You believed the gossip? You surprise me." He sat up straighter and moved slightly away from her.

She shivered at the chill of his withdrawal. "How could I not? He did not deny it or beg forgiveness. He only asked me to trust him."

"Blind trust?"

"Blind...?"

Phillip nodded. "Maybe you need to close your eyes and remember who that man really is. Ask yourself, would he do what the *beau monde* thinks he did? Appearances can be deceiving, and the *ton* delights in coming to the most damaging conclusions."

"What are you saying?"

"I have known Marcus for many years. I do not need to know the truth of what happened. I can see it in his eyes. He is innocent of the slander that has been spread."

"But if he is innocent, why will he not defend himself?"

"Doing so would only inflame the gossip more. Have you ever heard people protesting their guilt? It can often appear to be a defensive posture to avoid consequences, and it rarely works."

Josie stared at her plate. She no longer had an appetite. She laid her fork down on the table.

"He loves you, Miss Storm. Of that I have no doubt."

"I am confused."

"Do you think he does not understand you are human? I may not be a man of faith, but I have been around my friend long enough to ask this—whose sin is greater, the one who has the appearance of evil or the one who refuses to forgive?"

Josie's head snapped up to look Phillip in the eye.

"I would do almost anything for Lord Remington, Miss Storm. I would trust him with my life. I apologize if my plain speaking has offended. Up until this point, I had confidence that you would be the perfect wife for him. Perhaps I was mistaken."

Tears tickled the corners of her eyes. "He said he would die for me if he had to."

Phillip's raised eyebrows and widened eyes seemed to say, *I told you so.*

The musicians were tuning up in the other room. Phillip rose and presented his arm to escort Josie to her aunt. He gave them both a brief bow before he returned to the ballroom to claim his next partner.

Night after night, the dreariness of the dances and balls and parties continued. Josie wondered if Phillip were correct. Had she misjudged Marcus? Was she more blind to the truth now than when she had lost her sight? It was far easier to trust Marcus when she had no choice. And now?

Now she may have lost him forever.

~*~

Marcus spent time in Parliament and worked on writing his speeches and managing estate business.

Jared continued his daily visits to Whitehall and prepared for his return to the Peninsula.

Together they had arranged round-the-clock guard over Miss Storm.

Marcus had not told his aunt of the extra protection for them, as he did not want her anxious. He hardly slept. Marcus realized he would likely not rest until he knew Josie was free from all possible harm.

Not being able to be closer to her made the task more challenging. He had to be circumspect. If only she were his wife. He leaned back in his chair and put his hands behind his head as he stretched out his legs. *Wife*. She was the only one he could have ever imagined in that role. And even now, although she didn't believe in him, he still wanted her and only her by his side for the rest of his life.

Was this love or foolishness? She avoided looking at him when they were at the same social events. He was invisible to her. Yet he was aware of where she was at all times. She was in his dreams at night, and even before he would see her in a room amongst a crowd, he knew she was present. He could not help his attraction. It bordered on obsession.

He would honor her request and never approach her again. That was difficult when he was determined to protect her to the extent that he was able. He sighed. Love was brutal. He had started out in the spring determined that it was time to find a wife, and now that he had found her and was rebuffed, he had lost all interest in seeking a different bride.

~*~

Mr. Storm arrived in town and escorted Josie and Lady Grey for an evening of fêtes.

Josie was happy to have her father there to view her social success and only hoped he would not notice the sorrow in her heart.

She was surprised when her father led Lady Grey out to the floor to dance. She hugged herself as they danced perfectly in tune with each other. Sorrow overcame her at what she had lost. She had once

Susan M. Baganz

danced with in perfect harmony with Lord Remington.

The evening was tedious and long, and Josie just wanted to curl up in bed and have a good cry. She longed for Marcus, but how could she accept his convoluted non-apology? Nothing made sense, and even her heart disagreed with her head on the matter.

Mr. Storm leaned back in the carriage on the ride home, smiled, and sighed. "What a delightful evening with two of London's most beautiful ladies."

Lady Dorothea's corresponding smile was bright in the illumination by streetlights they passed. "It was quite agreeable." The older woman looked at Mr. Storm as she spoke.

Josie looked out the window and declined comment. She did not want to dampen her father's visit to town with her melancholy.

Mr. Storm helped the women from the carriage and escorted them inside. "Josie, would you mind spending a few minutes to attend me before I depart? You are tired. I shall not keep you long."

Her father give Lady Grey a speaking glance, and the hostess withdrew and closed the door to the drawing room.

Mr. Storm took his daughter's hand, led her over to the settee, and joined her there, setting aside her reticule and fan on the table nearby.

"What is it, Father?" Jose found comfort in his hand holding hers.

"Something is amiss. You cannot hide from me that you are unhappy. You are pale, and the sparkle in your eyes is gone. Would you care to share with me what is heavy on your heart?"

"Lady Grey did not explain what happened?" Josie blinked back her tears.

Her father nodded. His eyes were warm, and his brows furrowed in concern. "Will you tell me in your own words?"

Josie stared to weep softly, her father enfolded her in his arms, and she soaked his neck cloth. Emotionally spent, she hiccupped and raised her eyes. "I ruined it, Father. I did not believe him, and he will never forgive me, but everyone said it was true, and I do not understand why this happened."

"Now if I had not heard the more specific details from Lady Grey, I would say that you just spoke a bunch of nonsense." He smiled at her as his thumb came up to wipe away a stray tear. "Listen here, young lady. If Remington is half the man I think he is, he is worthy of your trust. I expect he would resume a courtship if you would only give him a sign of some kind." Josie started to talk, but he gently placed a finger over her lips.

"Hear me out. Do not tell me. I know what the gossips have said. I have seen the infamous drawing. My intuition tells me there is more to the story than society claims. 'Tis often the case with gossip, even what the papers report. I may not have been of as elevated status as your grandfather, but I've seen enough over the years to know when a man has integrity and when he doesn't. Lord Remington is of the first camp. He is sure to have his enemies in Parliament, and politics can be a dirty business.

"It is good for you to realize this now, my dear, because it is likely to be the first of many such scandals when you wed into the upper ten thousand. Deserved or not, it is the warp and woof of this society. What is more important than what everyone else says, however, is this—what is God telling you?"

"How do I know what is my own wishful thinking and what is truth?"

"Pray. Listen. Ask Him to show you and make it clear what you are to do when the moment is right. I will pray as well."

"Thank you, Father."

"I love you, daughter." With that, he kissed her forehead and said farewell.

Josie slept better that evening and awoke hopeful.

The rounds of visits took their toll even though the highlight was now on new scandals about some debutante being caught alone with a man or another eloping, or some titled gentlemen dueling on the Green over some perceived debt of honor that seemed to emerge daily.

Josie found it tiresome.

That afternoon, she had a barouche ride with Sir Tidley, whom she found enjoyable as he spun tales about people around them.

"Miss Storm, observe that young milkmaid over there by that tree? She is really the lost princess from Estonia, kidnapped and brought to London fifteen years past and raised humbly to keep her from discovery. And that young man, should he choose to marry her, will someday be a prince, even though right now he mucks out the stalls down at the stables at the east end of the park."

Josie grinned. "But, Sir Michael, should they be happy in their changed circumstances?"

Michael grinned and wiggled his eyebrows at her. "And why should they not be? A tidy fortune can cover a multitude of sins."

Josie's smile faltered. "Not all sins are easily wiped clean, Sir Tidley."

"Are you harboring some sinister secret? Is there a skeleton in your closet dancing merrily in eagerness to escape?"

Josie shook her head. "No, sir, but I do harbor my own failures, and sometimes the strictures on us in society make it difficult to make right the wrongs."

"And who, my dear, would you make restitution to?"

Josie glanced at him and searched his eyes. "I. That is to say…it is a private matter, and I cannot say more." She focused on her hands clenched in her lap. She would not use Marcus's friends as a go-between. She needed to find a way to speak to Marcus herself. She glanced up and out of the barouche to the pastoral scene beyond them. "I apologize, Sir Michael, for taking the enjoyment out of our ride." Josie pointed to a little boy punting a boat in the pond in the distance. "So, what tale belies that young man's existence?"

Sir Michael regarded her in silence for a few moments before he nodded, smiled knowingly at her change of topic, and began again to render another comical story about the young man.

Soon, she found herself smiling again. Josie prayed that somehow she would find a way to speak to Lord Remington should he happen to be present at one of the three balls she was scheduled to attend that evening.

Josie's plans were frustrated as she counted down the days until she could leave London.

She enjoyed the sights of town in the company of some of the young men who had been courting her. The Tower, St. Paul's Cathedral, and even an evening at Vauxhall Gardens for finely sliced ham and viewing the fireworks were exciting. Her enjoyment was tinged with regret that she was not experiencing these with a certain gentleman with dark wavy hair and chocolate colored eyes. She had tried to catch his eye, but he never acknowledged her presence. Her heart shrank. She would be leaving town in a few short days. Time was running out.

~*~

The next day, Josie took Molly with her on a walk to the small bookstore on Larson Lane, next to the confectioner's shop she had spied a few days past. She had hoped to purchase some books and treats for her siblings. Maybe she would purchase a book for herself for when she got home. It was a perfect fall day. The air was crisp, and for once, London did not smell as awful as it usually did with the wind directing the odor of the Thames away from them.

Even with all of her dancing, she had missed the exercise of her daily walks. Today she enjoyed lengthening her stride as they made their way. She stopped to purchase a posy from the small stall at the end of the street and paid generously for it. She inhaled the fresh smell of mums from a tidy garden as she walked past. She took in the sights of the street sweeps and horses pulling dray carts loaded with produce, young children herded by their nannies, and a few of the fashionably elite out to purchase items to take with them to the country.

Josie entered the bookstore and enjoyed the smell of leather and ink. After a short consultation with the proprietor, she made her selections and bought a bag of treats for her brothers and sister. She would miss the luxury of easy access to these things when she returned to Westwood. Molly carried her purchases, although Josie held her posy and occasionally lifted it to her face to inhale the scent and smile. It took her back to a happier time at Rose Hill. And Marcus. She frowned. All her thoughts brought her to the same place. Marcus.

Josie wondered if she would ever visit Rose Hill again and grieved the loss—not of that beautiful estate, but of the man who owned it. Lost in her thoughts, she did not notice the carriage that stopped alongside the curb or the large man who exited.

He approached her with all courtesy. "Youz be Miss Storm?"

This huge ox of a man with his bushy red hair and bearded face took Josie aback. She hesitated a moment before she responded. "Yes."

"Iz a message from Lord Chester. Hez wants youz to come right away if youz would. It be urgent like."

"My grandfather is in town?"

Molly shook her head. "I do not think—"

Another man grabbed the young maid from behind.

Josie screamed but found herself equally overcome by the red-haired oaf. Whatever he placed over her mouth smelled horrible. The posies slipped from her fingers as darkness descended.

Josie awoke on the floor of a moving carriage, confused. Her head ached from the repeated bouncing against the hard floor, and she struggled to right herself. Her stomach rebelled violently, and she almost retched. Dizziness overwhelmed her, and she tried to take deep breaths. She prayed. *Think, Josie. Lord, help!*

She was alone, and it was dark. From the uneven rhythm of the horses' hooves, she noticed how ill matched and tired they were. She inched her way up to the seat and found the outside shutters of the carriage closed. Trapped. She remembered the attack on Molly. A red giant. Obviously, Lord Chester had been a ruse. Her grandfather would never have treated her thus.

Josie cast up her accounts on the floor of the carriage. The smell almost caused her to do it again. Her head pounded, and she fought to think clearly. She weakly contemplated jumping from the carriage, until she discovered the locked doors. She prayed and leaned back into the corner and braced herself against the opposing seat in an unsuccessful attempt to stop the throbbing in her head and the roiling of her stomach.

The carriage rolled to a stop in a small village. Josie heard the difference in the sound of the horses' hooves on the cobblestones. There was noise in the stable yard and instructions given to change horses. The door unlocked, and the giant peered in.

"I suppose youz want to use the privy? I will escort you. No talkin' to no one or youz don't make it to the coast."

Josie nodded and experienced a flood of dizziness as she exited the carriage.

He roughly escorted her around the back of a little inn to an outhouse.

When she was finished, the giant half- jerked, half-walked her back to the carriage. He gave her a small piece of bread to eat.

She refused, afraid her stomach would rebel. The old ripped squabs were more visible, and someone had thrown straw over the floor where she had made a mess earlier. The stench overwhelmed, but she did find, to her relief, that the black covers were missing from the windows.

He shoved her into the carriage without ceremony, and the doors locked from the outside.

Josie leaned back in the corner and shivered in fear.

~*~

Lord Remington had trailed Josie discreetly when the attack occurred. He sent his tiger off to round up his friends and sprang his team in pursuit of the carriage Josie was in. He stayed a distance behind so as not to arouse suspicion.

Mr. Neville had also been trailing the pair and the man, at his signal, now saw to the welfare of the abigail.

Marcus's only hope now was that his friends would arrive, as prearranged, to help him out before it was too late. He doubted he could handle that giant and the other man alone. But he would do whatever it took to ensure Josie's safety.

25

Marcus drove into the yard and spied Josie. He was outnumbered and chose to continue to follow until the others caught up. He hoped it would be soon.

The red giant told his weasel-faced partner that if they didn't hurry, they would not make Dover by evening and he had too much money riding on this "prime piece" to miss their packet.

Marcus scribbled and left a note with the innkeeper for his friends. With new horses put to his carriage, he was ready to resume his journey behind the kidnappers.

They called her a "fancy piece," which indicated they intended to sell her to a brothel. Even if his friend did not arrive before the carriage reached Dover, Marcus would do everything in his power to prevent her from boarding any boat. The thought of what would happen to her if he failed was too horrific to bear.

That any other man would someday marry Josie galled him. She belonged to him. As the horses' hooves pounded the dirt road beneath him and the wagon bounced, he mourned again the loss of Josie's good favor and even the right to fight for her. Dust flew in his face stirred up by the carriage in front of him, causing his eyes to burn. Fight for her he would, even if she never chose to believe in his integrity. He prayed that his brother and friends would be there to help or

Marcus was most certainly riding to his death.

Prayer. When had he last prayed? In typical fashion, he took it upon himself to assume responsibility for the lives of those around him, including Josie. A dip in the road forced his bottom off his seat, and he came down with a hard jolt. He grinned and shook his head. *Yes, God. You definitely have my attention.* The miles flew past as he prayed fervently for God to intervene in some way and rescue Josie, while at the same time, Marcus surrendered himself to the possibility that he would be forced to sacrifice more than his reputation this time.

~*~

Josie watched the scenery pass at dizzying speed. They exchanged horses again in another small village. The giant had peeked in and leered at her. Terror overwhelmed her, and she wondered if death would be preferable to what they had planned. She was dizzy from the drug they had used. It made thinking about her situation nigh on impossible. Weak and helpless, she recited Scripture to calm herself and could almost hear Marcus's comforting voice from when he had read the words of Psalm to her only a few months past.

I will lift up mine eyes unto the hills, from whence cometh my help. My help cometh from the LORD which made heaven and earth.

He will not suffer thy foot to be moved: He that keepeth thee will not slumber. Behold, he that keepeth Israel shall neither slumber nor sleep.

The LORD is thy keeper; the LORD is thy shade upon thy right hand. The sun shall not smite thee by day, nor the moon by night.

The LORD shall preserve thee from all evil: he shall preserve thy soul.

The LORD shall preserve thy going out and thy coming in from this time forth, and even forevermore.

Josie's future was uncertain, and she prayed for rescue. She had a sense of peace that God was aware of what was happening and was there with her in the midst of it all. She shivered, hugged herself, and tried to fight the heaviness in her eyelids.

She awoke with the slowing of the carriage. Peering outside the carriage window, she observed a posting house. It was dark, and a thick fog had rolled in. From the cursing she heard from her captors, they had obviously not reached as far as they intended. She shivered in fear about what a night in an inn with them would mean.

Lord, please save me.

The giant roughly pulled Josie from the carriage, and she struggled to stand as the world spun wildly, around her. The air was cold, and she shivered. She wished she had worn her redingote to the bookstore earlier. It seemed she was in a nightmare until she heard a familiar voice.

A stable hand had come to take the horses and spoke with a cockney accent. She startled at him.

He glanced at her and gave her a cheeky grin and a wink. Sir Michael Tidley!

Red made it clear to the servant that the horses were to be ready very early in the morning.

Michael tipped his hat and led the horses off to the stable.

Josie glanced around. Was Sir Michael alone, or were there others?

Another carriage pulled into the courtyard as Red

escorted her to the door of the posting inn.

She sensed him. Marcus was here. Why would he come for her? Her spirit deflated as she remembered her cruelty to him at their last meeting. Did she dare hope that he would aid her?

Red deposited her on a bench by the front door with a growl to stay as if she were a dog. Not that she was in any condition to run. She couldn't stand on her own without blacking out. Red went to talk to his weasely partner. Soon Red came over and roughly hauled Josie back to her feet and moved her toward the door of the Inn.

Lord Remington blocked their entrance.

Josie gazed up at Marcus and feared what might happen. He flickered a glance at her but focused on her captor.

Red glared back, his hand that held her arm clenched even tighter.

"You're hurting me," she yelped.

"Maybe you should leave the lady alone," Marcus ground out. His fists clenched.

"She's mine."

"I beg to differ." Marcus did not flinch. His face had a fierce determination she had never seen before.

Josie swayed as dizziness and fear overwhelmed her, along with the scent of the slums that emanated from the brute beside her. She had the urge to retch again but dreaded doing that on Marcus. Before she realized what was happening, the brute shoved her onto the bench so hard she smacked her elbow against the wooden back support. The sudden move sent the world spinning wildly.

Wiping at her mouth with a handkerchief that somehow found its way into her possession, she looked up to observe Marcus's gaze on her, brows furrowed in concern.

Before she was able to respond, the red giant grabbed Marcus by the shoulder, spun him around, and leveled a punch into his gut.

Josie winced. She looked to the left and recognized Lord Westcombe arguing with Weasel.

A knife slipped out of the kidnapper's sleeve and barely missed Phillip's side as the aristocrat moved quickly and retaliated with force.

The refinement she had known these men for disappeared in the fierce battle that erupted. Lord Harrow, Sir Tidley, and Captain Allendale appeared from the stables.

"A good mill! Let us join them, men!" shouted Michael as the men ran to join their friends. Michael joined Philip in his battle against Weasel.

Jared and Theodore ran to assist Marcus.

Josie watched in horror as the men pummeled each other, feigned, and ducked as knives slashed through the air. It was a convoluted dance with the only music coming from the cheering of the crowd gathered from the town and inside the building where she sat shivering from cold and fear. She prayed fervently that Marcus and his friends would prevail.

Michael and Phillip soon stood over an unconscious Weasel. They bound him and left him in the dust. Their clothing was torn, and blood dripped from Michael's nose, yet he smiled as if energized. Together they turned to assist Marcus, Theo, and Jared.

Marcus fought well against the giant. But the large man was too much for him. The giant handled all three men coming at him with ease. He roared as he tossed Jared aside like a rag doll. Marcus roared back as he lunged for the giant's stomach in an effort to knock him over. The bigger man tripped over Theo's foot in the process but was quickly back on his feet and fought fiercely. Michael joined in the melee.

Phillip tended to Jared, got him up and dragged him over to sit next to Josie.

Jared's ripped shirt was missing a sleeve. He leaned his head back against the stone side of the building behind them and moaned. Blood trickled from a cut to his forehead, and Josie could only stare. Gently she placed a hand on his forearm. "Captain Allendale?"

"'Tis all right, Miss Storm. I cannot move my left arm. It hurts like the devil. I've been through worse." Jared gazed at the courtyard to where his brother and friends battled. "Lord, help them," he whispered.

Theo had taken a punch that had knocked the wind out of him, and he sat dazed to the outside of the imaginary circle within which the men fought.

Michael and Phillip had backed off when Marcus had yelled at them for getting in the way, "He's mine!" They gave Marcus his space, but it had not gone well. They were tense and ready to step in if necessary.

The giant started to lose steam.

Marcus moved slower. His knuckles were bloodied. His face was battered, but he remained focused and intent on Red. He had tossed his coat aside, and his ripped vest soon joined the dust. Blood spread across part of his back from a knife wound.

~*~

Marcus had never hurt so much in his life. The pain was cathartic as he sought to purge the hurt and suffering he had carried with him at the loss of Josie. He struggled not to look over to her. Jared was injured and sat by her side. He trusted his brother to take care of her. He had never faced so fierce an enemy, in fencing or in the boxing ring at Gentleman Jackson's, but then again, this man did not adhere to the rules of those sports. Marcus had abandoned all attempts at courtesy and quickly switched to fighting dirty. He did not know if he could take this man, but at least he had to try.

Michael and Phillip stood poised and ready should he need them.

Marcus spat blood out of his mouth. He was breathing heavy, and in spite of the cool damp air, he was sweating. He gasped for breath in between blows and ducked as much as he could. The giant tossed Marcus to the ground, and Marcus found his hand close to the gun that had fallen out of his coat when the fight began. In desperation, he reached for it and cocked the hammer back. He rose to his feet and found Red charging at him like a bull. They struggled for the gun, and it discharged as both men tumbled to the ground. Red went limp on top of Marcus.

The crowd stilled, not sure who had been shot in the scuffle. Marcus was not even sure himself, as every part of his body screamed in agony. Marcus growled to his friends, "Get this brute off me."

Phillip and Michael rolled the giant on to his back. With great effort, Marcus rose to his knees and pointed the gun at the man's chest. Phillip bent to take the giant's pulse and nodded to Marcus that he was alive.

Red's eyes fluttered open and he gazed at Marcus. The giant's breath shuddered in his body as blood seeped from the wound in his chest.

"Who paid you?" Marcus asked as his chest heaved in an effort to breathe. He thought he would pass out but wanted to finish what he'd started, hopefully without humiliating himself.

"Lord Widmore. Wanted 'er ded. I wern't gonna kill 'er, only sell 'er."

"As a prostitute?"

Red nodded.

Marcus fought back the urge to punch the man again.

Red weakly shook his head, and his eyes rolled back in his head.

Phillip checked his pulse and pulled his eyelids shut. He gave Marcus a grim look. "He's gone."

Marcus nodded, disabled his gun, and handed it to Michael.

Phillip rose to his feet, and they looked at each other across the dead body.

Marcus shook his head at Phillip. "Goodness, Phillip. I do not think I have ever seen you so out of fashion."

Phillip grinned. Dirt streaked his face, and his hair fell in his eyes. "You do not look very fashionable yourself, my friend."

Marcus's legs went weak. "Theo. Michael. A little help if you would."

26

Marcus, held up by Michael and Theo, stopped in front of Josie. Tears trickled down her cheeks at the sight of him battered and bloodied. As he came to stand there, her heart welled with love for this man.

"Are you well, Miss Storm?" he asked formally. His eyes were distant and glassy.

"I am as well as ever I could be. I am grateful to you for coming to my rescue." She was not sure Marcus ever heard those words as his head wobbled forward.

Theo and Michael dragged Marcus into the inn with Lord Westcombe getting the door.

Phillip returned, helped Jared to rise and offered his other arm to Josie, who shakily stood to her feet. Slowly, they entered the inn, where Phillip had procured a private parlour.

Jared slumped in a high-backed chair by the fireplace, leaned his head back, and closed his eyes. Josie stumbled to another chair on the other side of the fireplace and collapsed into it. She glanced at Phillip.

"Miss Storm, I' need to check on Lord Remington. I will arrange for food and drink to be brought in to you."

"Thank you, Lord Westcombe, but shouldn't Captain Allendale also be seen by the doctor?"

Captain Allendale opened an eye to look at her. "All in good time, Miss Storm. I believe my brother got the worst of it, and when he has been tended to, as well as the others, I will take my turn."

Josie nodded.

Phillip left the room.

The room soon bustled with the proprietor and his wife, who placed a feast for them on the center table. When they finished, they bowed, retreated, and closed the door behind them.

"Go ahead and eat, Miss Storm. There is no need to stand on ceremony with me."

Josie gulped. Her stomach clenched. "I am not sure I can."

"Try, at least. My brother would have my hide, were he able, if I do not see to your care." Jared opened his eyes as he regarded her. He did not smile, but he winked.

Josie went to the table and sat by herself. She had been lonely, abandoned, and terrified in the carriage. Now that the adventure was over, she was lonely and wanted to cry. She was also hungry. She poured some port, took a sip, and began to relax. The smells coming from the hot food at the table—fresh baked bread, soup, and a joint of beef—all tempted her. She began to help herself to some of the offerings when the door opened again and Sir Michael entered.

Michael grinned at Josie. "A feast to celebrate our success, eh, Miss Storm? Except that you dine alone." He glanced over to Captain Allendale. "Jared, what kind of host are you? You should be ashamed of yourself."

Jared growled.

Michael laughed and walked over to the injured man. "Come, let us get you settled upstairs to await the doctor's ministrations."

Theo entered the room and assisted Jared in rising to his feet. "I will escort him up, Michael. Please sit and keep Miss Storm company. We should not have any more trouble…"

"But 'tis better to be safe than sorry." Michael pulled back his torn coat to reveal the gun at his waist. Michael sat at the corner of the table closest to Josie.

Josie regarded Michael carefully. His hair was wet and freshly combed, and a colorful bruise was developing around his left eye. The clothes he had been wearing before were that of a servant, but now he was dressed as a gentleman of fashion although with a sloppily tied cravat. Any other injuries hid behind a smile, a twinkle in his eyes, and his natty attire.

Theodore and Jared left.

"Miss Storm," Michael began, "how have you fared through your adventure?"

Josie reached up and touched her hair, which had tumbled out of its pins. She had not even thought of repairing her appearance in the middle of all that had happened. She glanced at Sir Michael.

"'Tis of no consequence, Miss Storm, when one is among friends. You can tend to your appearance later. You look far better than the first time I ever saw you. I believe a carriage was involved in that, as well."

"Perhaps I should stay away from carriages, sir, since they seem to hold so many dangers for me."

Michael laughed and grimaced as a hand went to his side.

Josie raised an eyebrow.

"A rib, tis nothing that time will not heal." He bit into his buttered bread and closed his eyes as he hummed his contentment.

Josie grinned. How like Sir Michael to make

everything seem like a lark. She sipped her soup. The last vestiges of dizziness seemed to ebb away the more she ate. "How did you find me?" Josie had been stunned at how her rescuers had appeared.

Michael set his bread down. He poured a glass of ale, took a sip, and regarded her over the mug. Setting it down slowly, he finally spoke. "It was all Remy's doing, Miss Storm."

"Josie. Please. We were friends once, were we not?"

"Josie. Marcus worried that something bad might happen to you, even with Sir Bastian out of the way. Something was fishy with that first carriage accident."

"Accidents happen. Why would he worry about me? I would have thought he would have wanted nothing to do with me after the way I dismissed him."

"I cannot speak to that, but the first accident was not an accident. We didn't know, though, if you were the intended victim or not, and if the perpetrator would be bent on pursuing other attempts to harm you."

Josie set her spoon down and took a sip of her wine. Marcus had provided for her protection even after she had rebuffed him. All the time she had wanted to connect with him and he had her guarded and watched. It made no sense. "But how did you end up here?"

"Marcus followed you and sent for help when you were kidnapped. We took off in pursuit, and he left us messages at the inns along the way. We cut across country and managed to get here before the fog settled in. We had a great mill in the courtyard, you were saved, and here we sit." He raised a glass as if giving a celebratory toast.

Josie rose to stand by the window. She stared into the foggy night. Five men had come to her rescue, and all had suffered injury. For her.

Lord Westcombe entered the room and gently closed the door.

Josie glanced over to him, taking in his ripped shirt and the cuts on his face. He had washed up and had tried to repair the damage done to his person, but he still appeared careworn. Josie turned toward him. "I do not know how I could ever adequately thank you all for what you have done." She choked back her tears.

Phillip walked over, placed a hand on her shoulder, and guided her back to the table. "Everything will be fine, Miss Storm." He seated her, handed her the goblet, and bid her drink.

She complied.

Phillip sat next to her and filled his plate.

The two men glanced at each other.

Lord Westcombe shook his head.

"What is it?"

"Nothing," Sir Michael said.

"I do not believe you." She turned to Phillip. "Is it Lord Remington?" She did not need him to say anything, but the look of sorrow in his blue eyes spoke volumes. "He will recover." She whispered the words, almost as a prayer.

"He has not awakened yet. The doctor is concerned." Phillip focused on his food. "Josie, you must not blame yourself. He came of his own accord. We all did."

Josie sipped her wine. Marcus had fought valiantly. His friends as well, but Marcus had taken the brunt of the fighting upon himself. "I cannot believe I doubted him."

Theodore entered as she spoke.

"None of you doubted him, did you?" She glanced to all three of the men, who returned her gaze with steady eyes. "No, you would not. You trusted he would never betray his principles no matter what things looked like on the outside."

"We have known him longer than you, Josie," Michael replied gently.

She sighed. "Maybe so. But I was still wrong." Josie set down her glass, rose, and wandered back to the window.

Lord Harrow took a seat and pour something to drink.

Josie hugged her torso and silently cursed herself for doubting Marcus. If she had believed him, perhaps none of this would have happened. Now, how would she ever forgive herself if he did not survive? Tears streamed down her face. *Lord, please spare Marcus. Please heal him and his friends for they only sought to save me. Thank You for sending them.* She sensed an answer in her spirit, but it crushed her further to remember how many people had rejected and failed to believe in Jesus and how he had died for her sins. She became terrified that Marcus would also die because of her. The grief and fear overwhelmed her.

Phillip came to her with a linen napkin from the table. "I would offer you my handkerchief or even my cravat if either of them had survived the fight."

Josie turned and leaned into his dirty vest and ripped coat.

He tentatively placed an arm around her.

The contact only lasted for a moment before Josie backed away. "Thank you, Phillip."

"We will need to stay here this evening. The fog is too thick to attempt the drive back to London tonight. I will arrange for rooms and check on how Allendale and Remington fare." With that, he exited.

Sir Tidley rose, stirred up the embers in the fireplace, pushed a chair closer, and motioned for Phillip to bring Josie over.

She started to shiver uncontrollably as shock took over. The two gentlemen helped her settle in the chair and wrapped a blanket around her and gave her a sip of brandy. It did much to warm her up on the inside.

Theo returned shortly to state that a room for Josie awaited as they arranged a bath for her along with a servant to assist her for the evening.

"How are they?" She had to know how Marcus was doing.

Theo was sober and paused as if weighing what to tell her. "I wish I could give you a good report. Captain Allendale's collarbone has been re-broken. He will be home from war longer than he would like, but the doctor expects that if he stays away from any more fights, he will recover in due time."

"Lord Remington?" Josie asked hopefully.

Theo sighed and avoided eye contact. "The doctor is still with him. He has yet to regain consciousness. It is too early to tell."

"Oh." Josie's spirits plummeted.

"Shall I escort you to your room, Miss Storm? The landlady will personally see to your care. I have tried to explain what you have endured. In the morning, we will escort you safely home as I am sure your father, Lady Grey, and others are concerned for you."

Josie nodded and rose unsteadily. "Thank you. I owe you all a debt of gratitude that I could never fully repay."

The men nodded.

Theo led her out of the room.

Josie was treated with courtesy by the landlord's wife, and after a warm bath and oversized nightgown borrowed from her hostess, she was put to bed with the promise that her own gown would be washed and pressed by the time she rose in the morning. Josie fell asleep, but her dreams were disturbed. She awoke in the middle of the night in fear. She glanced around, and it took a few moments before she remembered where she was as all the memories of the previous day crashed in on her. She lay there in the dark, wondering and worrying how Marcus fared.

Why had he kept watch over her? Why did he go to such lengths to protect her? She shivered with the remembrance of Red and Weasel and her time in that carriage. Rolling over on her side, she hugged her pillow close and brought her blanket up snug around her shoulders as she shivered at the brutality of the fight she had witnessed and the way Marcus and his friends had suffered. All for her. It had overall been too eventful of a day, and she did not know how long she rested there praying for Marcus as he lay in another room that the men refused to let her visit. She didn't even know which one it was. There would be no nocturnal bedside vigils.

Shame overcame her as she remembered his faithful prayers by her bed. But here she was, alone and unable to act on any similar desire.

Tomorrow she would return to London. What would happen after that? She had already planned to return home. She hoped that her disappearance had not become common knowledge amongst the *ton* or her reputation would be in shatters. But what would that matter when the man she loved was near death? She closed her eyes in an attempt to fall back asleep and dreamed she was walking the gardens of Rose Hill with Marcus.

When she awoke later, she found that her fire had been stoked by a maid, her clothes had been returned, and a pot of tea awaited her. She rose, and her head pounded. She savored the tea, warmed herself by the fireplace, and managed to dress. The innkeeper's wife had provided her with a shawl to use as well, and Josie gratefully wrapped it around her before she exited the room to go down to break her fast.

She entered the private parlour and was surprised to observe Captain Allendale there before her.

He stood as she came in. His arm was in a sling and appeared to be bound to his torso. It was partially hidden by his jacket that lay loose on his shoulder on that side of his body. He deftly slid a chair back and helped her sit before he returned to his own seat. His blue eyes were bloodshot, and he had not shaved. His jaw was set, and he ate little.

"Did you rest well, Miss Storm?"

Josie shook her head. "How is your shoulder?"

"It hurts more than I care to admit, but the doctor says that now that it is immobilized, I can go home to recover in my own bed under the care of our family physician." He sighed. "I will not like having to explain this to Whitehall."

"How long now before you can return to service?"

"It might be two more months now." He frowned.

"I am sorry. I wish..." She shook her head. She wished many things. Foolish things. What was the point?

"What do you wish?" He looked at her now, his brows furrowed in concern.

"It is immaterial and foolish at present." She helped herself to some toast and jam.

"Sometimes dreams sustain us when life is hard." His voice was soft and gentle.

"Sometimes wishes taunt us with what may never be ours as well, and in that, they can be torture." Josie frowned. "I'm sorry you have suffered for my foolishness."

"Foolishness? You walked down the street with your abigail after a little shopping. Something many women of the *beau monde* do. What was foolish about that? You have nothing to apologize for, Miss Storm. In this situation, you were a victim. We are all glad that we were able to intervene before those brutes had completed their mission."

"I still fail to understand all that happened, or why." She looked at him and tilted her head. "Can you enlighten me?"

"It would not be my place to do so, and I am not as fully informed as some are. Be content that you are safe and will return to London and soon home to your family."

Josie set her toast down and sipped the hot chocolate before her. "How is your brother?"

"The doctor has advised that he not be moved. Michael will remain here with him while the rest of us escort you to London."

Josie noticed the wrinkles in his forehead. He had not made eye contact with her as he had spoken. It seemed scripted. "There's something you are not telling me." Fear started to rise within her heart, causing it to skip beats.

Jared continued to eat his eggs and refused to look at her.

"Will he live?" Her voice came out almost as a whisper as terror gripped her throat and squeezed off her air supply.

Jared swallowed, and she watched his eyes moisten. He looked her in the eyes. "I pray so."

Josie leaned back in her chair and sat down the cup she had held. She was hot all over, and she fought against encroaching darkness. She wouldn't swoon!

"Lean your head forward, Miss Storm. It will pass."

She did what he suggested, and slowly, the blood returned to her brain. She sat up and sighed.

27

The door opened, and a man entered the room that she had not met before.

"Good morning, Doctor Ipsen," Jared spoke up, "may I introduce you to Miss Josephine Storm, the young woman we rescued yesterday."

"A pleasure to meet you, Miss Storm." Dr. Ipsen sat down across from her and poured himself a cup of coffee.

"Have you been to visit Lord Remington this morning?" Josie asked.

The doctor glanced at Captain Allendale. She observed an unspoken communication pass between them. Why did these men persist in keeping information from her? The doctor cleared his throat as he looked to her. "I have been to see him. He was asleep."

Josie gulped. She knew this was not a good sign. "May I see him before we depart for London?"

The doctor shrugged. "I do not see any harm. Sir Michael reports he was in and out of consciousness during the night. Last night, he spoke a few words. He was asking for Josie. Would that be you?"

Josie bit her lip and nodded.

"I am medicating him for the pain. He may not respond or know who you are. I insist the visit be short."

Josie nodded and worked at finishing the food on

her plate.

Theodore and Phillip entered the room to eat.

Josie went upstairs with the Doctor Ipsen and Captain Allendale to see Marcus.

Sir Tidley let them into the room, nodded to them, and left to break his own fast.

Josie's gaze was riveted to the man in the bed. She moved over to him. A blanket covered him up to his shoulders. His arms rested, exposed, on top of the blanket, one bent across his torso and the other along his side. She spied the dark hairs at the top of his chest and the bruises along his skin. It seemed nothing was unscathed from what limited amount she observed. Her breath shuddered when she looked at his face all swollen and shaded in colors of red, blue, and purple. His appearance was worse than yesterday, although someone had washed the blood away. She wondered if he were able to open his eyes should he want to. They were swollen shut. His nose certainly had been broken. His hair fell onto his forehead. If she had not known it was Marcus, she would not have been able to identify him.

She sank into a chair next to the bed as Jared and the doctor moved away and spoke in low voices. Marcus's only movement was the gentle rise and fall of his chest. She reached out to touch the hand closest to her and held it tenderly in her own, observing the bruised, cut, and swollen knuckles.

"Good morning, Marcus. It's Josie," she whispered. She wanted what she had to say to be for his ears alone. She hoped he heard her or that at least somewhere deep inside his heart he would know she was there. And perhaps be glad? He had called for her during the night. That alone gave her hope. She leaned forward to whisper in his ear. "Marcus, you are strong, brave, faithful, and true. I was wrong to have ever doubted you. Please forgive me, Marcus. I love you and cannot imagine living my life without you in it." She lifted her head to watch his face and see if he would give any indication of having heard her, but there was nothing. She lifted his limp hand and turned it over. She placed a soft kiss in the palm and closed his fingers around it. She said a prayer for his recovery and left the room.

Jared found her waiting in the hallway with her back up against the wall, hugging herself.

"We must depart."

She shook her head as she leaned back.

"It would be improper for you to stay, Miss Storm."

"Did you think I did not realize that?" The words came out sharp, and she placed a hand over her mouth.

Captain Allendale smiled at her. "I'm glad you have not lost your fire, Josie." He put forward his good arm, she placed her hand on it, and together they went down the stairs and out to the carriage that awaited in the yard. Soon they were on their way to London.

Lord Harrow drove. Lord Westcombe rode alongside with the other horses tied to the back of the carriage. The Remington well-sprung carriage offered relative comfort even at faster speeds. Captain Allendale had refused some of the medication that the doctor had offered him for pain, and as a result, his suffering was etched on his face and seen in his tightened jaw. At their first possible change of horses, he purchased a bottle of brandy and spent the rest of the journey to London nursing his suffering with that.

Josie watched Captain Allendale as he numbed his

pain, and drifted in and out of slumber. Josie could not get her mind to rest. Would Marcus recover? If what she saw was not even the worst of it, he had a long road ahead. Society forbade her correspondence with a man who was not her husband or relative. There was no way to communicate her changed affections. She grieved and was grateful her companion was oblivious to her inner turmoil.

At the stops along the way, Lord Harrow and Lord Westcombe devoted themselves to her every need. They had not come through the fighting unscathed and looked worse for wear, with bruises and cuts and their clothing ripped and stained. Their spirits remained cheerful and ever focused on caring for her. Jared primarily slept and mumbled. Her heart ached for his pain and for the concern he must have for his brother, which was evidenced in some of his rambling. He never blamed her. No one did.

Except herself.

Somehow, this was all her fault. What more should she have done? She had not been aware of who had orchestrated the attack or what their intention was. All she could think of was that if somehow she had not rebuffed Marcus weeks before, none of this would have happened. And yet, she wasn't sure how true that was either. Four men were injured rescuing her, and a fifth one might die from his injuries.

She sighed deeply as they entered the outskirts of London. The further she was from Marcus the lower her spirits sank. What would life be like now? There was no medication for her pain, although she had been tempted to borrow a little of Captain Allendale's brandy to at least numb it for a while.

They reached London late in the evening and

found the Grey house fully lit.

Captain Allendale insisted on accompanying her inside and spoke with Lady Grey and her father. Josie was greeted with hugs and tears. They ordered a tea tray, and a meal of cold cuts was placed before her. She tried to eat, but she only wanted the solace of her bed. She forbore her interrogation well. Even her grandfather, Lord Chester, had been there.

Captain Allendale politely refused to stay but requested that Mr. Storm and Lord Chester call upon him in the morning for more details. He planned to follow doctor's orders and go home to rest. He bid Josie a weary farewell and departed with his friends who had awaited him outside.

Later in her room, Josie said goodnight to Molly, who was uninjured after her attack. Josie settled into a chair by the fireplace, held a glass of brandy, and watched the light from the fireplace dance and reflect in the glass and against the dark amber of the liquor. Trial by fire. Is that what this all was? Another test of her love and devotion to God? But what about Marcus? Was he only fulfilling a duty to her grandfather, whom she had discovered had asked for his help? Or had he done it because he cared? Would she ever know? Questions. So many questions and no answers. She sipped her drink, knelt by her chair, and prayed for Marcus and for God's leading if it was ever really His plan for them to be together.

Please, God? May I have him? Will You bring him back to me somehow? There was no answer. Her prayers seemed to hit the ceiling and bounce back down to crash at her feet. But God had answered her prayers for rescue when she had been kidnapped, at just the right time. If God could do that, surely He would bring her and Marcus back together if it was His will. If not, she would hopefully find another man to love. The thought was a hard one to accept. Tired and defeated, she crawled under the blankets and slept.

She awoke late. Josie came downstairs and broke her fast.

Her grandfather summoned her to join him in the study.

Josie entered the room cautiously and found that not only was the Earl of Chester present, but also her father and Lady Grey.

"Come in, Josie, and be seated. We need to discuss what happened." The Earl escorted her to a chair. The day was cool, the fireplace was lit and kept the damp at bay.

Josie waited as the Earl occupied the chair next to her.

"Now, my dear, we realize that the events of the past two days have been upsetting. We discovered who initiated the kidnapping." The Earl's voice was soft and low. His eyes shuttered, and his shoulders were more stooped than she remembered. He looked older than when she had seen him last night. When he glanced up to look at her, she observed deep sorrow there. "Who was it, Grandfather?"

He swallowed. "My son-in-law, Lord Widmore, was behind the original carriage accident, although you were not his intended victim. He's been arrested this morning for kidnapping, attempted murder, and for his unpaid debts. He is at the Tower pending trial. Lady Widmore and Lady Heticia will join me at my estate. Our family bears great shame and that this recent attack was against you, one of our own, puts a cloak of scandal over all of us."

Josie put her hand over her mouth. Her uncle, whom she had never met, had tried to have her kidnapped. "Why would he do this? What have I ever done to him? I've never even met the man."

Josie's father spoke up. "You have done nothing to deserve this treatment, my dear. Lord Widmore was a poor steward of his estate and gambled himself into the ground. He wanted to stop his wife and daughter from their trip to London. He thought he would benefit from a trust in their name. He would not have. His recent attack against you was because he discovered the dowry that your Grandfather established. He mistakenly believed that money should be his and if he eliminated you, he could somehow get his father-in-law to bail him out of his troubles."

Lady Grey, who sat next to her, spoke up and patted Josie's knee. "All to say, my dear, is that you are blameless and a victim of despicable evil that will now be rectified."

Her shoulders slumped. All of this because of greed? Now Marcus lay injured in a little Inn far from town because of it all. "What about Lord Remington?"

"What about him?" Lord Chester asked. "You spurned him, did you not?"

Josie swallowed hard, nodded, and looked down at her hands as they clasped at the skirt of her dress. "I was mistaken in my opinion of him. He is now wounded and far from home or people who love him. What if...?"

"My dear, Josie, the Lord is in charge of all the 'what ifs.' You need to trust my nephew to His care. I am worried about him too and will travel tomorrow to assist in nursing him back to health. He is a strong young man. I am certain he will rally." Lady Grey's voice held no censure, only gentle comfort in her soft tones.

"You will let me know how he fares?" Josie could not help the tears in her eyes as she glanced at Lady Dorothea.

"I will correspond with you." Lady Grey gave Josie a warm smile.

"This is so much to take in," Josie said.

"That it is, my dear," her father responded. "We will leave town early tomorrow morning. I want you to rest and recover from your adventures, but given the speculation there may be about the events surrounding Lord Widmore, it seems advisable for us to be absent from town. Perhaps there will be another season for you next year if you wish it."

Josie nodded and stood.

Lord Chester and her father also rose.

"Thank you, Grandfather, for all you have done." She came to him and gave him a kiss on the cheek. "I pray you have a safe journey home." He nodded to her. She turned to her father, and she gave him a kiss on the cheek as well. "I will do as you say and prepare to leave in the morning and rest. It will be good to be home." Josie walked to the door.

"I will come up for tea with you," Lady Grey said, giving Josie a warm smile.

"Thank you." Josie climbed the stairs to her room and proceeded to pack.

~*~

Marcus struggled against the images before him, of that giant of a man grabbing and manhandling Josie. He dreamt of fighting and gazing upon her horror-stricken face. He must have looked ghastly for her to view him that way. Pain invaded every breath he took and any movement he made. Even the blankets over him seemed oppressive and painful to the various wounds on his body, but the colder air from the room was even more so.

A concussion, some broken ribs, a damaged knee, and bruises everywhere seemed to be the major extent of his injuries. The doctor was certain that there had been no other internal injuries from his knife wound to be concerned about, since his fever left.

"You are awake again." Michael had been a steadfast companion, and Lady Grey arrived yesterday to help provide care for him until it was safe for him to be moved. "Bad dreams?"

"Bad reality, more like." Marcus gritted his teeth against the pain as Michael tried to lift him to give him something to drink. Bitter medicine he wanted nothing more than to spit out. But he didn't. "Water, please." The water followed but failed to wash out the bitter taste on his tongue. Michael helped him back down to his pillow, but everything hurt.

"Josie is safe?"

Michael nodded. "You have asked that question every time you have awakened. She is safe and probably at home with her father now."

"I had hoped…" Marcus sighed.

"Hoped for what? She could not stay here." Michael leaned back with a smile on his face as he crossed his arms.

Marcus frowned. "What do you know that you are not telling me?"

Michael chuckled. "Only what I have told you every time you have asked. Miss Storm was here to visit you before she left."

"What a wonderful image of a hero I turned out to be." Marcus groaned.

"She was grateful for our assistance and seemed genuinely concerned for your welfare." Michael offered.

"She had pity on me?"

"I think her feelings went beyond that."

"It's hopeless, and you do not want to tell me. I know it is. She rejected me, and while she may be grateful for our efforts on her behalf, it did not erase my alleged sins." Marcus closed his eyes, the light in the room suddenly being too bright as the sun shone from behind a cloud and streamed in the window.

"I would not say that, Marcus. Miss Storm is an exceptional young woman, and I would guess her feelings towards you have changed."

"Lot of good that does me when I am stuck here in a bed and she is days away at home. It is not like I can call on her and ask how she fares."

"Courtship might be difficult at present, I agree. But if Miss Storm is all you believe her to be, she will be worth the wait."

"She came to London to find a husband. Why would she wait for this?" Marcus motioned to his face with his bandaged hand.

"Women have done stranger things when in love."

Marcus chuckled, instantly regretting the pain it caused. "This, coming from an expert?"

"You wound me." Michael placed a hand over his heart and feigned shock.

"Then expound upon your wealth of knowledge." Marcus smiled weakly.

"Perhaps your aunt will be a better person to ask.

It seems to me that you and Josie were somehow meant to be together."

"I pray that it would be so."

"Well, you have crossed the first hurdle towards that end."

"Which would be?" Marcus asked.

"You survived."

Marcus nodded and fell back to sleep.

28

December

Josie resumed her routine back at home. She painted watercolors, played her music, and supervised the running of the Storm household.

Her brother Matthew remained at university, and the governess, Miss Perry, had Charles and Georgette well in hand.

In spite of all she had to keep her busy, she was restless and often irritated. She had a few letters from Lady Grey, enough to know that Lord Remington had recovered and returned to Rose Hill and that Captain Allendale would return to his regiment after the holidays. Of Lord Remington's heart toward her, however, she had no inkling, and this rankled her. Lady Dorothea had returned to her own estate, so her ability to provide any insight into Lord Remington was lost to her.

It was now early December, and Josie had begun to make a list of all that needed to be done for the upcoming holidays. She was so wrapped up in her notes, she was surprised when Molly came to inform her of a visitor awaiting her in the parlour.

Entering the room, she was surprised to discover a man she did not recognize.

"Good morning, sir. I am Miss Storm. And you are?"

"Mr. Neville, ma'am. We have not met prior to this, but earlier this year, Lord Remington hired me to investigate your carriage accident, and I was involved in that case until Lord Widmore's arrest."

Josie sat and bid her guest to do the same. "You have come from London? What brings you this far afield?"

His attire was that of a respectable man although not as high a quality of cut and material as seen amongst the *ton*. His brown jacket and buff trousers and simply tied cravat all bespoke a man of manners but limited means. His neatly cut brown hair was combed off his face. His face seemed older than his voice, filled with lines and darkened by the sun. His eyes looked old and weary but still held a twinkle.

She was at ease in his presence.

"You do, Miss Storm. I came to apprise you of the outcome of the case."

"And this could not have been done by letter?" Josie motioned for Molly, who had entered with the tea tray.

"Some news is best conveyed in person," Mr. Neville said.

A disturbance at the door preceded the tea tray along with her father, who came to greet Mr. Neville.

As the men regained their seats and Josie poured the tea, the men chatted a bit about Mr. Neville's journey west.

"It sounds as if you two have a prior acquaintance," Josie said.

"True, my dear, I met Mr. Neville when he was in town doing work for Lord Remington and Lord Chester."

"I see." Josie sipped her tea and waited.

Mr. Neville cleared his throat. "I have come to let you know that Lord Widmore was found guilty of the crimes of kidnapping and attempted murder as well as for his unpaid debts. However, his behavior became highly erratic and unusual even in court, and he was instead sentenced to Bedlam."

Josie gasped. "Bedlam? Is he truly insane?"

"He gave that appearance in the way he spoke and acted. He will never bother you again."

"I'm sad for my aunt and cousin. How tragic this must be for them."

"They are staying with Lord Chester, and he will provide for them I am sure."

Josie nodded. "My grandfather is a good man."

Mr. Storm agreed. "He has improved with age."

Josie couldn't help but grin.

"I also had business out this way doing some investigation of Sir Bastian's case. Since I was in the area, I was commissioned to deliver a special correspondence."

Josie put down her tea and saucer on the table. "For me?"

Mr. Neville smiled. "Most certainly for you, Miss Storm." He reached in his pocket for an envelope and handed it to her. "There is a gift that goes with that." He pulled a box up from the floor and handed it over to her. "The letter I think you will want to read privately."

Josie placed the box on her lap and undid the thick cloth ribbons. She lifted the lid off and set it aside. Peering in, she saw a blanket surrounding a multicolored puppy that looked a bit like her Yorkshire Terrier mother but with curlier hair from an unknown father. Josie lifted the puppy up, and the cream, brown, and white coloring on the dog shone on the glossy coat. The puppy whimpered and licked her nose. Josie snuggled it to herself, and her heart warmed. "You are like your mama, are you not?" She handed the puppy to her father. "Will you hold her while I go read this letter? In case a response is needed?"

"I would be delighted." Mr. Storm was already petting and getting his fingers licked by the little dog.

Josie excused herself as she left the room. She grabbed her cloak and headed out into the chilly December air. The garden was dead and ready for winter, but with a bleak beauty all its own. She sat on the bench by some bushes with brown branches but that still held a few berries. She took a deep breath, broke the seal on the envelope, and pulled out the paper.

Dear Miss Storm,

I pray this letter finds you well.

Please accept a gift I had longed to give you when you departed Rose Hill. She is a sweet puppy, and while I know you loved Charlie, she is currently helping me recover and cannot be spared. Please accept her daughter as a gift from me in remembrance of all we have shared and endured together. I was not initially aware of the plans my aunt had made for Christmas and wanted to assure you that I had no part in them, although your family will always be welcome at Rose Hill. I would never want you to feel pressured, or that I had failed to respect your decision and wish for me to withdraw my suit. I hope we might always be friends.

Respectfully,

MR

Josie laid the letter on her lap and sat in the cold a bit stunned. Marcus had written to her. She let her fingers touch the strong, masculine script and wished

Susan M. Baganz

she were able to touch him instead. Had he forgiven her? Would he still want her after all he had endured for her sake?

Could she really forget the scandal of London? Her fingers traced his initials with longing. There was no declaration of love, only an offer of friendship.

Christmas at Rose Hill? She wondered when her father had planned to tell her about that. Energy surged within her. They were going to Rose Hill for the holidays!

That had to be why her father had not given his blessing yet on her ideas and had been saying, "Wait."

She would meet Marcus again. She swallowed. She would see him again but potentially as a friend. Could she handle days of being at Rose Hill with Marcus, knowing he would never be hers? That this estate she had come to love would never be her home? It would be hard, but she had to see him. It was torture not being able to know how well he fared. How extensive his injures had been. She would get to thank him personally for his rescue of her. Her toes began to tingle with the cold. She rose, grabbed the letter, and returned to the warmth of the house.

Josie collected her puppy and invited Mr. Neville for lunch. She excused herself to write a letter to Marcus. She made a small bed for the dog, but the puppy chose to curl up in her lap. She pulled out a sheet of paper and began to write.

Lord Remington,

Thank you for the sweet dog. She is beautiful, and I will treasure her because she came from you.

I had been unaware of our holiday plans. I look forward to seeing you and your friends again.

I prayed for your recovery.

302

I regret my foolish words and actions the last time we spoke. I was wrong. I hope that you would forgive me. I had no right to judge. You have proven yourself brave, strong, faithful, and true.

My deepest regards,

J

Josie dusted the letter and carefully folded the lightly scented paper in an envelope, placed a wax seal on it, and scooped up her new charge to head downstairs to dine.

Mr. Neville left after lunch. He assured her that he would deliver her letter at Rose Hill on his way back to London.

When the door had closed on their guest, Josie followed her father into his study. "We need to talk."

He sat down at his desk, shuffled paper, and avoided her gaze.

"Father? When were you planning to tell me about Christmas at Rose Hill?"

The paper shuffling stopped, and her father looked up into her face. "I neglected to mention that?"

Josie laughed. "You know very well you did. No hiding it now."

He grinned and sat back in his chair as Josie, arms crossed, leaned against the solid oak desk. "I was planning to tell you soon, but I was afraid you would reject the proposal."

"I would be happy to return to Rose Hill."

He looked at her for a few seconds and nodded. "I am glad. I also look forward to it. I thought it would be good for the whole family."

"I agree."

"Are you certain? I didn't know how you would feel about seeing Lord Remington again."

Josie let her arms drop to her side. "I miss him."

Mr. Storm pursed his lips together and rose to envelop his daughter in a hug. As he let her go, he held her by the shoulders. "Josie, you will need to trust that God will work things out for you and Lord Remington should it be His will for you to be together. Maybe this will be a step in that direction, or it might help you close a door and move on."

"I don't want to move on."

"I know. We have a fortnight to pray and prepare."

"And train a new dog."

"Hmm?" Her father followed Josie's gaze to the floor where the puppy sat next to a puddle.

Josie scooped up the dog and turned to leave. "I'll go get a rag and take care of that."

Mr. Storm chuckled.

~*~

Marcus received Mr. Neville into Rose Hill, and they enjoyed a meal together.

Mr. Neville retired early for the evening after being convinced to stay as opposed to the posting inn.

Marcus battled fatigue since coming home, as he continued to heal. He took the letter to his suite and sipped a glass of brandy as he read the contents.

Charlie had joined him and curled up at his feet.

He sighed. She was coming to Rose Hill. She asked him to forgive her, and yet she had nothing to forgive. He never blamed her for her choice. Would he have done any better had he been in her shoes? When had pride and piety become a weight? He brought the page to his nose and inhaled. It smelled like her. He glanced

at her lovely writing and soaked in the words again—
"brave, strong, faithful, and true." It sounded familiar,
but he couldn't remember from where. The words gave
him hope. Would she be open to his attentions when
she arrived? Did he have the courage to try again?

Rising from his chair, he limped over to the bed
and prepared himself for the night.

Charlie jumped up and curled in a ball on his
pillow.

Marcus gently shoved her off. As he pulled the
blankets up to his chest, he thought he had a vague
memory. It had to have been a hallucination due to the
medication. He imagined that Josie had kissed his
palm. He lifted his hand, looked at it for a moment,
and dropped his arm in wonder. Had she? His heart
soared a little more with hope.

29

Today was the day the Storm family planned to arrive. A light dusting of snow overnight coated the grass and trees. Everything glistened in the twilight as the estate awaited its guests.

Jared laughed at Marcus as he paced before the fireplace. "Come, Marcus, stop acting like a lovesick fool. If I ever become like this when Cupid hits, please feel free to punch me in the nose."

Marcus reached up to touch the bump on his own nose that remained after it had been broken.

Jared noticed. "Do not worry about that bump either. It makes you look rougher and not so pretty, and that balances things out for the rest of us."

Marcus chuckled. "If you keep this up, little brother, you will find I can still mill you down. I refrain only because I do not want to get into further trouble for injuring one of Wellesley's staff."

"Sir Wellesley was not that angry when he understood the reason."

"Perhaps, but it was not nice getting a written reprimand from the man. I know you like him, but to be honest, Jared, the man makes me shake in my boots."

The Captain laughed at that. "I used to be that way too."

The sound of carriage wheels and horses' hooves reverberated in the courtyard.

Marcus limped to the window. "Josie has arrived."

Charlie got up from her spot before the fireplace and scampered to the door, barking and tail wagging, to greet the guests.

Marcus and Jared followed.

Jared grabbed Marcus's shoulder before they could exit. "Remember, you are still sworn to secrecy."

Marcus stared at his brother for a moment, stunned. "After all this time, I am still to live under a cloud of suspicion?"

"If Whitehall ever chooses to release any details, you will be free of your promise, but until then, I must ask again for your word."

Marcus swallowed hard and nodded.

Jared patted him on the shoulder. "You are a good man, and any woman who fails to understand and appreciate that is a fool and doesn't deserve you." He turned and walked out.

Marcus took a moment to assimilate his brother's words. He prayed that Josie was no fool.

Chaos reigned as he entered the foyer, where his staff collected cloaks.

Mrs. Hughes and Lady Dorothea bustled around, assigned rooms, and gave directions to a small army of footmen.

In the middle of it was Josie. She stood there with Charlie in one arm and a puppy in the other. She smiled as everyone talked around her. She glanced up and their eyes locked.

To Marcus, all the noise faded away. It was just the two of them. She was beautiful. Not the beaten down girl he'd fought for, but radiant and healthy. "Welcome to Rose Hill."

Mr. Storm stepped forward to clasp Marcus's

hand. "Thank you for having us. I'm glad to be out of that carriage."

As the luggage disappeared up the stairs, Marcus fought back the effort to scowl at the young man who protectively hovered over Josie. Before he might figure it out, Mr. Storm captured his attention.

"Lord Remington, allow me to present to you my two youngest children, Charles and Georgette." Mr. Storm beamed.

The children curtsied to him, and their nanny shuffled them off to their rooms above stairs.

The young man by Josie's side stepped forward and gave a bow. "I am Mr. Matthew Storm, my lord. 'Tis a pleasure to finally meet the man who saved my sister's life, twice."

Marcus smiled and relaxed. Her brother. Of course.

Josie smiled at him and gave a small curtsy as well. "Thank you for inviting us to Rose Hill, my lord."

"You are welcome. Rose Hill is a place for family and laughter. It is good to experience it again."

Lady Dorothea ushered Josie and her brother up the stairs.

Marcus could not help but follow their progress Josie's hips swayed as she climbed the stairs chatting with his aunt. She wore a green traveling gown, and her hair was starting to come loose from its pins. He recalled the way her hair looked when spread out against a pillow and the silky touch of it in his hands. He swallowed hard.

He turned on his heel to discover his brother standing there with a grin on his face. "You are a sad case, brother."

Together they ascended the stairs to seek their

rooms and prepare for dinner.

~*~

Marcus was forced to wait to visit with Josie. His sister, Henri, came into the drawing room. She and her husband, Charles, had arrived a few days prior. She was expecting their firstborn in the spring, and she looked plump and radiant. Marcus listened as she talked about her trip to the continent. She rested one hand on his arm.

Jared conversed with Charles about the war.

Josie entered the room. He sensed her presence before he heard her gasp.

Henrietta was laughing and noticed Marcus's gaze had moved to the doorway.

Marcus left Henrietta to approach Josie and bring her into the center of the room. "Miss Josephine Storm, may I present to you my precocious sister, Lady Henrietta Percy."

Josie gave a curtsy to Lady Percy but glanced at Marcus with her eyebrows raised.

Marcus raised his in return.

Lady Henrietta laughed. "Miss Storm, Marcus has been raving about you for months, and yet I suspect he neglected to mention me to you."

"That would be true, my lady." Josephine blushed.

"I was on my wedding trip for much of this year and have not seen my family often since we returned to London. It is a delight to meet you. I hope you will call me Henri and will soon grant me the right to call you Josie. I'm sure we will be fast friends."

Josie smiled.

Lady Percy led her away to become acquainted

while they waited for the others.

Marcus frowned at the distance placed between the Josie and himself, but they had time—plenty of time—to talk.

~*~

In a few more days, the household would burst with all its guests.

Josie chafed at how the hosting duties conspired to keep Marcus away from her. Early one morning, she came downstairs to find Marcus seated alone in the breakfast parlour. She detected a flicker of interest in his eyes when she entered the room and suddenly felt shy about being alone with him after so long apart.

"Good morning, Miss Storm."

"Good morning to you, Lord Remington. I would prefer it if you would return to calling me Josie." She went to the sideboard and filled her plate. The footman brought her hot chocolate, and she sat down to Marcus's right.

"I would be pleased to do so only if you would call me Marcus." He paused as he sipped his coffee. Catching her eye, he added, "I miss hearing my name on your lips."

Josie smiled and ate in silence. When she finished eating, she stood to leave.

Marcus reached for her hand.

She halted, looked at him, and raised one eyebrow.

"May we speak privately?"

Josie nodded and waited for him to rise. He escorted her out of the room into his study. Entering that haven, he closed the door and locked it.

Josie bit back a smile.

Marcus motioned for her to sit near the fireplace, and he chose a chair across from her. They sat there, silent, and stared at each other as if daring the other one to speak first.

"Thank you again for sending me one of Charlie's pups. She is adorable."

"I am glad you like her. The rest have all found good homes, but I had saved her specifically for you. Have you named her yet?"

"Charity, although I call her Cherry."

"Hence the red bow on her collar?"

"That, and it is Christmas."

They both avoided looking at each other.

Marcus leaned forward and turned his gaze to her. "I've missed you, Josie."

She looked at her hands. "I've missed you too."

"I have been eager to talk to you since you arrived. I have longed for your visit from the moment I received your letter. I hoped you had forgiven me."

"Forgiven you?" Josie looked at him with squinting eyes. "Marcus, it is I who needs your forgiveness. I was wrong to believe the gossip. I do not need to know why you did what you did, but I trust that you had a compelling reason. You would never have sacrificed your reputation and my affections for anything frivolous." Josie got off her chair and kneeled before him. She reached up to clasp his hands. "I was a fool to have spurned you, and if you only want to be friends, I will strive to be content with that, but I need to know you have forgiven me." She bent her head.

Marcus lifted her head up with a hand that he freed from her grasp. He helped her rise to sit beside him. "I wished I did not have to do what I did that night. I never wanted to do anything that would hurt you. Hurt us. Losing my reputation was nothing compared to losing you. Can you forgive me for not being able to tell you about it?"

Josie nodded. "Yes, I can. I have. Thank you for watching out for me. I did not know all you had done to try to keep me safe until after you rescued me near Dover. God showed me in that moment how He viewed us turning away from Him in our sin and yet He sent Jesus to die. Even though we did not know He was coming to rescue us. You also proved your faithfulness when you fought for me."

"My affection for you compelled me to no other action."

"Is it possible you might still care for me?"

"I love you, Josie, and I still desire you as my wife if you would have me. I have not fully recovered and cannot get down on one knee to ask you properly. I asked your father, and he has given his consent." His voice cracked as he spoke.

"But you will not be able to tell me about that brothel visit?"

"I cannot."

"Hmmmm."

"I thought you said you forgave me?" He frowned.

"I do, but that drawing in the newspaper is hard to forget."

"The girl I visited looked nothing like her."

"Excuse me?"

"They got it all wrong. She was nothing like in the drawing."

Marcus had a twinkle in his eye, and she suspected he was trying hard not to smile.

"What was she like?" She wondered how far he

would take this.

"Young, beautiful, and she really wanted to introduce me to the wonders of—"

Josie put her fingers up to his lips. "Don't you dare say it, Marcus, or I will slap you."

He chuckled.

"Was she nice?"

"The best, but are you really sure you want to pursue this line of questioning?"

"Why would you want me? I don't understand. I'm not experienced."

"Fishing for compliments? If I want experience, Madame DuBois has many young women who are more than willing to accommodate me. I am not interested in any of them. It's always and only ever has been you. I fell in love when I saw your face under a crushed chip bonnet in a teetering carriage on a stormy night."

"How could you possibly fall in love with an unconscious woman?"

"I don't know, except that since that day, a certain Storm has ravaged my heart, utterly and completely." Marcus pulled out a beautiful pearl and ruby ring set in gold. "This was my mother's. It was her wish that I would bestow it on my bride someday."

"Marcus." She leaned over, placed her hands alongside his head, reveling in the softness of his wavy hair. She moved his head toward hers and kissed him softly on the lips. He wrapped his arms around her as he returned the kiss.

Marcus was the one to pull back from the embrace. "Is that a yes?"

Josie nodded. "Yes. I would be honored to be your wife."

Marcus slipped the ring on her finger, and she reached up to kiss him again. Once again, he pushed her away and struggled to stand up. He took a few steps away from her.

"Marcus? What is it?"

"We cannot go on like this. I have already compromised you by locking you in here with me. You will have to marry me now, although your acceptance makes that much easier." He smiled as she tossed a pillow at him. "However, if you continue to kiss me like that, I fear we will be anticipating our wedding night."

"Hmmmm." Josie stood and walked slowly over to him.

He blushed as his eyes scanned her body.

She placed a hand on his chest and grabbed his cravat in her fist so he could not move away. "I suggest we get married as soon as possible. I really do not want to wait any longer." She reached up and gave him a lingering kiss.

He responded with his lips while trying not to touch her as he backed away.

She let him go and smiled.

Marcus laughed as he looked down at her. "I was hoping you would say that. I have a special license that would allow us to marry on Christmas Eve if you are willing. Reverend Wilson could perform the service for us in our chapel here. Our families and closest friends are already here. Do you have any objections?"

"You had a lot of confidence I would accept you."

"Not really, only a lot of hope and prayer. I knew if you said yes, I would not want to wait any longer. So, Christmas Eve?"

Josie pushed herself up on her toes to kiss his

cheek. Setting back down on her heels, she looked at him and smiled. "I would be delighted."

Dinner that evening was festive.

Marcus beamed as he announced his engagement to her.

Josie couldn't stop smiling. She was surprised when her father also had an announcement to make.

"I have the blessing of announcing that I too shall wed soon. Lady Dorothea Grey has agreed to be my bride." He sat next to Marcus's aunt and held her hand. Lady Dorothea bestow a kiss on her father's cheek.

Marcus sat back in his chair. "So that would make my new father-in-law also my uncle, and my aunt would also be my mother-in-law?"

Josie smiled. "It would also make your aunt my step-mother."

Laughter ensued as talk centered on the upcoming weddings to be had at Rose Hill.

30

Josie found the days before Christmas Eve passed quickly.

Marcus led a lively group in decorating the hall, and they all had ventured out into the snow to find the Yule Log, and the mistletoe to hang in strategic places around the manor.

Josie worked hard with Molly to prepare her wedding dress. Josie also enjoyed her acquaintance with Henrietta.

There were snowball fights and snow angels outside with her siblings. And cold lips warmed by stolen kisses under the mistletoe with Marcus.

Christmas Eve dawned with a fresh coat of snow covering everything, shimmering in the sun like diamonds.

Josie was delighted. She gazed out the window in the yellow bedroom, where she had lain eight months prior. She did not need Marcus to describe a sunrise to her now. After today, she would say farewell to this room and say hello to future sunrises with Marcus by her side. She sighed. She witnessed a pair of cardinals flying in the pine trees at the edge of the yard, each branch outlined with snow, giving sharp relief to the birds, which from a distance almost looked like the berries in the holly lining the mantle in the drawing room.

The house was ready, filled with guests and

thrumming with the anticipation of the wedding and Christmas.

Josie's own anticipation added to her joy. She could burst for happiness.

They had all purchased and wrapped gifts. The ballroom was decorated with red and green and white for the wedding breakfast to follow the ceremony in the Rose Hill chapel. Tenants and nearby neighbors were invited to this celebration of the wedding and Christmas, but only the houseguests would attend the ceremony. The afternoon would involve dancing and a wassail bowl, and the tenants and servants would receive specially selected gifts and a holiday bonus.

Josie sat by the fire, drying her freshly washed hair and eating a light breakfast when Lady Grey came to visit her.

"Dearest Josie. This is your day. How are you?"

"I'm in a wonderful dream I hope to never awaken from." Josie could not stop herself from smiling.

"You are marrying the best of men. I could not be happier for the both of you. I came to ask if I might fill the role your mother would have had if she had been here. There are some things that would be good for a bride to know before her wedding night."

Josie blushed. "I would love any advice you have to give. I've heard whispers. I admit to being nervous."

"The marriage bed can be difficult if a woman is not loved and cared for. I doubt you will have any problems in that regard with your husband. He is besotted. He may be innocent, but he is knowledgeable."

Josie cast Aunt Dorothea a withering glance.

"I'm not referring to that brothel incident. Trust him on that. He is innocent and probably just as nervous about this evening as you are. And probably just about as eager." She winked.

Josie's face grew warm.

"Relax, dear, and enjoy this day. You will do fine." Lady Grey went into more explicit explaining of the mechanics of consummation of the wedding vows.

When they had finished, Josie was eager to rush the process of dressing to get to the chapel. She couldn't help but anticipate the day, and the night, to come.

~*~

Marcus had finished shaving when he found himself accosted by his brother and three friends in his suite.

"We know you have little experience with the ladies and thought that maybe we should give you a few pointers." Jared's ears turned red.

"You doubt I learned anything during my time at Madame DuBuois'?" Marcus's anger rose within him, warring with embarrassment over such a private matter.

"Cut line, Remy. You've never been in the petticoat line, although they may have tried to lure you in. You wouldn't know what to do with a woman once you got her." Michael backed up a little as he finished.

Marcus stared at him intently and took a step forward. He was not smiling. "I appreciate your concern. I believe I will manage the consummation of my marriage without the assistance of you reprobates. You had all better leave, before I destroy this beautiful day with a brawl."

The men glanced at each other and departed with

no further comment.

Marcus fumed and went about finishing his preparations to meet his bride. As he stopped and went to the adjoining room, he looked in on the refurbished suite that Josie would be taking residence in starting today. He wasn't quite sure how to proceed this evening. Did any groom ever know? He only knew that Josie had a passion for him as much as he did for her, and he was confident they would figure it out together.

~*~

Josie looked in the mirror at the new gown she had purchased in London but never worn. It was a pale cream color, but for the wedding, she and Molly had added touches of a deep ruby red. She had a cloak in a slightly darker red that she wore over it that was lined with cream- colored fur. Out of all the gowns she had brought with her for the house party, she thought it would be the perfect dress for her wedding. Pearls and red holly berries adorned her hair, and she wore a pearl necklace that was her mother's, with the addition of a ruby pendant that was a gift from her groom.

Her bouquet consisted of pine branches, holly, and one sprig of mistletoe because she was whimsical as she put it together with Lady Grey. Altogether, she thought she looked well enough and hoped her groom approved. She wore cream-colored soft leather boots, as there was a short walk to the chapel in the newly fallen snow.

She had not seen Marcus that morning. She was anxious waiting in her room for her father to escort her outside. She had to wait until Marcus had already departed to the chapel with the other guests.

Her father's eyes welled up with tears when he came for her. "You look beautiful, my dear. Your mother would be proud of the young woman you have become." He held out his arm to escort her to the chapel.

~*~

Marcus entered the chapel, bedecked in holiday finery for the occasion. Bright sunshine streamed in the stained glass windows, casting a softly colored light of yellows, pinks, and blues over the front of the sanctuary. Marcus walked up the aisle with Reverend Wilson. He stood next to his brother, who was dressed in full military regalia.

The chapel resonated with the chattering of friends and family present, and Marcus responded to a few of the comments aimed at him as he waited. It took forever for Josie to come. She hadn't changed her mind, had she? His palms were sweating even though the temperature was cool in the small stone structure.

Finally, the door opened and Josie stepped in with her father. The door closed behind and left them in shadows.

Mr. Storm help Josie remove her cloak, and one of his servants began to play a soft melody on his violin. Josie and her father started forward.

The light from the windows bathed Josie in a rosy glow, and Marcus's heart beat faster. She was beautiful. Her eyes looked up to his, and peace washed over him. He couldn't help but grin. *Breathtaking*. He was grateful that God had brought her into his life. She smiled back, and then she winked at him. He chuckled to himself, and his brother nudged him and whispered, "Behave."

Soon she stood beside him, and he held her hand in his as they listened to the minister. The ceremony was long. Reverend Wilson gave them a charge to love and honor each other and to propagate the family line according to the Holy Scriptures.

Josie blushed next to him during that part, and he grinned. He spoke his vows strongly, and she responded as well in a clear voice. When pronounced man and wife, they turned toward their family and friends and the small chapel erupted in applause. Marcus held Josie to his side through the rounds of congratulations. He helped her put on her cloak and escorted her back to the house for the wedding breakfast.

~*~

Much later that day, Marcus and Josie were able to steal away to their suite of rooms, and they dismissed their servants to go and enjoy the celebration. Once they were alone, Marcus walked over to his bride and gave her a gentle kiss.

"Nervous?"

"Yes. There is no book that tells us what to do at this point, is there?"

"I am certain there are, but I do not think we shall need them."

"Thank you for the ruby." Her hand reached up to finger the blood red stone that touched her glowing skin.

Marcus's mouth went dry.

"I have a gift for you." Josie turned, left the room,

and returned with a large square but flat package wrapped with green velvet, a cream ribbon, and some mistletoe. She sat down on the settee by to the fireplace and patted the seat next to her.

Marcus sat and sneaked another kiss.

Josie accepted the kiss with enthusiasm and then placed the package on his lap.

"What is it?" His hand caressed the velvet wrapping.

"You will have to open it to see, won't you?" Her eyes were bright.

Marcus grinned. He unwrapped the package. The ribbon slipped off, and he draped it around Josie's shoulders. The mistletoe he stuck in her hair. The velvet came off, and he stopped moving as he contemplated what was in his lap. He looked at her with one eyebrow raised.

"How did you...? It is beautiful. I do not understand."

The watercolor painting on his lap was of him asleep in the yellow bedroom. The details were lifelike from his hair color, to his scuffed up boots, to the mutt sleeping in his lap.

Josie placed a hand on his and gave him a squeeze. "This was the first glimpse I ever had of the man I had fallen in love within my heart. The first image that greeted me when I emerged from my blindness. As soon as I was able, I tried to capture that memory on paper. I never want to forget that moment when I first saw you and knew you had kept watch over me. Protecting me. I knew then that you loved me."

"It is beautiful. I am touched that finding me sleeping on the job rendered so many positive emotions in you." She blushed as he set the picture down and began to unwrap her. "I don't plan to fall asleep on the job tonight."

Marcus and Josie discovered that they needed no instructions on how to proceed from there.

EPILOGUE

The Black Diamond paced. Bastian had failed him, and his back up, Widmore, was locked up as a lunatic. Probably a good thing, lest anyone give credence to murmurs about the existence of the Black Diamond. In time, all would recognize him and his greatness.

But not yet.

Lord Remington and his friends had robbed him of his object. Those men had proven to be patriots of England, and Captain Allendale had obviously not learned his lesson at the hands of the French.

Sir Michael Tidley. Oh, he had special plans for him.

All in good time. He'd be keeping an eye on these men who had stood in his way.

For now, Lord Wolton had struck a deal with Lord Follett. The Black Diamond looked forward to how this next season would unfold. He rubbed his hands together and fanned the flames of the fire before him as he chanted and prayed. The substitute sacrifice, while not as ideal, would suffice for now. He thrilled to hear her scream.

Yes. Being Emperor of England would be a sweet thing.

Don't miss the rest of the
Black Diamond Christian Gothic Regency
Suspense Series

Here's a sneak peek at
The Lord Phillip's Folly

Prologue

London

Across the misty sky flew a dark figure with wings flapping silently amidst the noise of the city of London where the elite of the *ton* prepared for this night's entertainments. As the black bird swooped and dipped amongst the chimneys, he found what he searched for. Make that "whom" he searched for. He spied her on the balcony gazing up at the sky awaiting him. He dove from his height only spreading his wings within a few feet to slow descent and land lightly on her outstretched arm.

"Duke," the young woman whispered. "You're back. I've been waiting for you."

His head bobbed but he refrained from speaking. His mistress frowned. He longed to see her smile. He tilted his head to the right, straightened it, and reached his neck forward to put his long dark beak to her cheek and rub gently.

Tears dangled at the edge of her eyelashes. "Tonight is the night, Duke. I cannot go through with what Papa plans. I must escape. All these years... I cannot endure any longer."

Duke was silent, listening. He bobbed his head.

She continued. "Lord Wolton has to be sixty, if not older and has the most nauseating odor. He is creepy and I'm certain he has some evil hold over Papa. But I cannot. I will not allow myself to pay the price for Papa's salvation. He's acted foolishly, and I love him, but I won't..." She glanced up at the sky. "Why would God allow this to happen?" She shivered, although the mid-April evening was warm. "Why couldn't I simply be loved for who I am? Why all this unrelenting...evil?"

Duke ruffled his feathers and shook them, once again rubbing his beak against her cheek.

"Watch over me tonight. I've no clue how I'll escape, but I don't want to lose you when I do. Wait outside in the garden and follow wherever I go. Can you do that, sweetheart?" Her intense golden-green eyes gazed into his.

"I love you," Duke squawked, nodding and making a kissing sound. He'd do anything for her.

"I love you too, Duke. What would I have done this past year without you?"

Movement from the dressing room alerted him to danger. Duke flapped his wings and took off, circling twice above her before settling on a nearby tree. She blew him a kiss.

He bobbed his head in acknowledgment as she turned to step back off the narrow balcony and close the doors to the bedroom behind her.

He would protect his mistress.

1

Spring 1810
Manchester

Despicable town. Infuriating family. Frustrating obligations. In spite of all that Lord Phillip Westcombe had returned to London. He enjoyed hibernating in the North Country the past few months. Peace and solitude had become a comfortable companion since his friend, Lord Marcus Remington, married Miss Josephine Storm at Christmas. Their happiness was something he did not begrudge them, but he found it difficult to be around. It pointed to a gaping hole in his own heart.

Instead, he spent the time studiously applying himself to his estate, and enjoyed managing the property. He was happy for Marcus and Josie, but the process of falling in love tended to be messy and complicated if their path to the altar was any indication. He did not want that in his life.

Yet here he was, back in London for the season.

If it hadn't been for his mother's pleas, his father's command, and his little sister's enthusiastic encouragement, he would still be at Stanton Hall. Avoiding the matchmaking mammas and the cloying attempts of young debutantes trying to trap him into the parson's mousetrap was one of his least favorite pastimes. At five and twenty he had spent the last few years gaining some town polish along with experience in how to avoid the snares of the marriage mart.

It was primarily his adoration for his sister, Penelope, that brought him here. He hoped she would find a man worthy of her hand. As one of her family, he owed her the courtesy of squiring her through the season, keeping a careful watch on the court of admirers she was sure to develop.

As Fenway, his valet, stepped away from tying his cravat into a spectacular waterfall, Phillip looked in the mirror. His blond hair carefully combed off of his face—every hair in its place. His ice-blue eyes scanned the image before him as he attached a ruby pin into the folds of the linen and smiled. Perfect white teeth set in a long face with a strong jaw and aristocratic nose and full lips. His new black coat fit like a glove. Perfection was an art. With the help of his tailor and valet, he was a master.

It was time to do his duty to his sister, please his parents, and dance with the wallflowers. With a final tug to his jacket, he nodded to Fenway. "Don't bother waiting up for me." He left his chambers determined to make the best of the evening.

~*~

The Earl of Manchester and his wife of thirty-two years stood ahead of him in the receiving line. They had asked only that Phillip, their second son, remain by the side of his sister Penelope for her come-out ball. He was the last person to greet people before they entered the ballroom.

Faces swam past him in a blur of color and stench. Why some in the upper ten-thousand refused to bathe perplexed him. He greeted each gentleman with a bow of his head and every woman with a lift of their gloved hands within an inch of his lips. His sister simpered next to him, giddy that this evening was in her honor and likely to be a 'crush,' to propel his mother into rapturous delight.

Waiting for an escape, he discovered an unknown face presented to him.

"I'm Lord Follett." The older man gave him a bow. Phillip could see the balding head, and the odor of alcohol on his breath warned him the man was already in his cups. "This is my daughter, the Honorable Elizabeth Follett."

Phillip sucked in a breath at the vision before him. Her soft red hair was pulled up and held in place by small white flowers. Her dress did not do her coloring justice. But it was the eyes, those green eyes that drew him. They spoke a message to him he couldn't quite decipher. It wasn't one of desire or seduction as he so often saw. More of abject terror.

Because of him?

He held her hand. "Welcome to Manchester Hall, Miss Follett." He allowed his lips to touch the glove and a shock traveled through him as she gasped. He straightened as one corner of his lips rose. *Ah, she'd felt it too.* Instead of terror, there was curiosity, and, as those lashes lowered, he sensed a mystery.

"You are too kind, my lord." Her husky voice whispered as the crowd pushed her forward toward the ballroom. He watched her go, the sway of her hips barely discernable beneath her gown.

"Phillip?" His sister nudged him.

"Yes, Penny?"

"Will you escort me in? Father said he would lead me out for the first dance. Anthony is to dance with me next and then you. You won't forget, will you?" Her brown eyes held an eagerness he knew would someday turn to *ennui* as the years marched on and she was subjected to these now exciting activities over and over again.

"How could I ever forget? You are by far the most beautiful woman in the room and I would be honored to dance with you."

She slapped him with her fan and giggled. "I'm glad you came home, Phillip. I've missed you."

He tapped a finger on her nose and lifted his elbow. She placed her hand on his forearm and he escorted her into the ballroom. Handing her off to his father he skirted the room, periodically shaking hands with people he knew but not stopping to chat. He wasn't in the mood for talk. His eyes scanned the mass of bodies. The Earl of Manchester determined it was late enough to begin the ball.

Phillip hated these events. When he was younger, he didn't mind attending and flirting with the available misses, but now it wore thin. Was he getting old or growing up? Managing the estate left to him by his maternal aunt, Martha, upon her removal to the hereafter two years hence had been a better use of his time and energy. He'd encountered success in turning a modest inheritance into profitable investments after Lord Remington took him aside and encouraged him that even as a second son, he could be prosperous and productive.

Phillip failed in his attempt to share his successes with his family. They persisted in the belief he was a ne'er-do-well, frolicking around aimlessly, gambling, and wenching his way through his monthly allowance and inheritance. As if he were still a callow youth fresh on the town.

Before Lord Remington's warnings and direction, that might have been true.

Yet his family considered him to be a wastrel, doomed to destruction if he didn't settle down with a wife soon. His father even suspected he was hiding in the north with a mistress. As if he'd waste money on such as that? He was long over his dalliances with ladies of the night. It irked him that his father would hold such a low opinion of him.

Phillip was fully cognizant that although his family loved him, he was far from the perfection of his older brother. He glanced around the ballroom and spied Anthony, only two years older than himself. Anthony tended towards portliness and while he pretended adoration toward his wife, Phillip knew that Anthony's excesses far surpassed his own when he was younger. He feared his father was misled in the belief that his heir was honorable and trustworthy to inherit the earldom someday. Phillip shrugged. Since Anthony's wife had presented him with two sons already, the title would never pass to Phillip. He found contentment in establishing his own path, and a wife was not integral to his success.

If his mother and sisters were any indication, women usually spent money, which did not help much in increasing wealth. Marcus's bride might be the exception, but it was really too early to tell on that account as they were fairly new to marriage. They had come in earlier and were on the dance floor, besotted with one another.

The orchestra finished playing the first dance. Phillip sought out his mother to lead her into the next one.

~*~

The Honorable Elizabeth Follett escaped the first dance with an excuse to check her hem but now she couldn't avoid the inevitable as she was led to the floor by Lord Wolton.

His face quickly grew red. He started wheezing with the execution of the steps of the dance. At over three times her own age, he was a prosperous landowner and neighbor. He possessed small dark eyes, bushy eyebrows, and very little hair on top of his head, which perspired terribly. His long sideburns only served to emphasize his jowls. His hands were plump and clammy to the touch.

A shiver of distaste overtook Lizzy every time his reached for hers as required by the movements of the dance, and even more at the lascivious look in his eyes as he would scan her body. His smile, crooked with a few darker teeth accompanied by his foul breath, made her fight against the bile threatening to rise inside when they drew close.

The only highlight of the exercise was the sight of the golden god dancing two couples down. Occasionally his eyes met hers in the course of the dance and she only hoped he could read her desperation. Ah, but beautiful sons of earls were not known to rescue the daughters of barons were they?

Led back to her father after the dance, she nodded her head and murmured a soft thanks to Lord Wolton.

Lord Follett had no real repute in the *ton* and felt his position keenly. He nudged his daughter and urged her, "Smile, Lizzy, for heaven's sake. Lord Wolton desires your hand, the least you could do is encourage him a little."

Lizzy once again tried to suppress a cold shiver at the very thought of any more interaction with Lord Wolton. Her father blustered and yelled when she stated her objection to the match. There would be no rescue for her from that quarter. She closed her eyes and took a deep breath, clenching her hands tightly together silently praying to a God she wasn't quite sure even existed, for a way out of the hell destined for her.

Opening her eyes, she glanced across the room to observe Lord Phillip Westcombe leading his sister out in the country dance. She could not take her gaze off of him. His kindly manner as he interacted with his sister was charming. And that smile. Would she even be able to breathe if he ever smiled at her like that? He was the stuff dreams were made of. She felt hope surge through her. Maybe, just maybe...

~*~

The evening dragged on with one dance after another. After supper, Phillip returned his young partner to her chaperone with an elegant bow. He found his attention captivated by the young woman who'd haunted him since her introduction earlier. She was difficult to miss with her red hair, although red was a bit strong to describe its softer hue. Hair that once curled around her face hung straight. She was pale, standing alone near a potted plant by the doors leading to the gardens below, as though she were hiding. She glanced his way and their gaze held. He read a silent plea and began to move in her direction.

He wove through the crowd surrounding the ballroom, stopping for brief handshakes and pats on the back as he maneuvered to that side of the room. He kept an eye on the young woman. She tracked his progress at times furtively searching the crowd. His curiosity was aroused.

"Miss Follett." Lord Phillip bowed over her hand and spoke softly so as not to be overheard in the noise of the ballroom. "May I be of assistance?"

"Lord Westcombe..." Elizabeth sighed. "Yes...I wonder..." Her eyes once again held a silent entreaty.

"Would you perhaps like to stroll in the garden?" Phillip extended his arm, and nodding, she wound her hand around it and walked outside into the fresh, cool evening air. Heat radiated up his arm at her touch. With every step, he was more aware of the woman by his side than any he'd ever known. It puzzled him. They stepped down into the garden lit with lanterns. Her lack of chatter perplexed him. Most women he met attempted to talk their way into a proposal. Few couples were in the gardens this early in the evening although lamps had been lit. He knew all the best places to engage in less than gentlemanly behavior due to his wayward youth. He led her down a path to an area by a small pond. Open and exposed. He would not compromise this young woman.

Phillip assisted Miss Follett to the bench, leaned against the tree next to it, and waited. She clenched her hands in her lap, took a deep breath, and began. "I need to escape. My father is forcing me into a marriage I do not want." Cautiously, she raised her eyes to meet his and he noted the tears at the edges.

He reached for his handkerchief and extended it to her as he came to sit beside her. "Is there no other way out of this marriage? Surely, they cannot force you to the altar. We do live in a civilized society."

"Civilized?" A short bark of laughter escaped the young woman. "My life has never been civilized. You'd be truly horrified if I told you the things I've endured." She turned slightly to look him in the eye and reached forward to put her hand on his arm. "Truly, if I do not escape tonight I have no other hope except—"

Phillip's eyes narrowed as she considered her words. Was she being overly dramatic? Was this a manipulation? Miss Follett wasn't trying to trap him into marriage herself, was she? From what he understood, she came with a healthy dowry, something he certainly didn't need. She was far from unattractive and given time during the season her own court of admirers would vie for her favors. Yet he sensed truth in what she claimed and that before him sat a desperate woman. The knight-errant in him fought its way to the surface disturbing the peaceful waters he tried hard to maintain. "What is it you require?"

"To disappear. Somewhere, anywhere they cannot find me."

"And then what? You re-appear elsewhere? How would that be explained? The scandal-mongers would have a feast that could destroy any hope you would have of making a respectable match. What about your future? Where might you live and how would you marry if you are cut off from your father and your inheritance?"

"You fully understand the complexities of my circumstances, Lord Westcombe. To me this matter is of life and death. My life. My certain death. If I am forced to marry, I guarantee I will be dead within the year. So, my only hope is to escape. Will you assist me?"

Phillip stared at her, considering, as the silence stretched taut between them. He tended to be a good judge of people and this woman told the truth. Finally, he came to a decision and nodded to her. "Can you remain here for a few minutes? Will you be all right?"

"You won't fetch my father?"

"No, merely a discreet friend who might assist. Trust me. I am a man of my word."

"I'll be fine. I'm not alone." Her face relaxed as she looked up past the tree to the stars twinkling in the sky.

Phillip wondered at her odd statement. There were other couples in the garden, but none near here. Giving her a short bow he surreptitiously returned to the ballroom. Once he entered he searched until he spied Lord Marcus Remington finishing up a dance with his bride. Phillip wove his way through the crowd to Marcus's side and whispered in his ear, "I require your assistance."

Marcus raised one eyebrow, nodded, and together all three made their way to the hallway and a private room. Phillip shut the door behind them.

"Well, Phillip, what is it?" Marcus relaxed one hand on his wife's waist as he stood beside her.

"I need shelter for a young woman in desperate need." *Now* who sounded melodramatic?

Marcus and Josie exchanged looks before staring at him.

"Phillip? Why does this woman need immediate shelter?" asked Lady Remington.

"I've done nothing wrong or to be ashamed of. She came to me for help."

"What do you want?" asked Marcus.

His wife nodded her head in agreement.

"I must spirit her away immediately. Could you depart and have your carriage go down to the corner alley? I'll bring her there unnoticed. After we arrive at your home, you can hear her story for yourselves."

Marcus nodded and escorted Josie out of the room.

"Dearest, I'm feeling tired and would like to go home now," Josie simpered as she fanned herself.

"Certainly dear. You look fatigued." Marcus's strong deep voice would suggest they were leaving for that reason alone.

Phillip slipped out the door of the library and wandered back to the garden, avoiding the few partygoers there. He accidentally came upon a few couples engaged in flirtation before he found his way back to Miss Elizabeth Follett. "Come," he whispered as he gave her his hand to help her stand.

"Where...?"

"You ask for my help yet now you resist? Trust me. I shan't harm you."

"I never doubted that for a minute." She rushed alongside him as they slipped through a spot in the hedge and made their way down the alley. Staying in the shadows they waited silently for the Remington coach to pull up. The rise and fall of her chest as she caught her breath was distracting.

He forced himself to focus elsewhere.

The carriage arrived and Lord Phillip assisted Elizabeth inside, entering behind her and closing the door. Marcus tapped on the roof to signal for them to start and they headed for the Remington home.

"Lord and Lady Remington, may I present the Honorable Elizabeth Follett to you?" Lord Westcombe intoned.

"Miss Follett, it is our honor to meet and assist you this evening." Josie reached across the carriage to squeeze the newcomer's hand. "You shall be safe with us."

"Thank you," Miss Follett whispered.

Phillip leaned back against the squabs and willed his pulse to slow. What had he done? He had acted on her behalf but belatedly wondered how this would reflect on him. Where was his neat, orderly life now?

2

Lizzy leaned forward to look out the window as they pulled up to the Remington house. Her awareness of the man sitting next to her caused her stomach to flutter. *Silly girl!* He was a kind soul helping a damsel in distress. Nothing more. Lord Phillip assisted her from the carriage and they followed Marcus and Josie to the entrance of the building. Leading her to the drawing room, Josie requested tea be brought. As Lizzy paced in front of the unlit hearth, Lord Remington moved past her to put the kindling in and strike the match to get a fire started. Phillip had gone to the sideboard for a glass of brandy and brought one for his friend.

Silence hung in the air until the tea tray arrived and the servants departed, closing the door behind them.

"I cannot stay long, my parents will miss me if I am not back before the end of the ball," said Phillip.

Lizzy stopped pacing as her heart raced. "What?"

Lord Remington went to her side to escort her to the settee next to his wife who handed her a cup of tea after quietly inquiring how she preferred hers.

"Phillip, you cannot rescue her and then abandon her here," Lady Remington protested.

"I will return once the ball is finished."

"But what is to become of me?" Lizzy whispered.

Phillip looked at Marcus. "Her father is forcing her to marry Lord Wolton against her will."

Lord Remington's eyebrows rose. He nodded. "You were kind to help her escape such a fate. But why would your father do that?"

A shudder shook Lizzy and she placed her cup and saucer on the table lest she spill it. "Wolton has some kind of hold over my father." She pulled off her gloves revealing red wrists with the marks of fingers on her pale skin.

Phillip growled. "Your father did this to you?"

Lizzy nodded.

Josie reached over to touch her arm gently above the injured area. "I'm eager to hear your story, but in due time. You may spend the night here until we can figure out how to best assist you." She glanced over at her husband who nodded in agreement.

"Phillip, I hope you realize what you're doing. We don't want to be caught interfering between a young woman and her legal guardian."

Lizzy piped up, "I am of age. I possess my own inheritance."

Phillip looked surprised. "Given that, how can your father force you to marry someone you dislike?"

Elizabeth wouldn't meet his gaze, looking down into her teacup as tears started to flow. "Trust me, he will."

Josie looked at Phillip with pleading eyes. "We shall figure this out in due time."

Lizzy pulled his handkerchief out of her reticule and used it to dab her eyes.

Lord Westcombe moved over to stand in front of her and she looked up at him. "I'm sorry I must leave. I promise you, I will return in a few hours. I could leave you in no better hands than Lord and Lady Remington's. You'll be safe here." He bowed to her and with a brief good night, he left the room to return to the Manchester ball.

~*~

Twice in one evening he had abandoned Miss Follett. It went against the grain of gentlemanly behavior. Being seen at the dance, however, would absolve him of any participation in the matter. In the end, it could possibly save her reputation and keep him from the parson's mousetrap.

The dancing was winding down and he took to the floor with another debutante. After the dance concluded he returned her to her chaperone's side and sought out his mother. Lady Manchester was short but retained her youthful figure. In spite of a few grey streaks in her light brown hair, she was still considered a beauty. Phillip tended to take after his father in looks and temperament.

"Oh, Phillip, there you are. I wondered where you had disappeared to." She tapped his arm with her fan. "Found someone you simply couldn't resist, did you? I heard the gardens were busy this evening." She giggled.

Phillip grew warm at the suggestion he'd been carrying on with a guest on his parents' property. It saddened him that she would believe something like that of him. Sometimes a past was a hard thing to live down. "You were searching for me, Mother? What can I do for you?"

"Lord Wolton was agitated earlier as the young woman he was pledged to dance with disappeared.

Lord Follett, the young lady's father, was unable to locate her. We had the withdrawing room checked and surreptitiously asked around but nobody remembers seeing her. It's as if she has vanished into thin air. I do not need to tell you that this is not the kind of notoriety we want associated with your sister's come out." She gave him a coy wink. His mother enjoyed the fact that along with being a squeeze her ball would be remembered for the disappearance of the Follett woman.

"What do you think has happened to her?" he asked, schooling his features to impassiveness.

She leaned toward him and was forced to look up as she whispered. "She is worth a fortune and has sole control of the money as of yesterday when she turned one and twenty. Rumor has it that Lord Wolton intended to marry her by Special License tomorrow." She paused and gave a shiver of disgust. "Personally, Phillip, I think the girl ran away and I couldn't blame her. I'd do the same if Wolton were my intended groom."

"If they were eager for her to wed him, why wait until she gained her majority? She no longer needs his permission for her marriage. I'm praying she is safe from that sorry end. But where would she go? Does she have relatives in town who might shelter and protect her?"

"None that I'm aware of. It troubles me. A young woman alone in this town is destined for only one thing and already her reputation is ruined by this event." Lady Remington shook her head sadly. "It's too bad, really, as she seemed to be a sweet girl and was passably pretty." Of course, she probably thought no one could ever be as beautiful as her own daughter.

Phillip listened to his mother and remained silent as he scanned the room for Lord Follett or Lord Wolton. He failed to locate them. "Where is her father and the potential bridegroom now?"

"I believe they left for the evening in an attempt to keep things quiet so when they find her they can whisk her away to the church and prevent a scandal."

"What if they fail to locate her?"

"I pray for that, Phillip, and I hope she is safe. At some point, however, she will need to access her fortune which will expose her to discovery."

"You are far too wise, Mother. Is there anything you need from me for the rest of this evening? I wouldn't mind calling it a night myself."

"Really? Phillip, you seriously cannot be thinking of going to your club or any of those other places tonight."

"No. However, I do plan to meet a friend."

"Fine. You may leave, Phillip, but remember, I expect you to accompany us to some of the balls this season to help keep an eye on a potential suitor for your sister's hand. I am counting on your support. I will send a list of entertainments I expect you to attend."

"I'll do my best, Mother." Phillip bent and gave her a kiss on the cheek. "Good night." He strode out the door and took a brisk walk to the Remington house. He wondered if Miss Follett was yet awake. He wouldn't mind seeing her again.

~*~

"Come, Elsa will help you change. You are a little taller than me but I'm sure I have a gown that will suit you for sleeping," Josie urged.

Elizabeth sank into the chair by the cheerful fireplace. "It's hopeless. There is no way out of this."

"Miss Follett..."

"Elizabeth please, or Lizzy."

"Elizabeth it is, then. A name that speaks of dignity, determination, and grace."

Lizzy looked up at that, startled. "Thank you."

"You may call me Josie. Now, what is concerning you?"

Elsa began pulling the pins out of Lizzy's hair and letting the heavy locks fall down around her shoulders. "My father has evil friends. He told me I needed to marry Wolton. I had no choice. But I'm tired of being a victim of men's schemes and debauchery."

"What *are* you talking about?"

Lizzy rose as the abigail put the pins on the dressing table and left to get a nightgown. She turned to Josie. "Maybe I can show you. Would you undo my dress?" Elizabeth turned around.

Josie rose to undo the fasteners going down the back of Elizabeth's gown. Letting it fall to the floor she pulled up the back of her chemise to reveal her back.

Josie's gasp echoed around the room.

Elizabeth walked behind a screen and finished dressing. She suspected her face was now the color of her hair.

Josie sat, mouth agape. "I'm so sorry, Elizabeth. I suspect there is much more you are not telling me."

"Yes, m'lady." Lizzy sat across from her with her head bent, awaiting condemnation from the Viscountess.

"Elizabeth, what you have endured was not your fault. It is a crime this can be done to a young woman with no one to protect her. God loves you, and Lord Remington and myself will do all in our power to protect you from further harm."

"You won't force me to leave? I am unworthy of your kindness."

"You are more than worthy. You are a precious young woman who has suffered evil. I suspect your battle will not be only one with your father and disappointed groom, but that a spiritual dimension underlies this."

"I don't understand." Lizzy folded and unfolded the handkerchief she still held, her thumb unconsciously tracing the initials embroidered in the corner.

"You've been subjected to great evil. More I'm sure than you've shared thus far. These things are not normal or in any way condoned by God. Like you, I don't understand what hold Lord Wolton has over your father that would force him to sell you in this manner. If your suspicions are correct you are destined for more of the same. I will need to share some of this with my husband, and possibly Lord Westcombe, so they can make discreet inquiries."

Lizzy panicked. "Must you?"

"I believe it is necessary if we are to protect you and give you freedom from the terror you've experienced." Josie leaned forward, put her arm on Elizabeth's, and looked her in the eye. "I want you to be free of the prison you find yourself in. Free to select a husband of your choice. Free to be all God has created you to be as a woman, a wife, and a mother someday."

"I never dared to dream that far." She hugged herself.

"I understand," said Josie kindly. "I believe it would be good for you to get some rest now. We will talk more in the morning when we can consider this with a fresh perspective as to what's to be done. By then Phillip might be able to give us information on what happened at the ball when they discovered you missing. I'm sure there was an uproar over that and his mother is relishing the notoriety it is giving her daughter's come out."

"Oh, I've ruined it for them, haven't I?"

"No. She will be in alt. Never fear. Phillip won't fail in keeping your secret. He has too much to lose by confessing anything."

"What do you mean?"

"A marriageable man kidnapping a young woman from his parents' ball? The only way he'd ever live that down would be to marry you himself."

Lizzy's heart sank. "I could never dream so high as to seek someone as fine as him for a husband."

"He is quite a figure of manhood is he not? A man of honor, as well. You can trust him. Now get some rest."

"May I keep the fire burning?"

"That's fine. I'll instruct Elsa." She rang the bell and the maid appeared.

"You've been all kindness, m'lady."

"Josie."

"Thank you, Josie."

"It is our pleasure. Sleep well and have pleasant dreams." Josie departed after giving discreet instructions to the maid.

Lizzy blew out the candles and strode to the window. She lifted the pane. Duke came to sit on the sill. "I'm well, Duke. Thank you. I'll see you on the morrow."

Duke nodded and flew off.

The windows were closed and the drapes were drawn. She settled into a chair by the fire, the vision of blue eyes and a strong chin were better dreamt of awake. *I'm in a safe place, I'll be fine.* She'd abandoned everything for safety. But in doing so she courted scandal. There was no way to save face after this. Even under the auspices of the Viscount and his wife, there was little cachet to be had as a runaway daughter of a baron. Even if she could gain her fortune, she'd expose her location. How would she live? Where would she go? Wearily she sought her bed and drifted into an uneasy sleep.

She ran away from one nightmare straight into unknown darkness with few options.

~*~

Duke flew to the top of the tree and settled in to sleep. The noise of the city made that hard. The gas lamps encroached on the darkness he was accustomed to in the country. His mistress was well. He spied the man who brought his mistress here, return. Duke bobbed his head. He'd do. Lizzy went with him willingly. She was safe and the terror he'd seen in her the past few days was momentarily gone. He could rest and wait to find out what would happen next. She wasn't clear of all danger yet. Evil lurked in the darkness and he would do anything to protect her.

Download the rest of Lord Phillip's Folly from your favourite online retailer.

ACKNOWLEDGEMENTS

It would be impossible to thank everyone who has helped me on my journey, so I apologize in advance for those I will miss. It doesn't mean you are any less valuable, and thankfully, God keeps better track of those things than I do, and His "well done, good and faithful servant" has more merit than any thanks written here.

So here it goes. Special thanks to:

Carol Hisel – can you believe it? I wrote the rough draft of this in NaNoWriMo reunited us after years of praying for you. And look what God has done! I'm honored He let me be part of your journey.

Elisabeth Herman – you amaze me. Thanks for all the ways you've invested in me.

Doris Pollard Wichern – another early reader and one of my most faithful cheerleaders in this writing adventure.

Lisa Lickel – thanks for being such a wonderful mentor, friend, and shoulder to cry on when the publishing process throws me those curve balls. I don't think I would have ever taken that first step in this journey to publication without your gentle push.

Pastors David Mundt and Ken Nabi – for your love and support and believing in me and the calling God has on my life.

Sally Shupe – my faithful editor. Thank you for finding all those silly errors!

Nicola Martinez – my beloved Editor-in-Chief, who continually supports my writing while allowing me the joy of helping others on their journey to publication. I'm grateful for our partnership and friendship.

ABOUT THE AUTHOR

Susan M. Baganz chases after three Hobbits, and is a native of Wisconsin. She is an Editor with Pelican Book Group specializing in bringing great romance to publication. Susan writes adventurous historical and contemporary romances with a biblical world-view.

This book is the first full-length novel in the Black Diamond Regency series. *The Baron's Blunder*, Henrietta's story, is a novella and prequel. Future stories include: *Lord Phillip's Folly*, *Sir Michael's Mayhem*, *Lord Harrow's Heart* and *The Captain's Conquest*. A Christmas Regency, *Gabriel's Gift* is due to release soon. She is also the author of contemporary romances in the Orchard Hill Romance Series, *Pesto & Potholes*, *Salsa & Speed Bumps*, *Feta & Freeways*, *Root Beer & Roadblocks*, and *Bratwurst & Bridges*. Future novels include *Donuts & Detours* and *Truffles & Traffic*.

Susan speaks, teaches, and encourages others to follow God in being all He has created them to be. With her seminary degree in counseling psychology, a background in the field of mental health, and years serving in church ministry, she understands the complexities and pain of life as well as its craziness. She serves behind-the-scenes in various capacities at her church and is a member of American Christian Fiction Writers (ACFW), and serves on the board of the southeast chapter. Her favorite pastimes are snuggling with her dog while reading a good book or sitting with a friend chatting over a cup of spiced chai latte. Learn more by following her blog, www.susanbaganz.com, her Twitter feed @susanbaganz or her fan page: facebook.com/susanmbaganz

Thank you

We appreciate you reading this Prism title. For other
Christian fiction and clean-and-wholesome stories,
please visit our on-line bookstore at
www.prismbookgroup.com.

For questions or more information, contact us at
customer@pelicanbookgroup.com.

Prism is an imprint of
Pelican Book Group
www.PelicanBookGroup.com

Connect with Us
www.facebook.com/Pelicanbookgroup
www.twitter.com/pelicanbookgrp

To receive news and specials, subscribe to our bulletin
http://pelink.us/bulletin

May God's glory shine through
this inspirational work of fiction.

AMDG

You Can Help!

At Pelican Book Group it is our mission to entertain readers with fiction that uplifts the Gospel. It is our privilege to spend time with you awhile as you read our stories.

We believe you can help us to bring Christ into the lives of people across the globe. And you don't have to open your wallet or even leave your house!

Here are 3 simple things you can do to help us bring illuminating fiction™ to people everywhere.

1) If you enjoyed this book, write a positive review. Post it at online retailers and websites where readers gather. And share your review with us at reviews@pelicanbookgroup.com (this does give us permission to reprint your review in whole or in part.)

2) If you enjoyed this book, recommend it to a friend in person, at a book club or on social media.

3) If you have suggestions on how we can improve or expand our selection, let us know. We value your opinion. Use the contact form on our web site or e-mail us at customer@pelicanbookgroup.com

God Can Help!

Are you in need? The Almighty can do great things for you. Holy is His Name! He has mercy in every generation. He can lift up the lowly and accomplish all things. Reach out today.

> *Do not fear: I am with you; do not be anxious: I am your God. I will strengthen you, I will help you, I will uphold you with my victorious right hand.*
> ~Isaiah 41:10 (NAB)

We pray daily, and we especially pray for everyone connected to Pelican Book Group—that includes you! If you have a specific need, we welcome the opportunity to pray for you. Share your needs or praise reports at http://pelink.us/pray4us

Free Book Offer

We're looking for booklovers like you to partner with us! Join our team of influencers today and periodically receive free eBooks and exclusive offers.

For more information
Visit http://pelicanbookgroup.com/booklovers